THE DREAMMONGER

EMMA T. SHANNON

ISBN: 979-8-9898487-3-7

E-book ISBN: 979-8-9898487-5-1

LCCN: 2025902306

Description: First edition. | United States, 2025. | Series: Le Cirque de la Rue; Book 1

Text is set in Garamond

Cover designed by Sagen Raven | sagenraven.wixsite.com

Interior art by Mgsdesiigns | melifluousgelatoo.my.canva.site

Published by Emma T. Shannon

Created with Atticus

To anyone who has ever wanted to run away and join the circus.

And to Dani.

Also by Emma T. Shannon

Song of the Hollow Duology
Song of the Hollow
Storm of the Gods

The Emerald Sea Saga
The Lost Moon

CONTENT WARNING

THE DREAMMONGER CONTAINS THEMES that may not be suitable for all audiences, including: blood, body mutilation, death, gore, and violence. It also contains mentions of self-mutilation, homophobia, transphobia, and sexism. Reader discretion is advised.

The Cast

Le Cirque de la Rue

Ilian Agreste – Beowulf. The beast tamer.

Aurelio Álvaro – El Cuélebre. The fire breather and sword swallower.

Alice Cécily – the Flying Fox. One half of the acrobat duo.

Sébastien de la Rue – the Dreammonger. The magician and ringmaster.

Noa Elie – Wonkus, the Gemini Twins. One half of the clown duo.

Sasha Elie – Goober, the Gemini Twins. The second half of the clown duo.

Odette Nadège – the Flying Fox. The second half of the acrobat duo.

Antara Shiva – Lady Kali. The knife thrower.

Louis Toussaint – the Seer. The fortune teller.

Svetlana Vasilievna – the Firebird. The contortionist.

PROLOGUE
1876 PARIS, FRANCE

IT WAS CHRISTMAS EVE, and it was to be the first Christmas the boys spent without their parents and without a roof over their heads. They were not the only children in Paris that would spend Christmas alone – and, quite unlike some of the other orphaned children congesting the streets of the city, they were not alone, as they had each other, just as they had for the seven years of their lives and the nine months in the womb before that – but for children who slept in warm beds and awoke to the magical festivities of Christmas day with presents and tinsel and sugar plums and chocolates, huddling together for warmth with backs pressed against the cold stone of a toy shop closed for the holidays wasn't something they'd ever expected. Just a year before, the boys lived in a different world, one where they were above the *poor folk*. Now, they *were* the aforementioned poor folk, with frostbitten fingers and toes and hollow bellies and lungs stricken with consumption. The boys were twins, but one had been born sixteen minutes (and thirty-two seconds, thank you very much) before the other and thus took the role of *elder brother* very seriously. In their possession, they only had one pair of threadbare wool gloves (with one of the thumbs missing entirely), so the elder brother graciously allowed his younger twin to wear them.

The elder twin's eyes – his mother used to say they looked like two spoonsful of honey on a warm spring day – tracked a teenage boy who pulled a sled with two younger children on it down the snowy street. With his worn jacket and patched cap, the elder twin might have thought they were another group of street urchins, but the boy's boots and the fluffy coats the younger children wore gave away that they had homes and families and money. Toddlers and babies did not last long on the streets, and judging by the youngest child's plump, rosy cheeks alone, they were well-fed and well-loved.

The twins had been well-fed and well-loved once, too.

The younger twin coughed harshly, the sound grating like sandpaper against slate. The elder twin cringed, but he was still the elder, so he pulled his brother close, raking his fingers through his tangled mess of black hair. Once, they protested baths, shrieking when maids poured hot water over their heads and scrubbed citrus soaps into their scalps. Now, they would kill for a proper bath. Perhaps not *kill*, but it had been weeks since they were last able to use the frigid waters from muddy puddles to wash their faces and underarms. With piles of slushy, muddy snow everywhere, any chances of getting cleaned had frozen over and wouldn't thaw until spring. At least they could scoop snow in their hands and eat it to satiate their thirst.

The younger twin coughed again. His breaths were wheezy and shallow, as if someone had punctured a hole in the hollow of his throat and forced him to breathe through a straw. By some miracle or another, the elder twin had not caught consumption, even with his younger twin coughing on him day and night. Yes, his fingertips and toes had blackened with numbing frostbite, and the chill had settled deep in his lungs, forcing his heart to pump harder to keep him warm and alive, but that was nothing compared to the chest-deep cough his younger brother suffered from. Another miracle, or something akin to one, as miracles simply did not exist for the boys anymore, had kept the younger twin alive, but it would take something stronger to make him see the end of the year. It would take two of those stronger-than-miracles for the younger boy to see the thawing spring and four stronger-than-miracles for him to make it to his eighth birthday on All Hollow's Eve.

The teenage boy and the laughter of his younger siblings faded from sight. The sun might have set, or it might still be low in the sky, but the depressing grey overcast shrouded Paris in a blanket of perpetual darkness, and with his pocket watch – the only thing remaining of his parents – stuffed deep in the pocket on the side of his patched jacket his younger brother lay against, the elder twin had no way of knowing what time it was. Surely it was still Christmas Eve, what with all the passersby still hurrying to get their last-minute purchases in, with the shopkeepers shooing their patrons out and locking their doors so they could make *their* last-minute run to the shops to get presents for their awaiting families.

God, the elder twin said silently, his spoonsful-of-honey eyes focusing on the sky, on the swirling flurries of snow twinkling like broken stars, *if you exist, please help my brother get better. Please. I'll be good next year. I'll go to church. I'll become a chasseur. I'll trade my own life if it means you'll help my brother get better.*

The twins were only seven years old, far too young to become the holy warriors sworn to protect France and spread the Word of God, but the elder twin had resorted to grasping at straws, desperate for any sort of help – divine or not – to heal his brother.

The younger twin coughed again, his tiny body shaking violently each time he tried to inhale. The elder twin wrapped his own small arms around the younger boy's body, doing everything in his limited power to keep his brother warm, even though his attempts were futile. His brother was going to die. And with a stomach-sinking realization, the elder twin came to terms with the horrors that his brother would likely not make it to see Christmas morning. It was, after all, no small feat that both boys had managed to survive as long as they had alone.

At least I will get my gloves back after this, the elder twin thought selfishly. Then, he scolded his own thoughts. *Don't say that! He's all you have left. God,* please. *Please, I'm begging you. Don't let my brother die.*

But God, whether he existed or not, did not listen. Someone else, however, did.

Heavy footsteps crunched in the snow. The boys were used to such sounds and long gave up hope of the footsteps stopping to offer the boys bread or money or a place to live like in a fairytale. The footsteps stopped, the crunching of snow shifting to the squeaking sound of snow compacting under a heavy weight. The elder twin, still shielding his brother from the cold, looked up. In the dark, it was hard to make out the features of the figure in front of him, but the elder twin deduced it was a man. A tall one, and an older one at that. He wore a top hat and a heavy coat, and he walked with a cane, though he showed no signs of a limp or favoring one leg over the other.

"Good evening, lads," the gentleman said. His accent was thick. Not French, even though his diction and pronunciation of the language were flawless. German, maybe? Or English. For all the elder twin knew it could be Spanish or American, or Russian. Even wealthy children weren't schooled in the different accents of the world.

The elder twin glared, trying to look as scary as a seven-year-old possibly could, his dark brow furrowed and his teeth – what few he had, since he was at that age where he lost teeth left and right – bared in what he hoped was a wolfish snarl.

Granted, it was likely more of a puppy snarl, but even puppies bite.

The man removed his hat and placed it over his heart as he gave a shallow bow. "Please, it is not my intention to harm you. My name is Monsieur Johan Engelstein. You, however, may call me Jack." *German, then.*

The elder twin had no desire to call the man anything. The twins' nanny used to tell them *don't talk to strangers, boys,* and even if Monsieur Johan Engelstein – *Jack* – gave up his name willingly, he was still a stranger.

The younger twin coughed so hard he gagged. The boy could not afford to throw up. He hadn't eaten more than a few stale scraps of bread in the past few days; losing even that would only speed up his inevitable end.

Jack took a step closer and crouched down. He put his hat atop his slicked blonde hair and removed his jacket. He put it around the boys quickly, retreating his hand as though he had just tossed a bone to a pair of rabid dogs instead. The elder twin shrugged off the jacket and wrapped the whole thing around his brother.

Jack said, "You look cold and hungry. Please, I have a carriage waiting. It's Christmastime, *ja?* My gift to you will be a bath, a meal, a warm bed, and medicine for your brother."

The younger twin coughed again, shivering within the confines of the borrowed jacket. Stranger or not, the elder twin had little choice but to trust M. Jack, if only to get his brother the medicine he needed to survive the night.

"Fine," said the elder twin. "Come on, A. We're gonna get you some medicine."

The younger twin groaned. His lips were chapped, his skin pallid and sticky with fever. Sweat glued his dark hair to his forehead. The only color on his face was the feverish flush on his cheeks, the frostbite on his nose, and the blood on his bottom lip.

Jack scooped the younger twin up like he weighed nothing more than a sack of flour. The elder twin rose slowly, a hatchling crane emerging from its egg, and followed Jack to the dark carriage waiting just outside the alley, its wheel tracks covering the indents from the earlier sled. It was pulled by two massive black Friesians, their manes threaded with red ribbons. They brayed, hoofs scraping the snow. Their breath came out in clouded puffs. Each one was taller than both twins if they stood one on the other – taller than the horses they used to have at their home before it was –

A butler – or a footman, or something of the sort, the elder twin was too tired to possibly think about servant rank right now – opened the door to the carriage, allowing Jack to climb up the steps with the younger twin still in his arms. The elder twin stared at the massive beasts, wondering if perhaps they were carnivorous to get as big as they were.

"Come along, boy," said M. Jack.

The elder twin looked away from the horses. He had half a mind to tap the sides of his holey boots against the wrought metal steps to shake the snow off before climbing inside the carriage. The seats were upholstered with velvet so deep red it looked black in the minimal light. It was Christmas Eve, of course, so the hired hands responsible for lighting the lamps lining the Parisian streets were off duty. Nobody would be out this late, anyway, and the street urchins were not real people in the minds of those who ran the city, so why would they need light?

The carriage jerked, then began moving slowly, the friction of snow against the wheels little match for the massive Friesians. The elder twin looked out the window, his breath fogging the frosted glass. They rode in silence, save for the creaking of wood, the huffing of horses, and the coughing of his younger brother.

"Your horses are real," blurted the elder twin. He pulled away from the window to look at Jack and his brother.

"That they are," said Jack. "Far easier to maintain than those steam beasts the aristocrats favor. Steam is hardly favorable in the cold."

With the Industrial Revolution came a number of advancements, the most prevalent being the creation of automatons – steam-powered beings that replaced horses and laborers. They took to the skies, cutting travel time in half. They lit the streets better than whale oil or kerosene could. They warmed homes, heated water, and provided soldiers with advanced weapons. The twins were among the spoiled ones who got running water and a staff that was half flesh, half metal. Their nanny had been a real woman, but their butler was an automaton – one whom the boys adored playing pranks on.

"Will you really help my brother?" asked the elder twin, deciding the life of his brother was more important than dwelling on M. Jack's preference for blood-and-bone horses over their automaton counterparts.

"Of course, my boy," Jack said. "While you bathe and clean up, I'll give him medicine. He needs rest, but he will be awake and healthy come morning."

Maybe God did exist, and M. Jack was an angel descended from the heavens to help the boys for the first time since the accident a year ago.

The elder twin looked out the window again. He knew better than to give up his name, especially since the tragedy staining their surname would only lead to complications the twins could not currently afford, but he offered something else instead, "You can call him A and me..." It was difficult coming up with a nickname since both boys had the same initials – *A. T. R.* – so the elder twin settled on being called "T. You can call me T."

"Interesting names for interesting boys," mused Jack. For a second, the elder twin considered Jack actually thought their names were A and T, but he realized soon that Jack was just doing that thing grown-ups did where they pretended children were serious.

"Are you German?" asked the elder twin, who was old enough and smart enough to know that asking someone their nationality was not the most respectful but simply too tired to care about decorum.

M. Jack, who should have been *Herr Jack,* but the elder twin decided not to question that, just chuckled. "Was it the name that gave it away or my accent?"

It was his name – the way he said his J's like Y's – that gave it away, and the elder twin said as much. M. Jack considered that and said, "I come from Berlin. I moved here about a year ago –" *a year ago!* "– because Paris called to me more than Berlin ever did."

The elder twin wanted to ask if Jack had come to Paris before or after last Christmas, but instead asked, "Are you rich?"

Jack laughed again. "Correct, young T. I'm a doctor. A surgeon, to be precise. Hence why I have medicine available for your brother here."

A doctor – a surgeon – was nothing short of a miracle. God must be real since a doctor was the only person in all of Paris capable of saving the younger twin's life. The elder twin supposed, with a slump of his shoulders, that this meant he was to become a chasseur now, to fulfill his end of the holy promise.

Wonderful.

The carriage came to an eventual stop, but the elder twin had fallen asleep by then, his cheek smushed against the cold glass of the window. M. Jack handed the sickly younger twin to the butler who rode with them. Jack picked up the elder twin and carried him inside. He wanted the boy to bathe, but things rarely worked out the way people wished, so Jack carried the boy upstairs to one of the many guest bedrooms in his sprawling manor and settled him on the plush mattress of a bed big enough for ten seven-year-olds. The boy stirred but curled up instinctively, the warmth lulling him to a deeper sleep.

"Well," said Jack aloud, in German since he was alone, "time to deal with the other one."

The elder twin, for the first time in a year, slept soundly. His dreams were not plagued by nightmares. In fact, he did not dream at all, save for the shadowy blur of a butterfly passing through his subconscious.

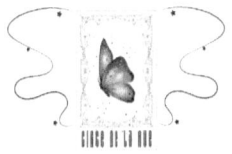

The elder twin awoke in a strange bed in a strange room that was most undoubtedly *not* the snow-filled alley next to the toy shop he and his brother had been in the night before. It was Christmas Day and the anniversary of his parents' deaths. The boy sat upright fast, the night prior coming to him in blurry snippets. The carriage and the horses and his brother and M. Jack and –

His brother!

The elder twin all but fell out of bed as he hurried to get to the door. He swung it open only to give M. Jack, who stood just on the other side with a tray full of breakfast, a startle.

"Oh, you're awake!" exclaimed Jack. "Your brother is resting. You need to eat and bathe before you can see him."

The elder twin did not like being told when he was allowed to see his brother, but his stomach, curse that traitor, grumbled loudly. He peeked at the tray and decided that his brother could wait a few extra minutes. He took the tray, minding the last vestiges of his manners, and sat down on the floor by the fire – stoked and roaring – to eat. Croissants, pains viennois, bread and thin slices of salted meats and cheeses, a cup of chocolat chaud that the elder twin quickly grabbed and gulped down, and a bowl of fruit with sprinkled sugar overtop reminded the boy of what he ate a year ago. He ate quickly, devouring everything in mere minutes, hardly pausing to savor any of it. Who knew how long M. Jack's charity would last and the elder twin wanted a full belly before being kicked back to the streets.

He licked flaky bits of pastry from his fingers and stood, turning to face the surgeon, who stood in the doorway with a bemused look plastered on his face. In the light, the elder twin got a better look at the man. He wasn't old, perhaps in his thirties, with milky pale skin and even fairer hair, so blonde it looked like spun silver.

He wore it slicked off his forehead, the back cropped close to his skull. He had a mustache but was otherwise clean-shaven. His eyes, dark brown – not like the spoonsful of honey eyes the twins had – had a glimmer to them that made the elder twin's shoulders relax. He wore a fine suit and finer gloves, his top hat nowhere to be seen but his cane propped against the door frame.

"I want to see my brother," said the elder twin as he wiped his mouth with the back of his hand.

Jack chuckled. "I do believe I said you could see him after you ate *and* bathed."

The elder twin scowled.

Jack said, "The washroom is through that door there." He picked up his cane and pointed to a door across the room. "We do have running water in this house, so please make use of it. You are a grown boy, and I believe you can bathe yourself. Unless you want me to call a maid?"

The elder twin's cheeks flushed scarlet. "No!" he exclaimed, and he ran to the washroom, slamming the door shut behind him. He pressed his back against the wood, breathing hard to quell his embarrassment. Once calm, he took inventory of the room – a spacious clawfoot tub, a toilet, a sink, a cabinet full of soaps and towels, a mirror –

He paused at the mirror, studying his face. His cheeks had sunken in, rendering him skeletal and ghoulish. The elder twin's heart skipped a beat at the sight. He looked like he belonged in a Penny Dreadful! His black hair had matted – it would need to be cut – and bruises lined the underneath of his eyes. Frostbite chapped his lips, blistering them and turning them purplish. His fingers and toes felt better, though, not as numb.

The elder twin turned on the tub faucet and dug around the cabinet until he pilfered exactly what he needed – a block of soap, a decanter, bottles of shampoo and conditioner, bubbles (for he was, after all, still seven years old), and a pair of scissors. He poured half the jar of bubbles into the tub and took the scissors to the mirror while the water ran.

He had to stand on his toes to see the mirror properly, but there was no precision when he chopped through the tangled, dirty mats of hair. Black tresses fell into the sink unceremoniously. When his hair no longer touched his shoulders but curled around his ears and across his brow, the elder twin set the scissors down, turned off the faucet, and stripped out of his filthy clothes to step into the bath. He did not throw a fit, even when he got shampoo in his eyes. He scrubbed until his skin glowed pink and the bubbly water was more of a rusty brown color.

Finished, the elder twin got out, dried off, and put his dirty clothes back on, since he couldn't just see his brother wearing naught but a towel, could he? His fingers brushed against his pocket, feeling the watch nestled there.

M. Jack was waiting in the bedroom when the elder twin emerged. He held a cup of tea in his hands, which he handed to the boy. "Willow bark," he explained. "It will help your frostbite."

For the first time in a year, the elder twin was not hungry, but he took the cup and gulped the bitter tea if only to ease the pain his injuries caused him.

"Can I see my brother now?" he asked, handing the cup back.

"You've rested and eaten and bathed, boy, so I do believe it is my turn to uphold our agreement. Come along, then. He's eating breakfast now." Jack left and the elder twin, with newfound energy, bounded after him.

The younger twin was in a bed just as grand as the elder twin's in a room just as extravagant. He sat upright, shoveling bites of croissant into his mouth. His cheeks had a flush to them, but not a sickly kind. A *healthy* kind.

"A!" the elder twin ran over, though he had enough restraint to not tackle his poor brother while he ate.

"Isn't this amazing?" the younger twin asked through mouthfuls. "I don't have that cough! It's a miracle!"

A miracle, indeed. Outside, the snow fell harder than it had the night before. The younger twin, against all odds, had lived to see morning.

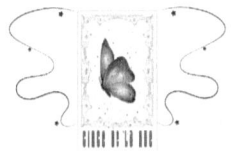

He would live to see the end of the year. He would live to see the bleeding of winter into spring. He would live to watch crocuses and tulips blooming in the garden outside M. Jack's manor. He would live to befriend the Friesian horses – there was a total of five of them – in the stables. He would live to try every dish the cook made (though he loathed snails and eggplant, as did the elder twin). He would live to see spring fade to summer. He would live to swim in the pond and scream when the elder twin told him that the rocks on the edge of the water were sunbathing snapping turtles. He would live to see the airships that passed through the Parisian night sky and decide he would one day ride one. He would live to see summer cool to autumn. He would live to see frost cover the grass outside. He would live to watch the trees surrounding the manor turn into a blaze of reds and oranges and yellows. He would live to see the nights get longer and the days shorter.

He would not live to see his eighth birthday on All Hollow's Eve.

He would get close, though.

It was the morning of October 30, 1876, and there was a dead body in the foyer.

It belonged to a woman, and she had not been dead long, not by the way fluids leaked from the wound in her stomach. She had been mutilated, though in the precise way a surgeon would mutilate their patient, with perfect lacerations slicing through each layer – flesh and yellowy fat, a thin membranous film over bright red muscle, a thicker chunk of globby fat, slimy intestines – but the woman – she was a woman, both boys knew, for she lacked the part both boys had – was missing one very vital piece of her, a hollowed cavity left in its wake. Her eyes stared lifelessly at the ceiling.

"Well, boys," came Jack's voice. The twins stiffened. The elder twin pulled his brother close, as if his weak arms could protect him from what was about to come.

Please, God, begged the elder twin as his eyes landed on Jack. He wore a leather apron over his impeccable suit, and his rubber gloves were slick with blood. *Please, keep my brother safe.*

"Looks like I didn't clean up my little project fast enough." Jack walked over – the boys flinched – and picked the body up. Viscera oozed from the mortal wound, dripping sticky onto the tile.

"What did you do?" whispered the elder twin.

"What I must," said Jack. "You see, boys, I made a deal quite some time ago, and I'm just doing what I need to in order to fulfill my end of things."

He turned and grinned, his lips stretching back to reveal teeth that were not human.

"The beast eats uteruses, God knows why, and hearts. This one is a bit too stale for its liking, though. Sorry, boys." He slung the body over his shoulder, then, with one hand, grabbed the collars of both twins. "I really was starting to like you."

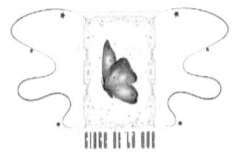

Many things happened within the infinite span of a minute.

The elder twin woke up strapped to a metal table. His brother was next to him, already awake and screaming.

Jack entered the room, his leather apron and gloves cleaned of blood, but not for long, a knife in his hand.

Jack stabbed the younger twin in the chest, slightly to the right and up, angled to slide between ribs perfectly.

The elder twin *screamed,* his rage raw and primitive.

The younger twin thrashed, sprays of blood spurting from his wound and spattering across Jack's face.

"Help!" screamed the elder twin, who was seven (quite nearly eight) years old, and did not know what else to do.

"What do you wish to give up in exchange?" asked a voice that did not belong to Jack nor the elder twin, or the younger twin. It was neither masculine nor feminine but rather both.

"Anything! Save my brother!"

"Very well, then."

A searing pain struck the elder twin's eye, though it was nothing compared to being stabbed, he thought.

And then Jack was thrown against the wall, knife clattering to the ground.

The elder twin did not see what happened next, but he did see a pair of unnatural blue eyes and an unnaturally tall figure standing over his brother.

The elder twin saw darkness and then nothing at all.

He did not see his brother again and for the first time in his entire life, he had his birthday alone.

Ten years came and went, and the city of Paris, France, remained as ordinary as it could possibly be. The night of Christmas Eve, 1886, was no different, as it was just as ordinary as it always had been. Those who were lucky snuggled up inside their warmed homes. Automatons worked mechanically to clear the worst of the snow from the main roads. The less fortunate huddled for warmth and did their best to stay out of the automatons' sight, as a slow death from the elements would be kinder than the fate the mechanical beasts had to offer. A muted, incoherent choir sang hymns and carols about the Birth of Christ, their angelic – albeit melancholy – voices filtering from Notre-Dame, filling the streets with lyrics of a virgin woman birthing a son. It was not until the day after that the balance shifted from ordinary to extraordinary, for in the middle of the night between Christmas Eve and Christmas day, that witching hour when the church choir no longer sang and the automatons no longer swept snow from the cobblestone roads, the circus appeared for the first time.

It was no ordinary circus by any means, which was a feat already, as all circuses were rather unordinary. There were no red-and-white striped tents and there were no adverts in every newspaper and magazine across France. There had been no train, no tram, no airship to deliver the troupe. There had been no con- struction of the tents, no clearing of the town square that seemed oddly vacant, as if it had been cut out and placed there for the purpose of housing a circus and nothing more. The people of Paris went to sleep on Christmas Eve with thoughts of presents and festivities and Mass in the morning, and when they woke up the following day, a circus had been set up right in the middle of the city. Paris had not been built to host a circus, but it had plopped itself down as if Paris's only purpose was to welcome it. Compared to the circus, Notre-Dame looked rather out of place.

One by one, the people of Paris ventured to peer at the circus, though the gate around it clearly indicated that it was, unfortunately, closed. But a meager fence did not stop anyone from watching the strange circus. It was, without a crumb of doubt, beyond ordinary in every sense known, and that quickly became realized by everyone who gathered around. The most obvious of those extraordinaries was the display itself.

Three pointed tents, colored black and white with spires sharper than swords as though they planned on spearing the sun and moon and stars right out of the sky, two smaller and one colossal, looming over the others like the Jotun of Scandinavia. Of course, there were vendor carts sprinkled around the tents, advertising caramel apples and sticky taffies and candied popcorn because what circus, extraordinary or not, would lack such things? There were games set up, too, though very few, and all targeted towards a younger audience. However, the vendors and games were not what drew the crowds to the circus on Christmas Day in 1886.

It was what lurked inside the tents that did.

The people of Paris waited all day for news of the circus, though it wasn't until the sun had set and the snow clouds dyed the sky black, and the automatons began their nightly snowplowing patrols that the gates opened, and the circus came to life.

Astrium was the fifty-seventh element discovered by chemists – chemists by license, alchemists by trade – in 1844, and it changed the world drastically. It gave the power to make things levitate and had been a pivotal turning stone in the Industrial Revolution. Steam and cogs and gears made automatons; astrium powered them. It had a bluish glow to it, so when the lights of the circus whirred on and gave a blue glow, it was clear astrium powered the extraordinary thing.

Tickets cost pennies, if that, and soon, the circus was overflowing with patrons. Children devoured chocolates and caramels as if they hadn't just devoured their weight in Christmas sweets, burning off the sugar by playing every game imaginable. The largest of the tents was closed, but the two others...

The first tent housed the Menagerie, which, in ordinary senses, was where the animals were kept. And, yes, there were animals within the Menagerie, but they were not the typical animals patrons expected. There were no elephants or giraffes, no beasts hailing from India or Africa. Instead, there were beasts driven from myth and legend. There was a unicorn with a blue mane and a pearlescent horn that, when victim to light, created a phantasmagoria of color. She let children and women pet her velvety muzzle but nipped at the hands of men. There was a tiger with four eyes who, if you listened *very* closely, spoke in an ancient tongue no tiger should speak. There was a griffon who liked to sleep in a spot of sun like a housecat and who adored the caramel apples her keeper refused to give her. She had a feud with the drake kept just a few stalls down, though nobody but them knew why. There were snakes larger than a train car with scales that shifted color the way a squid's mantle did; the drake with nubs on his forehead and back (the poor thing kept trying to lick his wings free); a rabbit with a proud set of horns who could, and most definitely would, chew on the trousers or skirts of anyone who stood too close; a chimera fit with the body of a lion, the hind legs and second head of a goat, and the tail of a snake; a sleepy fox with nine tails, a love of anything sweet, and a habit of escaping to be with the other foxlike creature, though this one had the head of a fox, legs of an eagle, body that was a mix between a dog and a lion, and the tail of a wolf.

The second of the two smaller tents was the Symphony Hall. There was no orchestra, but music played, nonetheless. Each person experienced something different when entering the Symphony Hall. Some walked on fluffy clouds, listening to lutes and zithers and mandolins. Others traipsed across the sea floor with an ensemble of timpani and steel drums, and woodwinds. Whether it be forest or castle, heavens or hell, each person experienced a different walk, and each person heard different instruments – violins and violas, bass, and cello. Pianos and brass and talharpa and xylophone.

Neither the Menagerie nor the Symphony Hall came close to comparing to the Big Top. There had not been any auditions for the roles the Big Top had to offer. Like the circus itself, the actors seemed to have appeared from thin air. And there had never been any finer actors in the history of performing arts. Acrobats flew as if they had wings, a contortionist squished her body into impossibly small vases like she had no bones in her fleshy vessel, a sword swallower who gulped down blades longer than his torso... Yet, as impressive as they were, they paled in comparison to the magician.

They called him Maître de Rêves, the Master of Dreams. A Morpheus turned real. His magic was a manifestation of the liminal unrealness only dreams had to offer. He created swarms of butterflies from thin air, made people levitate, and turned dirt and dust into gold and jewels...

The Circus had no name, but the street urchins gave it one because, like them, it belonged to the streets.

The Circus of the Street, they called it, and the name stuck.

By the morning of December twenty-seventh, 1886, when the circus finally vanished from Paris without leaving even a speck of dust behind, everyone had fallen in love with Maître de Rêves, or, as they started to call him once the newspapers published the circus's unofficial official name, Maître de la Rue.

All that remained was a butterfly with uncanny blue wings. Butterflies did not infest the airs of Paris in the dead of winter, but this was no ordinary butterfly.

It flapped its blue wings and began flying, weaving through the crowds, and finding a dank alley next to a toy shop. There, it landed on a chipped brick, its wings shuddering. It dropped to the ground, stiff and dead, lifeless, atop a piece of scrap paper. Nobody would find the corpse of the butterfly or the paper that became its coffin, but the butterfly knew what the words inscribed there on its tomb said.

If you long for adventure and wish to see something new, then take my hand and follow me now. Come visit le Cirque de la Rue.

Part One

CHAPTER ONE

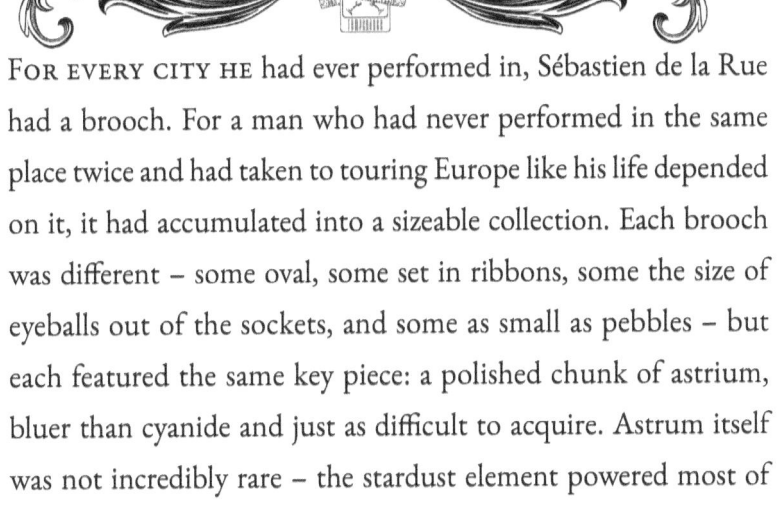

FOR EVERY CITY HE had ever performed in, Sébastien de la Rue had a brooch. For a man who had never performed in the same place twice and had taken to touring Europe like his life depended on it, it had accumulated into a sizeable collection. Each brooch was different – some oval, some set in ribbons, some the size of eyeballs out of the sockets, and some as small as pebbles – but each featured the same key piece: a polished chunk of astrium, bluer than cyanide and just as difficult to acquire. Astrum itself was not incredibly rare – the stardust element powered most of the modern world, after all – but finding polished pieces of it in its crystal form? There was a reason why it was more coveted than diamonds or rubies or emeralds. Most of the time, it came in a granulated powder, like sand or sugar, but like most things under pressure, it hardened and crystallized. While Sébastien's collection was sizeable, well over three hundred total, he could count on one hand the number of brooches he actually adored wearing. He kept his favorites in a stained wood box with a butterfly carved on the top.

A box, currently open, that he stared at in dismay.

None of the brooches were missing, of course – all five of his favorites were nestled in their velvet beds – but all five matched his outfit, and he could not decide which to wear. A travesty to rival every tragedy in the world.

He picked one up – an elliptical piece, set in silver with teardrops of *more* astrium dripping from the central gem – and held it up to his collar, catching a glimpse in the mirror. No, no, no. Too busy. He was wearing his striped pants and those were busy enough. He set the brooch down and picked another – this one was smaller and more circular, with chains and cuffs meant to affix to the collars of his shirt. Not busy enough.

" –his head off if he's not ready... Hey!" a voice – female, older, with a Russian accent so thick Sébastien tasted vodka and felt snow nipping at his nose – called from outside his tent. Nobody was allowed inside, save for Sébastien himself, but that didn't stop his momentary panic. He dropped the brooch and grabbed one at random, attaching it to his shirt without stopping to see if the plain circle with a smooth, polished gem would work. It had to.

The Russian woman yelled again, "Séb, I know you're in there. Do I need to bribe you? I have delicious coffee waiting for you. Mm... It's fresh and French – your favorite!"

Sébastien knew there was no coffee waiting for him, but he still tugged on his gloves and scraped his hair into a messy tail. The stubborn white pieces that tainted part of his black hair fell over his forehead. No time to fix them. If Svetlana had come to his tent with threats of ripping off his head and bribes of French coffee, he was in trouble.

He burst out of the tent, nearly knocking the woman over. Svetlana, like all other performers, was an enigma whose age was unknown. She could have been in her twenties with the generous curves she'd been blessed with, she could have been in her forties with the crow's feet wrinkles at the corners of her deep green eyes, and the grey hairs threaded through her thick brown locks; she could have been a teenager with the way she carried herself. She wore a heavy green gown – green was *her* color, after all – the color of evergreen trees in winter, the fur trim around the cuffs of her sleeves and collar so dark grey it looked black. Her hair was piled atop her head in a messy knot, exposing the harshness of her cheekbones and the severity of her emerald eyes. In her hands, to Séb's delightful surprise, was a tin cup of coffee.

He reached for it. She held it over her head. Svetlana wasn't any taller than Sébastien, even with her heeled boots, but even he knew not to tempt her.

"It's a calamity," she said calmly. "Let's see... Ahji and Dakov are having a lover's squabble of sorts, if griffons and drakes can *have* lover's squabbles. Noa and/or Sasha *borrowed* one of Alice's corsets, and Alice is absolutely *inconsolable*. The end of the world. Truly. Antara offered to practice her aim on the twins, and that went over about as well as you'd expect. Oh, and apparently, some duchess thinks she can rent out the entire Symphony Hall for her private amusement tonight."

Sébastien focused on grabbing the tin mug of coffee before any of it could spill. "Don't Ahji and Dakov hate each other?"

"Ilian seems to think otherwise. He caught Dakov in Ahji's enclosure a few times now. She was even licking Dakov's would-be wings." Svetlana began walking, her hips swaying with each smooth step.

Even though it was too early in December to be winter, Pärnu, Estonia had quite a bit of snowfall already. Sébastien loathed the snow almost as much as he loathed most other things in the world, like being responsible and spicy foods and work, but Svetlana had been made for it. Her heeled boots didn't so much as falter as she walked. This was a summer day for the Russian woman.

"Why is it my responsibility to sort out the griffon-drake squabble?" asked Sébastien over the rim of his mug.

"Darling, did you not listen to anything else I said?" he did not want to admit that he hadn't. "Noa and Sasha and Alice? The duchess? Do *you* want to let a duchess rent the Symphony Hall? She didn't even ask. I overheard her bragging that she got the reservation."

He finished his coffee in just a few more gulps, but even the caffeine did nothing to alleviate the exhaustion that always clung to his bones. The circles under his eyes nearly matched the black of (most of) his hair.

People could not just *rent* parts of Le Cirque de la Rue, the magical circus that never stopped in the same city twice. They especially couldn't rent parts of the circus without consulting the Maître de la Rue first. And Sébastien had spent the entire morning since the circus landed in Pärnu fussing over what to wear and what brooch would match his outfit. He had little respect for people who assumed they could simply walk all over him.

Séb pinched the bridge of his nose with the pads of his gloved fingers. The gloves had claw-like nails to them, even though his own fingernails were blunt. Supposedly, that is, as nobody but Sébastien himself saw his hands without the gloves on. He grumbled, "No. I don't want to let a duchess rent the place. I don't want to deal with her at all. Have her banned at the door. If she can donate...mm...an eighth of her wealth to whatever charity helps orphans and prove it, she can reserve the Symphony Hall for an hour. I'll even let her keep a Jar of Music for her troubles. I don't want to do auditions here. None at all. Not with duchesses tainting the air. I've changed my mind. No duchess at all, eighth of her fortune or not. Tell Ilian to tell Ahji and Dakov that if they don't kiss and make up by showtime, they're pulled from the Menagerie until we get to our next destination. And take Alice shopping. If Noa and Sasha have her corset, we all know she's never getting it back."

"See?" Svetlana looked over her shoulder and gave Séb a motherly-sisterly smile. "That wasn't too hard. No duchess, no griffon or drake, and Alice gets a new corset."

It would have been impossible without his coffee, and Séb was already grumpy that his cup was empty.

Before long, the pair stopped just outside the biggest of the three tents. Against the white backdrop of snow, the black stripes stood out even starker than before. Music and warmth radiated from inside. Svetlana pulled the tent flap aside and gestured for Sébastien to enter first. He ducked under her arm, finding himself in the backstage part of the tent. Astrium lanterns perched haphazardly atop crates and balanced on tightropes. Their blue glow made his eyes seem even more unnatural when they caught the light. He stepped over a box that smelled strongly of gunpowder labeled *AURELIO'S. DO NOT TOUCH.*

The main arena – a circular stage surrounded by velvet-lined seats with two massive towers on either side – was packed full of the circus's performers. The Gemini Twins – Noa and Sasha Elie, the circus's clowns – sulked in the shadows, a torn corset on the ground by their feet. Sébastien scanned the arena for Alice and found her in the air, swinging with her partner Odette on the trapeze. Either she was mad about the trick, or she was furious. She swung as if she had wings and a body that wouldn't shatter upon impact should she miss the next trapeze being tossed to her.

Svetlana hummed and plucked the mug from Sébastien's hands. She used part of her sleeve to clean the last precious drops of coffee from it, then set it down. She peeled off her blouse, then each skirt and petticoat until she stood in just her drawers, chemise, corset, and stockings.

Sébastien did not stare. Svetlana stripping to her unmentionables was just as normal as the Gemini Twins pulling pranks. It was, after all, rather difficult to squeeze into a small space with layers of heavy clothes weighing her down. Her performing costume was more tastefully risqué, but she couldn't have been bothered to go *all* the way back to her own tent to change, then come back to the Big Top to practice stuffing her body into a small receptacle.

Svetlana stepped one foot into the tin mug, then the other, her body folding with uncanny ease until she had squished herself into the tiny thing. She stayed there for a moment, then gracefully stuck one leg out, then the other, then rose from the mug like a burlesque dancer putting on a show.

"Oh, dear," she said calmly. "I smell of coffee now. Well, I suppose that's my cue to take a bath. Don't bother fetching me until showtime, dear. I have full faith that you will get this situation under control!"

She gathered her clothes and sauntered out of the tent, wearing nothing but her undergarments in the snow.

Sébastien looked at the somewhat organized chaos of his troupe.

He most definitely did not have the power to get the situation under control.

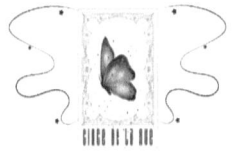

The moment the moon rose over the snowy city and stars speckled the sky, the troupe put on their costumes and waited, patiently, for Sébastien to announce them.

Sébastien dressed rather modestly for a ringmaster, wearing his striped pants, a plain shirt, and a tailcoat over the top of it all. He wore a top hat, his black-and-white hair pulled back with a striped ribbon. He fixed his astrium brooch and stepped into the arena, no longer Sébastien de la Rue but the Dreammonger.

"Ladies and gentlemen, boys and girls!" his voice boomed as if something was amplifying it. He spoke French, of course, since it was the only language he knew, but the circus translated it for the audience. "Those of you sitting here tonight are in for a treat. You've longed for adventure. You followed the butterfly. And now... Now, it is my pleasure to welcome you to Le Cirque de la Rue!"

He swept his hands out. At once, all the lights in the tent went out, but the darkness did not last long. A swarm of astrium-blue butterflies appeared from nowhere, glowing brightly. They fluttered around the tent before creating a cloud of wings that solidified into an *actual* cloud. Thunder crackled, and lightning flashed. Rain poured from the magic cloud, only...only it wasn't rain. It was rose petals, their perfume sweetening the air. Children laughed, reaching for the petals. Women gasped softly, and even the grown men couldn't hide their astonishment.

The lights went back on, a spotlight cast in the middle of the arena, lighting the Dreammonger. He took a step, though it was an *actual* step, an invisible not-there stair. He climbed the not-there staircase until he appeared to be levitating in midair.

"I am the Dreammonger!" he announced. "The Maître de la Rue. Your dreams are my realities, and I can grant miracles to those who believe. You, madame. Bonjour. You look as though you need a miracle."

He waved a gloved hand. A woman in the audience was suddenly lifted into the air. She gasped and quickly tried to push her skirts down as the Dreammonger pulled her close. She was pretty, in her mid-twenties, with brown hair and flushed cheeks. He kissed both of those cheeks. His gaze, impossibly blue, met hers, ordinary brown.

"Ah," he cooed, his lips curling into a grin. "A miracle I shall grant." He reached into thin air and pulled out a seashell, which he placed in the woman's trembling hand. "Put this beneath your pillow tonight, and tomorrow, you will receive that ring."

The Dreammonger winked and sent the flushed woman right back to her seat. He clapped his hands together and rushed to the ground. For a moment, it appeared like he'd fall, but his boots touched the ground gently.

"Look to the skies, ladies and gents! Watch closely – don't even blink! – for if you look away, you will miss the Flying Foxes." Sébastien pointed to the rafters.

On either raised platform stood a girl. They both wore white leotards with black corsets cinching their waists. One had pale pink stockings on, matching the pink ribbon in her white-blonde hair. The other wore purple stockings and had a purple ribbon in her brown hair. Alice and Odette, respectively.

Alice took a running leap, soaring through the air. The audience held their breaths. There was no net to catch the girl if she fell. And she *did* fall, careening towards the ground. Odette ran off the platform and dove after Alice. Only she didn't catch Alice.

Odette grabbed the trapeze that appeared out of seemingly nowhere. And Alice... Alice grabbed Odette's ankle. Alice swung and launched herself, holding the second trapeze. They crossed paths and landed on the opposite platforms.

The crowd cheered. Sébastien's blood pumped, his heart speeding up. Good. *Good, good, good.*

Odette took another leap at the same time as Alice. They passed each other in the air, both doing a perfect flip before grabbing the trapeze. Each girl held the bar with one hand, the other reaching out to take her partner's. Alice tucked one leg against her thigh and pressed her foot against Odette's, who mocked the pose. Suspended in the air, they stayed like that, the cheering only growing louder.

Their routine lasted another minute. Sébastien watched carefully. The second they passed trapeze for the last time, he announced, "And now, for our next act, we have a man of *many* talents. He can swallow swords, breathe fire, do stunts no man could ever think of doing... Please welcome *El Cuélebre!*"

Alice landed first, perfectly balancing on the palm of a Spanish man's hand. She lifted her arms in the air as Odette landed on the man's other hand. He wore no shirt, and his trousers were black and loose, held up with an orange sash (orange was *his* color). A dragon tattoo stretched across his back and shoulder blades, seemingly shimmering in the light. His curls were tied in a messy bun at the back of his head, his beard and moustache trimmed sharply. He flashed a grin; his wink caused a woman in one of the front-row seats to swoon.

Aurelio Álvaro, in a popular gossip column spread across the continent, had been dubbed the *most eligible and most sought-after bachelor in all of Europe.* While they had no idea Aurelio's relationship status, *most eligible and sought-after* was the proper way of stating he was the *hottest and most desirable man in Europe.* The ladies (and some of the gentlemen) ate it up. Standing well over six feet with rippling muscles and thighs that could crush rocks, Aurelio had the exotic beauty down perfectly.

Aurelio held both women effortlessly before setting them down. They ran off stage, hardly noticed now that El Cuélebre was there. Sébastien, who had positioned himself off to the side, grabbed the two props Aurelio needed. He handed the first to the firebreather – a lit torch. Aurelio took the torch and opened his mouth. His tattoo seemed to move in the firelight. He brought the torch down and down and down until he engulfed it. Then, he tossed the torch aside and *exhaled.*

Like a dragon, he spewed fire from his mouth, blazing rivulets igniting the sky. Warmth rumbled in his stomach. Sébastien couldn't help but smile to himself when the crowd erupted in applause. His heart sped up. Some of the exhaustion left his bones. *Good, good, good.*

Aurelio took the sword next. It was the size of his torso, if not longer. No human could ever guzzle such a blade without rupturing one vital organ or the next. He measured the blade for show. The audience hushed. They *knew* he would be fine – how would he make it into those gossip columns if he wasn't? – but that didn't stop the collective anxiety that smothered the crowd like a blanket.

He tipped his head back and unfurled his jaw. Then, inch by razor-sharp inch, he lowered the sword, swallowing the metal like air until the handguard pressed against his lips, and there was simply no more *to* swallow. He held the sword there for a few agonizing seconds before ripping it free and throwing it, only...

"Now, if that wasn't dangerous enough for you, perhaps Lady Kali will be. They call her that after the goddess of war, for she is nothing but ruthless," the Dreammonger announced.

From the shadows stepped a girl. She wore a unique costume – a *ghagra choli* that was white with black swirls. Her color was, of course, gold, and she wore it in bangles and bracelets and in the iris of the painted third eye above her brows. Her long black hair was braided over her shoulder, revealing the warm brown column of her neck. Her belly was soft, accented with a ring through her navel. Henna, blacker than night, decorated her hands and bare feet. She held the sword by the blade with two fingers.

Then, Lady Kali – Antara Shiva, as those in le Cirque knew her – threw the sword. It landed on a circular target across the arena. While the audience had been distracted by Aurelio, the Gemini Twins set up the next act.

Which, besides pushing out the target and arming Lady Kali with more knives than a butcher owned, involved strapping one of the twins to the board. Wonkus and Goober, the individual names given to the Gemini Twins by a younger audience member some time ago, were identical in nearly every way, and nobody (save for the twins themselves, perhaps) knew which of the two red-headed clowns was strapped to the target.

Antara did not care. She slid one of her jeweled daggers from the bandolier slung around her shoulder. She tested its weight and then, grinning, threw it. It landed a *hair* from the clown's ear.

The other twin, the one with buns atop their head (generally accepted as being Wonkus or Noa Elie), grabbed the board and *yanked*. At once, the target became a *spinning* target. And if that wasn't enough, Antara pulled a silk ribbon from the folds of her skirt and tied it around her eyes.

The audience watched in horror – in amusement. Antara took another knife and threw it. *Thunk!* Just barely missing Goober's – Sasha Elie's – neck. *Thunk!* Another knife, this one above Sasha's shoulder. *Thunk, thunk, thunk!* Three knives at once, all missing the grinning clown.

After Lady Kali came Beowulf, the nickname for Ilian Agreste, the master of the Menagerie and the beast tamer. He showed off his control over a few big cats and a bear before leaving the stage to the Gemini Twins. Their act was targeted towards the younger audience, but the adult members ate it up as well.

Then came Svetlana. The Gemini Twins had set up her act before tumbling off stage: a box, a tin bucket, a teacup, a thimble, all in a row. She walked onto the stage wearing a black robe over her costume – a black-and-white striped leotard with emerald lace, matching stockings, and green silk gloves that nearly reached her shoulders.

Svetlana was not announced, not like the other acts, so, her stage name wasn't known. The public took to calling her *Firebird,* likely only because she was Russian. She didn't mind. It was a powerful name, after all.

She shed her robe and approached the box. It was the sort of prop normal contortionists would use. A child could fit into it, as well as a particularly stretchy adult. Svetlana stepped into the box and folded herself down and down and down until there was nothing of her to be seen.

Then, she unfolded herself and stepped out of the box. She approached the pail next and did the same thing.

Then with the teacup.

At this point, the audience usually assumed *she* was a magician of sorts because nobody could fit into a teacup. They would eye the thimble, wondering how she could create an illusion to make it seem like she fit into the tiny thing. She wouldn't say a word; she would just step one foot into the thimble, then the next, then fold herself inwards until she was, somehow, within the thing.

And she would extract herself, bow, collect her robe, and saunter off.

And the crowd *devoured it.*

They rose to their feet, clapping loudly – God, Sébastien's heart thundered in his chest. He felt *alive.* The cast came to the center of the arena, giving one final bow. The applause would last for an eternity and a half before the audience filed out of the Big Top to visit the other two tents, or play games, or eat candies and gossip about how attractive Aurelio is or how Svetlana simply can't fit into a thimble.

And Sébastien would return to his own tent to put away his brooch and decide where the circus would go next.

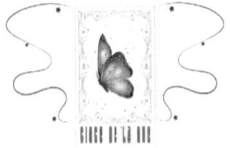

Svetlana Vasilievna took a flask of vodka (she was Russian, after all) from her robe and sipped on it as she went to the Menagerie. The people inside were too busy fussing over the unicorn or the kitsune to recognize her as the Firebird, and that was just as well with Svetlana. She wanted to be ignored right now. She wanted to blend in with the crowd.

She took another sip of vodka before putting the flask away and approaching the pen with Ahji, the griffon. The griffon was curled up, lounging like a housecat in a sunspot. Her wings covered her body like a blanket. Svetlana leaned against the glass wall.

Footsteps approached, followed by a figure that stopped just across from Svetlana. She peered at the man. Ilian was not unattractive by any means, with dark brown hair and deep blue eyes – nothing like the intense blue of Sébastien's. His color was maroon, and he wore it on his tie tucked beneath his waistcoat. His gloves were also maroon, but he forwent them now.

"Did they resolve their lover's spat?" Svetlana asked, casting a glance at the pen housing Dakov the drake. Dakov licked at his wing-nubs as best as he would. Soon, he would be Dakov the Dragon, but until those wings grew in, he was still a drake.

"I simply cannot keep up with the relationships between beasts," Ilian said with a sigh.

"Beasties and humans have that in common," said Svetlana. She took out her flask again and offered it to Ilian, who refused at first but begrudgingly took it when she gave it a little shake.

"Bleh!" he grimaced. "I don't know how you can drink this. Tastes like dragon piss."

"Oh? And you're an expert on dragon piss?" she took the flask and put it away. "I wouldn't say dragon piss. That's more...tequila. Just ask Aurelio."

Svetlana and Aurelio, supposedly, had had an affair a year or so ago. *Supposedly.* She refused to spill any details, and Aurelio never talked about his personal life.

"I suppose I could ask Ahji since Dakov is basically a dragon." Ilian looked at the sleeping griffon. She did not look like she was in the position to be answering any questions any time soon.

"So that's Ahji and Dakov along with Myōbu and Lorcan now?" Myōbu the kitsune and Lorcan the Enfield, two foxlike creatures about as inseparable as Sébastien was with his astrium brooches. Svetlana chuckled. "This place is turning into a brothel."

"There's a brothel in Paris that I wouldn't mind visiting again if we're ever in the area," mused Ilian, who seemed caught up on the wrong part of Svetlana's observation.

She chuckled, though. It wasn't her place to dictate whether the troupe could spend their wages at Parisian brothels. After all, she (allegedly) slept with another cast member.

"Got the time?" she asked. In the pen, Ahji let out a rumbling purr as she rolled over, exposing her belly. Her paws twitched, her wings fluttering. She must have been dreaming of flying. Or, perhaps, of a particular drake.

Ilian pulled his pocket watch from his waistcoat, flipping it open. Time was a malleable thing at the circus. Regular timepieces ceased working once guests crossed the threshold between Ordinary and Extraordinary. Only certain clocks, including the pocket watch Ilian had, worked within the confines of the circus grounds.

"Half an hour until midnight," he said. Time was *very* malleable, considering the circus began at six, and there was no way it had been nine hours.

"Mm," said Svetlana. It was time to force any stragglers out.

When each cast member signed a contract binding themselves to the circus, they had to agree to three rules: never go into the solid black tent that belonged to Sébastien, never leave their tent at night, and always have a strong belief in magic.

Midnight was the inarguable time all cast had to be in their tents. Svetlana pushed herself off the glass.

"I hope we go somewhere flashy," she said. "I would kill for a nice mink scarf."

"Your closet probably just curated three," Ilian pointed out.

"Mm," she said. "But that takes away the fun of shopping. Goodnight, dear."

She blew Ilian a kiss and sauntered out of the Menagerie. Ilian was quick to follow, going to his own tent. Each smaller tent was black and white striped, though they had splashes of color corresponding to *theirs*. Everyone except for Sébastien, that is. His tent, for whatever reason, was solid black.

Svetlana ducked into hers, greeted by the warmth of a roaring fire.

The tents were just as extraordinary as the rest of the circus, as they were all much bigger on the inside. Svetlana's resembled a cozy winter cabin with polished wood floors and walls. A staircase with intricately carved steps led up to a loft where her bed and wardrobe were. There was a washroom with an astrium-powered tub and shower and a stone fireplace that constantly had a fire going. She kicked the snow off her boots and hung her robe on a hook near the door. A bath sounded divine, but sleep called to her. She stepped out of her boots and walked upstairs, collapsing onto the pile of quilts and furs and knitted blankets that swallowed her mattress. Svetlana was asleep in minutes.

The only person still awake as the church bells tolled midnight in the distance was Sébastien, except he was still the Dreammonger.

"Let's see," he murmured. "Where are we going next?"

CHAPTER TWO

NO AMOUNT OF COFFEE, tea, or alcohol would help Enoch Irving reach his deadline, but he pretended each cup of caffeine would. He had never been very good at pretending. His final draft of the article set to be on the front page of the *Evening Standard* was due in... Twenty-three minutes. He hadn't even finished the last paragraph.

It was supposed to be a concise article about how the Thames had frozen over. Concise and Enoch got along as well as morticians and doctors; they acknowledged each other's presence but never truly crossed paths unless something terrible went wrong.

Enoch typed furiously, the click-clacking of his typewriter echoing off the walls of his tiny office. At least he had an office. After all the praise E. E. Irving received last spring, he was granted an overdue promotion that included an office and a secretary who brought him coffee (and tea, and sometimes alcohol). The typewriter *dinged,* letting him know the line was up. He grumbled incoherently about how the typewriter was a foul beast for interrupting his work, cranked the carriage return, pushed the page into place, and went right back to type type typing.

Knock, knock, knock.

"Busy!" Enoch called without looking up from his paper.

The door opened anyway.

"Just set it down, Miss Gertrude," he said, addressing his secretary.

"Mr. Irving, if you don't take a break, your fingers are going to fall off."

Not Miss Gertrude. Enoch looked up, shoving his glasses up his nose, and met the gaze of the chief editor, Mr. Slate. Enoch slumped in his seat, suddenly feeling very small.

"I'm nearly done, sir," he said in a much meeker voice.

"Bah!" Mr. Slate picked up the ream of papers that was Enoch's article. He skimmed through it. "Did I not specify concise?"

"Y-you did, sir, but..." but Enoch had no excuses. He just simply liked to write, and that was all. While Mr. Slate was distracted, he clacked out the last sentence of his paragraph and tore the page free, handing it to the editor.

"But you're E. E. Irving, and you simply do not know how to write less than five pages, even if your life depends on it." Mr. Slate looked over the manuscript to eye the collection of mugs and teacups on Enoch's desk. He felt very, *very* small.

Chief Editor Mr. Slate was not a cruel person, but he was a punctual one, and this was not the first time Enoch had gone even a minute past his deadline. He gazed at the photograph of an airship on the wall. It was from the first time he'd left Great Britain – for an article on cuckoo clocks powered by astrium in Germany. It was the only real piece of personalization in his office (aside from his hoard of mugs and teacups and his typewriter). *Well,* he thought. *There goes the promotion. It was nice having this office while it lasted.*

Mr. Slate tucked the manuscript under his arm. "Go home, Mr. Irving. You need a break. Get some rest. Take tomorrow off. There's that new pub downtown that everyone is talking about. Go visit it."

"Is that an order, sir?" squeaked Enoch.

Mr. Slate rolled up the manuscript and smacked Enoch on the head with it. "It damn well should be. Go home and go to sleep, Mr. Irving."

Enoch nodded. There was nothing else he could do. Mr. Slate left his office. Enoch quickly tidied up and left a note for Miss Gertrude. *Sorry about the mess. I appreciate your efforts.* After making sure everything was just how he liked it, he grabbed his coat and scarf and left the building.

The building wasn't too far from the flat Enoch rented, but he didn't want to be caught outside when the automatons – the Golems, as he liked to call them – came out to sweep stragglers off the streets. He wrapped his scarf tighter around his neck. His glasses fogged, but he knew the path to his flat by heart. Before long, he pushed open the blue door and stepped inside.

"Enoch, honey, that you?" his landlady, Mrs. Taffy, called. She lived in the bottom flat and rented the upper space to Enoch. It had its own kitchen and privy and everything he might need, but there was only one front door, so Enoch ran into the ancient woman more often than he cared to.

"Yes, Mrs. Taffy," he said as he kicked snow off his shoes. "Sorry to bother you so late."

"Would you like a cup of tea?" she hobbled out of her kitchen to greet him. Enoch was not a very tall man to start with, but he felt like a giant compared to his landlady. She had a hunched back, which only made her appear shorter. A child could stand taller than her. She was blind as a bat with spectacles even thicker than Enoch's, and that was a feat in of itself since *he* was blind as a bat. She wore a shawl constantly and had the habit of talking about her youthful days. Usually, Enoch wouldn't care. He loved listening to people talk about their youth. Not Mrs. Taffy, though. She would go *on* about how her dead ex-husband would ravage her in bed when they were newlyweds. In excruciating detail. Sometimes, Enoch had a hard time looking at her.

"No, thank you," he said. "I'm off to sleep now anyway. You ought to sleep, too."

"I'll sleep when I'm dead, thank you very much." She took a loud sip from her mug. Enoch did not believe it was full of tea. "And that will be never."

He believed that.

"Goodnight, Mrs. Taffy." He started up the stairs before she could delve into a story about her ravishing ex-husband.

Enoch's flat was small but very much him. It was chaos in all senses. Newspapers and notebooks littered the coffee table. He had a phonograph but no records for it. The dishes in his kitchen didn't match and were more cracked than not. He had an astrium radiator that rattled and clanked constantly. Mrs. Taffy had tried to fix it herself, but that seemed to only make it worse. When she asked about it, he would lie and say he didn't hear it anymore.

He shuffled to his bedroom and undressed quickly, putting on pajamas in place of his clothes. He sank into bed but pulled a notebook from his nightstand drawer. With the light from an astrium lamp, he flipped it open and began to write until his hands were stained with ink and his eyes were too heavy to stay open. He fell asleep, not for the first time, with his glasses still on.

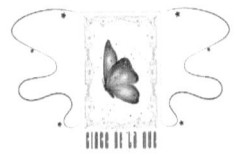

Enoch awoke to knocking at his door. Not his bedroom door, as that would be a whole other slew of problems, but the door at the top of the stairs that was *his* front door. He sat up quickly, his notebook and pen sliding off his lap. His glasses sat crooked on his face, and his hair was, no doubt, akin to a bird's nest. Not the delicate hummingbird's nest or the elegant nest of an eagle, but the haphazard nest pigeons made – a bunch of sticks and string and God knows what tossed together. He fixed his glasses and combed his fingers through his hair as best as he could.

"Coming, coming!" he announced when the unexpected visitor knocked again. He tripped over his bare feet, nearly falling face-first into the door.

Mrs. Taffy stood on the other side. Next to her was a woman Enoch recognized instantly. She was willowy and lithe, her hair the color of ink and her eyes just as severe, a harsh contrast to the deathly pale flesh of her face. She looked like she hadn't seen the sun in months, and that probably wasn't too far from the truth. She wore a smart day dress with pinstripes that only made her appear taller. She wore a crude apron over the dress and heavy leather gloves.

Lenore Therese was the only female undertaker in perhaps all of Europe, and she was, without a sliver of doubt, the damn best. Enoch had worked with her once when he'd been knee-deep in an article about a murder a handful of months ago. The body had shown up with black slashes through its eyes and a few fewer organs than usual. Why she was at his door again was beyond Enoch, and, quite frankly, he was a bit unnerved.

"Good morning, Enoch," said Mrs. Taffy. She sipped from a cup of probably-not-tea, then turned to descend the stairs. "Please keep the noise to a minimum. I'd rather not be reminded of my youthful days this early in the morning. Good for you, Enoch. I always thought you preferred blokes."

Enoch flushed crimson. He shoved his glasses up his nose and decided *not* to linger on Mrs. Taffy's crude comment. Instead, he stepped aside and gestured for Lenore to come inside. She did so. Only after closing the door did he realize she wasn't wearing the bird-beak mask that covered the lower part of her face that she usually wore. She stuffed the beak with herbs to block out the stink of decay and rot. When working with *very* decomposed bodies – or bodies of victims of consumption or illness – she'd add a pair of goggles to protect her eyes from any diseases or some other nonsense Enoch didn't care to take notes on.

"Blokes, hm?" She spoke with a rather posh accent, a stark contrast to Enoch's thick, harsh accent.

"Shut *up,*" he hissed. "What brings you here so early in the morning?"

"It's ten o'clock," she said simply like that explained everything.

Damn it! Enoch nearly rushed to his room to get dressed, only to remember he had the day off. "Would you like tea? If you want to sit, please take your..." he gestured vaguely.

Lenore removed her apron and gloves, setting them, regrettably, on the coffee table. Enoch hurried to the kitchen to put on a kettle. While he waited for the astrium stove to heat the kettle up, he gathered two mugs, his box of tea, sugar, and cream. He made the two cups quickly and brought them to the living room, handing one to Lenore.

"Someone claimed the body," she said without preamble. *The body? Oh! The body!* "Well, the ashes, anyways. I still had the photograph of the remains, and they compared it with a photograph they had, and it was the same person. Mister Lester Sanders. A street urchin. His third cousin or something like that recognized him. Apparently, they thought he'd been dead for years now."

"Oh," was all Enoch could say. He looked down at his tea. The case had closed quickly. Lenore had no idea what the cause of death was since a few vital organs were missing, so she, for the sake of getting the bobbies out of her morgue, just said he'd died from *organ failure.* ("Technically, his organs *did* fail him by not being there," she'd said.)

"Thought you might be interested. Could be a decent follow-up story. I could give you the photographs."

It would be a good follow-up. Far better than just sitting at home for a forced day off. What kind of person had to be *forced* into taking a day off? Enoch grumbled to himself and drank his tea.

"Is that all?" he asked, sounding far ruder than intended. If Lenore had been bothered by it, she didn't let it show.

She set her teacup down and grabbed her apron and gloves. "I hear that circus showed up in Italy."

That circus. Le Cirque de la Rue had only been to London once, a year and a half ago. Enoch stumbled upon it and decided to visit. He stayed up all night to write an article about it before anyone else in London did. He'd been waiting for it to return – he had so many questions, so much more to write – but it hadn't even been to Great Britain since.

"I doubt I can get on an airship and make it to Italy before it leaves," Enoch said glumly.

Lenore grinned. She had perfect teeth. He was jealous. After an accident involving ice and a severe lack of balance as a teenager, one of Enoch's front teeth was chipped.

"Maybe it's a sign it's going to show up in western Europe again soon," she said with a shrug. "Let me know if you want those photographs. And *please* don't put my name in anything you write. I like my anonymity. Have fun with your landlady. I'm pretty sure she's been listening this whole time. Oh, and you have drool on your chin."

Lenore waved with just her fingers and saw herself out. Enoch stood and rushed to the privy only to see that, indeed, he had a crust of dried drool clinging to his chin. The dark circles under his eyes seemed worse, and his hair was not a pigeon's nest but a rat's nest – a very messy rat's nest.

Enoch groaned and buried his face in his hands. It wasn't even noon, and he'd made a fool of himself already.

"How is it cold in *Italy?* Isn't it supposed to be *hot* here?" Alice shivered, pulling her coat tighter around her body. Sardinia, Italy, wasn't nearly as cold as Estonia – it felt more like spring with a gentle drizzle of rain – and it had been *her* idea to go shopping, yet Sébastien was still subject to her whining. He pinched the bridge of his nose.

"I know *you* know what seasons are," he said, exasperated. "It's *winter.* It's *cold.* Either stop complaining or go back to Le Cirque to practice with Cecily."

Alice puffed out her cheeks, pouting. "None of this would have happened if those damn clowns kept their hands to themselves."

A lot of things wouldn't have happened if the Gemini Twins kept out of trouble, but the circus wouldn't be nearly as entertaining. It was *because* of their trouble that the circus did so well, if nothing else. Still, Sébastien understood all too well how annoying the twins' pranks could get.

"And your wardrobe simply couldn't give you a *new* corset?" he asked, narrowly avoiding a puddle.

Above them, an airship flew low to the ground, the churning of its gears and pumping of pistons creating a droning hum. Sardinia had an airship port where smaller ships would take off and land. By the looks of it, this particular one had just taken off.

"It *could*," said Alice. "But I wanted to go shopping, and I was expecting Svetlana to come with."

Like everything associated with the circus, the wardrobes within each performer's tent would provide them with whatever clothes they needed – day clothes, evening clothes, costumes, pajamas, all of it. Alice most definitely had a new corset to replace the broken one sitting in her wardrobe. The oiled coat she wore to protect her garments from the rain was most definitely new.

Alice had originally asked Svetlana to accompany her. "Ask Séb to go," she'd said. "My manicure is drying, and he needs to get his brooch anyway."

Sébastien got his brooch fifteen minutes earlier and kept it safely tucked away in his pocket. Like every other brooch he owned, it was made of astrium. His newest addition was cut in the shape of a diamond and was the size of an eye – a human eye, that is.

Alice grabbed Sébastien's arm and dragged him into an atelier without warning. Save for his brooches, Sébastien utilized the unordinary wardrobes to the fullest. He'd never been fond of shopping, and most of the income from the circus went to the performers. Sébastien divided the wages up between his troupe evenly, then put two-thirds of the remaining money into savings and kept the last third for himself. Just enough for his brooches and his coffee addiction.

The atelier was warm inside, bright lights making it appear friendlier and more inviting. A woman with a tape measurer around her shoulders and tiny circle spectacles came over. She said something in Italian. Sébastien did not know Italian, but the circus translated for him – a helpful caveat of his contract.

Alice, to his surprise, greeted the woman excitedly and began talking about what he could only assume was corsets. Bored already, he flopped onto a chaise and waited impatiently for Alice to finish, wishing he had a mug of coffee to keep him occupied.

The woman, who must have thought Sébastien was Alice's husband since no respectable young lady would go out unchaperoned and Sébastien appeared to be the same age as her, brought over a newspaper for Sébastien to read. Even though it was in Italian and the circus worked to translate, he just picked out the names of the journalists and looked at the black-and-white photographs.

There were photographs of an airship accompanying an article written by G. Giovanna; horses before a race documented by a German journalist named Susanna Cooper; a frozen River Thames and an article by E. E. Irving; an article by K. Kukk with a photograph of the circus. Sébastien put all his attention on *that* photograph. The details were far too blurred for him to make anything out, but he could distinguish the three tents. A blurry ring of exposure created an aura around them.

The rest of the newspaper had articles that were all words and nothing else and a few adverts sprinkled here and there. Sébastien rolled up the paper and drummed it against his thigh, bored out of his mind.

"Pardon," came a voice in thickly accented French. Sébastien glanced up through his thick, dark lashes to meet the gaze of a young woman. She had to have been Alice's age – well, appearance-wise – with warm skin and black curls.

Sébastien arched a brow, silently prompting her to continue.

Her cheeks flushed. "I...I... Are you the Dreammonger?" she blurted. Those four words caught Sébastien completely off guard. Sure, he never hid his appearance when performing, but he never visited the same city twice and rarely did anyone pay any attention to the ringmaster.

"Perhaps I am, perhaps I'm not," he said slowly. "Why?"

That answer seemed to please the girl. "I saw the circus in town. I went when it visited Bonifacio a few months ago. I-I recognized your hair..." she pointed to her own hair, right where Sébastien's stripe of white would be.

He glanced over the girl's shoulder. Alice and the shop attendant spoke rapid Italian, gesturing at a corset as they spoke. He looked back at the girl.

"Maître de la Rue, at your service," he said as grandly as one could while slouching on a chaise with their legs spread and their shoulders hunched. "I take it you will be visiting Le Cirque tonight?"

Her eyes went wider than saucers, and she nodded excitedly. "Yes! I never thought I'd see it again. When I saw the tents, I nearly cried with joy. Tell me, Dreammonger, how do you manage to travel so quickly? Do you use an airship? Automatons?"

Sébastien grinned. "Magic," he answered in his ringmaster voice. "A true magician never reveals his secrets." Behind the girl, Alice paid for her corset. "We're staying two nights instead of one to host auditions. If you believe in magic and have some sort of talent, you should audition."

He stood, unraveling to his full, lanky height. "Ciao, mon Cherie. Oh, and check your pockets."

He walked off, joining Alice before he could see the girl's reaction when she reached into her pocket to find a black-and-white envelope with a blue butterfly seal.

You're invited to Le Cirque de la Rue. Follow the blue butterfly in your dreams. May we meet again, the letter inside read. It was signed simply as *Dreammonger,* as that was the only name Sébastien signed on anything circus-related.

"Let's get back," said Alice, who looked slightly less peeved now. "I need to take a bath before showtime."

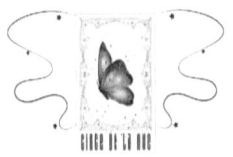

The following night, half of Sardinia showed up at the circus to audition. Sébastien instructed Svetlana to oversee the auditions while he watched from the shadows, away from sight. Svetlana was not too pleased about nannying a bunch of Italians, but it *was* Sébastien's circus, and she did have to follow his orders *sometimes*.

The auditions were held in the Big Top since it had the most space. The troupe sat in the risers, spread out to watch the people who had watched *them* the night before performing. Svetlana sat in a chair taken from her own tent, ankles crossed under the deep green skirts of her dress. She wore her hair up, pinned under a fur hat, looking very much like a stern Russian woman with more vodka in her veins than blood. Her deep red lips tugged into a frown as the next auditionee stepped onto the makeshift stage. The Gemini Twins had pushed together two pallets and threw a rug over them.

"Name, act, thirty seconds, go," Svetlana drawled, bored. She had a notebook and pen with her, writing down a list of names that had potential and doodling trees and bears and wolves and people with their spines and skulls torn from their flesh.

The auditions lasted until eleven thirty at night, when Sébastien emerged from the confines of the shadows, clapped his hands together and announced that the circus was over, and he would contact anyone he found interesting enough via letter. There were disappointed groans and sighs from the people still queued to audition, but they were herded out.

Sébastien hopped over to Svetlana and looked over her shoulder. He hadn't expected much from her but was surprised to see a fair list of names. He plucked her pen from her grip and scribbled out a few names. "This one is an acrobat. We already have two. Mm... This one had potential, but not for a long act. This one was just weird. If we had a sideshow, maybe."

"No sideshows, darling," said Svetlana calmly.

"No sideshows!" echoed Noa from the risers.

"No sideshows!" mimicked Sasha.

In America, sideshows had gained more popularity than the circuses themselves, with freaks of nature on display, like animals at a zoo. People would pay to point and laugh at misfortunate souls who had backward knees or hair growing all over their bodies or a twin stuck to them at the hip. Sébastien had never been interested in those crude displays, but every member of his troupe had been *very* vocal about their hatred for freak shows. *Especially* the Gemini Twins.

"Yes, yes, I know." Sébastien yawned, his jaw clicking.

"No more coffee, dear," Svetlana chided. "It will stunt your growth."

"I'm past the age of growing," said Sébastien defensively. He scribbled out a few more names until all that was left was Svetlana's grotesque doodles. Sébastien shivered. Seeing her art reminded him of how dangerous she was. Of how dangerous *everyone* in the circus was.

"Fifteen minutes to midnight," called out Antara from where she lounged in the risers, twirling a knife absently.

"Fifteen minutes!" said Noa.

"Until midnight!" said Sasha.

Fifteen minutes... Sébastien handed Svetlana back her pen. "Off to bed, then!" he chirped. His smile was forced. He had not smiled a proper smile in nearly fourteen years. Svetlana gave him a knowing look. She pinched her blood-red lips together and calmly stood. She sauntered out of the tent, followed by Sasha and Noa, Antara and Aurelio, Ilian and Alice and Cecily, leaving Sébastien alone in the Big Top.

He rubbed his eye absently, not worried about smudging the black line that split through eye and brow alike to curl over his forehead and cheek.

The Dreammonger stuffed his hands into his pockets and went to his own tent, greeting the shadows like old friends. He sat on the floor and closed his eyes. *Where to next, hm?*

Ah... France again? Been a while since I've been home... Let's see... His eyeballs darted beneath the thin membrane of his lids. *Lyon? Oh, haven't been there. I hear they have good astrium production. I'll find a good brooch there. A shame it isn't Greece or Spain. I don't want to listen to Alice whine again...*

He opened his eyes.

It had been two years since Sébastien de la Rue last stepped foot in France, and while it was not his hometown, it was far too close for comfort. He could not quell the unease that churned in his belly. He couldn't help but feel that coming here was a mistake, even though... Even though he felt that telltale pull of being on the right track.

Sébastien was looking for a new act, and he would find that act here in Lyon.

CHAPTER THREE

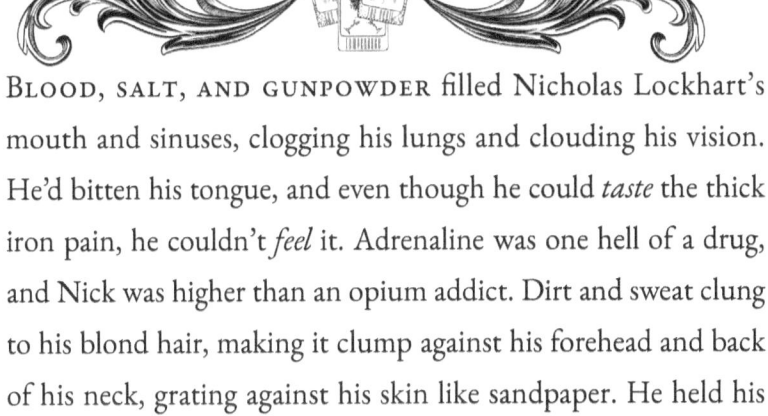

BLOOD, SALT, AND GUNPOWDER filled Nicholas Lockhart's mouth and sinuses, clogging his lungs and clouding his vision. He'd bitten his tongue, and even though he could *taste* the thick iron pain, he couldn't *feel* it. Adrenaline was one hell of a drug, and Nick was higher than an opium addict. Dirt and sweat clung to his blond hair, making it clump against his forehead and back of his neck, grating against his skin like sandpaper. He held his rifle with one hand because one hand was all he had left. His goggles hung uselessly around his neck, thumping against exposed clavicles. Somewhere during the fight his jacket had been lost and his undershirt torn. Sulfur and smoke and charred flesh burned acrid in the stagnant air. Blood spurted from the stump that had once been his forearm, slicking over the two jagged stakes of bone that tore muscle and sinew with a wet, sticky rip.

Thundering footsteps muted only by the squelching of boots squishing through bloated bodies and amputated limbs came closer to the hastily made trench Nick crouched in. He balanced his rifle between the sore muscles of his thighs, using his teeth to tear open a box of bullets. He loaded them in, his one hand trembling and slick with gore. He flipped off the safety and held the gun, pulling the trigger the second the enemy troops came into sight. *Bang! Bang! Bang!* Followed by three heavy, lifeless thuds.

Lieutenant Colonel Nicholas Lockhart was the only soldier left in his platoon, and that was quickly becoming a very temporary position.

His ears rang from the explosion caused by his gun, the tinnitus bleeding into his vision in the form of white spots.

Nick had come to terms with death when he enlisted in the army a lifetime ago, but now, staring into its maw and letting the inevitable slither over him like an oily layer of grease, he feared it.

Nick woke up screaming.

A woman rushed to his side. She wore a long grey dress covered by a pristine white apron and a matching cap atop her ginger curls. Her chatelaine clinked over the swish of her skirts. A shiny badge attached to the strap of her apron might have told anyone with a stable mind that she was a hospital nurse, but Nick hadn't been of a stable mind in a while.

She put her hands on his shoulders. "Lieutenant," she said calmly. "Lieutenant Lockhart, breathe. You are going to hurt yourself if you don't stop thrashing!"

Her words were garbled, jumbled, fuzzy. Nick could hardly hear her over the screams and gunshots and explosions.

"Nicholas Lockhart!" she slapped him across the face. In a different lifetime, Nick might have entertained the idea of a woman slapping him while pinning him to a bed, but the slap in *this* lifetime jarred him back to reality.

He was not a Lieutenant Colonel anymore because he had been honorably discharged after the wounds he'd received in battle a week ago. The letter had arrived three days prior. Nick's hand – a bronze prosthetic held together with rivets and powered with gears and veins of astrium that glowed beneath his bandages – refused to cooperate, and the nurse – Nurse Hattie, he remembered her now – found him on the verge of tears and silently tore open the envelope and unfolded the letter for him to read.

Nick went limp, flopping against the paper-thin pillow atop his paper-thin hospital cot. He wasn't the only patient in the room – there were six others, all separated by thin curtains, though the curtains didn't drown out the screams of his companions when the pain or the nightmares became too much.

"If you keep that up, Lieutenant, I will jab you full of laudanum myself," Nurse Hattie scolded. She was a girl, maybe nineteen or twenty – five or so years younger than he was – but her words forced him into submission. "I've half a mind to go into town and grab some opium if that'll shut you up."

Nick just stared at the ceiling, at the warped shadows cast by the gas-powered lights. Gas was cheaper than astrium, though not as cheap as steam, and was far more reliable than oil or kerosene. Soldiers were given the barest of minimums, even if they were honorably discharged. God bless the men and women defending England but don't give them anything more than stiff cots and hardtack.

"I wouldn't mind laudanum now," Nick grumbled, his voice hoarse from the screaming. His throat bobbed as he swallowed. "Or opium. I'm not picky."

Nurse Hattie tossed a rolled-up newspaper at him instead.

"Sorry, Lieutenant. Got to save the laudanum for those who really need it." She glanced at his hand sympathetically. When Nick had first arrived at the hospital, barely conscious and half-dead from blood loss, he'd been given healthy dosages of laudanum. Well, *generous* dosages, since nothing about the wonder drug was healthy, but the painkillers took away the pain and forced Nick away from the paper-thin edge between life and death.

As if on cue, the door swung open, and another nurse – a more senior one, a sort of zelatrix within the chain of command whom Nick hadn't met yet – barked, "Hattie, come on. New arrivals. Double leg amputee and some poor bloke missing half their face. Can't even tell if it's a he or a she."

Nick wondered if he knew them. They hadn't been on his platoon, that's for sure. But had they gone to basic training with him? Had he been in the infantry with them? Had he seen them on the battlefield, dodging bullets and bombs dropped by the enemy?

Thinking about it soured his stomach. As Nurse Hattie left, he picked up the newspaper and skimmed through it for anything important. The *Evening Standard* didn't usually publish anything about the war, but he'd been gone from home so long.

Footsteps echoed in the hallway as nurses and doctors raced to the operation theatre. Nick drowned it out and read the front-page column.

Murder Victim Identified After Months
by E. E. Irving

Three months ago, a body was found in the Whitechapel District of London with slashes to the eyes and several organs missing. The body was, at the time, unidentified and the cause of death was organ failure, even though most of the public agreed foul play had to be involved.

The body was that of forty-one-year-old Lester Sanders. Mr. Sanders's cousin, Albert Sanders identified the body.

Nick, bored, flipped the pages. Murders happened all the time in Whitechapel. There wasn't anything special about this one. He glanced over articles about the latest fashion (bustles never seemed to go out of style, God knows why), one about tea imports from India, some new restaurant that opened downtown, a circus in Italy hosting auditions, the annual Christmas market, Queen Victoria's new massive astrium ring –

Wait.

He flipped back to the article about the circus.

Mysterious Circus Casting Call?
by L. J. Cummings

It has been nearly two years since the allusive Le Cirque de la Rue appeared in Paris, France. Many people know of the circus, but hardly anyone knows about it. Well, that might change soon. When the Circus of the Streets appeared in Sardinia, Italy, just

LAST NIGHT, IT OPENED ITS DOORS FOR AUDITIONS. IT WAS NOT SPECIFIED WHAT ROLE THE RINGMASTER, KNOWN AS MAÎTRE DE LA RUE, IS SEARCHING FOR. AN ANONYMOUS AUDITIONEE HAD THIS TO SAY ABOUT THE ORDEAL: "[WE] LINED UP FOR WHAT FELT LIKE KILOMETERS, WAITING FOR A CHANCE [TO AUDITION]. THE CURRENT CAST SAT IN THE SEATS, AND A WOMAN WITH ORANGE HAIR AND ORANGE EYES SAT IN THE MIDDLE. I HAVE NEVER SEEN HER BEFORE, BUT SHE OVERSAW THE AUDITIONS."

IS THE CIRCUS EXPANDING ITS CAST? ALL OF EUROPE IS DYING TO KNOW HOW THE CIRCUS MOVES, THE TRUTH BEHIND THE MAGIC, AND WHERE IT CAME FROM. IF YOU ARE LUCKY ENOUGH TO JOIN, PLEASE SEND A TELEGRAPH TO THE *EVENING STANDARD* SO WE MIGHT LEARN THE TRUTH.

Nick frowned. He'd left for the military four years ago, before the arrival of Le Cirque de la Rue, but he'd heard rookies talking about it in passing. He hadn't believed them, of course. A magic circus that appeared and disappeared in the blink of an eye? It was simply impossible.

But, he thought as his green gaze shifted to his hand, *you've seen impossible things...*

Nicholas decided, right then and there, that he had to find this circus. Because something about it left a sour taste in his mouth. Something about it seemed too uncanny, too familiar.

Enoch slumped over his desk, his glasses crooked, and a piece of paper stuck to his cheek. His secretary, Miss Gertrude, knocked on the door and let herself in. She set a tray with tea and buttery scones on an empty space atop the desk. Enoch didn't so much as blink. He'd stayed up all night last night trying to figure out where the circus would appear next. His coworker, Lance Cummings, had gotten the scoop on the auditions before Enoch had, and that had irritated him to no avail. Tracking the circus was impossible, but Enoch had tried, and now, at ten in the morning, he regretted it.

Miss Gertrude sighed and poured a cup of black tea. She plopped in two sugars, just how Enoch liked it, and pushed the cup towards him as if the malty scent would snap him out of his dazed stupor.

It did, and *that* made him angry, too.

Enoch sat up, the paper still attached to his face, and grabbed the cup, gulping down the tea and realizing a second too late that it was *scalding*.

There was no polite way to spit the tea out, especially with Miss Gertrude present, so Enoch just forced himself to swallow, his eyes watering as his esophagus was thoroughly singed.

Miss Gertrude was a pretty young woman, a few years younger than Enoch, with dark skin and darker hair. She was British through and through and had started working at the *Evening*

Standard a year and a half prior. Enoch often wondered if she'd drawn a short straw to become his secretary.

"What do you think of the circus auditions?" she asked. Her voice was soft and sweet. She wore a paisley day dress with a pair of sturdy boots.

Enoch peeled the paper off his face and adjusted his glasses. He didn't bother attempting to tame the mess that was his hair. "There were no auditions for the original cast," he said. "They just appeared with the circus. It doesn't make sense why they're doing it now. Maître de la Rue has worked hard to keep the secrets of the circus just that – *secrets*. Why jeopardize that now by having auditions and letting a stranger in?"

It didn't make sense, no matter what angle he looked at it from. From what he remembered, the cast performed with near-inhuman abilities. He could picture the Firebird sinking into a thimble clear as day. Could some ordinary person do that? And why now, after nearly two years?

"The tea's still hot," Miss Gertrude said. "Maybe wait a few minutes to drink it this time. Would you like me to get you lunch from Sage's today?"

The dainty tea sandwiches from the restaurant down the street were some of Enoch's favorites, but he was too tired to even have an appetite.

"No, thank you," he said.

"I'll pick up those sandwiches you like this afternoon," she said, purposefully ignoring him. Enoch knew she had; she just refused to give in to his stubbornness. Enoch would, without a doubt, thank her later. For now, he picked at the crust of one of his scones and looked down at his notes.

All right, circus, he thought as he picked up a piece of paper and fed it into his typewriter. *Let's see if I can find you.*

Death. The Tower. The Hanged Man. Ten of Swords. The Devil and the World.

Louis Toussaint stared at the five cards he'd drawn, unease churning in his belly. Individually, the cards were rather neutral, neither good nor bad, but together, and drawn after Louis asked a rather specific question, they were harrowing.

It seemed he was going to die.

Three minutes prior, Louis had taken his worn deck of tarot cards from his pocket and shuffled them atop a stained wooden table in the corner of a pub that had no business being as lively as it was at noon on a weekday. He'd closed his eyes and asked, *what might the future bring me?*

Death, in a neutral sense, was change. It could be the literal change in the status of being alive or not, or it could be a smaller change. A haircut, a new house, a sudden move out of France.

The Tower was an obstacle. Sometimes, obstacles were small. One couldn't get a haircut because the barber was closed for the holidays. Sometimes, they were larger; Louis couldn't flee France because, well, he *couldn't*.

The Hanged Man meant a barrier, a challenge, a habit that refused to change. Louis did not like to dwell on his bad habits, so he glanced away from that card in particular.

The ten of swords... Well, there was no way around the black-and-white woman skewered by ten swords. It was simply a bad card. A card that left a bitter taste in his mouth.

The Devil *could* have been another obstacle. It could have been all the pent-up emotions Louis kept bottled away and hidden. It could have simply been something tempting. He'd always liked that card, not for its meaning but for the design. A shadowy figure with a massive, fanged grin. Only one of its eyes was visible, and it had been painted a brilliant blue.

And the World. Another major arcana, another decision, another terrible card piled onto the terrible fortune Louis had just spelled out for himself.

The fortune *could* have been telling Louis that the future might, in fact, bring him a new winter coat just *after* a snowstorm hit Lyon, and he wouldn't need it until *next* winter.

But Louis saw the future as it was on those five cards: he was going to make a decision that would leave him dead.

Sure, he could *avoid* that decision, but his own future was a muddled, garbled thing. He could see the futures of *others* plain as day, but his own? He was lucky to even get a vague answer out of the cards.

Sighing, he scooped the five up and added them back to the deck. He wrapped his ribbon around them and tucked them back into his pocket. He knew sitting at a table alone without ordering any food or drinks would eventually rouse suspicion, but Louis didn't want to venture outside just yet. Not when it was so damn cold, and his coat was more ragged scraps of fabric barely held on by a few flosses of thread than anything else.

Louis buried his face in his hands, his woolen gloves scratching his cheeks. He wore goggles like aviators would wear, even though he could not pilot an airship to save his life. The goggles were there to *hide* his eyes. His cloud-white hair curled around his ears and brushed against his forehead, almost annoying him.

Suddenly, the pub door slammed open. Louis glanced through his fingers to see a newsboy with a crooked cap and a scarf that covered half his face, panting in the doorway. The boy said, "The circus! Le Cirque de la Rue is *here!*"

He was standing before he knew it, already walking towards the door. For a circus that came from France originally, it had only been to the country once. And now it was here, in Lyon, and Louis felt a tether in his chest *pulling* him towards the three black-and-white striped tents.

Louis had no idea where the circus had appeared, but he walked down the streets as if he did. It wasn't until a butterfly emerged from an alley that he stopped.

A butterfly...? In winter...?

He frowned, watching the little creature flap its wings against the harsh cold. He reached out to touch it, to...transfer some of his warmth or something. The moment he did, a jolt of blue light appeared, streaking down the road in a beacon-like path.

The butterfly vanished.

Louis brushed his fingers over the pocket where his cards were. Maybe *this* was the decision that would leave him dead. Oh, well. At least it would be an interesting death.

He began following the path.

Louis didn't find out until *after* he'd discovered the circus (tucked into a city square where he was almost positive a fountain had been before) that the auditions would take place tomorrow. With nothing better to do and nowhere else to go, he decided to watch the circus. It didn't open for a few more hours, so he sat outside the gate and waited. He shuffled his cards and picked five at random.

Death. The Tower. The Hanged Man. The ten of swords. The Devil. The World.

Seventy-eight cards in the deck and he'd drawn the same exact ones he'd drawn earlier in the same order. Frowning, he shoved the five cards back into the deck, shuffled it thrice, then drew again. Death, the Tower, the Hanged Man, the ten of swords, the Devil, the World. He returned the cards to the deck and shuffled again. He split the deck and shuffled half, only drawing from there. The same five cards again. Well, the spirit of Tarot or whoever controlled the fates depicted on the worn cards was adamant about Louis dying.

By the time he tried for what seemed like the hundredth time, Louis realized he was being watched. He startled, dropping his cards when he saw a lanky man peering over his shoulder.

"Tarot?" asked the man.

Louis gathered his cards, wiping the snow off his trousers. "I – um – yes?" he choked out. "I... Keep pulling the same cards. Do you want a reading?" He fanned the entire deck out.

The man cocked one dark brow. Still, he leaned down and plucked one card from the deck. He turned it over so Louis could see without checking it himself.

That blue-eyed, sharp-teethed Devil stared back at him.

"My fortune?" asked the man, expectant.

Louis stammered, "Y-you are in danger. You've made a terrible deal. Your soul is not yours."

The man's slim shoulders sunk. "Well, I already knew that."

Louis's eyes went wide behind his goggles. "I-I'm sorry! You can draw another –"

But the man cut him off, shoving an envelope into Louis's face. He fumbled with his cards before taking the envelope. He looked up to ask the man what it was, but the man was gone.

He looked at the sleek black-and-white envelope. A blue wax seal with a butterfly stamped into it was pressed into the back. Louis carefully broke the seal and slid a piece of thick paper out. It was black and sleek, and the script was in glittery white.

If you long for adventure and wish to see something new, show this card to M. Svetlana at the doors tomorrow at precisely 3 o'clock p.m. for a V.I.P. audition.

-M. de la Rue

Six p.m. came before Louis knew it. He must have fallen asleep sometime after receiving the strange invitation, which he'd safely tucked into his one hole-less pocket because he looked up to see a dark (well, dark*er)* sky and finely dressed people walking into the open gates. He stood quickly, brushing packed snow from his clothes, and followed as a woman with a rather large bustle entered the circus grounds.

An amalgamation of smells and sounds and wonders hit Louis all at once like a tram. Spun sugar and melted caramel and popcorn, the ice-cold trigeminal petrichor of snow yet to fall. Children laughing, distant music, vendors luring guests in with the promises of chocolates never before tasted, and saltwater taffy made in the dragon palace Ryūgū-jō.

It was all rather...overwhelming. Every sense in Louis's being – sight and smell and taste and touch and hear, along with ones he didn't know existed, like proprioception and chronoception and kinaesthesia and electroception – was stimulated to the max, like they were sticks of dynamite and some ethereal being struck a match and lit them up.

Still, despite the overwhelming stimulation and the discovery of senses he didn't know existed, Louis felt drawn to the Big Top in the same way he'd felt drawn to the circus when he'd followed that butterfly-created path. The main flaps were pinned open, allowing guests to filter in as they pleased. It wasn't overly crowded, but Louis still climbed the stands to claim a seat at the very back, where he had a view of *everything*.

Another sense – one he *did* know he had, but not one he knew the name of – twinged. The hairs on his arms and the back of his neck stood on end. Adrenaline screamed *fight fight fight or fly do not freeze don't you dare freeze*, but Louis had never been one to listen to his instincts. At least, not when it was outside of tarot.

Time ebbed and gargled and twisted inside and out. A minute passed, or perhaps an hour, or an eternity, and Louis would step out of the tent not in 1888 but in 1988. Then, the lights dimmed, shutting off nearly completely.

And then the stage lit up *blue*.

A lanky man stood in the center, the spotlight drenching him in scintillating incandescence. His hair was long and black, tied back with a striped ribbon. There was a shock of white at the front, threading through the inky tendrils like a ghost. He wore black trousers and a black waistcoat over a white shirt. An astrium brooch sat at his throat, clear as day even from where Louis sat. The man wore long gloves, the ends sharp like he had claws beneath the fabric.

"Ladies and gentlemen, boys and girls!" the man announced. "Welcome one and all to Le Cirque de la Rue! You might know me as the Dreammonger. I –" There was a pause, a waver so faint that nobody would have noticed had they not been paying attention. Louis, though, caught it.

The Dreammonger threw out his arms, an eruption of blue butterflies filling the air. "I would like to be the first to say it is *good* to be back in France!"

There was a tightness to his voice, like a string wound taut. Once, a contrabassist tightened the string of his instrument too far, and it snapped, whacking him in the forehead and splitting his skull to the brain. Louis worried that would happen to the audience sitting closest to the Dreammonger.

His worries, though, were quickly disbanded when the show unraveled. First was the Flying Foxes, the acrobatic women with shimmers of silver trailing behind them as they flew from trapeze to trapeze. Then came El Cuélebre, a Spanish man whose tattoo seemed to slither in the light. Then, the Indian woman, Lady Kali, who tormented the Gemini Twins with her knives. And the Gemini Twins themselves, who chased each other around and sang songs and did acrobatics. And Beowulf, who let a hungry tiger charge at him only to get it to stop and lie down, belly exposed like a kitten with naught but a single look. The Firebird, who folded herself into a box, a pail, a teacup, a thimble.

And when the Dreammonger did his own act, performing miracles with waves of his hands and flashes of his teeth, Louis realized he was the same man who had handed him the envelope earlier.

The show ended with an eruption of applause. Then, the audience stood and filtered out, going to visit the other tents – the Menagerie, he'd heard whispers of, and the Symphony Hall. Both seemed interesting, but Louis felt strangely...rooted to this tent. To the Big Top, where miracles were birthed.

He left when that prickly uneasiness returned.

At *precisely* three o'clock p.m. the next day, Louis stood outside the circus gates, gripping the envelope he'd received the day prior so tight his knuckles turned the same color as the snow. There was a line of people stretching all the way through the gates and down the street. Louis had no right to be here. All these people had probably received the same invitation.

A girl with mouse-brown hair stood on the other side of the gate, staring at Louis. He didn't notice her until it was embarrassingly too late, and when he did, he startled.

"What's your act?" she asked, her voice fluttery and doll-like.

"P-pardon?" stammered Louis.

"Your act. You're auditioning, right?"

He blinked. "I... Well, I suppose. I was given this..." he held out the card. The girl snatched it up and read it through squinted eyes. Then, her eyes went wide.

"Oh, come along, then! He's waiting for you. Here, follow me."
The girl pointed to a gap between the line and the gate. Louis
hesitantly squeezed through it and followed the girl as she skipped
over the snow, light as a feather. He didn't think to ask who *he*
was. All his focus was on how it seemed like the girl didn't leave
any footprints, as if she was just *floating* over the ground instead
of walking on it. He sure made footprints, even if he was nothing
but skin and bones.

The girl didn't go to the Big Top, where the line of audition-
ees snaked out. She went to the Symphony Hall instead. In the
afternoon light, it lacked a bit of the ethereal whimsy it had at
night. There was no magic forest waiting for Louis, no high seas
adventure paired with a hurdy gurdy and fiddle. There was just a
table – circular, like King Arthur's, only smaller – and two chairs,
one empty, one occupied by a man who created miracles from thin
air and ephemeral dreams.

The Dreammonger tracked Louis with glacial-blue eyes. "Sit,"
he said, and Louis did.

"What's your name?" asked the Dreammonger.

Louis said, "Louis. Louis Toussaint."

"My name is Sébastien de la Rue, but you can call me the
Dreammonger. Or Maître de la Rue. Or, simply, Sébastien."

Louis couldn't help but wonder *why* the elusive Dreammonger
was offering up his name so freely, but he knew better than to ask.
Instead, he reached into his pocket to take out his cards.

"Why do you wear goggles?" asked the Dreammonger. "Are you
a pilot?"

Louis's hand stilled. He was not a pilot, even though he wore aviator goggles like he flew airships all day. Truthfully, he had never even *been* on an airship. When choosing between eating a hot meal or purchasing a ticket to fly over France, Louis tended to pick the former.

"I..." he paused. "I do not like my eyes."

"I don't like mine, either," said the Dreammonger, as if he didn't have the most *gloriously* blue eyes. Part of Louis wondered if they were real astrium and if plucking them free and selling them would be enough to pay for a hot meal *and* an airship ticket.

"I have never employed a fortune teller before," he continued, "so here is how the audition will go. You will lay your cards out and I will pick three. You will tell me what they mean and if they ring true, I will hire you."

Louis wet his chapped lips with the tip of his tongue. "And if it's false?"

The Dreammonger grinned. "It won't be."

Louis shuffled his cards thrice, then spread them out face-down on the table. He fisted his trousers under the table, watching like a hawk would a mouse as the Dreammonger hovered his hand over the fan of cards. He slid one out, then another, and finally a third. Louis gathered up the remaining seventy-five cards and set them in a pile off to the side.

He overturned the first card. The Hermit. Louis frowned. "You...lost something very important to you. You have secrets that weigh you down like anchors on a ship. You cloak yourself in false confidence."

The Dreammonger's grin did not waver.

Louis flipped over the second card. Temperance. "Something from your past is trying to catch up to you. You... You can't run forever."

This time, his grin slipped, only a fraction, so fast Louis barely had time to catch it.

The third card, unsurprisingly, was the Devil. "Your soul is stained. It can never be purified."

"Ha! I knew that last one. If I wanted a cleansed soul, I'd go to the Church and beg the Father to bless me, but I'm banned from every church in Europe, and I have *no* desire to step foot in one." The Dreammonger stood. "Tell me, M. Toussaint. *How do you do it?*"

How indeed.

He stared at his worn cards. Truthfully, he spoke aloud what words were whispered into his ears. He traced the threads of silver and responded to the cards with the interpretation they so desired.

To the Dreammonger, he said, "Magic, I suppose."

"Then!" exclaimed Sébastien de la Rue. "M. Toussaint, would you like to sell your soul to me?"

CHAPTER FOUR

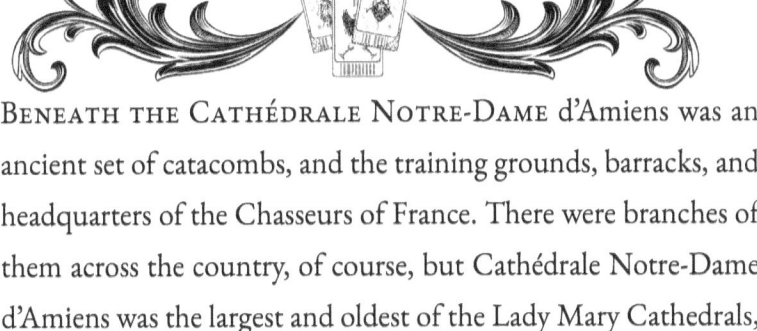

BENEATH THE CATHÉDRALE NOTRE-DAME d'Amiens was an ancient set of catacombs, and the training grounds, barracks, and headquarters of the Chasseurs of France. There were branches of them across the country, of course, but Cathédrale Notre-Dame d'Amiens was the largest and oldest of the Lady Mary Cathedrals, thus being the perfect place for a holy order of soldiers to be located. It might have been considered cruel to force an elite task force to train and sleep underground amongst ancient skeletons, but the whole purpose of the Chasseurs d'France (besides being *hunters)* was the *secrecy.*

Olivier Beaumont didn't mind the skeletons. They were just old bones. What harm could dead things do? Truthfully, the most dangerous part of *any* of the various French catacombs was the lack of direction within the sepulcher maze. Olivier had spent more than half his life down in the catacombs of Cathédrale Notre-Dame d'Amiens. He could navigate the twisting corridors with his eyes closed. Sure, he had only had the title of chasseur for about five years now, but he'd spent nearly ten years.

And many years before *that* as an orphan who sought out refuge at the church, but that was a different story.

What Olivier *did* mind, sans skeletons, was his partner, Claude. Claude Beaumont (all orphaned acolytes of the cathedral took on the surname *Beaumont)* was exactly one year older than Olivier yet acted like he was still in his prime teenage years. It drove Olivier right to the brink of insanity and kept taunting him to jump.

Olivier was in his room in the barracks, sitting spine-straight on his pallet with the Bible in his hands. He liked to read it whenever he thought of sinning (strangling Claude, reading raunchy romance novels, stuffing bones down Claude's throat, et cetera, et cetera). He was thinking very much about sinning right now, as Claude Beaumont decided that it was Annoy Olivier O'clock.

Claude sat on the floor, toying with his rosary, rambling as though he was confessing *his* sins.

"I *swear* the third corridor from the mess hall is haunted. Father, forgive me for using Your Name in vain, but I *swear to God* there is a ghost in there. The bones keep rattling and falling. Why else would bones do that, lest there is a ghost? Livi, are you even listening? Livi. *Liiiiiiiiiiviiiiiiiii.* I'm going to tell the ghost to haunt *you.*"

Olivier gritted his teeth together hard enough that he nearly sparked a migraine. "Maybe there's a rat."

"Then we need to fire Marie Antoinette," Claude said matter-of-factly. Marie Antoinette, full name Mademoiselle Marie le Chaton Antoinette The Third, was the wiry cat kept in the catacombs for the sole purpose of eating any mice and rats that found their way down into the mausoleum. She *technically* was a nun (if anyone bothered to look at a list of nuns from the cathedral, they would find, in small print, *Sister Marie le Chaton Antoinette the*

Third), but she was a cat, and she did not let anyone control her, God or not. (She did wear a collar made of prayer beads with a crucifix next to the tag that said her name.)

Olivier pinched the bridge of his straight nose. If he thought Claude could be any less annoying, he was, unfortunately, very, *very* wrong.

"Is there a *reason* why you decided you needed to come into my room?" Olivier asked, doing his best to keep from saying anything, ahem, *sinful.* A whole string of curses not fit for Mother Mary's ears coursed through his head. He had to bite his tongue to keep from saying a slew of four-lettered words.

"Oh!" As if suddenly remembering his purpose, Claude stood, abandoning the rosary. "Yes, actually! Father is sending us on a 'cism. Both of us and the newbie Jean."

The last thing Olivier wanted was to do an exorcism with both Claude and Jean, who had been a chasseur for less than a week and hadn't seen a soul purged yet. Exorcisms were messy work and usually required at least three *competent* people.

Olivier's competence made up for Claude's lack thereof.

He closed his Bible and stood, his loose tail of black hair sliding off his shoulder to rest on his back. "Fetch Jean, then. I'll meet you at the altar in fifteen. Do you have any *useful* information about the exorcism?"

"Fifteen-year-old girl, spewing tongues and trying to get her mother to sign a contract. Girl is illiterate. Apparently, she also ate a rat whole, bones and everything. Maybe we should hire *her* for our rat problem..."

Effective as that might be, Olivier thought, a possessed teenage girl wouldn't be as sweet and cuddly as the grey tabby mouser-turned-nun the church currently had.

Finally, by some small miracle, Claude left. Olivier picked up the rosary from the floor and pulled it over his head. He made a cross and murmured, "Father, grant me strength, not only to purge the poor child of her demon but to deal with Claude without sinning."

After slipping on his boots and arming himself with the usual exorcism tools – a pocket Bible, a vial of holy water, a box of matches, three knives, and a pistol with silver bullets – Oliver, regretfully, went to join Claude upstairs.

They took a carriage pulled by an automaton fashioned after a horse, if horses were made of bronze and gears and powered by steam and astrium. Claude talked the whole way, rambling nonsense that would kill brain cells if Olivier dared to actually listen. The new chasseur, Jean, bounced his knee and interjected at times, speaking even more nonsense than Claude. Olivier just stared out the window, watching the snow fall to the ground.

The house they arrived at was shabby, a single-story residence with a patched roof and broken stairs. Curtains had been drawn over the windows. Inside, though faint, was screaming.

"Let me take the lead," Olivier said as he climbed out of the carriage. "Claude, you can hold the girl down if need be. Give her holy water and trap the demon once I've lured it out. Jean, you're in charge of cleansing the area with sage and incense."

Jean nodded and dug through his pack, pulling out a smudging stick of bundled, dried sage and a handful of frankincense and myrrh incense. Olivier knocked on the door.

A woman who looked thirty years older than she likely was opened it. Dark circles clung to her pale, sallow skin. Her hair was threaded with greys and messy, falling over her face. Her dress was wrinkled and stained.

"Are you with the Church?" she asked. "Oh, thank God! Please, come in. Please. Andrea is in her bedroom."

Before any of the chasseurs could step foot inside the house, a blood curdling scream sounded from somewhere inside. The woman flinched, though she didn't look surprised.

Claude grabbed Jean's wrist and dragged him in. The room needed to be purified before Olivier could work. Left behind, Olivier stepped inside and turned to the woman. "I need you to tell me everything you can about your daughter and the demon that is possessing her. When did this start? Do you know how she invited the demon in? Usually, if she signs a shoddy contract, the demon can take over. But sometimes, if they're more powerful than their host's soul is pure, they can corrupt them."

The woman, whom Olivier presumed to be Andrea's mother, clutched at the rosary around her throat. He did not tell her the truth – that religious iconography, that religion in general, did nothing against demons. It was a presentation, a tactic to ease the minds of those who learned that demons did, in fact, exist. Hell was real (though Olivier had yet to see proof that heaven existed, too). The only thing that could combat demons was their own tricks. Magic against magic, devils against devils.

The Bible and holy water helped, sure – any religious text would do the same thing – but it was the words Olivier spoke that would draw the beast out. The serum that would allow him to grab it.

Andrea's mother said, "It's been nearly two weeks now. I don't know how this happened. Andrea is a sweet girl. I couldn't afford to send her to school, so she cannot read, so I doubt she signed anything. Unless she signed something without reading it – *oh*, is my poor girl going to be okay?"

Olivier did not like lying. "We will do our best, mademoiselle."

Andrea screamed again. Olivier pushed past the older woman, following the sound of the scream.

It was not hard to discern which room belonged to Andrea because only one of the bedrooms was soaked in enough blood to resemble a butcher's shop. The walls were dyed red, as were the warped floorboards. Clothes and furniture lay scattered about, soaked in gore. Claude stood with Jean, holding a fistful of incense while Jean saged the room.

Sitting in the middle of the bed was a naked girl. Olivier had seen many naked girls before, but there was always something unnerving about seeing one drenched in blood – especially if he could not tell if the blood belonged to her or not. She might have been blonde. Or brunette. Or had black hair or ginger. It was red now, just like her flesh. Her eyes glowed red, too, though not from the blood. Her spine protruded from her back, either as a result of malnutrition or the possession. Or both since demons always forgot to eat when inhabiting human hosts. They didn't need to eat in their regular forms.

The demon possessing Andrea turned its head slowly to face Olivier. In a tritone voice, split into a devilish chord, it said, "Son of God. Have you come to banish me? Or have you come to strike a deal?"

Answering that question would only invite the demon in, so he asked a question of his own. "Is the blood yours? Ah, your host's, that is." Slowly, he slid his Bible from his pocket and opened it to the ribbon-marked page.

"Wouldn't you like to know, pretty boy?" The demon twisted, contorting until it was on its hands and feet, only its knees bent backward, and its head hung down in a way no head should hang.

Olivier balanced the Bible in one hand. He used his other to trace a cross in the air. "E nomine Patri et Fili et Spiritus Sancti."

Claude stepped up, copying Olivier's motions. "E nominee Patri et Fili et – Jean, you too – et Spiritus Sancti." Poor Jean quickly did the same.

Religion did nothing against demons, but it made them look official to Andrea's mother, who lingered in the doorway with a look of exhaustion mixed with horror plastered on her features. It also angered the demon because while religion did not harm it, the chasseurs were backed by religion, and chasseurs *could* harm it.

Claude handed the sticks of incense to Jean and stepped closer to the bed, doing his best to keep from slipping on the blood. With Andrea distracted, he grabbed the demon's wrists and pinned them to the wall. The demon screamed, thrashing in a desperate attempt to get free. It gnashed its teeth, snapping and hissing.

"Now, Olivier!" yelled Claude.

Olivier thrust out a hand and said, "Most glorious Prince of the Heavenly Armies, come to the assistance of men whom God has redeemed from the tyranny of the devil! In the Name of our God and Lord, strengthened by the Mother of God, Mary, of Blessed Michael the Archangel, of the Apostles Peter and Paul, I undertake the attacks and deceits of the demon. Behold! The Cross of the Lord!"

Olivier traced a symbol in the air that was, if one paid close attention, *not* a crucifix. It was a more circular, runic symbol, one that, once completed, caused the demon to arch its back and writhe, screaming in blood curdling agony.

"May thy mercy descend upon us, Lord!" Olivier drew another runic symbol. The demon screamed again. It thrashed, trying desperately to free itself from Claude's grip.

"Hurry it up, Livi!" hissed Claude. The demon clawed at his wrists, drawing parallel lines of crimson blood against his olive flesh.

"I drive you from us, unclean spirit! I drive you from us, infernal beast! In the Name and by the power of God, may you be driven away from this world!" Blood began to trickle from Olivier's nose, as often happened when he put a strain on his own powers. His hand shook as he drew the third symbol.

The demon screamed a raw, inhuman roar. It brought up a naked foot and kicked Claude square in the chest. Chasseurs had to be strong – they were warriors, after all. Paladins of the new age – but demons were not inhibited by mortal limits. Claude flew back, hitting the wall with enough force to shove the bricks out of place. He choked out a cough of blood. Olivier had no time to see if he was okay; the demon had turned its head and stared directly at Olivier.

With speed no human should ever be capable of, the demon was off the bed and had Olivier pinned to the ground. It pried the Bible from his grip. It didn't matter. Not really. The final part of the binding ritual didn't need any words to cover up what he was really doing, but with Andrea's mother watching...

Olivier grabbed the demon's wrists when it grabbed his throat, squeezing the sides in an attempt to crush his trachea. He coughed, sputtering out spittle and blood and nonsensical gasping words. There was a faint *crunch* of glass breaking.

The most effective way to kill a demon was to slice off its head, but when the demon was inhabiting the body of a vulnerable fifteen-year-old girl, Olivier had to do the next best thing.

Trick the demon out.

An exorcism consisted of three steps: binding the demon, pulling the demon out, and banishing the demon. Olivier preferred to draw the final sigil for binding on the demon's forehead – usually with ash or holy water, just for show – but the back of its wrist worked just as well.

The demon suddenly froze, its eyes going wide and its hands slackening. As if paralyzed, the demon slid off Olivier and fell stiffly to the floor.

Olivier rolled onto his side, gasping for air. He silently thanked God that his throat had not been crushed. Still, his voice was weak. And with Claude out...

He shot Jean – poor Jean, who stood trembling like a leaf, clutching his incense and sage as if they would somehow save his life – a look. In a croaky, whispery voice, he said, "Take the shot. Pull it out."

Jean dropped the incense and sage, then dug through his coat pockets until he produced a syringe full of glimmering gold liquid. His hands, which had been shaking only moments ago, steadied as he shoved the needle into his jugular, filling his bloodstream with the serum. His eyes shifted to a molten gold color. Without the serum in his own blood, Olivier couldn't see the demonic soul that Jean grabbed and *pulled,* but he knew what was happening all the same. Jean struggled like the demon was heavy but managed to hold it long enough for Olivier to trace a final sigil into the blood on the floor.

Jean slammed the demon into the pentagram, sealing it away for good.

At first, nothing happened. Then, at once, the blood faded, seeping back to its hellish origins. Andrea, who was Andrea yet again, groaned softly and sat up. It did not take long for her to realize she was naked as the day she was born with three strange men in her room, and she screamed.

Her mother ran in, ripping the duvet from her bed and covering the girl with it.

"Is it gone?" her mother asked.

Olivier picked himself off the ground, dusting the glass from his broken syringe off his trousers. He did not bother helping Claude up.

"It's gone," Olivier confirmed. "Back where it belongs." To Andrea, he said, "Now, don't go signing contracts with people you don't know, *especially* if you're not even literate in the first place."

Andrea's mother began sobbing. She grabbed Olivier's sleeve, clinging to him like *he* was *her* mother. "How much do we owe you? I don't have much – oh, please, I cannot thank you enough!"

He forced a smile that almost looked more like a grimace. "Nonsense. We can't accept payment. If you truly wish to repay us, consider donating to the Church."

Jean hurried to help Claude up. Olivier was all too eager to leave the crying mother and her daughter and get back to an afternoon of *nothing*.

He rubbed his throat, already feeling the necklace of bruises coming on.

"The contract is simple," Sébastien said. He produced a stack of papers from seemingly nowhere and slid them across the table, facing Louis. "You will work under me for a minimum of one year. The rest is outlined there."

This agreement between the Maître de la Rue and M. Louis Toussaint, commencing the 21ˢᵗ of December 1888, will henceforth bind the Dreamer, M. Toussaint, to the Dreammonger, Maître de la Rue for exactly one year and one day, unless otherwise specified. The Dreamer agrees to accept payment once a week, every Friday, in exchange for a performance every other night, except on Sundays. The Dreamer agrees, under no circumstances, to not break this binding contract, lest they forfeit their essence. The Dreamer additionally agrees to the following: s/he will not speak of the internal works of Le Cirque de la Rue with anyone outside the employ, s/he will not leave his/her designated tent between the hours of 12:00 a.m. and 6:00 a.m., s/he will not, under any circumstances (including life or death) enter the Tent Noir, belonging to the Dreammonger himself.

As Louis read, Sébastien continued to talk, "You will be getting your own private tent, of course. Food, clothing, et cetera will be supplied to you. I will have a new tent installed for your act. Fortune telling isn't exactly something that can be done in the Big Top. Do you need new cards? Please use the blank sheet of paper at the bottom of the stack to list anything you need. I think I'll start you at a base of five francs a night, plus extra depending on how much the circus makes."

Louis looked up. Sébastien couldn't see his eyes, but he knew they were wide behind those goggles.

"F-five francs?!" sputtered the fortune teller. "I – you must be joking. *Five francs?!"*

Sébastien frowned. "Is that not enough? I can give more..."

Poor Louis seemed like he might faint. "Five francs is *beyond* enough!" If he was worried about the whole *selling his soul* bit, that went away as soon as he knew how much he'd be paid. Louis scribbled his signature at the bottom of the contract.

Sébastien swept the paper up, rolling it into a scroll and allowing it to disappear into its nowhere place yet again. "Come!" he said, standing suddenly. "Let me give you the grand tour. We will be leaving Lyon tonight, but for now, let's celebrate!"

Sébastien had two talking speeds: normal and impossible. When giving the tour, he clung to that *impossible* speed. Louis struggled to keep up with his pace – Sébastien was all leg and a good several inches taller than Louis – and keeping up with his speech? It was beyond difficult to do two impossible things at once, so Louis just grabbed whatever bits he could.

They were in the Menagerie currently. Sébastien tried to introduce Louis to each creature, but the creatures seemed uninterested. A tall man stood in a pen with a lion-eagle-beast and a doglike...lizard. Louis recognized him as Beowulf.

"Oh! Perfect timing," said Sébastien, abandoning the idea of Louis needing to know the names of each chimeric being. "Louis, this is Ilian Agreste, our beast tamer. Ilian, this is Louis, our newest.

Please be polite." Louis wasn't sure who was being referred to, and he didn't want to ask.

"A pleasure," said Ilian. His accent was French but...more southern, like he came from somewhere that bordered Spain. He gestured to the beasts. "Ahji and Dakov. They're having another lover's spat."

"Isn't it dangerous to be in there with them?" asked Louis tentatively, as if he hadn't seen Ilian face a vicious tiger the night before.

"Nonsense," said Ilian. Then, in a more austere tone, he said, "Ahji, back."

Ahji, the bird-lion-thing, hissed but lowered herself to the ground submissively, taking a few steps back. Dakov huffed, steam coming from his nostrils, and sat down, craning his neck around to lick the nubs on his back.

"Ilian is excellent at controlling any and *all* animals," Sébastien exclaimed. He reached into the pen to pet Ahji, but she hissed again. He recoiled quickly. "Come along. The others are in the Big Top."

The others, indeed, were in the Big Top. Sébastien led Louis up to the first person they encountered: a large Spanish man with a perfect mustache and a glimmering dragon tattoo. He held a box of gunpowder, the box labeled *AURELIO'S. DO NOT TOUCH.*

"Aurelio!" Sébastien said. "This is our newest, Louis. He's a fortune teller. How exciting, no? Louis, this is Aurelio, resident fire breather, strong man, and sword swallower."

Aurelio balanced the box on one hip and thrust a hand out. Louis hesitantly took it, his own gloved hand swallowed by the massive size of Aurelio's.

"I do stunts, too," he said. He didn't speak French. He spoke... Spanish. Yet, somehow, Louis was able to understand it perfectly, as if he'd been speaking Spanish all his life.

Stunned, he just nodded, his eyes wide behind his goggles. Had he not been so thrown off by the languages, he would have stopped to appreciate the man's beauty.

"Séb!" came another voice. She didn't speak French, either. Louis looked away from Aurelio to see an Indian woman with a dark braid wrapped around her head, turning the corner. She tossed a knife into the air absently.

"Antara!" Sébastien grinned. "Antara, this is Louis. Fortune teller. Louis, Antara. Knife thrower. Word of advice from someone who did it once: never volunteer to be strapped to the board."

"Why? In case she misses?" Louis asked hesitantly.

Antara beamed. "I never miss. You get dizzy after the spinning. Séb had to end the show early so he could go backstage and puke his guts out."

Sébastien groaned. "Don't remind me of that, please. Worst mistake of my life."

Antara nudged him with her shoulder. "Hence why I remind you of it. I think the twins are messing with the Foxes. Might want to break that up before they start a fire or something. Nice meeting you, Louis! I'll have to stop by for a fortune one day."

"Likewise," added Aurelio.

Sébastien led Louis into the main arena, grumbling under his breath about throwing up and hiding knives.

The area was chaotic, and only four people occupied it: two redheads who looked almost exactly the same, and two acrobats who stood on trapezes, yelling at the clowns.

"Give it back!" the blonde acrobat yelled. She noticed Sébastien then and added, "Séb's here. He won't let you get away with this!"

The two clowns turned at the exact same time to face Sébastien and Louis. Louis shivered, their resemblance too uncanny to be anything less than unsettling. The clowns dropped whatever they were holding and walked up to the two.

"Stop messing with Alice and Odette," said Sébastien. "Or no blood milk for a week. Also, meet Louis. He's a fortune teller."

"I'm Noa," said the clown with buns atop their head.

"I'm Sasha," said the clown with buns at the nape of their neck. "Or, perhaps *I'm* Sasha," said Noa.

"And *I'm* Noa," said Sasha.

They looked exactly the same, save for how they styled their red hair. Each had snow white skin with a red nose and cheeks. Each had one black eye and one white eye with a star pupil. Each had black and red makeup. Each had a tear on their cheek, though Noa's was on their right and Sasha's was on their left. Noa wore mostly black while Sasha wore mostly white.

"We generally accept that the one with the tear on the right is Noa and the one with the tear on the left is Sasha," explained Sébastien. "But who knows? I doubt even *they* know sometimes."

"Not true!" barked Sasha.

"True that is not!" mimicked Noa.

They even *sounded* the same, talking in a way that Louis couldn't figure out if they were male or female by voice alone. He was trying to figure out how to politely ask when a woman with brown hair and an elaborate green gown sauntered over. She gave the twins one look – a single look – that sent them running off. Her lips were so dark red that they looked black. The same color as dried, aged blood.

"Your fortune teller?" she asked in Russian that Louis could somehow understand. "I'm Svetlana Vasilievna, contortionist. I'm sure Séb didn't give you the full rundown of things, so I will. Do not agree to do anything with the Gemini Twins. They love pranks more than anything. You can bribe them with milk and honey but don't fall for any of their tricks. Alice and Odette love loopholes. If you see them falling, don't catch them. It'll bruise their egos. They are not related by blood, so please don't mistake them for sisters. Ilian cares more about his animals than any of us. His sense of direction is nonexistent, so don't go into town with him alone unless you know the area well. Never eat anything Aurelio cooks unless you want to eat the spiciest thing you've ever consumed. Also, he burns pretty much everything he does cook. His tent is the warmest if you want a nice place to sleep. You can trust Antara with her knives. Don't volunteer to be on the board, though. You will throw up. Her tent is also very warm, but don't touch any of her jewelry. And most importantly, if Sébastien tries to convince you that he does, in fact, need more coffee, ignore him. His blood is more caffeine than anything else at this point. He needs water or tea only right now."Louis stared up at Svetlana in awe. She reminded him of an elder sister, if he had one, or an aunt. He decided quickly that he adored her.

Though that might have been ruined when he blurted, "How do you fit into the thimble? Is it an illusion?"

Svetlana's blood-colored lips curled into a smirk. "Didn't you know? It's the same way you can tell the future – *magic.*"

CHAPTER FIVE

EMRYS WILDE STARED AT the betrothal papers, unable to settle on one emotion; disgust, betrayal, anger, frustration, vexation, disgruntlement, desolation... He settled on simply feeling *numb*. Written in elegant script on thick, cream paper were the words spelling out his doom.

Lord and Lady John Carnegie Thomas
announce the betrothal of their daughter
Eulalie Rose Thomas

to

Lord Emrys James Wilde
Duke of Cornwall
to take place on
Twenty-sixth of February
Eighteen Eighty-nine

Emrys was twenty-one years old, and apparently that made him a spinster because his parents – who had no political power anymore, not since Emrys inherited the duchy a year and a half ago after his father, the previous duke, fell too ill to continue his work – gave up on him finding his own marriage partner and chose one for him.

He wanted to speak to the clergy, to a lawyer, to anyone with a crumb of power to see if his parents were even *allowed* to arrange a marriage for him, but the various signatures on the paperwork proved every person of power who mattered sided with the previous duke and duchess. Emrys Wilde was a duke, sure, but he had not been duke long enough to make acquaintances where it mattered, and his parents still used whatever vestiges of their influence they had left to arrange the betrothal.

There wasn't even a *portrait* of this supposed Eulalie Thomas accompanying the paperwork, so as far as Emrys was concerned, she was an ugly old hag. He had no idea who the Thomas family was nor what sort of social standing they had. *Lord* and *Lady* were titles so common that it was almost rarer to find someone who simply went by *Mister* or *Missus* nowadays.

Emrys collapsed into his seat, still holding his damnation in one hand. At least he had two months to prepare himself. It could have been worse, he tried (desperately) to rationalize. The wedding could have been held tomorrow. At least Eulalie Thomas seemed like a normal enough name, and Emrys wouldn't find himself whisked away to Prague or Sankt Petersburg or Istanbul – somewhere he didn't know the language or the culture.

Eulalie Thomas... It sounded almost...French.

The numbness tingled into pins and needles, giving way to a *different* emotion, one Emrys couldn't quite name. He liked French things. He liked crêpes and Tarte Tatin, he liked Van Gogh's paintings and Georges Bizet's compositions. Most of all, though, he liked Le Cirque de la Rue.

Tracking the circus down to attend multiple performances was next to impossible, but Emrys was a duke with quite a bit of money and access to a rather fast airship. He'd seen seventeen performances and would happily sell his soul to the Devil to see another seventeen more.

Perhaps she knows more about the circus…

Or, perhaps, Emrys thought as he slammed the paper onto the desk and stood so fast his chair toppled to the ground, he should do everything in his power to void the betrothal and go about living his life happy and single without a woman – French or not – tying him down. Because with women came heirs, and heirs were *not* something Emrys, who had barely made it into adulthood, wanted to even remotely think about.

Just then, the door to the study swung open. The page – a young boy with an artificial eye and leg, courtesy of the war somewhere or another he'd fought in for a brief month before being honorably discharged and ending up in Cornwall looking for work – whom Emrys hired to learn about the Circus's whereabouts burst in.

"It's in Oxford," the page gasped. "The airship is already waiting for you if you want to go –"

Finally, some good news!

Emrys grabbed his top hat and plopped it atop his black curls. "Of course I want to go, don't be daft."

Anyone else would have assumed Emrys's words to be insulting, but the page just grinned. He stepped aside, allowing Emrys to hurry into the hallway, the duke eager to get to his airship to see the stupefying magic for the eighteenth time.

The private airship belonging to the Duchy of Cornwall was small compared to the commercial vessels used for transporting hundreds of people. Only capable of holding two or three people, it was more of a schooner in style, with an exposed deck, a covered area for steering (and to protect the astrium pumps from the elements), and a narrow blimp with sails. It was fast, thanks to its size, and Emrys knew how to pilot it.

Once aboard, Emrys swapped his top hat out for a pair of goggles and a snug cap. He wrapped his scarf around his nose and mouth with one hand, using the other to flip the switches to power the ship up. The engine hummed, sputtering a few times in protest to the cold. A good kick to the controls got it working just fine. Tubes surrounding the cabin lit up blue as astrium pulsed through them, forcing the gears to turn and the pistons to pump.

"Atta girl," murmured Emrys as the ship lifted itself off the ground. "Steady now..." He adjusted his goggles, waiting for the ship to get up high enough before glancing at the compass (astrium-powered, mounted on the wall) and the map (hand-drawn, also mounted on the wall). With both hands gripping the pegs of the wheel, Emrys directed the ship southeast. He grabbed the lever that opened the astrium supply, causing the ship to speed up or slow down, and coaxed it forward. Quicker than a train, the airship sped off, heading straight for Oxford.

Le Cirque de la Rue had just opened its doors when Emrys landed his ship. He locked it up and switched hats, fitting his goggles around the brim of his top hat (he'd had a pair stolen before and rather liked these ones). Emrys squeezed into the throng of people weeding into the circus. Stepping over the threshold was like a breath of fresh air. His shoulders relaxed. *He* relaxed, an easy smile finding its way onto his face.

Visitors who had never been to le Cirque de la Rue seventeen (eighteen, now) times might not realize that the smaller black-and-white striped tent to the right of the Symphony Hall was new. It appeared to be the same size as the personal tents belonging to the cast that always lurked in the shadows *behind* the circus (but weren't accessible as far as Emrys knew. He'd gone behind the fence once to see if he could get a better look, but no matter how far he walked, he always ended up at the main entrance). There was a painted sign hanging over the entrance.

The Seer

There wasn't a line at the new tent – Emrys glanced around and saw that most people were still wandering the grounds and filtering in and out of the Symphony Hall and the Menagerie, as the main act had yet to start – and if Emrys was right about the time, he had enough to spare before the *real* act started. His feet moved on their own, leading him into the tent.

The tent was bigger on the inside but...eerily simple. A rug covered the floor. There was a circular table in the middle, a chair on either side. A crystal ball full of astrium sat in the middle of the table, shrouding the tent in blue.

A man sat in one of the chairs. His hair looked pale blue in the uncanny light, his eyes obstructed by goggles not unlike the ones Emrys had on his hat. He wore a black shirt and waistcoat with a white tie, along with white leather gloves. After visiting the circus so many times, Emrys learned that each cast member had a unique color assigned to them. This...*seer*...didn't. Unless his color was white.

Emrys hesitantly sat down. A deck of Tarot cards was placed in front of him.

"Shuffle it as many times as you'd like," said the Seer. Beneath whatever translation spell the cast members had lacing their tongues the Seer sounded...French.

Emrys nodded and picked up the deck. He shuffled it seven times (it seemed like a lucky number). He didn't know about Tarot etiquette and how to properly shuffle a deck, so he did it the way he would a regular deck of cards. When he finished, he handed the deck to the Seer.

The Seer fanned the cards out in a semi-circle. He said, "Pick three."

Emrys did so, his fingers brushing against the smooth backs of the black-and-white cards. The Seer gathered up the unused cards and took the three.

He flipped them over, one by one. "Your past, your present, your future." The three of swords, the seven of pentacles, the Lovers. The cards were simple yet beautiful, each one painted black and white with streaks of glimmering gold ink throughout – gold drops of blood from the heart the swords stabbed into, gold stars in the middle of each pentacle and on the palms of the idol, like ichor seeping through their fingers, a gold cord binding the lovers' wrists together in some sort of handfasting ritual. Maybe *gold* was the Seer's special color. Except, gold was Lady Kali's color...

The Seer touched the first card. The three of swords depicted three blades stabbing into a white heart that had begun to wither and turn black. It was an anatomical heart, ventricles, and aorta hanging limply from where it had been pulled from a ribcage.

The Seer said, "You didn't have a rough childhood, but it wasn't as kind as it could have been." Emrys flinched. How had this man gotten that from a *card?* "You were very close with someone – your nursemaid? – but she...left when you were young. You had a lover when you were a teenager, but you walked in on her kissing someone else."

Emrys hadn't doubted that the Seer was legitimate, but... He sat back in his chair, eyes wide. He'd always thought that *maybe* there was some logical explanation to the circus, yet it would have been next to impossible for the Seer to know those things about Emrys. Then again, he *was* a duke. His childhood wasn't the most protected thing. Perhaps this Seer had simply done his research...

The Seer moved to the seven of pentacles. A figure stood in the middle, palms outstretched as if reaching for the seven coin-like objects in the sky. His brief interest in the occult a few years ago had taught Emrys what a pentacle was, and it was still widely accepted that pentacles were able to trap demons. He didn't believe in demons, though, and always thought pentacles were just some ancient rune.

"You recently came into money," said the Seer. "A hell – ahem, sorry, a *lot* of money. You inherited a title you hadn't been expecting to inherit yet. Still, you're conflicted." The Seer looked Emrys up and down before continuing, "You're not confident in your role yet. Huh."

Okay, thought Emrys, feeling a bit more on edge now. *He must've read something about you. That's all...*

The final card, the Lovers, showed two figures – one masculine and one feminine – wearing wedding robes, hands fasted. They were stark white against the black backdrop, the only color the cord that bound them. The Seer said, "I would congratulate you, but the marriage isn't going to work out the way it's planned to. You're going to fall in love, but it will end poorly. You're going to hold on when you shouldn't and let go when you should keep holding on. Do *not* let her onto the ship if you want what's best for her."

Emrys blinked twice. All he cared to pick up was *the marriage isn't going to work out.* That was good, right? He didn't *want* to be betrothed to Eulalie Thomas. He didn't want to be betrothed – or engaged or married or even courted – at all.

The Seer's shoulders slumped a fraction of an inch. "You can ask me three questions about your past, present, or future. Only three. And hurry because the main show is going to start soon, and I know you don't want to miss it."

"Am I going to marry Eulalie Thomas?" he asked without thinking things over.

The Seer's eyebrows raised behind his goggles. "No," he said. "Not *Eulalie* Thomas."

"Oh, thank God," murmured Emrys. Then, he paused, thinking over his next two questions. It felt like a genie – he had to word things just right to get what he wanted. When again would he have the chance to ask a Seer to see into the future? How far did the sight go? Could Emrys ask what the world would look like in a hundred years? Or could he ask about the greatest mysteries of the past – how the pyramids of Giza were built, what was in the Library of Alexandria, where Camelot truly was?

Instead he asked, foolishly, "How *do* you see the future?"

The Seer said, a bit surprised but in as flat of a tone as he could muster, "I have six eyes."

A not answer, then.

Outside, Emrys could hear the commotion as people began filing into the Big Top. He blurted out his final question, "Where is the circus going next?"

The Seer's hand twitched, but he answered without hesitating, "Paris."

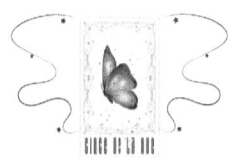

The day before, Sébastien had brought Louis to the new tent that seemingly popped up out of nowhere, stating it was *his* and he would find everything he needed inside. Louis glanced around, noting that all the other tents were black and white with stripes of color – green and orange and red and purple and pink and gold and maroon – save for one, which was blacker than pitch. Louis's tent didn't have any stripes of color. It was just...white.

He went inside and dropped his Tarot cards, not bothered in the slightest as they scattered across the ground. The tent was *much* bigger on the inside, and it did not resemble a tent at all.

The walls might have been red, but they were covered with so much *stuff* it was hard to make out the precise shade of the wallpaper. Frames holding paintings and pristine Tarot cards scattered amongst shadowboxes with dry specimens of butterflies and bat skeletons were only some of the decorations. There were sconces with dyed astrium, warming the place to a dim glow. Rugs covered the dark wood floors. There was a kitchen smothered in hanging herbs, a living room with a low chaise, a coffee table, a hearth, and a plethora of potted plants. A winding staircase led up to a full washroom and a bedroom. Bookcases stuffed to the brim lined the walls of the bedroom. There was even a wardrobe full of clothes – casual and fancy together – and an astrium-powered kettle atop the desk.

But best of all, the lights were *dim.* Which meant Louis could *see* without getting headaches, as he often got when under bright lights for too long. He made sure Sébastien wasn't behind him before ripping off his fingerless gloves and yanking his goggles over his head. He flopped onto the bed, sighing heavily.

The next day, they were in Oxford, England, and Sébastien was showing Louis *his* fortune-telling tent. "You're going to be the Seer," he'd said. "Give readings to whoever comes in here. I believe in you."

"W-wait," said Louis. "My...my color. Every performer has a color, right? What's mine?"

Sébastien went quiet for a moment. Then, he simply shrugged. "I guess le Cirque hasn't decided on one for you yet."

Now, after giving his last reading of the day to some strange English duke, Louis lay in his bed, staring at the ceiling. Stars danced across what should have been the peaked top of the tent, an entire night sky within his bedroom.

Le Cirque de la Rue never went to the same place twice, yet it was going back to Paris. His eyes didn't lie, and neither did the whispering threads. Le Cirque would land in Paris the next time Sébastien moved it – however he did that. Did *Sébastien* even know where they were going? Louis had only been a member of Le Cirque for less than two days, but he'd already wracked his brain trying to figure out *how* the damn circus moved. He stayed up that first night, hoping to hear something, but without any windows in his tent and the contract binding him from leaving, he couldn't figure it out.

Well, he decided, rolling onto his side, cheek squished into his fluffy goose-feathered pillow (Louis didn't actually know what feathers filled the pillow, but goose feathers sounded fancy), *I suppose I just need to figure out a loophole to the contract if I want to figure it out.*

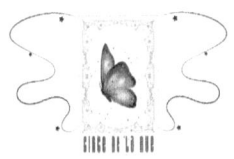

Enoch just about had an aneurysm when he heard the circus had arrived in Oxford. Oxford was *close*. Close enough that he could board the taxi airship that went from major city to major city with his notepad and pen and arrive before the main show even started. The snow delayed the air taxi by forty-five minutes, which stressed Enoch out *more*, but it wasn't enough of a delay that he missed the show. He arrived right on time, squeezing himself into a seat next to a man with a top hat and fine lines under his eyes from pilot goggles.

The man whispered as the lights began to dim, "First time?"

Enoch shook his head and whispered back, "Second. You?"

"Eighteenth," the man said with a grin. "I'm Emrys."

"Enoch," said Enoch. Emrys had a distinct accent – it was posher, smoother than Enoch's own. He decided immediately that he liked it, especially paired with the silky baritone Mr. Emrys spoke in.

The Dreammonger stepped onto the arena, black-and-white save for the blue of his eyes and the blue of his brooch.

"Ladies and gentlemen, your hero has returned yet again for another spectacular evening of magic, make-believe and the impossible!" the Dreammonger threw his gloved hands out, an eruption of blue monarchs swarming, lighting the tent in cyan. "I am the Dreammonger, and it is my pleasure to share this dream with you, ladies and gentlemen. I welcome you to Le Cirque de la Rue!"

The Gemini Twins tumbled onto the stage, followed by El Cuélebre, spewing fire from his mouth like a dragon. From the eaves came the Flying Foxes, leaping and falling as though they were truly flying. Astride a *unicorn* came Beowulf, and balanced on the back of the unicorn, twisted into a shape no human should ever be able to achieve with all their bones and muscles and organs in the way, was the Firebird. The Dreammonger conjured up a bright blue knife, which he threw only for Lady Kali to catch. She threw it into the air. The blade exploded into a firework of light.

"You've seen it eighteen times," whispered Enoch, careful not to disturb Mr. Emrys. "Do you know anything about the circus that normal people don't?"

Emrys didn't seem disturbed in the slightest. If anything, he seemed eager to talk. Not taking his eyes off the stage, he excitedly whispered, "They recently hired a new act. The Seer. He's more of a sideshow, though. The circus never goes to the same place twice, *except* the Seer said it's going to *Paris* again after this. My working theory is that they use astrium to somehow move the circus, like how engineers get airships to fly, but I haven't been able to confirm anything. Oh, and if you try to recreate any of the recipes from the vendors or the songs from the Symphony Hall you *can't*. It's impossible. And I think the drake and the griffon are mates. Same with the kitsune and the Enfield."

Enoch slipped his notepad from his pocket, scribbling everything down. Between taking notes, he glanced up to watch the various acts: the Dreammonger performing miracles; the Flying Foxes leaping through the air; El Cuélebre spitting fire and swallowing swords; Lady Kali tossing blades blindfolded at the spinning target, where one of the Gemini Twins ("the one with buns on top of their head is Wonkus. The other one is Goober," Emrys had whispered) was strapped down, grinning as each blade barely missed them.

A man wearing a heavy coat, a scarf, and a hat tilted to obscure his face sat next to Enoch. He murmured an accented apology before focusing on the show. When he left, there was an envelope on his seat that neither Enoch nor Emrys noticed.

The headline for the *Evening Standard* the following day read: Le Cirque de la Rue: Just What is the Mysterious Magic Circus?

By E. E. Irving

In it, amongst gossip about the relations between various Menagerie beasts and details regarding the new Seer, was the line

It is a well-known fact that Le Cirque de la Rue doesn't visit the same city twice, but insider information provided by an anonymous source states that Le Cirque will be returning to Paris after its visit to Oxford.

Le Cirque de la Rue hadn't moved yet. After listening to Odette and Alice whine about wanting to visit some of the shops in London (which was only an airship flight away), and Svetlana saying casually that she *also* wanted to visit London for tea, Sébastien caved.

The circus was safe, even when unattended, as no one save for those bound by contract could get in or out outside of operating hours. So, Sébastien – and the rest of the troupe, dressed in civilian clothing – boarded an air taxi and made their way to London.

Louis, dressed in a sweater and trousers, his goggles and gloves on, stepped over to the window where Sébastien stood. Sébastien had been watching the landscape below, eyes tracking the minuscule details as the airship flew across the English countryside.

"Why couldn't we have just moved the circus to London? Wouldn't that have been easier?" Louis asked.

"The circus doesn't visit the same place twice," Sébastien answered almost instantly. He gripped the window ledge tightly. "And it's good for the others to get out and travel like this. Makes them feel normal."

And he knew the twins and Antara liked airships. He glanced over to see the twins with their faces smushed against the window. They were the only ones who still looked like they came from a circus – both wore jodhpurs and poet blouses, their red hair styled as usual. Their faces still had the clown makeup caked on, but their eyes were filled with a different sort of whimsy and wonder. Antara, dressed in a British day dress, leaned against the wall, trying not to look excited as she gazed out the window. Sébastien knew her too well, though. She was, without a shred of doubt, teeming with excitement.

"Why?" asked Louis. "Why doesn't it visit the same place twice? I bet people would want to see it again..."

Séb clenched his jaw. It was an impossible question to answer. Only one person in the entire circus knew more than a few scarce details *why,* yet even then, she didn't know the entire reason.

Well, Séb thought, that wasn't the whole truth. There technically *was* one other... He brushed his fingers against his cheekbone, where the black paint he always wore cut through his eye.

Before Séb could come up with a half-truth answer, Sasha screeched, *"London! London, London, London!"*

Noa echoed, *"London, London, London, London, London!* There's the clock! The clock, the clock!"

Sasha pounded her palms against the window. "The clock, the clock! The palace, the palace!"

Every member of the circus was a full-grown adult, yet everyone rushed to the windows like children, like they had never seen London before. Sébastien couldn't help but smile at their antics.

Svetlana leaned against the glass on Sébastien's other side. "Have you ever been to London?"

Louis shook his head. "They speak English, though. I don't know how I'll do today."

"The circus allows you to speak and understand every language. I'm speaking Russian right now," said Svetlana. "Yet you understand me perfectly. Sébastien, darling, if you come with me to tea, I will treat you to coffee. I was supposed to go with Ilian, but he canceled. There's some exotic reptiles exhibit he wants to see, and you know I'm not a fan of anything that cannot handle the cold."

To Louis, Sébastien said, "Svetlana believes anything impervious to the cold can't be trusted. Aurelio and Antara beg to differ. As do I. I'd much rather be warm."

Svetlana stroked the mink stole draped over her shoulders. Like always, she wore green, her emerald earrings matching the taffeta of her dress.

"I know you do, darling. You can feel the heat radiating from your tent just walking past it," she said. "I say we go to Russia soon to show Louis *why* I don't trust anything that is phobic of the cold."

"Fine," grumbled Sébastien. "I'll go to tea with you. Louis, you're free to explore as you see fit. I'll find you later and we can explore together. Here. Your pay. Spend it wisely." He reached into his jacket pocket and pulled out a purse stuffed full of money. It was more than the five francs the contract stated he'd be paid.

Sébastien saw how he faltered and quickly said, "Some gentleman tipped the Seer well last night. It's all yours. Private acts like yours typically get more tips than the rest of us."

Louis didn't look any less gobsmacked, but he tucked the purse safely into his pocket.

The airship landed smoothly. The second the doors opened, the twins barreled out, vanishing into the throng of people waiting to get on. Antara and Aurelio followed, though they parted ways quickly (Antara wanted to visit a Buddhist community while Aurelio had plans to see the British Museum). Odette and Alice linked arms, practically skipping as they headed, no doubt, for the most expensive atelier in London. Ilian zipped after them, a map in his hands, already muttering about some species of snake or another.

"Shall we?" Svetlana asked, taking Sébastien's arm.

"Let's just get this over with," mumbled Sébastien, who did not like tea nor tea houses and the *parties* within them.

Svetlana led Sébastien through the snowy London streets like she'd been born and raised there, never once faltering as she turned down a different avenue and passed by alleys. The Golden Rose Tea Room was a delicate building, painted cream with gilded accents, a sign with a rose hanging from the awning. Svetlana kicked the snow off her boots and stepped inside. Sébastien followed, feeling instantly overwhelmed the second the heat and smells and chatter suffocated him.

An automaton the size of a cat with whirring wings approached them at the door.

"Two, please," said Svetlana calmly in Russian. The automaton didn't respond, but it turned and began buzzing off, leaving the two to follow until it stopped at a round table on the second floor of the Golden Rose. Svetlana sat down, looking at the menu on the table.

Sébastien watched the little automaton as it flew off. The second floor wasn't as crowded as the first, but he still did not like all the eyes on him. While he doubted anyone recognized him (he did, reluctantly, style his hair so the white streak was hidden), there was still that lingering anxiety that someone would.

"What would you like, darling?" Svetlana asked. "Oh, they have Russian Caravan."

"Don't you have that every day regardless?" Sébastien grumbled. He put his elbow on the table and rested his chin on his palm.

"That's terrible manners, love," she said without looking up. "But you are correct. Perhaps I should try something new. Green does sound good. Odette had me try this lovely lavender tea recently. But that would only make you sleepy. Darjeeling? Oolong? Chai? That's such a funny word. Chai means tea. Antara would simply set this place ablaze if she saw that."

Sébastien picked up the small teaspoon and tapped it against the table, bored. "Pick something for me that isn't sweet."

The automaton returned them, holding a pad of paper and a nub of charcoal in its two pincers. Svetlana set the menu down. "Afternoon tea, please," she said. "A pot of Russian Caravan, sandwiches, and a sample of desserts. Oh, don't give me that look, darling. They're for me."

Any other woman would have passed on the desserts, especially if they were concerned about their figure. Not Svetlana. She was slim, though her thighs and stomach had a bit of extra softness to them. She had the curves of an ancient statue, and that didn't stop her from indulging every now and then.

After scribbling down the order, the automaton flew off. It returned less than five minutes later, a spread in tow. It laid everything out and flew off again. Svetlana picked up the teapot and poured two cups. She added cream to hers. Sébastien did not. He picked up the cup, sniffed it, and frowned.

"I found a letter," Svetlana said. "In the stands. I already burnt it."

Sébastien slowly set his cup down. If Svetlana burnt a letter... No. That was never a good sign. She always – *always* – showed him whatever things were left behind. But this letter?

She spoke before he could, reciting the words on the note. "'And oh! I pine to see his face, and hear his gentle tone; and he is near – yet comes not here – and I must weep alone.' Frances Osgood. A line from one of her poems."

Sébastien had not bothered reading poetry since he was a child, yet the words struck him in the chest. It was uncanny. Not what he'd been expecting. *And I must weep alone.* Surely, the poem hadn't been meant for him. Right?

...Right...?

Svetlana sipped her tea as if nothing was wrong. He hated her for it. He hated the control she seemed to have over him.

"Poets and you have a lot in common, dear. You are both delusional. You both get power from adoration."

"You know that's not how it works."

"Isn't it? Oh, and I should mention, the note was not written in French."

Instantly, Sébastien knew what language it had been written in. His stomach sank to his feet, killing his appetite for even coffee.

"Sit down, darling," she said as she waved the automaton waiter over. "One pot of your strongest coffee, please. No cream or sugar."

He sat slowly, hesitantly, staring at the lace tablecloth with wide, empty eyes. "Svetlana," he said. "Why would he be in London? In England at all?"

Louis darling. It was written in Latin, though."

Sébastien didn't want to read anyone's mind nor look into the future, and he didn't want to drag anyone else into his mess. Svetlana knowing just the very tip of the iceberg that was Sébastien de la Rue was bad enough as is. Nobody in the circus was trustworthy, but Svetlana, at least, wouldn't share Sébastien's business with anyone.

The automaton returned, setting a pot of coffee on the table. Svetlana picked it up and poured a cup. Sébastien stared down into the deep brown liquid as if the frothy bubbles and swirling deliciousness held all the answers. Appetite or not, he was tired, so he picked the cup up and took a long, deep drink.

It had been a long time since he'd slept.

CHAPTER SIX

NICK HAD BEEN DISCHARGED from the hospital with a note saying he was healed enough to return to society. Really, they had just run out of beds, and since Nicholas could function for the most part, he'd been given the boot. At least the hospital had been nice enough to arrange an airship ticket and a week-long stay at a decent hotel in London while Nicholas got his life back together. He didn't know if he had a home to return to.

The hotel was...well, it would do. It wasn't the nicest hotel in all of London, but it was better than a hostel and far better than the barracks or a makeshift bed of dirt and scratchy blankets in the trenches. After spending a day bathing until the water went cold (then waiting for it to warm up again and repeating), trimming his hair and shaving the stubble along his jaw, and lying in bed to stare at the ceiling for hours on end, he was thoroughly bored.

It took one day for Nick to gather up the strength to haul himself to his feet, to put on clothes and venture outside. For the first time in years, he went clothes shopping. It was so mundane, so ordinary that it felt like a trap. Any time anyone moved too fast in his peripheral, Nick found himself reaching for a gun that wasn't there. When people stood too close, he would tense up and their words would distort. If anyone tried to touch him, he would be thrown right back onto the battlefield. The most embarrassing was when anyone tried to address him, and he would stand up straight, give a salute, and ask for his orders, sir.

Old habits died horribly hard.

He bought himself two plain civilian outfits, a set of pajamas that were so soft he couldn't stop rubbing the silken fabric between his fingers (they didn't have pajamas in the military, of course), and a pair of leather gloves that were so buttery and smooth and hid the bronze mechanics of his artificial hand perfectly. With a bit of leftover money, he purchased a Webley revolver just so he felt a little less exposed.

By then, it was noon, and even though he had been trained to last hours and hours without sustenance, Nicholas was hungry. The closest eatery was the Golden Rose Teahouse, which seemed too fancy and girly for him, but his stomach simply did not care, so he went inside.

A buzzing automaton greeted him. Nicholas stared at the automaton. The automaton stared at Nicholas.

"I... Can I eat here?" Nick asked.

The automaton turned and buzzed off, weaving around tables and heading towards the stairs. Nick realized he was meant to follow, so he did, trying his best to focus on just the automaton, not the people around him.

He was led to a table on the second floor, the chair angled to face the banister that overlooked the first floor. Before sitting, he took stock of his surroundings. A mother and her two daughters having tea. A couple gossiping over tiny sandwiches. A fretting man and a curvy woman engaging in a conversation in two different languages. A lone blonde woman writing in a journal as she sipped on her drink. Slowly, Nick sat down. He could apprehend any one of the other patrons should they pose a threat.

The automaton took his order, buzzed off, and returned minutes later with a plate of sandwiches, a pot of tea, and a newspaper. The *Evening Standard,* of course, because it was the most popular newspaper in all of London.

THE EVENING STANDARD

I888   DECEMBER 23   LONDON

LE CIRQUE DE LA RUE: JUST WHAT IS THE MYSTERIOUS CIRCUS?

by E. E. Irving

For the first time in months, the infamous "Circus of the Street" made an appearance in England, appearing in Oxford last night. By six o'clock, when the gates open, half of England had to have been lined up outside. For those unaware, the main acts are as follows: the Flying Foxes, two women who seem to defy gravity with their heart-stopping acrobatics; the Gemini Twins, adoringly called Wonkus and Goober, the clowns who never fail to make the crowd laugh; El Cuélebre, the fire-breathing sword swallower (who has the hearts of every woman in Europe in his possession); Beowulf, the animal-tamer, who can get a ferocious tiger to bend to his will; Lady Kali, the vicious knife-thrower; the Firebird, whose name has nothing to do with her contortionist act; and the mastermind behind it all, the Dreammonger, Maître de la Rue.

However, there is a new addition to the cast, a fortune teller with the name "the Seer." Not much is known about this new act, only that he has a separate tent and can see into the future with a deck of Tarot cards.

Besides the main cast, the beasts of the Menagerie seem to have complex relations of their own. There are rumors that the "griffon" and the "drake" are in a relationship, however that may be. The beloved Kitsune is also fond of the mysterious Enfield. Whether these creatures are actually the real beasts from myth is still up for debate, but either way, is it possible for the two unnatural beings to have relations? Perhaps the only one with answers is Beowulf himself.

It's a well-known fact that le Cirque de la Rue doesn't visit the same city twice, but insider information provided by an anonymous source states that le Cirque will be returning to Paris after its visit to Oxford.

Just who is the Seer? how accurate are his readings? If anyone has any information about the inner workings of the circus, or if the prophecies told by the Seer are correct, please contact E. E. Irving at the Evening Standard.

There was a photograph as well, a grainy image of a black-and-white tent with a sign that read *THE SEER*. The flaps were pinned to the side, but only darkness loomed within, an uninviting void that sent a strange chill down Nick's spine. He turned the pages quickly, skimming over headlines of *"is this the latest silhouette fashion for women?"* and *"new bakery opens downtown," "local girl goes missing after engagement announcement," "body found without organs in East End,"* and *"new airship construction underway. Travel to Antarctica a new possibility?"* Nick bit into one of the tiny cucumber sandwiches. It had been so long since he'd eaten a fresh vegetable. If he wasn't in public, as he still had *some* decency, he would have shoveled the entire tray of sandwiches into his mouth.

He painstakingly ate one at a time, relishing in the crispy freshness of the cucumbers. Nick hadn't even liked cucumbers before joining the military.

When the sandwiches were gone, Nick set the newspaper down and took to scanning the room. There were no threats, but the habits that came with being on the frontlines for so long were damn near impossible to kill.

No matter how many times he scanned the upper floor of the teahouse, Nicholas's gaze kept landing on the man and woman who kept arguing in two different languages. The man didn't bother him – if he could even be called a man. He barely looked older than a teenager. It was the woman that Nicholas kept looking at.

She was beautiful, with dark hair piled atop her head, exposing the milky column of her pale neck. Her cheekbones were sharper than razors, her lips were full, and her eyes were hidden behind thick lashes. She was curvy, and her deep green dress hugged those curves wonderfully. But when she glanced at Nicholas, her eyes had a fuzzy quality to them, and her teeth looked...uncanny. She gave him a smile, but it was not a kind one.

Crash!

Porcelain shattered against the ground, bringing with it a horribly tense silence. Too late, Nick realized *he'd* dropped his cup, sending shards of porcelain and sticky tea everywhere. He stood too fast, barely remembering his bags, before he turned and rushed out of the Golden Rose Teahouse.

That woman... She was not human. Nicholas knew that without even a *sliver* of doubt.

And she knew that Nicholas knew it.

Nicholas went all the way back to the hotel without stopping once. He locked the door and closed the drapes. He was not afraid of demons or devils. But he *had* spent four years fighting them – he'd lost his hand to them, his entire platoon to them. As he started to pace, he couldn't help but worry. Did that other man know about the woman? Nick hadn't gotten a good look at him. Was he inhuman, too? What were they doing just sitting and drinking tea and pretending they weren't bloodthirsty *beasts*?

The person in the room below him smacked the end of a broomstick against the shared floor-ceiling. Grumbling, he sat on the ledge of the bed and stared at his hands.

His flesh-and-blood-and-bone hand and his metal-and-astri-um-and-steam hand.

"Wait a second." He stood again, clearly to his downstairs neighbor's dismay. The newspaper! Nobody ever knew where the circus was going next, but it said it was returning to *Paris*. Nicholas had no interest in the circus, but that one photograph he'd seen of the cast in the hospital...

They all had that same inhuman blur to them.

Nick did not speak a lick of French, but that didn't stop him from shoving all his belongings into a single bag, which he slung over his shoulder. He made two stops: the first to purchase two airship tickets for that evening, and the second to the *Evening Standard* building.

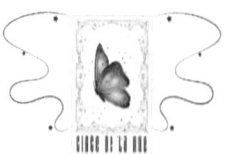

Miss Gertrude knocked on Enoch's door before inviting herself in. "There's someone in reception looking for you."

Enoch sat up quickly, trying to play off the fact that he had been asleep just moments before. His glasses sat crooked on his nose. Bruises limned under his eyes. A week-old corpse looked more alive than he did.

"Who is it?" he straightened his glasses and stacked the askew papers he'd been using as a pillow.

"He didn't give his name. He just wants to speak with Mr. Irving. I'm *assuming* he has information on your little circus article. He's giving poor Miss Mary at reception a fright."

A squeaky door or a puffed-up kitten would give Miss Mary a fright, but Enoch didn't need to say that since Miss Gertrude gave him a knowing look. Still, if someone was looking for Enoch, it *had* to be because of his article.

"If I get any calls, tell them I'm out of the office." There was a telephone on the wall, powered by gears and steam and astrium, that rang once in a blue moon if even that. All private offices at the *Evening Standard* building had them. The only time Enoch ever got a caller asking for him was when he'd left the sink on in his flat, and Mrs. Taffy wanted him to know she'd gone to shut it off (and that his place was a mess, and that no lady would want to be his wife, and no bloke for that matter).

Enoch stepped out of the office, making his way past the rows of writers busy clacking away at their typewriters through the frosted-glass door to the reception area. Miss Mary sat behind her desk, looking like the puffed-up kitten she would've been frightened of. Frizzy hair escaped her tight bun, and her skin looked far too pale. It didn't take a genius to see *why*.

The man on the other side of the desk wasn't giant in height, but compared to Enoch and his less-than-average stature, the man, who couldn't have been more than six feet, was massive. He was all toned muscle and harsh angles. A scar cut through his upper lip, his blond hair slicked against his head, his eyes piercing and viridian. The kind of green that ancient sultans conquered worlds for, the kind poets had orgasms over.

He held himself like a soldier, spine pin-straight and shoulders back. He wore a loose shirt tucked into slacks, but he donned them like a uniform.

He took one look at Enoch, glancing him up and down, and said, in a rich baritone, "Are you Mr. Irving?"

Enoch stood as tall as possible. "I am. And you are...?"

"Lieu – Mr. Lockhart." Behind him, Miss Mary about near passed out. Mr. Lockhart cleared his throat. "Is there somewhere we can speak in private?"

Either Mrs. Taffy was onto something, and Enoch was interested in blokes, or this Mr. Lockhart was the perfect male specimen.

Enoch pushed up his glasses. "My office. Right, yes, this way, Mr. Lockhart." Stumbling over his own feet, Enoch led Mr. Lockhart back through the frosted-glass door and the maze of desks to his office (where Miss Gertrude was not waiting in case he got any calls). Enoch sat behind his desk and shoved all his papers aside, moving his typewriter so he could get a good look at Mr. Lockhart, who sat in the chair across the desk (which was usually reserved for excess stacks of paper but was, thankfully, void of any messes for once).

"What can I –" Enoch started.

Mr. Irving slapped two rectangular tickets on the table. Enoch caught a glimpse of the word *France* before Mr. Lockhart spoke, drawing his attention to those perfect green eyes. "I read your article. The circus is going to Paris. I'll keep this brief. I want you to come with me so you can write an article."

Enoch's brow furrowed. That was it? He couldn't go to Paris on such short notice. Tickets were – well, there *were* two. But he'd have to take time off work or get permission... Not to mention, *every* journalist in the world would be there.

Mr. Lockhart continued, "I need you to expose the true nature of the circus."

That caught Enoch's attention. "You...know the true nature of it?"

The man nodded. He leaned close, lowering his voice to a whisper, "Not a single one of them is human. *That's* how they do it."

It was a terrible day, because it was Olivier's one day off, and he had a horrible headache. He also had a tender ring of bruises around his throat that ached each time he swallowed, but it was nothing compared to the throb behind his honey eyes. Olivier was prone to headaches only twelve months of the year. It had to do with his stress or something like that, according to a few of the nuns at Notre-Dame d'Amiens.

He'd snuck out before anyone (namely Claude) could notice his absence, deciding fresh air would do his headache better than being surrounded by bones would. He was wrong. The air was not fresh. It was cold, thick with snow, and his civilian clothes were far less warm than his church clothes.

Or so he told himself, which wasn't the truth, as his long coat and woolen trousers were just as warm, but he'd forgotten to grab a scarf in his haste to leave.

Olivier didn't know where he was going, but that was fine. He stuffed his hands into his pockets and trudged through the snow, trying to get as far from Notre-Dame d'Amiens as possible before his absence was discovered by a certain annoying chasseur who would only make the headache *worse*.

There was a certain grey drabness to Amiens, especially in the dead of winter when everything was covered in snow. Astrium lights and the floodlights from overhead airships reflected blue, but for whatever reason, muted colors were *in* fashion, making even the bright blue seem washed out and sickly. Olivier never cared much for colors – he wore red, blue, and gold for a uniform – but it was impossible *not* to notice the foxtail flash of red against the drab, beige-washed palette of Amiens.

He stopped in his tracks, blinking a few times. A wisp of red – like the end of a scarf, or the hem of a dress, or the tail of a sly cat – had vanished around the brick wall of some building, disappearing into an alleyway he usually would have no business going down. He furrowed his brow, taking a crunching step closer. Nobody else seemed to have noticed, and if it was dangerous... Well, it was Olivier's job to eradicate demons. He crossed the street, stomping through slushy puddles, and peered into the alley.

Nothing. No scarf or dress or sly crimson cat. Just...an advert pasted hastily to the dead-end wall, pristine though threatening to fly off in the wind. It was cream-colored, the text such a dark red that it looked black. He frowned. With the minimal light in the alley, he could hardly read what it said. Part of him thought he should just abandon it and leave. But for whatever reason, Olivier carried the advert out into the open street, where the astrium-gas lamps gave enough light for him to make out the words.

Hell is empty and all the devils are here.

Saints or sinners, who will prevail?

C. o. S.

M. S. A.

Besides the *Tempest* quote, Olivier hadn't the slightest clue what the words meant. Still, it was curious, so he tucked it safely into his pocket for later.

Stepping onto the street once more, Olivier made his way to the one place in Amiens he liked, outside the church – a bookstore with a small café tucked into the corner of the first floor, giving him both a chance to drink tea and look at books that *weren't* the Bible. Even with the cold weather, the small shop wasn't crowded – only a few other patrons sat at tables and perused the shelves. Olivier smacked his boots against the side of the wood door to shake the snow off, then he stepped inside, greeted instantly by the warmth from astrium radiators and the inviting scent of fresh-ground coffee beans and old paper.

He ordered a cup of Earl Grey and held it in his hands at the table he'd sat down at. The sweet mix of bergamot and black tea lulled him into an easy calm. Steam wafted from the ceramic cup, curling like cigar smoke. Atop the table was a newspaper – a local paper with an article, front and center, translated into French from London's *Evening Standard*. Olivier set his cup down and picked up the paper, skimming over the words until...

Paris.

He'd never cared for the circus, but he knew those who lurked beneath the black-and-white tents were unholy. It was his sacred duty as a chasseur to eradicate every demon in the world, yet he'd never had reason enough to visit Le Cirque de la Rue.

Except for now.

Olivier abandoned his Earl Grey, standing up so fast his chair nearly toppled over as it scraped against the ground. A few patrons turned to stare. He ignored them, rolling up the newspaper and stuffing it, too, into his pocket. Then, abandoning the warm sanctum of the bookstore in favor of someplace far less favorable, Olivier all but ran back to Notre-Dame D'Amiens.

The Archbishop did not meet with regular people on random whims in the middle of the day without being notified even thirty seconds before, but he made an exception when Olivier burst in, panting and wet from the melted snow.

Olivier raked his fingers through his long black hair, getting it off his face and out of his honeyed eyes. He said, "Your Excellency, I would like to be assigned to Paris."

The Archbishop, an old man with powdery hair and more wrinkles than verses in the Bible, looked up over his thin-framed spectacles, lowering the holy book in his hands. "Paris? Why Paris? Sit, Olivier, please. You're getting water everywhere. God bless you, but *sit.*"

Nobody could ignore the Archbishop, not even Olivier, so he sat right on the floor. "There are demons in Paris. A troupe of them. It is my duty, as a soldier of God, to exorcise them. Please, your Excellency. Send me to Paris. I need to go *now.*"

Very few people in the world had the authority (and ability) to boss the Archbishop around – the Patriarchs, the Supreme Pastor, the Pope, God Himself – but in his eager moment of desperation, Olivier inserted himself into that hierarchy.

Then, as if to sweeten the deal, Olivier added, "I'll pay for my own lodging and airship ticket."

The Archbishop took off his spectacles and pinched the bridge of his nose.

"Olivier, for the love of God. I would never ask you to spend your own money on work. Take the evening airship and either seek sanctuary at Notre-Dame D'Paris or go to L'Hotel. Ask them to bill the church." The Archbishop put his glasses back on and opened a ledger, using a rather dramatic feather quill to scribble something down. "I suggest you take Claude –"

"No!" Olivier interjected, once again invoking his nonexistent Power of Authority. "I mean, it would be best if Claude stayed here. What if another possession comes up while I'm away? God willing, his powers are needed here."

The Archbishop gave Olivier a skeptical once-over before saying, "Then I ask that you go to D'Paris and ask the Archbishop there for one or two chasseurs to aid you. Before you go, please clean up. You're dripping water everywhere like a drowned dog. Go on, then. God be with you."

Beneath his feet, a puddle of melted snow had accumulated. He hadn't even felt it soak through his clothes until the Archbishop pointed it out. Again. Scrambling to his feet, Olivier thanked the Archbishop (and God for not smiting him on the spot for defying authority) and hurried to pack and get ready to go.

Louis had never been to London before, and he had been excited to explore the streets of the famous city until he found himself in the Whitechapel district. Louis, before joining the circus, had been poor himself, living on the streets and feeding himself with whatever scraps he could find, reading fortunes for the occasional coin or two. He ought to have fit right in with the derelict urchins.

The living ones, maybe.

The dead ones, not so much.

Bile rose in his gullet, acrid and scraping as it bit into his esophagus, making his eyes water and his chest heave as he swallowed
wave after wave of nausea until he simply couldn't hold it back. He
barely managed to turn and fall to his knees before emptying his
stomach and then some into the snow. It sizzled, hot acid melting
it in the grossest way possible. Louis coughed and wiped his nose
and mouth with the back of his gloved hand.

Breathe, he told himself. *Breathe, damnit!*

He stood slowly and looked at the body again. It was fresh, or
so he assumed, as the blood oozing from underneath it continued
to creep closer and closer to his boots. It belonged to a woman
who might have been pretty in life, with blonde hair and a supple
bosom, but in death, she resembled a horror from a Penny Dreadful. Her torso had been split, bisected with precision, each layer of
dermis and fat and muscle peeled back like the flesh of a fruit. Her
ribs had been cracked, split neatly, and her heart was missing, her
lungs looking rather flat without the fatty muscle nestling against
it. Her aorta had been sliced, too, and while the cold had mostly
stopped the gushing blood, globs of it still trickled out. She had
her stomach, her intestines, her gall bladder, and her liver. Her
pancreas and kidneys were both missing, as was her uterus.

And her eyeballs. Those were gone, too, leaving bloody sockets
to stare empty at the overcast sky.

The body was fresh. It hadn't been snowing, though the skies
threatened it.

There were no footprints, save for Louis's own, around the
body.

I have to tell someone. But who? The authorities? He'd be the prime suspect, and Louis did *not* want to sit in a cell while he waited for someone (Sébastien) to sort things out. No, authorities were out of the picture. But...

Sébastien. Sébastien was...weird. There had to be something he could do. Some miracle or another. Taking one last look at the body, Louis took off running, hoping the Dreammonger would know what to do about the dead girl.

Chapter Seven

"Emergency meeting!" Sébastien announced an hour later, once everyone had returned to the airship that would take them back to le Cirque. Louis had found him and Svetlana as they were leaving the teahouse, panting and out of breath as he explained, poorly, what he'd found. It took him leading Sébastien to the backstreets of Whitechapel for Sébastien to finally understand what was going on.

When he saw the eviscerated body, his skin went as pale as the snow, and he began running without a word. Louis told Svetlana twice to go after him.

Now, the troupe was aboard the airship, and Sébastien paced the length of the cabin.

"Darling, you need to sit down," said Svetlana over the rim of her teacup.

"Sit down!" cried Sasha, who hung from the rafters like a monkey.

"Sit down!" repeated Noa, who eyed a chair suspiciously, either planning to force Séb into it or to throw it at him.

He did not sit down. He continued to pace. His head throbbed from exhaustion. When had he last slept? Three nights ago?

Four? A week? It had to have been a week, at least. But it wasn't good enough. It was never good enough. The Seer brought in more revenue, more guests, more applause, but it *wasn't enough*. The ground beneath him blurred, tilting in a dizzying slope. He grabbed the ledge beneath the window to steady himself.

His heart slowed – or perhaps it sped up – into an arhythmic thudding that he could feel in his ears. His sinuses ached, feeling clogged and tender.

"We're moving the circus," he said. "As soon as we get back. Everyone, to your tents. Do not come out until I say so."

Antara crossed her arms and leaned against the window. "We never move during the day. What's the reason for the change?"

She was a clever girl, but only one other person knew why.

"Are you even *able* to move it during the day?" Ilian interjected. "I always thought it *had* to be at night."

"At night!" announced Sasha as they landed with a thud.

"At night!" mimicked Noa as they turned and hissed at Odette, whose only crime was standing too close.

Odette grimaced and stepped away, shivering as if even being *close* to Noa would somehow taint her. She nuzzled her chin into her mink stole. "Is anyone else concerned *why* we suddenly have to move in the middle of the day when *anyone* could be watching? No? Just me. Of course..."

The world tilted again, creating a phantasmagoria of coppers and bronzes and astrium blues. Something warm trickled from Sébastien's nose. His eyes went wide, a gloved hand flying up as if covering the blood would somehow prevent his troupe from smelling it.

They smelled it all right. Nine sets of eyes narrowed in on him, pupils constricting and dilating the way a cats would when they homed in on their prey.

The contract forbade any of the members of Le Cirque de la Rue from attacking Sébastien, which was why they all stood grounded in place. He wiped his nose with his gloves. Did exhaustion even cause nosebleeds? Probably. At least, it did with his luck.

Or lack thereof.

Sébastien glanced around the cabin. He didn't know too much about Louis's background yet. The contract *did* prevent anyone from attacking, but the least stable ones were Svetlana, Ilian, the Gemini Twins, Odette, and Alice, and Louis, since he was too much of a wild card.

"Let's see..." he said, slurring his words together. "Antara, Aurelio, you're the least likely to eat me right now, so you're in charge of making sure the others don't get a bite."

With that, the exhaustion simply became too much, and Sébastien collapsed to the floor, unconscious.

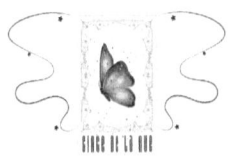

"We won't eat him," said Noa half an hour after Sébastien collapsed. They perched on the back of a chair, eyeing him like a vulture.

Svetlana hummed and placed a tablecloth over Séb like a blanket. Louis had sacrificed his coat, rolling it up to stick under his head like a pillow. He'd been worried at first that all the jostling would wake the Dreammonger up, but Sébastien was out cold. Nothing would pull him from his much-needed sleep, it seemed.

"We won't, we won't," emphasized Sasha. The glint in their eyes said otherwise. Sasha rocked back and forth on their feet, staring at Sébastien.

"Now, dears, that isn't very nice," said Svetlana calmly. She smoothed out the tablecloth-blanket under the scrutinizing gazes of Antara and Aurelio.

For two people tasked with keeping their boss safe from...potential cannibalism, Louis thought, they weren't taking their job very seriously.

Still, even he was staring at Sébastien – at the crusted flakes of blood on his upper lip, at the mysterious gloves he always wore. Curiosity itched at him, making his palms ache and his fingertips tingle. It would be too easy to reach over and pull those gloves off to see what he was hiding.

Louis sat on his hands instead.

"How are we supposed to get him back to his tent?" he asked. Was he the only one banned from the Tent Noir where Sébastien lived?

"I'll handle it," Svetlana said.

"He put *us* in charge," Antara said, gesturing between herself and Aurelio.

"Where did Ilian go?" Alice asked as she glanced around the cabin.

"Ilian, Ilian!" chanted Noa.

"Outside, outside," giggled Sasha.

Louis sighed. At least he'd been given six eyes and not six ears. He would have gone positively mad if he had two extra sets of ears being forced to listen to the banter.

Drowning them out as best as he could, Louis focused on Sébastien's sleeping form. He'd told Sébastien he'd found a body minutes before the emergency meeting was called, minutes before the ringmaster passed out from exhaustion. If not for the very subtle rise and fall of his chest, Louis might've thought him dead.

As he watched the steady rise and fall, his eyes darting to Sébastien's gloved hands, he wondered, what did the Dreammonger dream of?

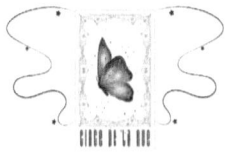

Svetlana was not a weak woman by any means, even if her body didn't have any visible muscle. She could have easily hauled Sébastien back to Le Cirque from the depot, but she was a lady, so she asked Aurelio to do it. Aurelio slung Sébastien over his shoulder like a sad sack of potatoes, grumbling about how damn bony the ringmaster was. Sébastien didn't wake, not even as he flopped limply against Aurelio's muscled back. Svetlana kept pace with them, ignoring Antara's glares.

"Are we supposed to trust that you won't eat him?" she asked. Svetlana caught a glimpse of metal in Antara's hand. A knife – a small one, concealed but ready to be thrown.

"The contract states I'm not to cause him any harm, dear," Svetlana replied calmly. "I'm just going to nudge him inside his tent and make sure it's closed. It would be a shame if he caught a cold."

"We can't just *toss him on the ground,*" Antara ground out. Svetlana tried to put herself in the girl's shoes. Like everyone else in the circus, Antara had a strong connection with Sébastien – a bond that went deeper than any other bond, and that was before the contract came into play.

"Oh, he'll be fine. But if you would rather, Aurelio can just set him down and push him in. I won't touch him, dear, if that will make you happy."

Antara crossed her arms, grumbling something under her breath. She spoke in an ancient tongue that would be completely untranslatable if not for the helpful filter the circus gave her. It was a tongue that hardly even had a written language, one that predated any of the other languages spoken by the rest of the troupe. Sometimes, when she grumbled under her breath, it was impossible to translate. Still, Svetlana liked languages, so she found it pleasant even though Antara was, most definitely, calling her every foul word there was.

"Um," Louis spoke up. "Does... Sébastien not sleep often?"

Silence fell over the group. The only sounds were the crunching of snow beneath their feet and the occasional giggle from Noa or Sasha.

Then, Alice answered, "We don't know."

Odette added, "We aren't allowed in his tent."

"He does drink quite a bit of coffee," Svetlana mused, though she wondered how Sébastien was able to sleep after he'd downed two and a half pots of coffee in London.

"He moves the circus at night and works all day," Ilian murmured.

"Circus at night, yes, yes, it moves at night," Noa said.

"Nobody knows how it moves. But it moves! It moves, it moves, it moves!" Sasha giggled.

"I don't ever see any light coming from his tent, but he's weird like that," Antara said.

Aurelio adjusted his grip on Sébastien. "He *has* to sleep. There's no way he can survive without it."

"Does the Dreammonger dream?" Louis whispered.

Nobody had an answer for that.

They arrived at Le Cirque de la Rue only minutes later. The fence erected around the perimeter hadn't been touched. While there was fresh snow on the ground, a fluffy white blanket of it, no snow touched the tops of any of the tents.

Svetlana followed Aurelio and Antara to the Tent Noir. Antara peeled off her jacket and set it on the ground, so Aurelio wouldn't have to put Sébastien in the snow. Svetlana *could* have offered hers, but she rather liked it and didn't want it wet.

With Sébastien on the ground, Aurelio crouched down and carefully pushed him through the tent flaps until he disappeared from sight. Svetlana raised her eyes to dare a peek inside.

Nothing but darkness. She hadn't expected any less.

"Place your bets on whether we're moving tonight or not!" Antara called as she stood, brushing melted snow from her knees.

As the others raced to the Big Top to place their bets and exchange their stories from London, Svetlana lingered by the Tent Noir. The contract stated she was not allowed inside.

But it said nothing about *looking*.

When she was sure she was alone, she picked up the edge of the tent flap with two fingers, pulling it aside just enough to peer inside.

There was a faint glow of something astrium blue amidst the darkness.

Strange, she silently mused. *Just what is he hiding?*

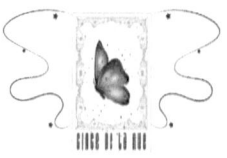

That night, every member of Le Cirque de la Rue retired to their tents before midnight, as they were contract-bound to do. Svetlana made herself some Russian Caravan and sat by the hearth, sipping as she doodled pictures of disemboweled humans in a notebook. Odette sat down with some honey milk to read an old book of poetry. Alice combed her hair until it shone like spun gold, eating sugared berries between steps in her routine. Noa and Sasha chased each other around the living room until they got tired enough to sprawl by the fire like kittens. Ilian retired to his bed, his room darker than pitch, just the way he liked it. Aurelio curled dumbbells until his biceps screamed, then went to lay on the rocky ground of his cave-like room. Antara enveloped herself in warmth, sand and sage filling her senses and drowning out the overwhelming concern she felt for Sébastien. Louis, who was still getting used to his own personalized tent, stared at the fire in his hearth, goggles and gloves abandoned.

What did the Dreammonger dream of?

The Dreammonger did not dream, not really.

You know you are not to sleep, said the voice that followed him.

Forgive me, but sometimes there are necessities I cannot control, he said.

It is your choice to not sleep. That was your regulation. Your rule.

Unable to wake and stop it, Sébastien could only unconsciously writhe, squirming on the floor as the circus, for the first time in its existence, returned to a location it had already been to.

Louis's prediction had been correct.

The people of Paris, France, woke up that next morning to a set of three discoveries: another half-foot of snow had fallen, there was a dead body partially frozen stuffed into an alley, and Le Cirque de la Rue had returned.

"You were right," the girl with the Venetian mask said. She sat on the edge of the magnolia desk, head cocked to the side. The porcelain mask hid her features, painting them instead in gold and red. Her dress was that reddish-purple of fresh bruises or coagulated blood.

"When am I not?" the man in the black-and-red Venetian mask replied. "But remind me what I was correct about this time."

The girl twirled a golden curl around her finger. It wasn't gold like polished coins or satin slippers, but gold like the first rays of sunshine obliterating dawn, like the air at noon in the middle of July, like the straw spun by Rumpelstiltskin in the old fairy tale. It was a celestial gold, not a natural one – white and gold and like the stars in the heavens.

"That circus," she said. With her high-collared dress and gloves, the only visible features about her were the mass of curls atop her head, held back by a single red ribbon. "It's returned to Paris."

The man in the mask looked up slowly.

"Then it is time," he said, "for the Carnivale to arrive."

THE EVENING STANDARD

I888   DECEMBER 24   LONDON

HORROR IN WHITECHAPEL
by L. J. Cummings

Last night a body was discovered in the Whitechapel district of London. The body underwent an autopsy with undertaker Dr. Lenore Therese, who determined the cause of death to be another case of organ failure. The body was identified as belonging to M. A. Nichols, a forty-three year old prostitute living in Whitechapel at the time. The killer has not been identified at this time.

According to lead detective Thaddeus Jones and Dr. Therese, the culprit is most likely male, with background in either surgery or butchery. There were no signs of struggle on the victim or in the immediate area, so the culprit likely knew Ms. Nichols. This marks the second murder in London of its nature.

As the murders have only taken place in Whitechapel, a curfew has not been instated, but authorities encourage women walking alone to be wary of their surroundings. On behalf of the Evening Standard, we ask that you report any suspicious activity to the proper authorities.

WAR EFFORTS OVERSEAS
by A. R. Pike

In an interview with Queen Victoria last weekend it was revealed that the increased tariffs and taxes have been going towards the war efforts overseas. The queen has not announced which country is fighting, but it is believed Russia might have a role

cont. on page 3

Theodore's Bakery opens this Saturday. First fifteen customers receive a complementary dessert of their choosing. Located on Main between the Hatter's and the Atelier Lucy.

Hell is empty and all the devils are here.

C. o. S.
M. S. A.

IF YOU KNOW ANYTHING ABOUT THE INNER WORKINGS OF LE CIRQUE DE LA RUE PLEASE CONTACT E. WILDE VIA TELEGRAM, POST, OR TELEPHONE.

CHAPTER EIGHT

THE CIRCUS HAD RETURNED to Paris, which caught Sébastien off guard when he awoke the following morning, only slightly *less* sleep deprived than before. He sat up slowly, realizing he was on the floor but not caring too much about it, and rubbed the sleep from his eyes. The last thing he remembered was Louis desperately telling him about a body he'd found and begging Sébastien to do something about it. Then, getting on the airship, and then...

Waking up.

It was a rule that he was not supposed to sleep.

Yet he'd done it anyway.

Yawning, Sébastien stood and pushed himself out of his tent only to be greeted by a thick blanket of snow and nine grown adults hovering outside like toddlers. The troupe scrambled back, though it was too late for them to play it off casually.

"Where are we?" he asked. The dull hum of *Paris Paris Paris* was just as annoying and unhelpful as a pesky gnat.

"Paris, darling," Svetlana answered tightly.

"Paris!" shrieked Noa.

"Paris!" screeched Sasha.

"Well, shit," said Sébastien, and he went right back into his tent.

Exactly two years ago, during its debut, le Cirque de la Rue appeared in Paris – in the same spot it was in now, nestled in the heart of the city like it had always belonged there, the distant tolling of Notre-Dame's bells, the whirring of airships above, the crunching of snow as children and carriages pulled through the city's streets... It was *exactly* as it had been two years ago, only this time it hadn't been planned.

Sébastien didn't plan where to bring the circus each time it moved except for the very first appearance. That had been part of the deal – *Paris first, then never again.* He'd never wanted to return to Paris. And now, as he marched up the spiral staircase in his tent, his stomach roiling with nausea and his heart fluttering inconsistently against his too-tight ribs, he wondered if he could move the circus despite it being the middle of the day. Despite the fact that there would be onlookers, that people would be watching, that someone was bound to figure things out...

Once in his bedroom, he began to pace. There was a rug – a Persian rug, expensive and artfully woven (Antara would have approved, though, really, anyone with eyes would approve) – on the floor, in the space between his bed and his desk, that had a frayed path in the middle from the months and months he'd spent pacing in the same spot. He reached up and tore the ribbon from his hair, letting the locks fall over his shoulders and chest.

"There's a body – a woman, oh, God, she's been torn open." Louis had said.

"Oh, and I should mention, the note was not written in French." Svetlana had warned.

"And oh! I pine to see his face, and hear his gentle tone; and he is near – yet comes not here – and I must weep alone."

Sébastien tripped over his rug, falling knees-first into his privy, hardly making it to the toilet in time before he threw up, emptying his stomach of everything in it – coffee and tea and bile and tiny blue motes that he flushed away before he could look at them properly. The fatigue that hit him like an airship explained it enough.

It's just a city. Just one measly city. You control who's allowed in and out of the circus. It's for one night. This is what happens when you sleep. The circus defaulted.

He threw up again, though it was mostly bile this time. His liver ached. His stomach clenched over and over until he was sure he'd have abdominal muscles like Aurelio.

Groaning, Sébastien flushed again and slumped over the toilet bowl. The acrid, sour taste of bile lingered at the back of his throat.

They can't know you have emotions. You can't let them find out you're weak.

Right. He wiped his mouth with his sleeve and forced himself to his feet, going to the sink to brush his teeth twice. Then, he went to his bedroom and peeled off his clothes, opting for a black suit instead, adding the simplest of astrium brooches in his collection to his collar. He tied his hair back with his ribbon and descended the stairs. He threw open the tent flaps dramatically, putting on a grin that would never reach his eyes.

"Well!" he announced to whoever cared to listen (the troupe was hiding, but they were all within earshot. They'd gotten better at pretending to not be nosy in the past five minutes). "It seems we've made a homecoming. Tonight, we will remind Paris what le Cirque de la Rue is made of!"

"Ladies and gentlemen, we ask that you please remember to collect all your personal belongings and make your way, at your leisure, to the main deck. The *Lucille* will be landing in Paris, France shortly. The weather is below freezing, with a high likelihood of more snow this evening. We thank you for flying with us today, and we hope to see you again soon."

The announcement played throughout the airship, the *Lucille,* which had flown from London, England, on an express trip.

Mr. Irving would not stop bouncing his leg. His knee kept hitting the round table he and Nicholas were seated at, causing it to shake. He toyed with the chains drooping down from the arms of his spectacles, slicked his hair back a few times before adjusting his top hat, twisted his gloves, and straightened his waistcoat... All of it was driving Nick to insanity.

He kept his mouth shut, though, because he knew better.

"Do you speak French?" Mr. Irving suddenly asked.

"What?" Nick asked. Then, when he realized the question, he answered, "No. I can count to ten and say 'yes' and 'no,' but that's it. Can you?"

"Not a lick," Mr. Irving said. He groaned. "How are we supposed to navigate around *Paris* if neither of us speaks *French?*"

"We find a guide?" Nick suggested.

Mr. Irving groaned again, louder this time.

The announcement played again. Outside, the buildings of Paris became more detailed the closer the airship got to the station. A heavy overcast blocked out the sun, a dark contrast to the snow that smothered everything.

"It's fine," Mr. Irving said as he stood. "It'll be fine. Everything will be fine. I'm sure there's some sort of automaton that translates things. Let's go. Every hotel in Paris is probably booked right now, and I want to find one close to the circus."

Nick wanted to sleep as far from the circus as possible, but maybe the proximity to the devilish fiends would remind him of his time at war and help him sleep.

Likely not, considering he hadn't ever been as sleep-deprived in his life as he had been in those trenches.

The *Lucille* landed minutes later, and Mr. Irving and Nick managed to squeeze through the bottleneck. Mr. Irving started shivering almost instantly. Without a word, Nicholas slipped off his jacket and draped it over Mr. Irving's shoulders. He'd dealt with colder weather before – and now that he was subject to the winter air, he'd be motivated to find a hotel faster.

The only hotel with any vacancies within walking distance of Le Cirque de la Rue (which Nicholas got a glimpse of and tried to figure out what, exactly, was so special about those black-and-white tents) – which had been a non-negotiable stipulation enforced by

Mr. Irving – was L'Hotel. It was a luxury hotel, one neither of them could afford, yet Nicholas found himself standing awkwardly in the foyer as Mr. Irving tried to haggle a price.

"Fine. *Fine.* Do you have a room with two beds? Two very *separate* beds?" Mr. Irving argued at the counter. Somehow, he thought speaking slowly would get the very French concierge to understand him. It, rightfully so, only angered the poor man behind the desk.

"Est-ce que cet homme est avec vous?" came a deep baritone from next to Nicholas.

He peered at the newcomer from the corner of his eye. The man stood at around the same height, his long dark hair braided over one shoulder and his pale skin flushed from the cold. He wore a heavy jacket and had only a single suitcase with him. He stood with his spine straight, like a soldier, though his shoulders were slumped, and there was an air of casualty around him. His spoonsful of honey eyes, framed by thick black lashes, met Nicholas's.

"I don't speak French," Nick said. Then, bashfully, "Sorry."

"Ah. You must be from England, then," the man said, this time in English, his French accent so horrendously thick that it was almost easier to understand him when he spoke the foreign language.

"Yes," he said. "I just arrived from London. Do... You perhaps think you could help my..." friend wasn't the right word, and neither was comrade. Partner? Associate? Pal? "My...acquaintance is having translation troubles. Do you think you could help?"

The man looked at Mr. Irving, who was now spewing some nonsense about a Mrs. Taffy and not being interested in blokes.

He sighed. "For both our sakes – and our sanities – I'll see what I can do. Two rooms or one with two beds?"

"Whatever is cheapest," Nick said.

The man nodded and approached the counter. He began speaking in rapid French, much to the concierge's relief. They exchanged money and keys before both men returned to Nick.

"What brings the two of you to Paris?" the Frenchman asked as he handed the room key to Nicholas (Mr. Irving had grabbed his two pieces of luggage – one of which was holding his typewriter – and had no free hands).

"The circus," Mr. Irving answered. "Mr. Lockhart here knows something secretive about it, and I'm a journalist who wants to write an article on it."

"Ah," mused the Frenchman. "I'm here for it, too. Olivier Beaumont. A pleasure."

"Nicholas Lockhart," grumbled Nick.

"Enoch Irving," said Mr. Irving. "A pleasure indeed. Say, since we all have a common goal, do you mind sticking with us to help us translate?"

M. Beaumont gave a tight smile that said he would rather do literally anything else in the world, but he agreed, nonetheless. Nicholas didn't say anything; he'd much rather have a grumpy translator than have to deal with Mr. Irving's nonsense for a second longer.

Nicholas glanced at the number etched into the key – 307 – and headed towards the elevator. The three of them piled in. Nick pressed the button for the third floor while M. Beaumont called for the fourth.

"Room four thirteen," the Frenchman said. "You're welcome to visit me this evening if you want to go to the circus together."

"Right, then!" Mr. Irving said with a grin. He had a chipped tooth. Nick stared at it for a split second too long.

The elevator dinged, and the doors slid open, spilling them out onto the third floor. Mr. Irving gushed a farewell before stumbling after Nick.

Their room was grand – grander than the hospital he'd been staying at. The room was easily the size of a small apartment, with red carpet and matching silk drapes around the walls. A heavy chandelier hung from the ceiling, astrium powering the gas lights. A sofa and two chairs huddled around a table near a giant window overlooking Paris. The bed itself was massive, easily able to fit three or four people, with plush sheets and a mountain of pillows piled atop a soft mattress.

The problem, however, was that there was only one bed.

Mr. Irving dropped his luggage. "Right," he said. "Apparently, this was the only room available on such short notice."

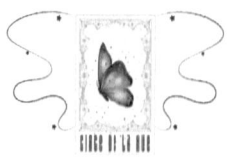

It had been less than a month, and Lie still hadn't gotten used to the musty, incense-thick malaise of the catacombs. Bones didn't have a smell, not like the sickly-sweet stink of rot fresh bodies had, but they were so old they were practically dirt, and dirt *did* have a smell.

Better the bones, Lie tried to reason, than the cloying sweetness of Frederick Stearns & Co.'s Heliotrope, which she'd been gifted for her birthday. She *hated* Heliotrope. She hated Frederick Stearns in general. Now that she thought about it, the bones made for a much nicer eau de parfum.

She stalked through the twisting corridors of the catacombs that stretched beneath Cathédrale Notre-Dame D'Paris, her boots click-clacking rhythmically against the compact ground. Even though she was hidden by the darkness the catacombs had to offer, she kept her hair tucked into a cap and slouched her back just so as to further conceal her bound breasts.

Lie was not a man, and she was not a chasseur, even though she was pretending to be one. Her French was excellent, thanks to tutoring hounding it in at such a young age, but she decided it was easier to pretend she'd taken a vow of silence. Faking paperwork and stealing a uniform from the church's laundry was enough to get her in under the fake name *Blaise Beaumont* (because, apparently, all orphans were given the surname Beaumont, for whatever reason).

"Now how I came to get this hat 'tis very strange and funny," Lie sang under her breath as she stepped over a discarded femur, mak-

ing her way deeper and deeper into the bowels of the catacombs. *"Grandfather died and left to me his property and money..."*

The chasseurs had one job: eradicate demons and cleanse humanity. When Lie got word that she was to be married off to some rich man she'd never met, heard of, or seen, she decided the only thing to do was swear herself to the holy order and slay demons. Between facing monsters every day and being a housewife, the choice seemed easy. So, she hopped on an airship to Paris and became Blaise Beaumont.

"And when the will it was read out they told me straight and flat," she sang softly, *"if I would have his money I must always wear his hat."*

It wasn't until she'd been shown the catacombs – well, the barracks where the chasseurs slept in the most superficial level of the catacombs – that Lie realized maybe being a housewife would be less dangerous. The catacombs shown to the people of Paris as a tourist trap – a popular one, especially with the booming interest in the occult – held the bones of long-dead people, crammed together to create a maze of death. But the deeper parts, the ones only the chasseurs had access to...

Those bones were not human.

Some of the bones belonged to creatures too big to be human, with bulking skulls and protruding jaws and snouts that smushed flat against their skulls. Some had teeth that were needle-thin and just as sharp, while others still had sockets for more than two eyes. There were spines that stretched into long whiplike tails, femurs that were long and willowy, bones that were blacker than pitch amongst bones that were crystal clear.

She walked amongst those bones now, following the chalk markings she'd made with each escapade she ventured on. The chalk coated her gloved hands with a fine powder, crumbling under her grip.

"If I go to the opera house, in the opera season, there's someone sure to shout at me without the slightest reason…" Alone with no one but the post-mortem to keep her company, Lie's voice became echo-soft and horribly loud at the same time.

Thunk.

Lie's heart leaped to her throat, her stomach turning to useless, watery goop that sank to her feet. She spun around, thrusting out her astrium lantern to illuminate the eerily still corridors. Her other hand drifted to her bandolier, to the arsenal of holy weapons there – precisely to the pistol resting against her hip.

"Hello?" she called out before remembering she was supposed to be mute. *Oh, well,* she thought. *Too late now. If you were being followed they just listened to your horrible rendition of* Where Did You Get That Hat?

She shoved her chalk into her pocket and drew the pistol, just in case. "Hello?" she called again. "Is anyone down here?"

Silence stretched throughout the catacombs. A chill ran down her spine.

"Helloooooooooo?" she called out again. Then, in English, just in case. Lie spoke a grand total of three languages, so she called out in each of them. "Hello? Bonjour? Salue?"

On edge and thoroughly perturbed, Lie ventured deeper into the bowels of the catacombs.

"At twenty-one I thought I would to my sweetheart be married... The people in the neighborhood had said too long we'd tarried," she continued to sing, albeit softer and with a shakier voice. She couldn't shake the feeling that she was being watched.

Lie came to a fork in the corridors and shone her light down both. Both seemed equally dark and unnerving, so she picked one at random, drawing a line with her chalk to mark the way before slipping through the passage of skulls and bones.

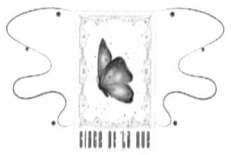

When Lie emerged from the catacombs a handful of hours later, dusty and shrouded in cobwebs, she was quickly pulled into the choir booths in the upper levels of the church, and she swiftly realized something was wrong. She hunched her back just right before she could get caught and huddled around the other chasseurs.

"Two things," said one of the chasseurs, Pierre. He was a reedy man in his early thirties with a cloud of curls and a thin nose. "The first: apparently, D'Amiens sent one of their chasses here. He's going to do a massive exorcism or something and will need a couple of us for assistance. The telegram didn't include many details. The second... Well, there was a body discovered not too far from here this morning. A woman. She was missing her...ah...*female organ.* And her heart, liver, both kidneys, tongue, and eyeballs."

Lie blanched. She'd read about a few slayings in England before leaving of the same nature. And so close to Notre-Dame...

"Do they think it's demonic?" another chasseur, Benoit, asked. "Grand. I don't want to deal with a demon capable of killing people like...*that.*"

Neither did Lie, who hadn't dealt with demons at *all*. She was a fraud and had managed to avoid any exorcisms so far, and she wanted to keep it that way for now. At least until she knew *how* to handle otherworldly entities.

"Either way, it's awful," said a redheaded chasseur named Jacques. "A demon capable of killing a person and stealing her organs or a *human* doing just that..."

Lie shifted her weight from one leg to the other uncomfortably, biting down on her tongue to keep from saying anything. Was there a black market for human organs in Paris? She wouldn't be surprised. The city's beauty was nothing more than a veneer meant to entice people but not trap them. The culture and history only barely managed to veil the filth beneath.

"Did they identify the woman?" Benoit asked.

"Not that I'm aware of," Pierre said. "She did have a brand, though."

A brand. The woman was a prostitute. Brothels would typically brand their workers with their house's sigil. Usually on their inner thigh, the mark would stay there until the girl was freed and it was cut off, or she died. It was typically the latter.

"Did you figure out the name of the brothel she's from, at least?" Jacques pressed. Chasseurs, unlike most church officials, did not take a vow of celibacy, and though it was frowned upon to sleep out of wedlock, the church tended to look the other way when its holy warriors did such a thing.

"Some place called *Le Jardin de Rêve*. It's in Pigalle. Never heard of it, though," Pierre explained. *The Dream Garden...*

Lie's frown deepened. Pigalle, the red-light district, was hardly a quarter hour away by carriage, an hour or so on foot. Not far, but... How had someone managed to bring a desecrated body all the way from Pigalle to Notre-Dame without being caught by the night guard, without leaving a trail of blood, without leaving behind *anything* that would lead back to them? Why drag a body from Pigalle to Notre-Dame? Unless she'd been lured away from the Dream Garden... But...

The night guard – the bestial automatons who swept snow off the streets in the winter and swept garbage off the rest of the year. To them, urchins and anyone out past curfew counted as *garbage*. They had obligations to report to the authorities if they saw anything amiss. Certainly, a *murder* would be something. And if they had seen the woman and dealt with her, her wounds would be...different. She wouldn't be on the streets at all. None of it was adding up. Lie gnawed on her cheek as she thought, trying to piece the puzzle together.

Where had the girl come from...?

Prostitutes were not treated like real people – just as street urchins weren't considered to be real people. Whoever the woman was, she wouldn't be given justice. Her case would be swept under the rug and forgotten about.

It didn't sit right with Lie.

"It's a shame, though," sighed Jacques as he shook his head. "Nobody deserves to die like *that.*"

Lie had to bite down on her tongue to keep the mute charade up. She came from a wealthy family, but that didn't mean she lacked a heart. Prostitute or not, that woman had been slaughtered, butchered like an animal. Jacques was right – nobody deserved to die like that.

Pierre waved his hand to dismiss the subject as if the woman's life was nothing more than a juicy tidbit from a gossip column. "I wonder who the chass they're sending in from D'Amiens is. Ben, you've been to D'Amiens before, right? Any guesses?"

Apparently, Benoit had gone to Norte-Dame D'Amiens the summer before to help with a rough exorcism in the countryside just north of Amiens. He'd been picked only because of his physical strength, as the demon was not only strong itself but had possessed a lumberjack with biceps the size of Lie's thighs.

Benoit just lifted his shoulders in a shrug. "It depends on what they're looking for. Claude was the one I worked with. He's not the best with the words, but he can fight a demon physically. Olivier is the best over there, but I doubt the Archbishop would be eager to send *him* to us."

Olivier. The name was smooth, delicious. Yet...she'd heard rumors about Olivier – nothing more than whispers about how he was devilishly handsome and devilishly cold. She could only silently pray to God that it wasn't Olivier heading to D'Paris.

Olivier stood outside of D'Paris later that day after he'd left his luggage at L'Hotel - and a note on the Englishmen's door telling them he had to go out, but if they wanted his help getting to the circus that evening, he'd be back before six o'clock.

He wore his chasseur uniform – the blue-and-red coat over a white shirt and deep navy pants, tall black boots, a bandolier with his collection of Holy weapons – his dark hair braided over one shoulder. His winter coat had been thrown hastily over his shoulders, and he buried his chin into its warm confines as the wind outside picked up.

D'Amiens, he decided, was far more beautiful than D'Paris.

He kicked the snow off his boots before going through the massive, heavy doors.

Warmth greeted him instantly as he took in the interior of the cathedral. The nave stretched for seemingly forever, the altar atop the apse a lifetime away, bathed in colorful light as the outside bled in through the ample stained glass windows. Few people knelt at the pews, heads bowed in prayer. Olivier kept his steps light so as to not disturb their peace with God.

It was not the Archbishop of D'Paris that greeted him once he reached the apse, but a nun. Her dark habit flowed around her like living shadows, her eyes shining bright, fanned by crow's feet.

"Bless you, child," she said by way of greeting.

"Thank you, sister," Olivier said. "I'm Olivier Beaumont, a chasseur from D'Am –"

"From D'Amiens, yes," the nun cut him off. "I'm Sister Marie. I'll take you to the Archbishop and I can collect the chasseurs for you. How many do you need?"

Olivier followed Sister Marie as she led him to another large door. His own Archbishop, had requested Olivier take a few Parisian chasseurs with him, much to his reluctance. These were the chasseurs of Cathédrale Norte-Dame D'Paris; they were some of the best in the world.

"Just one," he said, then silently sent a prayer to God that his Archbishop not flay him alive for being disobedient when he returned home. "Preferably one that's quiet. My partner in Amiens is...not."

Sister Marie laughed, her eyes scrunching up and her teeth showing. "I know just the one, then. The Archbishop is through here. I'll send Blaise in shortly."

Olivier thanked the sister and watched as she disappeared down the corridor. With a sigh, he pushed open the door.

"Good afternoon, your Excellency," he said, approaching the Archbishop and taking his hand and kissing his episcopal ring. Holy soldiers as they were, chasseurs were not above respect, and since Olivier had never met the Archbishop of D'Paris, it was crucial he establish that respect.

"You must be Olivier Beaumont," the Archbishop said smoothly. "I trust the flight from Amiens was well?"

As well as it could be. Olivier nodded. "Sister Marie said she would fetch a chasseur for me to work with while I'm here."

"I must say," the Archbishop, a man with an almost uncanny face, said, "I was surprised to hear that there was such a massive scale outbreak of demons here. I take pride in the work my chasseurs do."

It was an unspoken command. The Archbishop wanted Olivier to divulge as much information as he could about the demons. He hesitated. Would the Archbishop even believe him if he said he was here on a hunch alone? To eradicate the demons that made up the cast of Le Cirque de la Rue?

He was saved from answering when the door swung open, and both Sister Marie and a lithe chasseur stepped into the room. Sister Marie bowed in greeting before leaving.

Olivier stared at the new chasseur. He was...small. Barely five-and-a-half feet, if that. His blond hair had been stuffed into a cap, though a few pieces hung loose over his violet eyes. His shoulders were hunched in, giving him an air of self-consciousness. While there weren't any wrinkles in his uniform, a few dusty cobwebs hung to the navy fabric.

"This is Blaise Beaumont," the Archbishop introduced. *Another orphan.* "He is mute, so he can't help with the vocal part of exorcisms, but his hand is as steady as can be, and he can draw sigils with the accuracy of a printing press. He's fast and clever."

Olivier's lips flattened into a straight, thin line. He'd wanted a chasseur who didn't annoy him like Claude, not some mute wraith who barely looked old enough for the job.

But he couldn't refuse the Archbishop, so he thrust out his hand. "Olivier Beaumont, fellow orphan. I have a hotel room not far from here and plans this evening that will require you. I'm willing to wait if you need to gather your things before we return to L'Hotel."

Blaise Beaumont said, of course, nothing, and just patted his bandolier – his Bible, rosary, salt, holy water, dagger, and pistol on clear display.

Olivier said, "It is below freezing outside. You might need a coat."

Heat flooded Blaise's cheeks. He glanced at the Archbishop, who dismissed him to fetch a jacket with nothing more than an absent wave of his hand.

There was simply no way this would end in anything less, he realized with a sinking stone of dread, than absolute disaster.

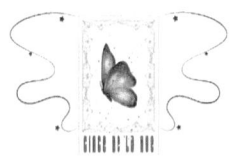

Had Emrys not asked the Seer where Le Cirque de la Rue would be going next, he would have, in no way, been able to make it to

Paris in time. The only hotel with any vacancies was L'Hotel, but they had a private area for him to store his airship and a room that overlooked the pavilion where Le Cirque was.

Despite the wind and snow, Emrys stood on the balcony and watched the city lights dance across the black-and-white tents, making the white seem almost blue.

His plan was to visit the Seer first to figure out where the circus would be going next so he could arrange lodging ahead of time.

Maybe he'd also ask about the details of his betrothal. Every time he saw a woman (which was, unfortunately, quite frequently, given about half of the population of Paris was female), his stomach turned sour, and his palms burned with anxiety over the realization he would be getting married soon.

At least, for now, he was alone. No nagging parents, no butlers or servants, no future wife... Just himself and, in a few hours, the circus.

Emrys shivered when a particularly cold gust of wind nipped at his exposed nose and ears. With one last glance at the circus, he hurried inside and closed the balcony door. He forwent the warmth from the blazing hearth in favor of taking a bath hot enough his skin was pruned and red by the time he finally dragged himself out.

He dried off and wrapped his towel around his waist, letting it sit low on his hips. There was still about an hour until Le Cirque opened. His appetite was nonexistent, yet he still went to the telephone hanging on the wall to request dinner be sent to his room. It would be good to at least get something in his belly since he knew he would be gone until late in the night.

Emrys sat before the fireplace, his towel sliding over his thighs as he crossed his legs.

Two years ago, when Le Cirque de la Rue first appeared in Paris, he had not gone. He'd been tracking it, though, and knew it never went to the same place twice. So...why had it returned to Paris on the two-year anniversary?

Why was it back?

A soft knock on the door, followed by a feminine voice calling, "Room service!" interrupted his thoughts.

"Come in," he called, making no move to get up from his spot on the floor.

The door opened, and an automaton hovered in, pushing a cart loaded with covered trays. The automaton's multiple tentacle-like limbs worked quickly to set the various trays and cups on the table near the bay windows.

"Anything else, sir?" The automaton asked, its mouth not moving as that feminine voice came through.

"No," said Emrys. "Thank you."

The automaton left, taking the cart with it. The smell of roast meat and melted butter dragged Emrys's attention to the table. Maybe his appetite wasn't *completely* gone... He stood, adjusted his towel, and went to the table, curiously peeking at the platter.

Roast lamb in a thick, dark sauce, vegetables drowning in butter, a bowl of pale-broth soup, bread still steaming from the oven, tea, coffee, wine, and deliciously dark chocolate.

Emrys bit off a piece of chocolate first before delving into the rest of his meal.

At a quarter to six, Emrys was dressed and finally leaving his room. He placed his top hat over his mess of half-dried hair and slung his jacket over his shoulders. He locked the door and turned to leave, only to run into something solid.

"Pardon me," came a voice in English – a welcome surprise in the foreign country.

Emrys glanced up (and up and up, God, the man was tall) to meet the green gaze of a blond man. He had a scar through his lips. Next to him was a shorter, mousier man – one Emrys recognized quickly.

"You!" Enoch said, shoving his circular spectacles up his nose. "I wondered if you would show up. Mr. Lockhart, this is Emrys. He's seen the circus eighteen times now. Emrys, this is Mr. Lockhart."

Mr. Lockhart stared down his slightly crooked nose at Emrys, one thick brow raised. He said, in that deep voice, "Where did our escort go?"

"Escort?" asked Emrys. "Are you going to the circus too?"

"Why else would a couple of Englishmen be in Paris tonight?" Enoch asked with a crooked grin, his chipped tooth on full display.

"Apologies!" This came from a different man, one speaking English with a heavy French accent. Behind Emrys came another pair of men – both dressed in blue-and-red uniforms, one with dark hair and the other with pale hair.

"Our escort," said Mr. Lockhart flatly.

"Will you be joining us as well?" The Frenchman glanced at Emrys. "Oh, doesn't matter. This is Blaise Beaumont. He and I are...colleagues of sorts."

Blaise's violet eyes only stared. He didn't say a word. There was something...oddly familiar about him. Emrys tucked that uncertainty away. There would be time to dwell on the uncertainties later.

For now, he had a circus to get to.

CHAPTER NINE

IF SÉBASTIEN WAS THE father of the circus, then Svetlana was its mother. Even the Dreammonger himself felt a surge of anxiety before asking her for permission to go into town for a cup of fresh, hot coffee. Not that he *wanted* to wander the streets of Paris (even though the cafe that brewed the best coffee in Europe was there), but he was far too exhausted to host the circus that evening if he didn't have *some* caffeine in his system. But, as the mother of the circus, Svetlana knew when things were wrong.

Just as she knew now, when Séb holed himself up in his tent, throwing up until there was nothing left in his stomach. Forbidden from entering the Tent Noir, she stood outside, hugging her fur-lined coat tighter around her body. Snow clung to her hair and lashes, though her skin didn't take on the flushed appearance most normal people got when standing out in the cold for so long. Perhaps it was the Slavic blood in her. Perhaps it was because she was anything but a normal person. Perhaps it was because she was too focused on trying to draw Séb out of his tent to allow herself to be cold.

"Darling," she called. "Please come out. We hardly have any time before the circus is supposed to open. Are you trying to figure out what brooch to wear?"

He was. He'd narrowed his options down to three. He did not tell her as much.

Two things were keeping Sébastien confined to the safety of his tent: the crippling anxiety rendering him immobile and the nausea that continued to force his stomach to lurch, even if he'd already regurgitated anything and everything in his system. He needed to eat before he could perform, but just thinking about eating anything made that damn nausea worse.

"Dear," Svetlana said flatly, tone void of any emotion. That's how Sébastien knew he was in trouble. Not that Svetlana ever showed any real emotion, but if she withdrew it completely...

He grabbed a brooch at random and affixed it to his collar. He knew, even without looking in a mirror, that he looked terrible. Dark purple smudges limned his under eyes, his skin was clammy and wan, his hair hung like limp noodles in the tail he'd scraped it into... His breath stank of vomit, of sickly sweet ketones that clung to the back of his throat like a film.

Sébastien stumbled out of his tent, nearly crashing into Svetlana.

"Darling," she said slowly as if speaking to a child. To her, Séb *was* a child. He was the youngest member of Le Cirque de la Rue. "Do we need to cancel tonight's show? You look terrible."

She licked her thumb and wiped something from Sébastien's cheek.

"You know I can't." he batted her hand away. "It's fine. See? I'm fine. I just have to announce the acts, perform a few miracles, and everything will be..."

He stumbled again. Svetlana caught his arm before he could fall face-first into the snow.

"You are hungry," she observed.

"If I eat anything, I'm going to puke again," he warned.

"Aim away from my shoes, then. I quite like these."

The rest of the troupe had already gathered inside the Big Top. Odette and Alice swung from the rafters, narrowly dodging the knives Antara threw and the snowballs the Gemini Twins somehow managed to sneak in. Aurelio rifled through one of his boxes of gunpowder, licking the dust off his fingers as he worked. Ilian lounged against the purring body of a massive tiger. It was Louis who approached as Svetlana and Sébastien entered. He wrung his gloved hands nervously, his eyes entirely hidden by his aviator goggles.

"I...um...I didn't want to look into the past or future without your permission, but..." Louis dropped his hands to his sides. "Why does everyone seem on edge about being here?"

The sickness all but left Sébastien's body. He grabbed the front of Louis's shirt, yanking him close.

"There is a door blocking my past from the rest of the world, and so help me, God, if you find the key to unlock it, I will kill you," he said in a low, grave voice. "I will carve the eyes from your body if that's what it'll take to keep you from looking. Do *not* snoop through things you don't understand."

Louis stared at him.

The Big Top had gone deathly silent.

Then, in a terrified, meek voice, Louis squeaked, "How do you know about the eyes?"

Sébastien shoved him back. "This is a circus full of demons. None of you are human. But I, the creator, *am.*"

Lie trailed after Olivier like a dog, her head down and her eyes focused on the snowy ground. He didn't look pleased about having to chaperone two Englishmen – three now that they'd joined with another last minute. One who looked...oddly familiar. She couldn't help but notice how attractive he was.

Such sinful thoughts for a so-called holy warrior.

Olivier seemed to want to get rid of her. He'd said on their walk, "Blaise. I want you to go with Mr. Irving and Mr. Lockhart. I have my own things to attend to first."

She wanted to ask about where Emrys would be, but he didn't seem to need chaperoning.

Her mother would have a heart attack if she learned *Lie* was doing the chaperoning when she was hardly *close* to being old enough to go without a chaperone herself.

At six o'clock, they entered the circus grounds. Lie sidled up to Mr. Irving and Mr. Lockhart. A brief glimmer of overwhelming whimsy crossed Mr. Irving's face, but it vanished when he saw Mr. Lockhart's hand drift to his belt. Even though his jacket concealed it, Lie knew Mr. Lockhart had a weapon hidden there. Her hand often went to the weapons on her bandolier without her even realizing it.

"I'd like to check out the Symphony Hall before the main show starts," Mr. Lockhart said, his deep voice so sudden Lie nearly jumped out of her skin.

"Right," said Mr. Irving. "I haven't seen that. Is that all right with you, Mister... Ah, what would you like to be called? Mr. Beaumont?" Lie shook her head quickly. Mr. Beaumont was *Olivier.* "Blaise?" At that she nodded, because here, she was Blaise. Here, she was a mute Frenchman who fought demons and served God.

"Then let's shed formalities completely," Mr. Irving was saying. "I'm Enoch."

Mr. Lockhart was quiet for a moment until Enoch Irving nudged him, and he grumbled, "Nicholas."

Lie nodded again. There wasn't much else she *could* do.

The Symphony Hall loomed before them, no line of people waiting to get in because any number of people could go in at once. It almost existed on a different plane, welcoming its guests to different realities that existed all at once.

"Whose brain are we delving into?" Asked Enoch as he peered into the black void behind the curtains. "I'm not particularly fond of the idea of having you two peek into my subconscious. No offense."

"None taken," grumbled Nicholas. "Well, since Blaise is incapable of giving his consent one way or another, I suppose it'll be my brain we pick at."

Enoch took his sleeve – his cheeks flushed crimson when his fingers brushed against Nicholas's bare wrist - and Lie was left to grab ahold of Enoch.

Together, a train of three, they slipped into the Symphony Hall.

At first, there was nothing. Just darkness that stretched on and on and on.

Then, the timpani sounded, a low rumble as they built up and up, a crescendo leading into a clash of tubular bells and low strings. It was the opening to a song that did not exist for anyone except Nicholas, an A-flat minor of arpeggiated scales and deep trills. A piano played a faint melody that did not exist within the *main* melody strummed by cellos and basses. Woodwinds and brasses accompanied the main song, though a faint drumming and harp created a different harmony.

And as the melodies – all cacophonous and clashing in a dissonance like waves against rocks – came to a climax, the world opened before them.

A grassy knoll was before them, wildflowers speckling the green of it. Stringy white clouds cut across the blue sky like fairy floss. A gentle breeze made the grass appear liquid. Wild strawberries turned to juicy pulps beneath Lie's boots. There was even a creek racing parallel to an old wooden fence, crooked and mossy with age.

"This is your subconscious?" Enoch asked over the triplets of violas.

"Apparently..." murmured Nicholas, that one word alone holding more emotion than anything he'd said before.

Lie watched a bird tumble through the air. It flew carelessly, but...there was something...off about it. Something in the mechanical way it flapped its wings.

The timpani thundered again, the song becoming harsher. Sharper. Darker. Those fairy floss clouds clumped together, heavy and black. Lightning sliced across the sky.

"This...seems a bit more accurate," Nicholas said.

A droning buzz drowned out the music, the bubbling of the creek.

"Get down!" Nicholas yelled, yanking both Lie and Enoch to the grass with him. Lie glanced up to see a shape flying above them. Not an airship...

No, it had a body, long and powerful, and wings. And when it opened its mouth...

Fire spilled across the heavens.

"Your subconscious is a bloody dragon?!" Enoch hissed.

"Shut up!" Nicholas barked.

"Demons are real, and it is your job as a chasseur to eradicate the threat they pose." Those were the words the Archbishop said to Lie that first day she arrived at Norte-Dame D'Paris under the guise of Blaise Beaumont.

It was not a dragon that infected Nicholas's subconscious. No, it was the same being whose bones were in the catacombs Lie had traipsed through only that morning. It was a demon.

"Now," he said, smushing his body flatter against the grass, "would be a good time for me to tell you who I am. Lieutenant Colonel Nicholas D. Lockhart. Until a few days ago, when I was discharged, I served in the military, fighting a war against demons."

Deep down, Lie already knew that. Obviously, demons existed, or else the chasseurs wouldn't have a purpose. But... She'd heard whispers of a war overseas. English newspapers seemed to think it was the Russians who were battling. Without any real evidence, she was left to speculate whether there *was* a war after all.

Now, though, there was a soldier before her. A soldier who confirmed the existence of demons. A soldier who had been *there*, fighting against the monsters.

"*Clearly!*" screeched Enoch. "What other reason would there be, Mister Barge-In-To-My-Office-And-Claim-The-Circus-Is-Run-By-Demons?!"

That, Lie realized with a twisting sense of dread, was also reasonable. There was just no other explanation as to why the circus moved so quickly so often.

"This isn't real," Nicholas said as he grabbed Enoch's shoulders. "If there was actually danger here, the circus would have been shut down long, long ago."

"Then why would you react like there's danger?!" Enoch hissed.

"Because I'm a *soldier*. Some habits die hard!" As if to prove his point, Nicholas stood and brushed invisible blades of grass from his knees.

Lie stood, too, tipping her head back to look at the sky. Sure enough, the dragon demon had vanished, and the dark clouds parted, returning to the stringy white bits of fluff. The violins and cellos, with their spiccato runs, gave way to a final surge, a final climax of winds and brass and deep strings.

And then, just as soon as it had started, it was over. The grassy knoll and burbling brook vanished into a shroud of darkness and silence.

Then, there was the other side of the tent, flaps parted to give way to the snow outside.

Lie stumbled out, her heart pounding and her lungs aching like she hadn't been breathing the entire time.

"Well?" came a voice in English. Emrys stood with his hands on his hips, grinning proudly like *he* was the mastermind behind the Symphony Hall. Next to him was Olivier, looking sullen and irritable. Lie avoided his gaze completely.

"Nicholas's subconscious is the worst thing I've ever had the misfortune of experiencing." Enoch adjusted his crooked glasses. Besides his messy hair, he didn't look disheveled at all.

Lie noticed grass stains on his knees that had not been there before.

"Enoch is dramatic," Nicholas grumbled.

"Enoch!" Emrys exclaimed. "E. E. Irving. You know, I've always wondered what that second E stands for."

Enoch grimaced. "Ezekiel," he said, sullen.

"It looks like the performance is going to start soon," Olivier said in English, disrupting Enoch (Ezekiel Irving)'s moping.

Lie glanced at the unnoteworthy black-and-white Symphony Hall once more before trudging after the band of men.

They sat near the front, of course. As the lights began to dim, a woman sat next to Lie.

"This seat isn't taken, is it?" she asked in French, her voice lyrical and entrancing – a siren's spoken voice.

Lie shook her head.

"Oh, good." She smoothed out her crimson skirts.

As the final astrium lights died, Lie caught a glimpse of the woman's face.

Or, rather, the porcelain mask she wore, concealing her features completely.

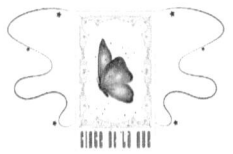

Sébastien stood in darkness, facing a crowd he could see but who could not see him.

In the few minutes he had to spare between eating and guzzling enough coffee to power an airship, he'd debated going into the arena at all. Ultimately, he decided he had to. It was one random night. Nobody knew the circus would be appearing in Paris. The chances of his past catching up... They were slim at best.

He held out a palm, face up, and allowed a single astrium blue butterfly to appear. It flapped its wings, hovering stationary.

"Once upon a time," he began, speaking loudly despite the invisible collar around his throat, "in the caves deep in Spain, there lived a serpent named Cuélebre."

The butterfly morphed into a lengthy, coiled serpent. Bat-like wings sprouted from its back, and its mouth was full of needle-thin teeth. The dragon grew until it was nearly the size of the tent, and though it glowed blue, it did not illuminate its surroundings.

Sébastien continued, hidden safely in the darkness, "The Cuélebre liked to be alone, but like all creatures, it needed to eat. So, it would fly from its cave, whistling as it flew, and fed on the livestock in the villages of Asturias."

Three blue horses appeared in the air, only for the Cuélebre to attack them, tearing into them and devouring them whole.

"Its scales are too thick for weapons to penetrate," continued Sébastien. The dragon let out a silent roar. "The people of Asturias did not like the Cuélebre. So, they waited until Midsummer, when the Cuélebre would be vulnerable, and they attacked."

Blue people appeared, attacking the serpent with guns and swords, with spears and trebuchets.

"And the people thought they won."

The dragon collapsed, writhing in agony.

"But they were fools to think such a creature could be defeated."

The people vanished, leaving the dragon behind. It stopped writhing, going completely still.

"Ladies and gentlemen, it is my pleasure to welcome you to Le Cirque de la Rue," Sébastien said. "And it is my pleasure to show you that humans will *never* compare to the might of a dragon."

The serpent vanished as a blast of fire obliterated it. The overhead lights flashed on, illuminating Aurelio – El Cuélebre – who stood in the middle of the arena, his dragon tattoo shifting in the light.

Aurelio inhaled deeply, and when he exhaled, a plume of fire shot out. The flames licked the faces of those sitting in the front row, but the fire didn't get close enough to burn.

The orange and yellow bounced off the porcelain mask of a woman sitting in the front. Sébastien's breath caught in his throat when he took those bottomless eyes in.

He faltered, enough so that the collar around his neck tightened, and he nearly missed the cue for the next act.

"Not far from Spain, where our dragon was found, there was a lamp in the Arabic deserts, not unlike the one found by the hero Aladdin. In that lamp was a woman so beautiful she couldn't be human. And she wasn't, for she was a djinn. A creature of fire and luck, one who may never need to open her eyes to see that her strike lands true."

Aurelio breathed out a final plume of fire, lighting two torches on either side of the rotating target, which Noa was currently strapped to and Sasha stood next to. Antara sauntered out of the darkness, flipping a pair of knives through the air. Her eyes were hidden by a blindfold. Aurelio approached her and, reaching into his mouth, pulled out a massive sword. He made a show of wiping the saliva off on his trousers – earning a laugh from the audience – before handing the blade to Antara.

She threw her knives into the air first before taking the sword. The knives hung suspended in the air for a moment before gravity took over, and they came surging down.

Antara, fast as lightning, brought her slipper-clad foot up and kicked.

Thunk! Thunk!

The knives buried themselves deep in the board, one on either side of Noa's head. The clowns both grinned and grinned, not afraid at all.

Antara threw the sword next, heaving the heavy thing like it was nothing. It hit the board right between Noa's legs.

Sasha grabbed the edge of the board and yanked.

Aurelio pulled two more knives from thin air. They glowed miracle-blue. Instead of handing them to Antara, he tossed them up and up and up.

And when they came down, Antara, once more, kicked them.

Thunk, thunk!

Right on either side of Noa's slim neck.

One by one, Sébastien introduced each act with a story – Ilian, the Beowulf who could charm any beast; Odette and Alice, the fairies whose lithe bodies were not affected by gravity; Noa and Sasha, the Gemini Twins who seemed to have spawned from nowhere...

Then came Svetlana's turn. As the stage was set for her, a spotlight appeared.

It bounced off the porcelain mask again.

Nausea soured Sébastien's stomach.

"F-from... The permafrost of S-Siberia..." he began, choking on his words. Iron filled his mouth. He brushed his fingers against his upper lip. *Blood.*

He sucked in a shaky breath and tried again, "Came a shapeshifting..."

The masked woman was staring right at him – right where he was standing, supposedly hidden by the shadows.

The lights flickered as his vision blurred.

"A..."

Sébastien fell to his knees. Blood spurted from his nose. The tent creaked, its foundation shifting and settling.

"Svetlana," he whispered, voice hoarse. Hungry eyes were pinned on him.

He collapsed, unconscious.

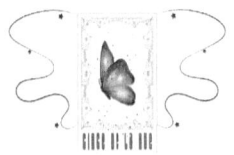

A ghost of blue sat on the shoulders of the Dreammonger, and nobody else seemed to notice it. Nobody except for Lie, who couldn't stop staring at the static outline of raw magic suffocating the Dreammonger. It gripped his throat and had entwined itself wholly around him. The other performers had magic coating them, too, but not nearly as much as the Dreammonger.

"You see it, don't you?" that soft voice asked. The masked girl next to Lie. Slowly, she nodded.

"Then," the masked girl continued, "watch this."

The circus shuddered, the lights flickered, and the Dreammonger collapsed.

The astrium-blue magic that had been smothering him flickered once before drawing back like it was a sentient being.

"What the...?" Murmured Enoch, who leaned closer, straining to get a better look. *He can't see the magic...*

"They'll kill you if they find out," whispered the masked girl, not unkindly. "You and him are cut from the same cloth, you know."

Lie watched as the sentient magic moved slowly as if lost before it settled atop the Dreammonger once more.

"In a certain tsardom, in a certain country, there lived and dwelt a girl." There was a new voice – a woman's voice, speaking in thick Russian that Lie could somehow understand despite never having learned the language.

A hushed silence fell over the crowd.

"This girl," the Russian woman continued, "was not an ordinary girl, like you might think. For she was of the earth and trees, the snow and ice, the tundra and Siberian wastes itself. She danced in the darkness and ate bread and potatoes with Baba Yaga three. She feared no bear or wolf or beast but lived in terror of humans, for the tsar of this certain tsardom, this certain country, was not unkind to his people, but did not extend that kindness to the beasts of the taiga. And this girl...well, she did not look like a girl. Sometimes, she was a raven."

A breath of orange fire illuminated the flapping form of a massive raven, its feathers oil black save for a plume of snowy white on its breast.

"Sometimes, she was a magnificent stag."

The raven was gone in a blink – a blink that the audience experienced all at once - and in its place stood a tawny stag with massive antlers that reached for the sky and dapples of starlight on its pelt.

"Sometimes she was a hag – she reserved this form for her meals with Baba Yaga."

Another collective blink. A hunchbacked old woman with a shawl with threads that brushed against the ground and a scarf over her grey hair stood firm in the middle of the arena.

"And while none of these were her true form – as she couldn't be in that body for long, lest she face the wrath of the tsar – her favorite was that of a girl."

And a girl stood there next – brown hair, green eyes, a somewhat thicker, softer waist with an ample bosom and ample hips to match. Though for a flash so fast it was missed by nearly all during that collective blink, she was not a raven or a stag or a hag or a girl. She was a beast of darkness, massive with moss and brambles clinging to its eldritch form.

"And the girl," said the girl, in her leotard that emphasized her curves, "who had once been trapped in a bottle found herself in Paris in the middle of winter. They gave the girl a name - and that name was *Firebird.*"

Fire exploded around the Firebird, creating shadows that gave the phoenix appearance of wings. She threw out her arms, relishing in the show that had not been made for her but would forever belong to her.

In the chaos of the Firebird taking over the show, the magic and the Dreammonger had vanished, pulled aside while Lie wasn't paying attention.

Olivier didn't care about the types of demons, only their class, and by the time the show had ended, he had ranked each circus member in order of who was the most dangerous.

The Gemini Twins, who didn't seem malevolent, but not benevolent, either.

Lady Kali, who could be malevolent but didn't seem interested in it.

El Cuélebre, whose energy was massive but whose will seemed nonexistent.

The Flying Foxes, both tricksters of a higher caliber, both with the potential to devour their prey.

The Seer, who he'd glanced at briefly but whose energy rubbed him the absolute wrong way.

Beowulf, who was teeming with evil energy.

The Firebird, who was the most dangerous of all.

And... The Dreammonger, whom he couldn't exactly rank since he wasn't even sure the Maître de la Rue *was* a demonic beast.

"I was right..." murmured Nicholas from Olivier's side. "They aren't human..."

"You think so, too?" this came from a woman, a voice Olivier didn't recognize, even though she spoke French. He turned to see a woman with a porcelain mask sitting next to Blaise.

"Pardon...?" Nicholas leaned forward to get a better look at the strange woman. She turned, her uncanny features flat in the dim light.

"They aren't human," she said. "Well. I would love to linger – truly. But..." she reached into her pocket and pulled out a single card, which she handed to Blaise. "I wouldn't be opposed to seeing you again, strangeling."

She stood and walked away, disappearing into the throng of people instantly.

Olivier glanced at the sleek card in Blaise's gloved hand. It was red – bruise red, blood red, the color of organs. Across the face of the card in black, sprawling script were the familiar words

Hell is empty and all the devils are here.

C. o. S.

Beneath the words was an address and a date – two nights from now.

"Who was that?" Enoch asked as he pushed his glasses up his nose.

Blaise looked up, violet eyes wide, and simply shook his head.

The girl in the mask did not leave any footsteps in the snow as she vanished seemingly into thin air.

She left another card in the blanket of white outside the Symphony Hall tent. It didn't have the Shakespeare phrase like the other. Instead, it had a different poetic line, one that would only make sense to a single person despite being written in Latin.

I cannot keep the tears back,
And yet they should not flow
For one who wantonly could wound
A heart that loved him so.

CHAPTER TEN

LOUIS WAS NOT USED to receiving mail, much less mail that came in a thick, crimson envelope sealed with gold wax and his full name – *Monsieur Louis Toussaint, the Seer*. How someone had been able to figure out what, exactly, his name was when he only gave out his stage name was the least of Louis's concerns. Had the letter arrived in his tent, just as the newspaper did, he wouldn't have been surprised. The strange magic of the tents was something he had yet to figure out, but he rarely found himself questioning its convenience.

He had yet to open the envelope, finding it wasteful to crack the beautiful seal. It had been stamped with what looked like a Venetian mask, though he'd never been to Venice, so he couldn't be certain. There was no return address, no name indicating whom the letter came from.

"Well?" Odette leaned over Louis's shoulder, her dark hair brushing against his neck. "Are you going to open it?"

"Who's it from? A secret lover?" Alice squished in on his other side. They sat huddled in the risers, along with Antara and Aurelio, though Antara was there to chase away the Gemini Twins (or so she claimed, but Louis could tell she, too, was curious).

"If it was from a secret lover, I don't think he'd be sitting out here with all of us to read it," Aurelio said as he picked at one of his claw-like nails. "The love letters *I* get certainly don't look like that. They usually have hearts and lipstick stains all over them."

"Well, I don't think this is one of *your* obsessed lovers," Antara said. She pulled a knife from her belt and threw it in the direction of Noa, who had started creeping up the risers. For the past fifteen minutes, both Sasha and Noa had been trying to sneak up on Louis to take the letter from him. The knife sailed past their head, causing them to scurry back.

"Do you need me to open it?" Alice asked, her breath hot against Louis's cheek. "You *do* know how to open a letter, right?"

"Maybe he can't read," Antara said. "Sasha! You devil, go away!" She threw another knife, causing Sasha to screech.

The risers creaked as another person walked up them.

"What's this about?" Sébastien. Louis looked up from the letter. Sébastien had looked terrible ever since the performance last night. The circles under his eyes appeared black, his hair hung limply down his back, and he claimed that the circus would have to spend another night in Paris because he simply could not move it.

"Louis got a letter," Odette said.

"A love letter," Alice chimed in.

"A rather dull love letter, if you ask me," grumbled Aurelio.

"It's not a love – get your clowns out of here, Séb!" Antara put her thumb in her mouth and flicked her nail against her teeth.

Sébastien turned to Noa and Sasha. They backed off, cowering under his gaze.

"Are you going to open it?" Sébastien asked, returning his focus to Louis.

The letter felt like lead in his grip. He sucked in a breath and snapped the seal, unfolding the envelope to pull out a single sheet of thick, cream paper. Gold filigree adorned the edges. A picture of a mask stood out in the middle, surrounded by the words

M. Louis Toussaint (the Seer)
Your company is requested at
Carnivale of Saints Masquerade Ball,
Which will begin at 6 o'clock p.m., on the twenty-sixth of December,
1888.

Yourself and three additional guests are invited.

"It's...an invitation..." Louis said after he'd read it twice. "To a masquerade ball. It says me and three others are invited..."

"A ball?!" Alice exclaimed, ripping the invitation from Louis's grip. "Oh! I want to go! Please, let me go!"

"No, I want to go!" Odette yanked the invitation away from Alice. "Please, Louis? Please, please, please?"

"Don't make deals with them," Sébastien said calmly. "But, if you need ideas on who to invite, Svetlana loves parties. And she's excellent at dancing. When is it?"

"Tomorrow," Louis whispered. "Why me? I... I don't know how to dance. I don't know who this is from. I just found it in my tent this morning – the Seer tent."

"Can't you read the future?" Antara asked as she flipped a knife casually. "And the past?"

Louis could, but for whatever reason, it was...*blocked*. Like someone had taken shears to his mind and snipped out that particular vision into the past. When he tried to peer into the future, the same thing happened. Nothingness with raw edges, hastily scraped away and hidden.

"What's this about me?" Svetlana held her skirts up as she ascended the risers, sitting down next to Aurelio.

"There's a masquerade ball tomorrow. I can bring three people."

Svetlana clapped her hands together. "Oh! I would love to go! But if I go, I want Séb darling to go. He needs the socialization."

A contorted look plastered itself on Sébastien's face, telling Louis that Sébastien did not, in fact, need the socialization.

"So, Séb darling, you, and me," Svetlana continued. "Who else should go? I think we need one more lady, so it's an even split."

"Me!" cried Odette.

"No, me!" Alice shoved Odette aside.

They lapsed into a furious argument, speaking Gaelic so fast the circus couldn't translate it.

"I'm the only other woman," said Antara. "So..."

"You don't even like Western dancing!" Alice broke out of the argument first.

"Or Western parties!" hissed Odette.

Antara just lifted her shoulders in a shrug. She tossed the knife she'd been playing with, watching as it soared through the air to bury itself in the wooden target clear across the tent – right in the bullseye.

"What's the dress code?" Svetlana took the rumpled invitation from the ground where the Flying Foxes had abandoned it. "Ah. Here. Tiny script near the bottom. *Masks are required. Formal attire. Please wear your color.* Oh, I can do that. I've plenty of green ballgowns I've been *dying* to wear. Nothing about wearing Western attire, Antara dear. Just *formal.*"

"The Western standard for *formal* doesn't typically include the *Indian* standard for formal," Antara grumbled, though she didn't try to talk herself out of going.

Louis still didn't know *what* his color was. He decided he'd just ask his wardrobe to produce something suitable. If he didn't know his color, he doubted whoever sent the invitation knew.

"I don't know how to dance," Louis said.

"I will teach you," Svetlana assured him. She gave a smile that sent a chill down his spine.

"I don't need *you* to teach me how to dance," Antara glowered.

Sébastien held his hands up in defense. "I wasn't about to offer. Svetlana, are you *sure* I have to go? We're in *Paris*. I... I *can't* go out. You know that."

"You'll be in a mask, darling."

Louis frowned. "What do you mean you can't go out? If you don't want to go, I can invite someone else. Ilian, maybe..."

Sébastien whipped his head around to stare at Louis – to stare deeper than deep, through his soul. Too late Louis remembered the rule that he wasn't supposed to ask about Sébastien's past. He swallowed hard and said, "Doesn't matter. I'm...sorry."

Svetlana handed him the invitation as he stood. "I'll investigate the area where the ball's being held, darling. You'll be fine."

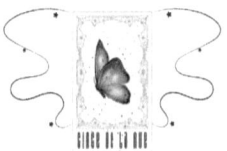

Amongst the dozens across Paris to receive a mysterious envelope, three stood out: Lie, who was granted a single guest – Olivier; Emrys, who was to go alone; and Enoch, who decided his guest would, of course, be Nicholas.

The girl in the mask could hardly wait.

"Why did you invite the Seer?" the man in the red mask asked, sitting next to the girl on the ledge of the building whose roof they were on.

"And not the Dreammonger?" the girl twirled a celestial-gold curl around her gloved finger. It matched the color of her slippers. "Because I know the Seer will bring the Dreammonger."

"And how do you reckon?"

"I gave him three guests. The Firebird will want to go. He won't bring the Gemini Twins, and the Flying Foxes will end up arguing. Beowulf doesn't like social outings. That leaves the Dreammonger, El Cuélebre, and Lady Kali. Assuming they want to pair one man and one woman, Lady Kali will go."

"That's still a decent chance the Dreammonger won't show."

The girl in the mask stopped twirling her hair and turned to face the man. "He'll show. Trust me."

"Then I will trust you, Saint Geneviève," said the man. "But if he doesn't show…"

Her voice turned cold. "He will. Besides, it's the Seer I want to trap. He's a fool, after all. And he can look into the past. Isn't that what you want, Gabriel?"

It was, and both Saint Geneviève and Saint Gabriel knew it.

The girl in the mask fixed her gaze on the snowy cityscape of Paris once more.

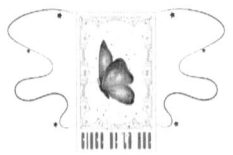

Sébastien decided his wardrobe had a vendetta against him. He already knew the circus hated him, but his wardrobe, too?

He'd asked for an outfit for the ball. Something inconspicuous, something he could blend in with. He'd put the clothes on and now stared at himself in the mirror.

His shirt was white, his trousers and tailcoat black. His waistcoat, though, was blue. Astrium blue. Stand-out-in-a-massive-crowd blue. So was the ribbon around his top hat, the gem atop his cane. He ripped the waistcoat off and threw it into his wardrobe. "Black," he demanded. "Or white. Or anything that *isn't* blue."

His wardrobe spat out another waistcoat, this one bright pink. He kicked it back in instantly.

"*Black!*"

The wardrobe finally relented. Sébastien buttoned on the black vest and grabbed a brooch from his box – a large gem inlaid in silver. He tied his hair with his ribbon in a low tail and put on the top hat. His mask, a black-and-white half-mask that would cover his eyes and nothing more, was in his pocket.

Outside, Svetlana, Louis, and Antara were waiting. Svetlana wore an emerald gown, the silk moving like water over her form. Antara wore a gold dress – Western in style – with henna up to her elbows and kohl smudged over her eyes. Louis...

He wore white, though only a small splash of it, and a black strip of fabric over his eyes and cheeks. A strange mask, but Sébastien understood why he'd needed it. Not much else would cover his gaze.

"This is going to be awful," Antara said as she pulled her coat tighter around her body. She took out her mask – gold, of course, and in a masquerade version of a Buddhist mask. It took the shape of a dragon's face, a massive headdress flowing into her dark hair.

"Have some faith, darling," Svetlana said. She put on her mask – porcelain, made to look like a Russian doll with massive eyelashes, thin brows, and rosy cheeks – and gave a full grin.

Sébastien cast a longing glance at the circus tents. It was just one night. One night, and they'd be back before midnight. They *had* to be.

"Let's get this over with," grumbled Sébastien.

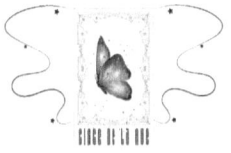

There was an eerie familiarness to the hall where the party was, one that unsettled Sébastien so deeply he nearly turned around and went right back to the circus. He hadn't been to a ball in many, many, *many* years. Even with his mask, his bright eyes, and the white streak through his otherwise dark hair (hidden by the top hat or not), he was rather recognizable. He just hoped his appearance had changed enough through the years that he wasn't *too* recognizable. At least not to the wrong people.

A man with an exaggerated curled mustache and a domino half-mask stood by the door. Bright lights from inside the hall spilled out onto the street. Guests pulled in on foot, with automaton-drawn carriages, *riding* automatons designed after elephants and camels and other *exotic* beasts. Sébastien was overly aware of the thin layer of snow clinging to the soles of his shoes – a layer none of his entourage had to deal with.

"Invitations," said the man, who was not a man upon closer inspection but an automaton with shiny bone china skin and an unmoving mouth. Its mechanical astrium eyes – nearly the same shade as Sébastien's – blinked uncomfortably.

Louis held out the crumpled invitation. The automaton stared at it before saying, "The Seer and three guests. Welcome to the Carnivale."

The automaton stepped aside. Svetlana picked up her skirts and ascended the marble steps, entering the foyer first. Louis and Antara followed; Sébastien watched the automaton-drawn carriages for a second more before hurrying after.

The foyer was decorated like a cathedral, with vaulted ceilings painted with Biblical frescoes – only...*wrong*. There were Adam and Eve in the Garden of Eden; only Eve had a whiplike tail and Adam had curling horns. There was Jesus on the cross, but with more blood than any church relief should have. There was Gabriel and Mary, but Mary held a knife over her womb, and Gabriel had eyes on his palms, on his cheeks, on his wings. There were other scenes, too. Scenes that weren't rooted in Biblical mythology but *other* mythologies. There was Koschei the Deathless hiding his soul under a tree. Scheherazade telling her stories to the sultan. A vampire being slain with a stake to the heart. San Jorge climbing the mountain in Montblanc. A slew of fairy creatures from Celtic lore.

Columns were painted in an alternating black and red with veins of gold snaking through the otherwise solid colors. The marble floor had the same patterns. Astrium chandeliers hung from the ceiling, casting shadows that made the frescoes dance.

They were led to the ballroom, where people dressed in an array of masks were already dancing. A banquet table was against the wall, piled high with foods so temptingly delicious they had to be straight from Elphame. Servers in Venetian masks handed out slim flutes of champagne. An automaton orchestra played a minuet.

"Coats?" asked another automaton, this one designed to look more feminine. It held out a hand, gesturing to the coatroom behind it with the other. Svetlana hummed and peeled off her coat, handing it and her gloves to the automaton. Antara did the same. Louis toyed with his jacket before holding it out.

Sébastien faltered. He didn't want to hand over his coat. Handing it over meant a delay in getting back to the circus. The automaton kept its hand thrust out. Sighing, Sébastien removed his coat, then, reluctantly, his top hat, which the automaton took happily.

"Dance with me, darling," cooed Svetlana as she took Sébastien by the hand, dragging him to the polished dancefloor before he could argue. Helpless, he shot Antara and Louis a pleading look, but they'd already decided the banquet table was far more interesting than saving their ringmaster.

"You know I can't dance," hissed Sébastien.

Svetlana tutted and placed a hand on Sébastien's shoulder. Usually, she was taller than him. Not now. With a groan, he slid his hand over the generous curve of her waist.

"I'll lead," she promised.

The automaton orchestra finished the minuet and launched right into a waltz. Svetlana wasted no time sweeping Sébastien into a dance that he did, admittedly, know. He would never confess to it, even as his feet glided flawlessly over the floor – step-two-three, step-two-three, small turn, gentle dip, forward and back, twirling Svetlana with grace. Beneath her mask, Svetlana beamed, those small wrinkles creasing at the corners of her eyes. Perhaps in a different lifetime, he would court her. She was beautiful, after all.

"For someone who can't dance," she said over the swelling crescendo of violins and violas, "you haven't stepped on my feet once."

He stepped on her foot then, just to prove a point.

"I missed dancing," she said, almost mournfully.

"You've been able to dance for two years," he pointed out.

"Two years! What is that compared to the lifetime I'd lost?"

Sébastien dipped her low, her skirts fanning out around her like a pool of molten forest.

"Did you dance a lot before...?" he didn't say the words aloud, knowing just how traumatic it had been for her. She bristled, nonetheless. He twirled her expertly, trying to get that smile back.

"Oh, yes, darling," she said. "All the time. I'd be in the snow dancing barefoot. I'd dance on the tree branches as a bird. I'd dance through the snow as a fox. I'd dance a slow dance as a bear, a fast one as a rabbit. I'd dance with the hunters who came into my wood even if they didn't know it."

She grinned, and even though her eyes crinkled again, Sébastien shivered. He knew what happened to the hunters who stepped foot in Svetlana's wood. He could only hope the dance she was leading him in wasn't one of *those.*

"You should dance," he said as the last melody of the song began. "At the circus, I mean. Add it to your routine. People would like it."

Her eyes lit up, but she didn't smile. He knew of all the acts she liked to be the least flashy. The one who drew the least amount of attention to herself. Adding a dance to her routine would only make it that much more memorable. When Sébastien first found her, she'd protested the idea of having an act at all. He had to beg her – had to tell her the situation behind him needing her – before she relented.

The song ended with a final chord. Sébastien bowed and Svetlana curtsied.

"I'm going to drag Louis darling out next," she said and disappeared into the throng to find him.

Sébastien turned, hoping he could disappear and just sit as a wallflower until midnight when a hand slid into his, and the whole world stopped.

"May I have this dance?"

The world slipped into slow motion. Each of his vertebrae shifted, one by one, as Sébastien turned around to face the person whose hand he held.

It was...a woman. Her entire face was hidden by a porcelain mask – painted bone white. The lips were thin and crimson. Red and gold filigree adorned the cheekbones and forehead, making the commoner *Volto* mask seem like it belonged to a princess. Her dress was red, too – not a bright red, like the color of cherries or fruit, but the darker red of blood long-since dried. The sleeves went off her shoulders in ruffled bunches of taffetas. Black Chantilly lace had been draped over the body of the dress, falling in perfect waves, ending in a strip of ribbon just above the brocade hem that brushed against the floor. She had a bustle and a train that swept out behind her like a mermaid's tail. Black gloves inched up her arms. At her neck was a velvet streamer with a chunk of ruby so massive it put Sébastien's own astrium brooch to shame. Her hair, like spun gold – the color of the sky during sunrise – was a cloud over her shoulders and down her back, held in place only by a single red ribbon

Beneath her mask, he could see her eyes – *green.* Not a jade green or a forest green, but a blazing green so unnatural they matched the intensity of Sébastien's blue eyes.

She blinked, her lashes thick and pale, angelic against her dark skin.

"I –" Sébastien faltered. He'd never seen anyone as beautiful as her.

"Oh!" the woman said. She spoke *French,* though with an accent he couldn't quite place. Kenyan? Arabic? Swahili? "I didn't mean to intrude. Is that woman you were dancing with your wife?"

Sébastien's face burned the color of her dress beneath his mask. "No! She's...she's more like a sister to me. I... Um... I'm terrible at dancing."

"So am I," she said, lifting her slim shoulders in the smallest of shrugs. God above, that *body.* An ample bosom with hips to match, a soft stomach, long fingers, a slender neck...

Sébastien swallowed hard, his throat bobbing. Somewhere in the crowded room, the violins picked up, starting a mazurka. *A mazurka!* Why did he have to dance a *waltz* with Svetlana but a *mazurka* with this angelic woman?

He couldn't even *remember* the steps.

The woman giggled, and Sébastien nearly died.

"Oh, this is going to be *terrible,*" she whispered. Regardless, she held out her hand, which Sébastien had dropped. He took it delicately, unable to move as she dipped into a shallow curtsy.

As the melody began, so did the dance. The woman led, skipping with fairy-like precision, heels clacking against the polished floor. She spun – Sébastien held onto that soft curve of her waist, mouth dry as he desperately tried to remember the steps.

Finally, he got the hang of it and took over, leading her around the circle the rest of the dancers had formed. He held her hand as she twirled, skirts fanning out around her. Each of her steps got lighter, and so did his. He couldn't tell if she was smiling beneath that mask, but her eyes crinkled at the corners.

All too soon, that dreaded song ended. She curtsied again, and he bowed.

"Zarifa," she said, sounding breathless. "My name is Zarifa Njoroge."

Zarifa!

"Sébastien de la Rue," he said before he realized how giving his name might be a terrible idea. But she just giggled again.

She had to be some sort of siren, for the emotions encompassing Sébastien – desire, lust, *love* – were so uncharacteristic he could only think to blame it on the supernatural.

"I was hoping you'd come," Zarifa said. She pressed her body against Sébastien's to let a couple pass. He felt *everything.* Every soft curve, every jut of whalebone in her corset, every rapid beat of her heart against her ribs.

"I –" he started.

"I was at the show last night. Le Cirque de la Rue."

The show where he'd made a complete fool of himself. The show where he'd fainted and been chewed out so harshly it was a miracle he could even slip away to go to the ball. *That* show.

"It's amazing," she continued. "Your performances. All of it. I *love* circuses, you know."

Sébastien bit down on his tongue to keep from spilling every single secret he had about the inner workings of Le Cirque.

"Do you want a drink?" he blurted, noticing a server walk by with a tray of champagne. When Zarifa nodded, her curls bouncing, he reached out and grabbed two flutes.

Zarifa pushed her mask aside, revealing her chin and full lips. She raised her glass to those perfectly soft lips and drank. He *watched,* enraptured by the simple motion. Jealous of the crystal that got to touch her mouth.

He quickly downed his own champagne, the bubbles stabbing his sinuses in sharp pops.

"How does it work?" she asked, taking his glass from him and placing both on another passing tray. She fixed her mask. "The circus. Where is it going next?"

"I don't know," he answered truthfully, even though part of him desperately wanted it to stay in Paris forever just so he could dance with Zarifa Njoroge one more time. "I *don't* know until right before it moves."

"Do you want to step outside with me for a moment? It's hot in here." She gestured to an open door that led to a balcony. Even with the snow outside, he nodded, eager to spend even a *second* longer with her.

Zarifa took Sébastien's hand and pulled him through the crowd.

CHAPTER ELEVEN

"THIS IS TERRIBLE," GRUMBLED Olivier as he downed another glass of champagne. "Horrible. I'd rather spend a week with Claude than be here."

Blaise ignored him and stuffed another petit four into his mouth, licking the sugar off his fingers. Both chasseurs had shown up to the ball in their uniforms since it was the nicest thing either of them had with such short notice. Blaise wore his hair in a low tail and had a simple black mask over his face. Olivier opted to braid his hair down his back, wearing a plain white mask. They'd only found the two, and with Blaise snagging the black one, Olivier was left with the uglier one.

"Why did we even show up," Olivier continued to moan, "when we could be investigating the circus?"

Blaise pulled his glove on, finished with the desserts (for now), and pointed to a woman standing on the other end of the banquet table, a glass of champagne in her hand and a pastry in the other. At first, Olivier didn't know why Blaise had decided to target her.

Then, he recognized her. Her...aura, at least. Olivier had gotten so good at recognizing the difference between humans and demons over the years that it didn't take long for him to realize that the woman nibbling on a tart was Lady Kali from Le Cirque de la Rue.

His eyes went wide. "I'll be back," he said to Blaise. "Stay close in case I need backup." Thank *God* he'd brought his exorcism tools, namely the syringe full of golden liquid, just in case. He could eradicate the demon without, but in a place as crowded as this, it was good to have *some* sort of cover.

Blaise nodded and, realizing he was to be confined to the area for the foreseeable future, removed his glove and went right back to tasting all the desserts.

Olivier marched right up to Lady Kali with purpose. She was shorter up close, though she radiated a warmth no human could withstand.

"Can I help you?" she asked after popping the last bit of tart in her mouth and chewing. "I'm not versed in Western dances. Please don't make me prove it."

Olivier blinked, stunned. Never in his years of being a chasseur had he ever had a demon speak to him so...casually. There weren't even any threats – veiled or not – in her words. Of the demons at the circus, he'd ranked her to be one of the least dangerous, but a demon was a demon, and it was his holy duty to eradicate them.

Lady Kali unceremoniously brushed the bits of crumbs and sugar from her fingers on her golden skirts.

The only danger she seemed to pose was a danger to the etiquette of high society.

"What...dances *are* you versed in?" he found himself asking.

Her face lit up, if only for a brief second. It was...human the way her eyes went wide behind her mask, bright and excited.

"*Gaudiya Nritya* is my favorite," she said, speaking much more animatedly, her voice limned with excitement. "But I know all the martial and harvest dances from India. I know others, too. I lived in India for a *long* time before moving to..." she gestured vaguely.

Olivier had no idea how to spell that dance, much less how to perform it. He said, "I won't ask you to dance, then. You're with the circus, aren't you?"

She groaned loudly. Dramatically. Very unladylike. "I was promised I wouldn't be recognized. What gave it away?"

"The fact that you're the only Indian woman in this entire ballroom," he said, though it was only *half* the truth. He couldn't confess to knowing she was a demon. Yet.

"Are you going to demand I leave because I'm dirtying the air? Because my *kind* isn't wanted here?" her voice took on an edge, sharp as the knives she threw.

"No," he said quickly. "It's just..." just *what?* He could not care less if she was Indian. It was the fact that she was a demon that rubbed him the wrong way. She could have been a French woman with pale hair and paler skin, and he'd still single her out because, beneath the veneer of a human appearance, she was a *demon*.

"Antara, darling, it is unsightly for you to linger by the banquet all night," a new voice said.

A woman sauntered over, her green dress swishing around her ankles. She was *tall*. Taller than Olivier, and *he* was tall.

And she was *dangerous*.

The Firebird – the most dangerous demon at the circus. *She* was here. Oh, God, if she was here, *no one* was safe. What could two chasseurs do against a monster teeming with the raw, visceral power the Firebird held? Olivier's heart thundered against his ribs. His breath caught in his throat. At once, his mission was forgotten.

"What am I supposed to do? *Waltz?*" Lady Kali – Antara – scoffed. "I'm perfectly fine here. I'm keeping an eye on Louis and Séb."

"Where are they, then?" the Firebird glanced around the ballroom.

"Louis is over there." Antara pointed at a wall across the room, where a man with a Venetian mask spoke with a man with white hair. "Séb left with some woman a few minutes ago. Was I supposed to stop them?"

The Firebird's gloved hands flexed into fists, only relaxing when she finally noticed Olivier. She slunk over, fluid like a cat, and traced her index finger along his jaw, tipping his chin up.

"Oh," she said in that thick Slavic accent. "A chasseur. How *darling*. What church are you with, dear?"

Olivier blinked. "Pardon?"

"What church?" the Firebird asked again. Her eyes darted to his throat, watching with a predatory gaze as he swallowed hard.

"Notre-Dame," he stammered. "D'Amiens."

"You traveled all this way just to attend a ball?" She let go of his chin and crouched down to his level. "How darling. Did you bring a sweetheart?"

God, please grant me the strength to deal with this infernal woman.

Heart thumping, Olivier went over every type of demon he knew, trying to figure out *what* this woman was. If not for the conservative neckline of her gown, he would have deemed her a succubus. Her voluptuous curves certainly pointed her in that direction.

"He came with another chass," Antara said. She grabbed a lemon and lavender cookie, stuffing the whole thing in her mouth. Then, speaking with her mouth full, she added, "he's over there. Scrawny little thing."

"Manners, Antara," the Firebird chastised. "It's rude to point. It's rude to talk with your mouth full. It's rude to take such large bites. Remember: dainty bites, but not too many. Go find Louis and make him dance."

"I'd rather not."

"Antara, darling," the Firebird warned. "Go find entertainment. You're a grown woman. I'd like to speak with our chasseur friend without having to be your governess."

"I'm older than you," Antara argued. Still, she wiped her fingers on her skirts again and stomped off to join the throng of partygoers.

The Firebird turned to the table of delectables, humming as she inspected each treat until she found a single white-and-red striped candy, which she popped in her mouth. There was a stretch of silence as she crunched on it, eyes closed as she savored the peppermint taste.

While she was distracted, Olivier traced a sigil onto the ground with the toe of his shoe – a binding sigil to keep the demon in place.

As soon as he made that last line, her eyes shot open, absinthe green – *poisonous.* His heart skipped a beat. Dangerous as she was, she was trapped. She couldn't leave the confines of the binding circle he'd cast, not unless he broke it – which he would *not* do until he'd exorcised the demon.

Where in God's name is Blaise?! Olivier turned to where the chasseur had been lingering, but the boy had vanished. *Blast it!*

The demon was secure. For now. He could go find Blaise and exorcise the demon before things got out of control... He took a step, and another, far enough away from the binding circle that the demon –

A hand gripped his shoulder. Every last drop of color drained from his face. He couldn't will his legs to move, to run. He was *stuck.*

"Precious," whispered the Firebird, her lips close to his ear. "But a circle that weak won't be able to hold someone as powerful as me, love."

Enoch hadn't thought to bring anything fancy enough for a ball and the borrowed suit Emrys had so graciously lent to him was half a size too big. He'd been forced to choose between wearing the dress code mandated mask and his glasses, ultimately being forced to go to the ball blind – his spectacles tucked safely in the inner pocket of his tailcoat. His hair refused to cooperate, so he gave up on slicking it back and decided to deal with the mess of curls that fell over his deep green half-mask.

It bothered him to no avail that Nicholas, in his polished uniform and slicked hair and perfect posture, looked like a storybook prince, even with the solid white mask that covered his eyes and looked tacky on everyone else.

Emrys was...well. Fine. Fine enough for someone who dressed for parties regularly. Enoch couldn't care less about Emrys's appearance, especially when the man took off, disappearing into the crowd the second they entered the ballroom.

Enoch groaned inwardly. "This is terrible," he grumbled to himself. "I hardly remember how to dance."

"Aren't you here to interview guests for your column?" Nicholas asked, his deep voice almost entirely devoid of emotions.

"Who wants to be interviewed this early into a party?" Enoch argued. "Nobody, that's who. Where is that Frenchman? How are we supposed to do *anything* when we can't speak the language? I won't be able to interview anyone without a *translator.*"

Nicholas lifted his shoulders in an infuriating shrug. Enoch fought the sudden urge to tackle him and skin him alive.

Instead, he grabbed a pair of champagne flutes from a passing server, handing one to Nicholas and downing the other in two gulps.

"I saw a staircase," Nicholas offered. He swirled his golden champagne around absently before handing the glass to Enoch, who took it and drank it without a question.

"Congratulations," huffed Enoch. "I suppose you'd like a medal of honor for that? It's a big building; of *course*, there's going to be a staircase. Look, there's one right there." He jabbed his thumb toward the large staircase leading to the upper level of the ballroom, where an automaton-powered orchestra was in the midst of a polka.

Nicholas shook his head. "I saw someone sneak through it. They looked like they were trying to be inconspicuous. The staircase was hidden in the wall."

"What? Like some hidden passage? This isn't a mystery novel, Nicholas."

"It *was* a hidden passage."

"Well, I'll be damned. Where do you think it leads? Should we investigate?"

Nicholas nodded once.

"If we get attacked," Enoch said as he hurried after Nicholas, "I'm counting on *you* to protect me. I'm a journalist; I don't know a *thing* about self-defense."

"I've a revolver," he said nonchalantly. *Damn him! If he's going to announce he's armed, he should at least pretend to have some chalance!*

It wasn't until Enoch tried to spell *chalance* that he realized it wasn't a word.

Nicholas led him through the tight throng of people, sweaty bodies and heavy skirts pressing up against Enoch, suffocating him to the point of claustrophobia until they were through the door and in the much cooler – much *emptier* – hallway.

Enoch glanced around, trying to find the staircase.

Nicholas, without waiting to see if anyone was watching, walked right up to a stretch of wall adorned by rather tacky floral wallpaper and a portrait of a man dressed for Carnivale in Venice. Nicholas grabbed the portrait and pushed it aside, revealing a narrow, dark staircase.

"Do you have a light?" Enoch asked, peering over Nicholas's shoulder into the gaping maw of darkness.

He reached into his pocket and pulled out a lighter, which he flicked open, producing a tiny flame. "I'll lead," he said, and that took *some* of the stress off Enoch's shoulders. Then, before delving into the darkness, Nicholas pulled a revolver pistol from his belt, flashing it to Enoch quickly enough to take a bit more stress off.

Nicholas went up the first step, then the next. "They're small," he warned in a low voice. For whatever reason, that sent a burning flush down Enoch's neck. He was grateful for his mask – for the darkness he stepped into.

Nicholas was right; the steps *were* small. He could barely fit half his foot onto one. He brushed his fingers against the wall – wood, raw and untreated – counting each step silently as he focused on *not* tripping.

"There's a curve," Nicholas whispered when Enoch counted the thirteenth step. Sure enough, the stairs curved, spiraling up further and further.

The lighter fizzed out, plunging them into extreme darkness that lasted an eternity – rather, a second – before the familiar blue of pure astrium bled into the edges. They'd made it to the top of the staircase, greeted by an open door that...

That opened into a...

"A library?" Enoch pushed past Nicholas, squeezing his way through the threshold. No, not a library. At least, not the typical kind, with shelves of books. There *were* shelves, though they held other curio, ephemera with occult influence – skulls, wet specimens in jars, swords and helms, a skeleton of conjoined twins... There were books, too, scattered around tables and piled in precarious stacks on the carpeted floor. Astrium sconces lined the walls, but there were candles as well, burning low in puddles of wax. A circular window overlooked the snowscape below.

No.

No, no, no.

Enoch hurried over to the window, smushing his face against the chilled glass. That wasn't Paris. That wasn't the city he'd trudged through less than an hour ago. There was snow, yes, but... But the city was upside down, hanging from the sky like wrought iron bats, spires reaching like stalactites towards a liminal world of snow and darkness. Tiny motes of astrium floated around, starlike against the black sky, falling in time with the snow that fell in reverse to coat the not-Paris city.

The massive outline of a zeppelin floated lazily in the distance, like a whale slicing through the deep. Enoch shivered.

Nicholas was flipping through a book, his brow creased as he turned each page. Enoch abandoned the window, joining Nick instead.

"*Histoire Admirable de la Possession et Conversion d'une Penitente,*" Enoch read aloud, butchering the pronunciation terribly.

"Michaelis," Nicholas explained absently. "Demonology. The classifications used by most people come from this."

"How do you know?"

Nicholas turned the page. A grotesque creature, fat and grinning with too many teeth, was illustrated there. "One of my men read it every night. *Why read the Bible when the answers are right here?*"

Enoch swallowed hard. Right. Nicholas had fought demons. He turned the page again.

Thunk.

Enoch froze, breath caught in his throat. Someone was walking up the stairs. Nicholas acted faster, slamming the *Histoire Admirable* shut and grabbing Enoch's wrist, dragging him down an aisle of shelves stuffed full of wet specimens and mummified remains. He caught a glimpse of a fetus, its eyes bloodshot and seemingly watching Enoch as he ran by.

"– one more waltz, I think I'm going to cut my feet off and feed Gabriel to the wolves," a woman grumbled. She spoke English, surprisingly, her voice indicating she was young – a teenager, perhaps. Far too young to be out in society without a proper chaperone.

"Then you'll be without a boss and without feet," a man – also young. Too young to be a chaperone – said. "And no boss means no paycheck."

The girl groaned. "Only four showed up. Gen was right, though. *He* did show up."

Gen? He?

"Firebird, Kali, Seer, and Dreammonger," the boy – because, truly, he was a boy and not a man – said. "Gen basically guessed it."

Chair legs scratched against the floor, followed by the *whump* of skirts being dramatically thrown aside so the girl could sit. Enoch's heart thundered against his chest. Nicholas had shoved him against one of the shelves, his entire body pressed against Enoch's to keep him hidden.

"Were you reading Michaelis?" the girl asked.

Enoch's stomach sank.

The boy snorted. "Me? Read? Mags, you've got it backward. I don't *read*. Maybe Gen was up here earlier. Or Gabriel. Or Benedict. I haven't seen him in a while."

"Well, well, well," a third voice crooned.

"Benedict!" the girl exclaimed.

Enoch dared to glance up. Perched atop the shelf was a man with too-long limbs and goggles covering his eyes. Beneath his mustache, he grinned, his teeth too sharp. The man – Benedict – said, "Looks like we have a couple of rats among us."

CHAPTER TWELVE

LOUIS USUALLY WOULDN'T TURN down a free drink, but in such an unfamiliar place, he needed his senses sharp as ever. His palms ached, desperate for a glimpse into one of the thousands of futures flitting around him like butterflies. Tomorrow's headache would be tremendous. He knew going to this ball was a mistake, but...Svetlana was smiling. Sébastien was dancing with a stranger. Even Antara seemed to be enjoying herself as she tasted two of every pastry. Louis stared at the champagne in his hand. A server had given it to him without him asking, but he couldn't bring himself to drink, so he just watched the golden bubbles popping as they rose to the top of the chalice.

"Not much of a drinker?" a man's voice came from next to him. Louis looked up to see a man in a Venetian mask with an ensemble to match – black and red robes like he'd stepped right out of the Tudor era. His hair was just long enough to be held back with a red ribbon.

"Ah. Not tonight," Louis stammered. "I'm not one for parties." Beneath the magic of whatever translator spell the circus had placed on him, Louis realized the man was speaking French.

"Neither am I," the man confessed. "It was my assistant who insisted on throwing this one. I'm just the funds behind the whole thing."

Somehow, Louis realized he should have seen this coming. Still...he'd been so focused on seeing with his regular eyes to see through the others to predict the man behind the masquerade cornering him.

"Gabriel," the man offered. "And you are...?"

"Louis," he answered, taking Gabriel's hand.

"My assistant, Geneviève, should be around here somewhere. She's impossible to miss." Gabriel paused, taking a sip from his champagne flute. "You're from the circus, no? Le Cirque de la Rue?"

Louis bristled. He dropped his hand to his side, thumb pushing up the edge of his glove.

"No," a version of him said. "I'm not."

"A terrible liar you are," a version of Gabriel answered. "Though I suppose your kind struggle with lying."

His eyes blinked, and he peered again.

"Yes," a version of him said. "I am."

"Ah," a version of Gabriel answered. "The Seer, no? Tell me, how do you do it?"

"Yes," Louis answered, deciding that future was the least terrible of the two. Prolonged conversation, yes, but it was better than Gabriel digging too deep... "I am."

"Ah," said Gabriel, satisfied in his guess. "The Seer, no? Tell me, how do you do it?"

Louis sighed through his nose. "I have six eyes," he said, monotone. "And I use Tarot cards. People like those."

"Yes, I suppose they do," Gabriel mused. "So, you can see into the future with your six eyes?" *Well. This wasn't supposed to happen...* When Louis didn't answer, Gabriel pressed further, "Can you also see into the past?"

A slew of curses rushed through Louis's mind. No. No, no, no, no, no. Gabriel wasn't supposed to dig like this. His palm throbbed, but he knew looking would do little good now that he was in too deep. He was a terrible liar, so his best bet was to stay vague.

"Sometimes," he answered because it *was* true. He could only see into the past when those eyes were open. And right now, he kept them closed because he was dizzy enough with just two eyes taking in his surroundings.

Gabriel reached into his pocket, and Louis tensed, prepared to fight or die. But Gabriel didn't pull out a weapon. He pulled out an envelope, black, with a red wax seal. He held it out and said, "I think you would enjoy this."

He pushed himself off the wall and walked off before Louis could even think to question what the envelope was.

Louis set his champagne down and slipped out of the ballroom, hands trembling as he clutched the envelope. Once in the cool hallway, he snapped the seal and pulled out the letter.

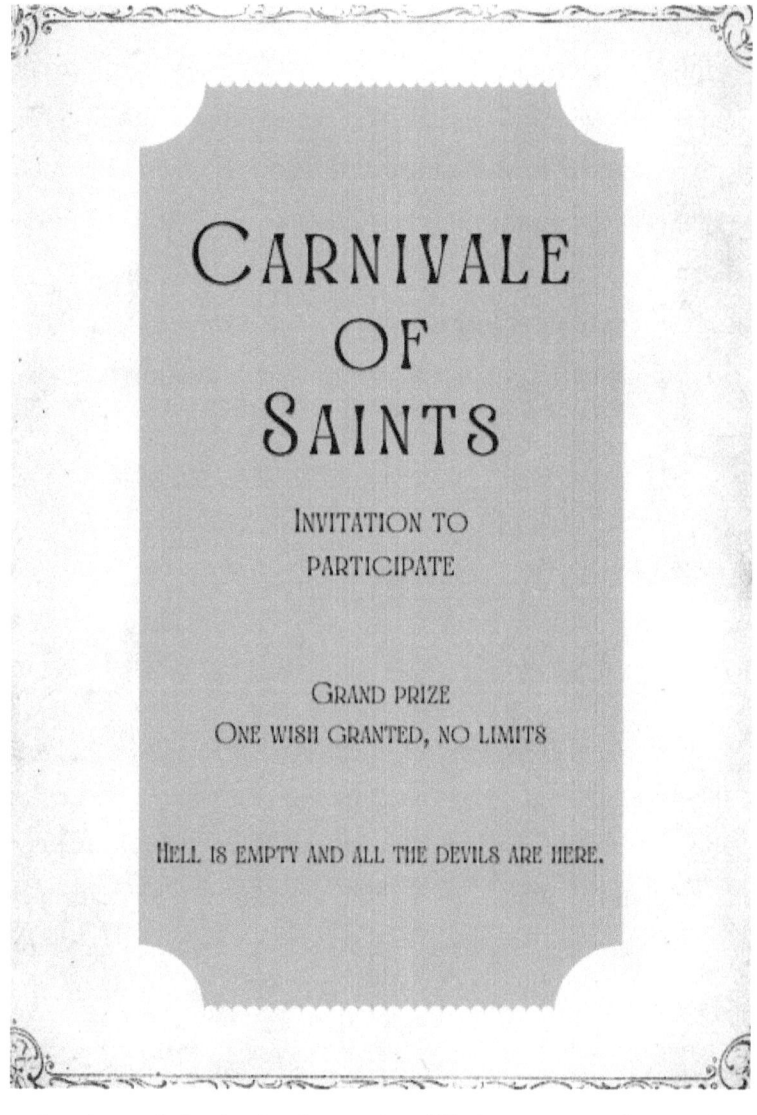

CARNIVALE OF SAINTS

INVITATION TO
PARTICIPATE

GRAND PRIZE
ONE WISH GRANTED, NO LIMITS

HELL IS EMPTY AND ALL THE DEVILS ARE HERE.

Louis read the invitation twice. Thrice more, a dozen times, until the words burned the back of his eyes, and he simply had no choice but to believe them.

One wish granted, no limits.

He thought back to the cards he'd drawn – the ones he kept drawing: the Tower, the Devil, Death, the Hanged Man, the ten of swords – and what they meant. What it *all* meant. Le Cirque de la Rue could slow down his inevitable demise by giving him food and shelter and warmth, but it wouldn't save him in the end. It was useless.

But the Carnivale of Saints...

Maybe, just *maybe*, he *actually* had a chance to not just survive but to *live*.

Sébastien hung over the side of the balcony, gloved fingers slipping on the snowy railing, wondering if he could somehow survive the second-story fall. He probably could but with a few broken bones and a bruised ego, which was, to him, a fate worse than death.

"I'll help you up," Zarifa cooed, "if you tell me how the circus works."

Sébastien would have told her regardless, as she had some sort of power over him, but that was beside the point. He *couldn't* share the secrets of the circus with anyone who wasn't a part of the circus itself. Svetlana had been the only exception two years ago before the details of the contract had been smoothed out. Beautiful as Zarifa was, a knot formed in Sébastien's throat whenever he tried to say *anything*.

"Join my circus, and I can tell you," he said, since for the past five minutes, he'd been trying, desperately, to get her to join.

"I'm perfectly content where I am," she said. "So, tell me."

"I can't!" He tried to pull himself up, but his fingers slipped.

"If you take off your gloves, you can get up," she pointed out unhelpfully. Sébastien cursed under his breath.

"I," he stressed, "cannot."

"Do you have a phobia of germs?" that cursed beauty was *toying* with him like a cat did its prey!

"No," he hissed through his teeth.

"Are they stuck to your flesh?"

"No!"

"Then take them off."

Oh! If she wasn't so beautiful, he would have *lost it!*

Only five minutes earlier, they'd been standing together, leaning over the balcony's railing to watch the city below. Then, Zarifa had pushed Sébastien, and now...

Now, he was stuck, unable to pull himself up because he lacked the upper body strength necessary, and Zarifa refused to help until he gave her answers.

There *had* to be some sort of loophole to get out of this mess! His arms screamed, the minimal muscles there protesting holding up his body weight. "Fine!" he exclaimed. "What *exactly* do you want to know?"

Zarifa twirled a curl around her finger. "What, exactly, are you?"

There were many things the people of Europe wanted to know about the circus: how did it move? Where would it go next? Where did it come from? Was any of it real? How did it work? *Who* is the Dreammonger?

But only those who lacked the very essence that made humans *human* didn't ask *who*. They asked *what*.

"I am Sébastien de la Rue," he said, still struggling to get up, "and I am completely, one hundred percent human."

Zarifa's face was hidden by her mask, but he *knew* she was grinning a wolfish grin. He could hear it in her voice when she said, "Sébastien of the Street... No one would have guessed the Dreammonger is a human."

She grabbed his hand and, with strength that surprised him, pulled him up. She wrapped her arms around his body and buried her face in the space where his neck and shoulder met, breathing deeply.

"Human..." she murmured, like his scent alone convinced her. It probably did.

When he'd first met Noa and Sasha, stealing them away from that sideshow in the dead of night, they'd sniffed him like a pair of puppies and declared him human. They'd also said he'd smelled wrong, but he always took their words with a grain of salt. A whole fist of salt, really.

"*Yes,*" panted Séb, exasperated. "I'm human. See? Human."

Zarifa reached towards him. He flinched, expecting to be pushed again, but she simply straightened his coat and adjusted his brooch, though she recoiled quickly when her fingers brushed against the astrium. Séb didn't notice – he was too focused on the way Zarifa's curls fell over her face. For whatever reason, he forgave her for

her attempted murder. Beautiful people couldn't be held account-
able.

Her green eyes met his. Svetlana had inhuman green eyes, but
they were the green of ancient forests, of knowing moss, of creatures who kept to the dark. Zarifa's were feline, absinthe, the color
that drew you in only to kill you.

He would not mind being killed by her.

"Then you must have a pact," she said. "An oath. A contract.
Whatever word you want to use. There is someone above you,
pulling your strings like a marionette. Who is your puppeteer?"

Sébastien opened his mouth, but only a choking sound came
out. He tried again, twice more, before simply saying, "I'm at the
top of the chain. I don't have a puppeteer."

Zarifa tapped her nails against her arm. "How interesting…" she
mused. "For the sake of my dignity and pride, I must return inside.
You know what sort of rumors stem from a lady being alone with
a gentleman, don't you?"

He did, but he was not a gentleman. A scoundrel, maybe. A
roguish fiend. A dirty street urchin who used his misfortune to
make a name for himself. But not a gentleman. Never a gentleman.

Zarifa pushed her mask aside just enough to expose her lips. She
leaned close and pressed a kiss to the highest point of Sébastien's
cheek, right next to the black scar that cut through his brow and
eye. Then, leaving Sébastien more breathless than ever, she vanished back inside.

Emrys had always hated parties. When he was younger, his parents threw constant lavish balls, and Emrys had been expected to mingle and dance and try to find a wife. He'd once spent a season reserving dances with a young lady – Elizabeth Tudor – but never went past a few flirty kisses. Maybe he should have pursued her. At least then he wouldn't be in an arranged marriage with someone he didn't even know.

He'd danced with a total of two ladies at the masquerade before guilt weighed down on him like an anvil, and he excused himself to the sidelines, becoming a wallflower who sipped at champagne and tried to drown the wrongness churning in his gut. He'd never met his betrothed. He didn't want to marry her. He *wasn't* married to her, so a few dances with strangers who didn't know him – didn't know that he was engaged – couldn't hurt.

He finished his champagne and decided fresh air would do him better than being trapped in the crowded room with his suffocating thoughts. He placed his empty glass on a passing tray and squeezed through the throng.

Outside, he found solace leaning against a stone half-wall that blocked off the garden. Covered in snow, it looked desolate, but in the spring and summer, the hedge maze would be immaculate, the smell of gardenias and roses and lilac cloistering.

He tipped his head back, blinking against the lazy snow, and watched as a massive airship droned overhead. Even at its altitude, he could practically hear the gears and cogs grinding, the pumps filtering pure astrium into the engine to power it and give it the ability to fly. Fog lights sliced through the dark – a submarine turned astral.

The astrium core – the tank in every airship, every automaton, which held the raw element – on the ship must have been *huge*. One day, he promised himself, he'd fly an airship that big.

"Go to a ball, Lie. That's a great idea, Lie. You'll have so much fun!"

Someone speaking English tore Emrys away from the airship. He glanced over his shoulder to see someone dressed in a uniform trudging through the snow, eyes focused on the ground – not noticing Emrys. As they got closer, he recognized the navy blue uniform.

"Blaise?!" Emrys exclaimed before he could stop himself. He could have *sworn* the chasseur claimed he couldn't speak!

The chasseur looked up, startled. He quickly clapped a gloved hand over his mouth.

"I... Don't worry," Emrys said slowly. "I won't tell anyone you can speak. What are you doing out here?"

Blaise hesitantly lowered his hand, opting instead to wrap his arms around his slim body. "I can speak," he grumbled. "Just... Keep it between us. I don't need anyone else knowing that."

Emrys wanted to know why the chasseur insisted on pretending to be mute, but it wasn't his place. There was a feminine quality to Blaise's voice, his English accent unmistakable.

"Who's Lee?" Emrys asked, relaxing his posture enough to lean against the stone wall again. "I heard you grumbling about a Lee."

Blaise's cheeks burned scarlet. "It's... Lie. L-I-E. That's my real name. Blaise is a..."

Understanding hit Emrys all at once. It wasn't uncommon for young men to change their names and flee to the military – or, in Lie's case, the holy order – to avoid one responsibility or another. Maybe Lie was like him and avoiding an arranged marriage. Though he must *really* not want to wed if he's willing to run away to a completely different country to avoid it.

"Do you like airships?" Emrys asked, grateful he had someone he could *talk* to. When Lie lifted his shoulders in a small shrug, Emrys said, "I like them. If my circumstances were different, I'd be a pilot. I like all automatons, really, but airships are my favorite. There's something about flying one that's just...freeing. Humans don't have wings. We shouldn't be able to fly. Yet, somehow, we figured out how to."

The massive ship above had disappeared into the clouds, the faint glow of the fog lights the only sign it had ever been there at all.

"I've only been on one a few times," Lie confessed. "Not enough to form a strong opinion either way. You're the one who's been to the circus a million times, aren't you?"

Emrys's two favorite topics were airships and the circus, and somehow, Lie managed to encourage Emrys to talk more.

"It *feels* like I've gone a million times." He held out his hand, catching a rouge snowflake in his palm. "I love the circus. I could see every single show, and I'd never get bored."

Lie leaned over the railing, hugging himself tighter. "I've heard," he said carefully, "that they're all demons."

That didn't surprise Emrys. There *had* to be some divine power – holy or not – at play. No human could do the things any of the actors did. Most people chose not to believe in demons, but Emrys did. When he was a child, one of the maids on his parents' staff had gotten herself possessed. It took two priests to get it out, as the English didn't have the chasseurs the French had.

"Is that why you and that other chasseur are here?" he asked. When Lie nodded, he sighed. "A shame. I wouldn't want the circus to be shut down. But...you follow God's will, so do as you must, I suppose."

Lie snorted. "Thanks for your permission."

Emrys cracked a smile. He shrugged off his suit jacket and draped it over Lie's trembling shoulders. He swam in the fabric, but his violet eyes went wide. He murmured a thanks and wrapped the jacket tighter around his body.

"I have an airship," Emrys suddenly said. "A small one. You don't look eager to go back inside. Want to take it for a spin?"

Lie nuzzled his face into the jacket. "Sure," he said softly. "I'd love to."

Lie knew nothing about airships, but when she saw Emrys's, her eyes went wide all the same, and she eagerly climbed aboard. It was small, but that meant it was fast (or so Emrys had claimed). He flipped a switch, turning the astrium engine on, and bright blue veins of light surged through the bronze body of the ship.

"Here," said Emrys as he handed her a pair of aviation goggles. "Wear these, just in case. You'll be able to see better with them."

"Don't you need them?" she asked as she slipped the goggles over her face. They fit snuggly across her eyes, casting a greenish tint to the world.

"I can fly with my eyes closed." He grinned. "But I have a spare." He grabbed a second pair of goggles from a hook on the wall, sliding them over his face. He shoved his hair out of the way, slicking it back.

Emrys pulled a lever, and the airship lurched. Lie smushed her face against the window, watching raptly as the ship rose, leaving behind an indent in the snow. Her heart thundered against her ribs. Paris grew smaller and smaller, the massive buildings becoming little more than dark specks against the blanket of white.

"Hold on," Emrys said.

Lie grabbed at the ship as it leaned to the side, taking a sharp turn smoothly, its portside nearly parallel to the ground below. Lie's stomach slid with it, her heart rising to her throat and leaving her breathless.

The tap-tap-tapping of Morse code pulled Lie's attention away from the window long enough for her to see Emrys sending a message. His hand stilled as another came back. She didn't know Morse code, especially not *international* Morse code.

"I'm asking that ship in the distance if I can cut in front of them," he explained, gesturing towards a looming mass on the horizon. "They said I could."

He grabbed the wheel and yanked, sending the airship speeding up and up and up until –

They cut through the clouds, blocking Paris out completely.

Lie's eyes went wider than saucers.

Without the clouds blocking her view, she could see *everything*. Constellations twinkled in the sky – Orion and Taurus, Gemini, and Eridanus – a smattering of diamonds surrounding the crystal moon. Emrys killed the fog light, making the stars seem brighter.

She sat down, too breathless to stand. The cosmic heavens wrapped her up in a celestial blanket, bringing her one step closer to the stars humans craved to touch.

She was among the stars, so close she could practically reach out and grab them – oh, to cradle Betelgeuse and Polaris in her hands like baby birds. Every moment in her life had been leading to this climax. She had been born to be here, to live with the astral world stretching out around her, an endless sea of stars. *This* was her purpose, to view the *opus perfectum* she'd come into the world under.

She didn't realize she'd started crying until she blinked, and her lashes were wet against her cheeks.

"It's beautiful, isn't it?" Emrys breathed. "Big ships can't make the climb this high. It's just you and me and the stars."

Lie pushed her goggles up long enough to wipe her eyes. "It's incredible. Just...*incredible.* I've never seen anything like it."

"See that blue star there?" he pointed. Lie followed his gaze – there. A bright blue star nearly muddled by the indigo sky. "The stories say that's the star that gave us astrium. Sirius is its name. I mean, it is the right color, but it's just a story."

Lie knew the story. A scientist – rather, an alchemist – a few decades ago watched a star fall from the sky. When he went to inspect it, he found a bright blue rock that made everything surrounding it – the scientist included – float. Through trial and error, the scientist managed to harness the rock – called *astrium* – and discovered a way to use it to make airships fly and automatons run.

"Why is it the same color as the blue fuzz?" young Lie had asked her tutor.

"What blue fuzz are you speaking of?" her tutor had asked, confused.

Magic. The aura that shrouded some people, that sat on the shoulders of the Dreammonger, that only *she* could see.

"Want to see something else?" Emrys asked suddenly. "It's not as spectacular, but it *is* beautiful, especially this time of year."

With no desire to return to the ball and every desire to stay out here where she didn't have to be Blaise or anything *but* Lie, she nodded.

Emrys turned the fog light on again and, with a whir of the engine, the airship took off, speeding into the night.

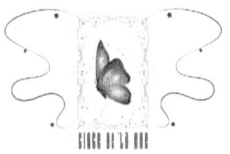

Olivier's vision tunneled, the swirling colors of the party blurring into a kaleidoscope of dizzying smears before everything was dark, and it was just him and the Firebird, her lips against his ear, every hair on the back of his neck erect, his heart all but stopped.

"Let go of the woman you're possessing," he hissed through his teeth, his body too paralyzed to do anything else.

The Firebird exhaled slowly, sending spider shivers down his back until warmth pooled in his stomach. She reached a hand around, flexing her fingers in front of his face.

Black fingers, tapered into claws, the inkiness of it spreading past her elbows.

"Foolish boy," she crooned. "This *is* my body. One of them."

She nipped at his ear – *God*, her teeth were *sharp*, wolfish, predatory. Olivier had gotten so comfortable in his false throne at the top of the food chain that he forgot apex predators still hungered for the taste of human flesh.

This woman, whatever she was, was going to devour him.

"What are you?" Olivier breathed.

"I am the forest, the trees, the earth," she sang. "I am Gaia personified, I am decay, I am hunger. I am the bitch you should be afraid of."

Olivier swallowed hard, his throat bobbing. "You're the Firebird."

"And you must fancy yourself *Ivan,*" she growled. "Or are you Koschei, destined to keep me your prisoner? Though... Ivan turned out to be Koschei in the end..."

Where in God's name was Blaise?! Paralyzed, Olivier couldn't trace any sealing sigils. The best he could do was stall until that useless partner of his appeared or until someone else came to his aid. Though, the shroud of darkness seemed to only envelop Olivier and the Firebird. He hadn't the slightest clue what they looked like to the onlookers.

"I am Olivier," he said, ignoring her Slavic nonsense. "Not Ivan or Koschei or any of that. And you are...?"

The Firebird stilled, surprised and...and caught off guard. Slowly, one of her clawed fingers traced his jaw, its sharpness sending tingles throughout his body, colder than ice.

"Svetlana," she answered finally. "Svetlana Vasilievna."

Olivier knew *just* enough Slavic mythology to make the connection. "Like Princess Vasilisa."

"Clever, Livi," she breathed. "You're smarter than you look."

Come on, *Blaise!*

"You can't kill me," Svetlana continued. She brushed the pad of her thumb over Olivier's lips. "I am the second oldest being here, and I am the most powerful. I rip the spines of men who wrong me out of their bodies and hang them with their intestines. I feast on their eyes and drink their blood. I *am* death incarnate, and I will destroy anyone who dares to try and stop me again."

Again. So she had been stopped before.

At once, she let go, and in a reverse tunnel, the darkness fled, and the masquerade returned. Olivier spun around to face the demon, expecting to see her true form, but she was just…a woman. A curvy, tall woman with a Russian mask, a smirk, and a miniature cake in her gloved hand. She bit into it, a moan of delight slipping from her mouth as she savored the strawberry and cream dessert.

"Don't be so afraid, Livi," she said after finishing the cake. "I'm bound by contract not to hurt you, and I only hurt those who have wronged me. Unless you become my Ivan or my Koschei, I will not do a thing to you. *Unless* pain is your pleasure."

Olivier's face burned hotter than the summer sun.

In all his years of training, Olivier had been taught that demons could only possess those with weak wills. While some were more powerful than others, they could never take on forms of their own. But Svetlana could. So, what did that make *her?*

As if she'd read his mind, Svetlana said, "You humans – you *men* – deem anything you can't explain to be unholy. Have you ever stopped to think that *your* God might not be the deity that created *me?*"

"Stop it," hissed Olivier. "I will not listen to the words of a devil who insults God. Without Him, I wouldn't be here. I would have died years and years ago."

Svetlana examined her nails, even though she wore gloves and could not see them. "Pity, darling. Do you think that, perhaps, it was not your *God* who saved your life but yourself? Perhaps it was fate. Perhaps it was coincidence. Does everything need to be divine, Livi dear?"

Everything *did* need to be divine because without God... Olivier would be lost. He'd begged God to save him all those years ago. Maybe it was just a coincidence, but it was easier to blame everything on a higher power than to believe he was alone.

"Why shouldn't I exorcise you?" Olivier asked. Svetlana was too powerful for him right now, but with backup – with that blasted *Blaise* – maybe he could do it.

"You don't kill humans, do you?" she looked up from her nails. Before Olivier could answer – before he could say she *wasn't* human – she said, "Because if you kill me, you will be damning Sébastien, and *he* is human."

CHAPTER THIRTEEN

EMRYS LANDED THE AIRSHIP in a patch of pristine snow and killed the engine, watching as Lie stepped off the deck. He followed, shoving his goggles up onto his forehead.

"What...is this place?" Lie whispered, taking in the scenery – the abandoned manor he'd brought him to.

Once, the place must have been incredible. The manor was massive, bigger than Emrys's, and his wasn't small in the slightest. Dead shrubs lined the path to the front door, but what Emrys really wanted to show Lie was the fountain. For whatever reason, it still worked, pumping water out of the vases the three masked figures in the center held. In the summer, it would be pretty, but in the winter, when the water froze and snow covered the stonework, it was *beautiful.*

"Over ten years ago, there was a fire," Emrys said. Even in the dark and snow, the soot could be seen on the face of the manor. "Authorities said it was an accident, but it's impossible. There were four people who lived here. The lord and lady had sent the staff home for the weekend, so it was just them. Only two bodies were found, and neither of them showed signs of smoke in their lungs. They'd died long before the fire."

"What about the other two?" Lie asked.

"The bodies were identified as Lord and Lady Rene. Their two sons were never found." Emrys wanted to believe that the boys got away, but he knew that was just wishful thinking. They'd be a bit younger than he was now if he remembered their ages correctly.

"That's awful," Lie whispered. "Who would do such a thing?"

Emrys shrugged. Aristocrats were notorious for having enemies. He could count on both hands the number of people who would willingly kill him and set his house on fire just to nab a bit of his fortune, and his wealth was a *fraction* of the Rene fortune.

Though, if he was remembering the details correctly, the only things missing from the manor after the fire were the two boys. Unless the murder-arsonist had staged the whole thing to kidnap the children. Neither Lord nor Lady Rene had any living relatives. If the culprit truly wanted to get away with it, the smartest thing to do would be to hold the children hostage until the eldest was of age and could sign the fortune over.

Emrys silently calculated the approximate age of the eldest Rene child. If he was still alive, he *would* be of age. Yet the Rene fortune remained untouched, as far as he knew.

Lie stepped closer to the fountain, his boots crunching under the snow.

Then, he stopped abruptly, going as still as the ice-encased statues.

"Lie...?" Emrys frowned. "Are you cold? We can go back. I just thought you'd like to see the fountain, but I –"

"We need to leave," he whispered. *"Now."*

"Right. Let's –"

Then, he saw what had Lie so shaken up. He hadn't seen it at first, the fountain obscuring it, but now... He saw the bare feet poking out from behind it, the thinnest layer of snow over them. He stepped closer to get a better look and instantly wished he hadn't.

The body had been torn apart like a pack of wolves had gotten to it only moments prior. Intestines hung limply from the abdomen; the woman's legs had been *ripped* apart, tearing her nearly in two. Her ribs were cracked and snapped, her lungs deflated, and her heart gone. One of her femurs stuck out, stark white against the blood and gore. Her face had been shredded, eyes gone, cheeks slashed into a grim smile, nose smashed to bits, and teeth plucked free. Her skin hadn't yet taken on the waxy sheen of death, and her limbs were not trapped in rigor mortis.

She had not been dead long.

Emrys grabbed Lie's wrist and ran for the airship, dragging the petrified boy behind him. Lie collapsed to the ground once they were on the ship, body shaking as he sobbed. Emrys didn't falter, didn't waste a second trying to comfort him, as he started the engine and forced the ship to take off.

As they rose higher and higher into the air, Emrys stole one last glance at the manor. The woman's blood was so bright against the snow but, surprisingly, that wasn't what he focused on.

He only noticed the figure standing behind one of the columns, watching where they had just been standing as the airship passed through the fog and the manor vanished from sight.

Nicholas shoved Enoch against the bookcase, shielding him with his body. The man, Benedict, twisted his head like an owl, craning to get a better look. Nick reached, slowly, for his revolver.

"Irving," he whispered. "When I say to, *run*. Run for the window."

"Wait –" Enoch started, but he didn't finish the sentence.

Nick yanked his revolver free, aiming it between Benedict's eyes. *"NOW!"*

He fired. Smoke erupted where Benedict had been. Nick spun around, trying to figure out where the beast had gone. He wasted no time trying to see if Enoch had actually run.

There! Benedict clung to the ceiling like a spider, head turned at an unnatural angle.

Nick's stomach sank like lead. Whatever Benedict was, he wasn't human. He'd spent *years* fighting these monsters on the front lines. He'd watched as his platoon had been –

Nick fired the pistol again, hardly waiting before shooting another round where Benedict had last been.

Then, he ran.

He ran straight for the window. Enoch struggled against the lock, trying desperately to pry it free as the other two not-humans prowled closer.

No time!

"Brace!" Nick shouted.

"What –"

Nick grabbed Enoch, holding him close to his chest as he crashed into the window, shattering the glass with his shoulder. Shards of glass flew around them, slicing into Nick's cheek, his neck, but he held Enoch close, protecting him as they plummeted towards the ground. Enoch screamed, but Nick swallowed his fear. He was a protector. He couldn't show any fear. Not yet.

He watched the window grow smaller and smaller. Benedict stuck his head out, spidery limbs brushing against the jagged bits of glass.

Nicholas grinned. He aimed his pistol one more time and fired.

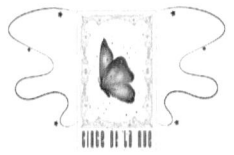

Sébastien returned to the party, seeking out any familiar faces. There was Svetlana, harassing some poor fool. There was Louis, being a wallflower. There was Antara, skirts hiked up past her ankles as she hurried to Louis. Deciding it was safer *not* to interfere with Svetlana and her prey, Sébastien squeezed through the crowd, reaching Louis just as Antara did.

"How come Svetlana can eat as many sweets as she wants, but when *I* do it, it's unladylike," Antara grumbled, throwing her weight against the wall dramatically. She mimed throwing a knife at Svetlana, who looked up with green eyes and a wicked smirk.

"Svetlana is a lawless woman," Sébastien grumbled, though the only woman he could think about was Zarifa. Where had she gone? He couldn't find her anywhere in the crowd. "Even *I* can't argue with her."

"I'm much older than she is," Antara huffed.

Louis chewed on the inside of his cheek, debating outcomes before deciding to ask, "How old are you?"

Had he asked Svetlana, Louis would have been chastised for even daring to ask a woman her age. But he asked Antara, who simply could not care about age anymore, not when she'd lived as long as she had. She lifted her shoulders in a shrug and said, "One thousand eight hundred ninety-five."

Louis choked. "You're not serious."

Antara twirled a dark curl around her finger. "I'm the oldest in le Troupe de la Rue. One thousand. Eight hundred. Ninety. Five."

"B-but that means –" Louis ticked off on his fingers as he counted. "You were born *before Christ died.*"

"Yes," she said simply. "In the year seven. I'm a few centuries older than Svetlana. How much older am I than you, Séb?"

Sébastien hadn't been listening, too focused on trying to find Zarifa. Antara asked the question again. This time, he answered, "It doesn't matter how old I am. I'm old enough. Have you seen a woman with gold hair? It looks like a cloud. I bet it feels like a cloud, so soft... I bet the rest of her is soft, too."

"Dark skin?" Antara asked.

"Red dress?" Louis added.

Sébastien stared at them both.

"She's standing on the podium with another man." Antara nodded in their direction.

Sébastien followed her gaze, his stomach sinking when he saw Zarifa next to someone else. A man, tall and lanky, with a red tailcoat and a Venetian mask. He wore a top hat, black with a sash of red, and a ruby brooch at his throat, just as gaudy and expensive as Sébastien's astrium one. Though he couldn't see the man's face, something about him was...familiar.

"Ladies and gentlemen!" the masked man announced. The music had stopped, and with it, the chatter died, forcing everyone's attention on Zarifa and the man.

The masked man clapped his hands together. "It is my honor and delight to have you all here tonight. While I'm sure you are all happy to have lively music and champagne, I am willing to bet you've been wondering *why* I threw this ball. And I will tell you, in time. But first! First, I must make an introduction. Ladies and gentlemen, meet Saint Geneviève, the coordinator of this ball. The one who is responsible for what is planned down the road – a twisty road, mind you."

Geneviève. It took Sébastien a moment to realize *Saint Geneviève* was *Zarifa.*

He hardly had time to process it before the masked man continued. "My name is Saint Gabriel, the Angel of Death. Tonight's ball is an opening ceremony of sorts. You have all heard of *Le Cirque de la Rue,* no?"

The Angel of Death turned a fraction, eyeless gaze landing right on Sébastien. Dread, cold as ice, filled his belly.

"Tonight... Tonight, I have hidden forty-nine invitations to participate in something *new*. Something far better than the Circus of the Street." Even though his face was hidden by the mask, Sébastien knew Saint Gabriel grinned. "Ladies and gentlemen, there are forty-nine spots left. Find the invitation, and you can participate for the chance to win a *wish*. Somewhere in this building, there is a red envelope waiting for you. Find it, and your entrance to the Carnivale of Saints will be granted. Remember: Hell is empty, ladies and gentlemen."

He tipped his hat, eyes never once leaving Sébastien, not even as chaos erupted, the guests scrambling to find one of the precious invitations. "And all the devils are here."

PART TWO

CHAPTER FOURTEEN

NICHOLAS HANDED ENOCH A chipped teacup filled with melted snow. Enoch, parched, took the cup, and gulped the freezing water down, not caring that it burned his throat or froze his belly.

"Thanks," Enoch murmured around the lip of the cup.

It had been two days since they had jumped from the window of the hidden library to escape the creature known as Benedict. Two days since they'd landed in this...place. It looked so much like Paris, yet...wrong. Uncanny. The sun never shone, and the streets weren't filled with people. Nicholas had found an abandoned house and, after thoroughly inspecting it, deemed it safe *enough* for Enoch to stay in.

The *Otherland,* Nicholas called this place.

Hell, as some people called it. Purgatory. The nowhere, the everywhere, the waiting space in between. Alice's Wonderland come to life. *Enoch's Otherland.* A place above or beneath the real world not quite existing on the same plane.

Enoch handed the teacup back to Nicholas, who took it and set it down. There was no heat in the house, but they had found a few moth-eaten blankets. They also found that sitting with their hips touching was warmer than sitting on opposite sides of the cold floor.

"I've been here before," Nicholas said. He looked *awful,* yet still...horribly perfect. His blonde hair fell over his face, no longer slicked back, and dark circles marred the pale skin beneath his green eyes.

He looked at his hands – one flesh, one mechanic.

"The war," he continued. "It's here. On the border between Earth and the Otherland, wherever that is. We aren't told where we're fighting when we enlist. We're put into airships and taken here without being told where – or what – *here* is. We are told to kill all enemies without hesitation, and it wasn't until we got to the frontlines that we learned the enemies aren't human, even if some of them *look* human. It was only because of my rank that I learned where we were fighting."

Enoch didn't speak, not for a while, his mind racing with the realization that demons and hell were real.

"Is..." Enoch started, slowly, carefully, "Is the war how you lost your...hand?"

"It was blown off," Nicholas said. He picked up the teacup and rolled it from hand to hand. "I was honorably discharged. There's nothing *honorable* about being told you're too incapacitated to hold a gun and defend your country."

Enoch watched the mechanical joints of Nicholas's prosthetic move, the gears churning as astrium pumped through false veins around metal tendons.

"Do..." Enoch's experience with soldiers fresh from the battle-field was limited only to Nicholas. "Do you want to talk –"

"I don't want to talk about it," Nicholas said sternly.

Enoch just nodded.

He wished, not for the first time, that he had a notebook and a pen with him, or a book, or *something* other than the uncomfortable suit he'd been stuck wearing and the cheap masquerade mask that had snapped when they fell and he only just decided to throw out.

Nicholas set the teacup down and buried his face in his mismatched hands. He groaned and raked his fingers through his blond hair, shoving it off his forehead. Whatever product he'd put in before the ball kept it in place, a few pieces sticking up.

Without thinking, Enoch reached over and smoothed a few of those pieces down.

"I'm sorry," Nicholas murmured. "I didn't mean to snap."

"I sort of expect soldiers to snap at annoying journalists who won't leave them alone."

Nicholas gave Enoch a sideways look – one of...pity. "You're not annoying. I just... I am not ready to talk about the numerous mistakes I made leading up to the explosion that cost me my hand."

Enoch could understand that very well. He said, "Well, I won't ask about your hand, but could you tell me more about the demons you fought? If we're stuck in this...Otherland...I want to know what we're up against."

Nicholas lowered his hands. At first, Enoch didn't expect him to talk. Maybe talking about *any* aspect of the war was lumped into that *I-don't-want-to-talk-about-it* subject.

But then, he said, "There are three types of demons: the ones from Elphame, the ones from the Otherland, and the ones from earth. The demons from Elphame aren't what people usually think of as demons. They're the faeries, the mermaids, the dragons. The tricksters who would rather gamble your soul from you than outright devour you.

"The ones from the Otherland are the more dangerous ones. Vampires, succubae, incubi, powerful demons. But the ones from earth... They're the worst of them all. It's the demons from the Otherland who tend to possess humans, but the demons from Earth... They're the monsters of folklore, the wicked beasts that haunt your nightmares. They can blend in with humans, and *that's* what makes them so dangerous."

Enoch swallowed hard. Just last week, he didn't truly believe in demons. And now... Now, they were his entire existence. He was trapped in their realm, a helpless mouse in a den of bloodthirsty, starved tigers.

Had he fallen from that dimension-shifting window alone, he would not have survived.

"Wait." Enoch sat upright. "You said the war is here."

Nicholas blinked once. "Yes..."

Enoch said, "Why don't we find *them* and see if they can bring us home?"

Louis sat at the table in his fortune-telling tent, a single tarot card placed in front of him, and an entire circus troupe circled around, peering over his shoulders as if the card would spring to life and bite them.

The card did not belong to his deck, nor the deck he received when he stopped being just Louis and started becoming *the Seer*. It was black and silky, edges painted gold to match the filigree decorating the back. The front was a card he recognized as easily as he recognized his own reflection, if not more so – a single eight-pointed star, red as blood, against a black backdrop of inky night. Though where he expected to see the Roman numerals *XVII* and the card's name, *the Star*, there was...something unfamiliar. Something strange. Something that, apparently, required the entire Troupe de la Rue to huddle around like curious kittens.

Once there was a traitor hidden at the table
Another cursed to sit under a snake in a gable.
A king to return with a coven of knights
A blue moon to bathe the world in its lights.
It is near yet far
Unto all it shall mar.
It is the beginning that gnashes its teeth
It is the ending, a pale, wicked beast.

"Where did this come from again?" Sébastien asked. He'd gone straight to his tent after the masquerade two days ago and refused to leave. The circus was on hiatus, and only Svetlana seemed concerned, but the elusive ringmaster *finally* dragged himself out, missing all the context behind the mysterious card.

"Séb, darling," Svetlana said, cupping his cheek. "I told you. Louis dear was invited to this...game. The Carnivale of Saints. This is the clue to the first game."

"I'm lost," said Sébastien. "How is a tarot card a clue?"

"It came in an envelope," added Louis, unhelpfully. "There was an address on the inside – easily missed – and the back just said *the Crimson Market.*"

"Treasure hunt, treasure hunt!" chanted Noa.

"Scavenger hunt, scavenger hunt!" sang Sasha. "Pipe down, darlings," cooed Svetlana, though there was a sharpness to her motherly tone that shut the Gemini Twins up in an instant.

Louis turned the card over, studying the back. He slipped one of his hands beneath the table, hidden by the lengthy tablecloth, and nudged his glove up and up, just enough to take a peek...

Nothing nothing nothing, said the future.

He frowned and tried peering again, but there was nothing. A wall of solid black, an endlessness of nothingness, just like when he tried to look into Sébastien's past.

"What was the address?" Sébastien asked, drawing Louis back to the present. He set the card down, face-up, on the table.

"It's not a Paris address," he said. He could see into the future there, a glimpse enough to know the address of the *Crimson Market* wasn't in Paris, but he could get there *from* Paris.

The glimpses of the future were choppy: a corridor of skulls, a narrow passage, an antechamber with a wall of clocks, a dark sky and a crowded street... It wasn't much, but it was enough for him to figure out where to go.

"Wait, wait, wait." Antara held her hands up. "Noa, Sasha, what do you mean by a *treasure hunt?*"

"Scavenger hunt," corrected Sasha, much to Antara's annoyance.

"Clues," said Noa. They climbed onto the table and held their arms above their head. Then, in a voice carrying far more clarity and sanity than anything they had said before, Noa said, "On the shores of the west, where the great hills stand with their feet in the sea, dwelt you, and therefore, dwelt me. It was you and I, I and you, me and my and my and thee, together as one and forever as one."

Maybe not completely lucid...

Sasha, from their post on a tilted chair, balancing precariously, said, "Tricks and treasures loved we and thee. Treasures and tricks, in the queendom by the sea. We know tricks, you see, we and thee. We know treasures. We know clues when clues appear and when they don't. *Once there was a traitor hidden at the table. Another cursed to sit under a snake in a gable. A king to return with a coven of knights. A blue moon to bathe the world in its lights.* A *clue.* A trick. A *treasure,* Six Eyes."

Noa scooped up the card and held it to the sky. "Six Eyes, Six Eyes, can't you see? A treasure, a scavenger, a *hunt,* knows me and thee and we."

Svetlana stretched her arm to pluck the card from Noa before they could bend it. A wordless look had both Gemini Twins scrambling to sit quietly on the floor, their nonsensical rambling ceasing.

"A treasure hunt..." breathed Louis. Of *course.* Of course! It made perfect sense. If the Carnivale of Saints was offering up a *wish,* of *course,* it would be hidden, only found through a treasure hunt.

But...*what was it?*

Louis raked his hands through his hair, yanking on the roots as if the sudden pain would give him all the answers he needed. It didn't.

He knew Tarot better than he knew himself (which wasn't saying much, but the sentiment still stood), yet the truth behind this *one card* kept slipping through the cracks of his fingers. All his life, he'd been able to draw a card and *know.*

Death. The Tower. The Hanged Man. Ten of Swords. The Devil and the World.

He was going to die, and he knew it because those six cards promised him. But this one... This mysterious card – this clue – made no sense. Someone – maybe Saint Gabriel – didn't want Louis peeking into the future to figure it out.

Which meant someone *(Saint Gabriel)* knew what he was. What he could do.

And how to block his abilities.

Just like Sébastien could…

Through his goggles, Louis glanced at Sébastien, who had stopped listening as Svetlana lectured him, half asleep with his cheek in his hand and his eyes glossy.

Louis stared harder, thankful for once that his oversized aviator goggles protected his gaze. Sébastien didn't seem to notice, not that he was awake enough to, as he absently nodded along to whatever Svetlana said.

Louis closed his eyes only to open his eyes and stare. He stared and stared, trying to pry into Sébastien's past, but…nothing. Just a wall of black.

So, he shifted and began prying into Svetlana's.

There. Glimpses of a world he did not know – dense trees and thick snow, warm bread, a hut surrounded by skulls on stakes, the rush of wind in feathered wings, a jar –

"Get out."

Louis startled out of the past, only to realize Svetlana was inches away from him, her green eyes cold.

"Do not pry where you are not welcome," she said coldly, her voice glacial and stern. "I will breach my contract and pull you limb from limb if you even *think* about looking where you are not supposed to. Sébastien cannot do a thing I haven't already lived through."

(Sébastien sleepily grumbled something that might have been an agreement but might have been a protest).

Louis threw up his hands, swallowing thrice to clear the lump in his throat. "I-I didn't see anything. Honest! Just...just some snow and trees and –"

And there was a hand around his throat, its grip far stronger than anything he'd expected from Svetlana.

"I will kill you, Louis Toussaint," she said with a harshness he had never heard from her, "if you do something that stupid again."

He closed his eyes, all of them, and whispered, "Yes, ma'am."

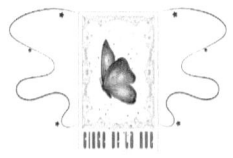

Exhaustion throttled Sébastien, and it wasn't just because he wasn't sleeping. It wasn't because le Cirque de la Rue was stuck in Paris, either, like a fly in a pot of honey.

It was Zarifa.

Zarifa.

She clogged his mind, swallowing his thoughts whole and replacing them with *her.* Her curves, her voice, her touch... *Zarifa, Zarifa, Zarifa.*

She had tried to kill him, but he had already forgiven her for that tiny mistake. He wasn't dead, obviously, so why hold a grudge against her? There were only two people in the world Sébastien held a grudge against, and Zarifa didn't come *close* to that list.

He wondered what she looked like beneath that Venetian mask. He wondered if she liked coffee, or if she liked tea. Or drinking chocolate. Or champagne. He wondered if she had freckles, if she painted her cheeks with rouge, if she kept her stockings up with garters or ribbons.

He also wondered, briefly, what she looked like nude, and that thought nearly destroyed his already fragile mind, so he quickly focused on something else, like how her golden curls would fall over her face and if her brows were just as pale. How she would taste if he kissed her, what sounds would fall from those plump lips if he suckled on her throat –

Enough!

"I'm going out to get some air," he announced as he stood.

"No, you're not," Svetlana said suddenly. "Alone? In Paris?"

Sébastien snapped, "You're not my mother. I can do as I please. And I am going out."

Svetlana flinched, recoiling as though she'd just been struck. *Nothing* made Svetlana flinch. She was far too proud.

Antara put her hand on Svetlana's shoulder. "She's just looking out for you, Séb. She's older than you, and you're not really in your right mind. You're *exhausted.* Go take a nap."

"I can't," Sébastien hissed. "You're *all* older than me. Every single one of you. Every creature within this damn circus is older than me, but don't forget, Antara, who holds your soul. I'm going out."

The words tasted like ash as they left his mouth, settling like a film on his tongue, heavier than lead, but he couldn't take them back. Not that he wanted to. His words were true, every one of them, and even though he was frustrated beyond belief, he'd done nothing but state facts.

Svetlana was not his mother.

Every single creature within the confines of le Cirque de la Rue was older than Sébastien.

Sébastien held their souls.

And he was going out, whether it was a good idea or not, because as much as he loathed Paris, he needed to *breathe,* and he needed to find Zarifa.

He made it just out of the tent, no more than five paces before he was stopped. Aurelio stood in his path, shirtless despite the snow, arms crossed over his bare torso. The gentle, lazy snowfall seemed to sizzle off his exposed flesh like he was made of brimstone and fire instead of blood and bones.

"One day," Aurelio said without preamble, "you are going to explain to us who you are. Never have we *stopped* performing. Why now?"

Yes, hissed a voice that was not Sébastien's in his ear, a cold breath against the back of his neck. *Why stop? Why stop* now *when things are getting dangerous?*

Why stop when you know it will be the undoing of you?

Death will be a mercy, and you do not deserve mercies.

Sébastien's mouth suddenly went dry.

"Do not pretend we are friends, Aurelio," Sébastien said. "You don't deserve anything from me. I am the Maître de la Rue, and this circus performs when *I* want it to, not a moment sooner."

Before Aurelio could protest, Sébastien turned on his heel and walked not back to the Big Top, nor to the Menagerie or the Symphony Hall, but through the cluster of smaller tents to his *own* Tent Noir. His feet, unlike those of everyone else within le Cirque de la Rue, left footprints in the snow.

Alone in the darkness of his tent, Sébastien began to pace and pace and pace. He tore his gloves off, tossing them onto the back of a chaise lounge. One slipped, falling to the ground, but he didn't bother to care, not as he kicked off his shoes and ripped the brooch from his throat. He yanked his ribbon out of his hair and raked his bare fingers over and over his scalp, forcing the long tresses off his forehead and onto his back.

"Newspaper," he demanded the circus like it wasn't mad at him. "And coffee. *Now.* If you want me to keep you running, I need both."

A pot of coffee and a warmed tin mug appeared on the coffee table between the chaise lounge and the hearth that housed nothing but long-cold ashes. Next to it was the folded *La Loi* newspaper dated that morning.

Sébastien climbed over the chaise and sat down, pouring himself a cup of coffee and drinking it all in a few greedy, scalding gulps. He poured another and picked up the *Loi.*

There were three articles within the newspaper that caught Sébastien's unfortunate attention.

THE CARNIVALE OF SAINTS: A STRANGE COMPETITION WITH A WISHFUL PRIZE.

Le Cirque de la Rue in Paris: The Mysterious Circus Hasn't Moved in Days.

Body Found at the Ruins of the Rene Manor.

Sébastien finished reading the third headline when bile rose up his throat, too fast for him to stop, and he vomited all over the wood-plank floor.

He slid off the chaise lounge, coughing out the remnants of coffee-tainted spittle. His stomach cramped, twisting like snakes in a hibernacle.

You're going to die you're going to die you're going to die you're going to die you're –

Rather pathetic, aren't you, Sébastien de la Rue?

"Please let me sleep," Sébastien whispered, his voice hoarse from the bile that he'd just spewed. *"Please."*

You know the deal. You know the consequences.

Sleep, and everyone will die.

"I am *human*," Sébastien breathed. His voice grew softer and softer, drowned out against the *other*.

You lost your humanity the day you –

"STOP!" He clapped his hands over his ears, trying to shut the *other* up. Then, softer, he whispered, "Please stop."

Tears splashed on the floor, one fat drop after another. No amount of coffee would curb the exhaustion and keep the creeping insanity at bay. It didn't matter, not anymore. As tired as he was, the show simply had to go on. His own life was meaningless, but Sébastien couldn't damn the lives of his troupe.

"You win," he croaked. He pushed himself to his knees, then stood as wobbly as a newborn fawn. "I won't let the Carnivale get in my way."

Good good good good good good good.

Sébastien grabbed his ribbon and tied his hair back. He found his gloves – one still on the back of the chaise lounge, one swept partially beneath it – and tugged them on. He affixed his brooch to his throat and grinned to himself in the dark.

"I am Sébastien de la Rue," he said to himself, to the darkness of the tent, to the circus itself. "I am the Maître de la Rue. *I* am the *Dreammonger.* I will not let the Carnivale of Saints keep me from my dreams."

Suddenly, a tiny bit of blue light appeared hovering before him, a will-o-wisp suspended in the air.

Sébastien reached out and plucked the light from its suspension. Opening his mouth, he placed the mote of magic on his tongue and swallowed.

CHAPTER FIFTEEN

LIE STARED AT A stringy pile of dust tucked into a forgotten corner of the Parisian catacombs – an amalgamation of spiderwebs and human hair and bone dust and dirt, no doubt – watching as it tumbled beneath a human maxilla, trying not to flinch as Olivier scolded her.

"Where *were* you?! There was a demon at the ball, Blaise. A *demon. A powerful one,* and you were off...off galivanting somewhere." Olivier raked his lithe fingers through his hair as he paced, but Lie kept her focus on the dust bunny.

She *had* gone off galivanting with Emrys. She'd abandoned Olivier, abandoned her false post as a chasseur to fly in an airship and see the stars and –

A sharp pang of nausea punched her in the gut, sudden and violent as a bullet.

And there had been a dead body. The morning newspaper already got the scoop on the murder, dubbing the nameless woman the *Rene Doe.*

She had been a real person once. She'd had a real name not tied forever to the tragedy of the Rene family. She had a mother and a father, grandparents, people who had been there for her birth but gone for her death. She'd had wants and needs, hopes and dreams, aspirations, things she hated, things she loved. Had she liked sugar or cream in her tea? Did she eat scones with strawberry jam or blueberry? Did she have loved ones waiting for her only to learn she would never be coming home after seeing her mutilated corpse in the grainy photograph on the front page of the *Loi*? Someone *else* had found her because Emrys and Lie had just *left* her there –

"Are you even listening to me?"

Lie looked away from the dust bunny to face Olivier. He had his arms crossed over his chest, tapping his foot impatiently, waiting for her wordless answer.

Deciding being lectured for not listening would be better than being lectured for lying, she shook her head no.

"Of all the people at Paris, they pair me with the least competent one," grumbled Olivier as he scrubbed his hand over his face. Lie flinched. He was right, though. They'd paired *her* because she was quiet. Lie had no real chasseur training. She'd never actually exorcised a demon.

She was just a charlatan playing dress-up, pretending to be someone she wasn't just to avoid being tied down in a marriage with a man she'd never met.

Maybe marriage *would* be better than demons. Maybe marriage would protect her from ending up like the Rene Doe.

Maybe maybe maybe –

"Blaise Beaumont, what are you *thinking about* that is *so much more* important than this?!" Olivier snapped.

Lie blinked, not saying anything. Olivier sighed and reached into his pocket, digging out a notebook and a stub of a pencil. He handed both to Lie, who flipped to a random blank page and scribbled the words:

I accompanied M. Emrys Wilde to the ruins of the Rene manor. I am thinking about the body of the Rene Doe. We saw her.

Lie handed the notebook back. Olivier scanned her smudged handwriting before pinching the bridge of his nose. "If you saw a dead body, Blaise, why didn't you *contact the authorities?*"

She'd wanted to, even though, technically, she *was* an authority figure, but the moment she and Emrys had arrived back at the masquerade, chaos had erupted, and any chance of going to the authorities was quashed. It didn't matter, anyway, since they'd been contacted later that night, and the Rene Doe had been found. An undertaker from England, Lenore Therese, had flown up on an airship to get her hands on the corpse.

Meanwhile, Emrys had stumbled upon a red envelope and, after asking a few other masked guests, learned of the *Carnivale of Saints.* He'd snagged an invitation, something everyone was fighting over, and promised he'd meet Lie again later, only to flee before the invitation could be ripped from his hands.

Leaving Lie to make her way back to Cathedrale Notre-Dame D'Paris before the snow made the trip impossible.

She pointed at the notebook, but before Olivier could hand it over, another chasseur bounded into the section of the catacombs Olivier and Lie were in. Lie didn't know all the Paris chasseurs by name, but she recognized the red hair of this one. Paul? Raoul? She couldn't quite place his name.

"Pardon the intrusion," Paul-Raoul-Whatever said awkwardly. "The Archbishop is looking for you, Monsieur Beaumont. A-ah, Olivier Beaumont, that is."

Olivier sighed heavily through his nose. Tucking the notebook and pencil back in his pocket he said, "I'll be right there." Then, to Lie, he said, "You're coming with me, Blaise. Don't think I've forgiven you for abandoning me to deal with that demon alone."

I think I'd take dealing with a demon over seeing that dead body again, Lie thought as she hurried to follow Olivier.

Emrys's room at L'Hotel resembled a madman's cave. Loose papers with rambling scribbles covered every empty surface like a blanket of snow, and in the center of it all, clutching the strange not-a-Tarot Tarot Card was Emrys himself.

> *Once there was a traitor hidden at the table*
> *Another cursed to sit under a snake in a gable.*
> *A king to return with a coven of knights*
> *A blue moon to bathe the world in its lights.*
> *It is near yet far*
> *Unto all it shall mar.*
> *It is the beginning that gnashes its teeth*

It is the ending, a pale, wicked beast.

He'd deduced quite easily that it was a clue for a sort of treasure hunt, but its meaning eluded him. He grabbed the leaf of paper closest to him and scribbled out a new note, trying to decipher the meaning of each word.

The envelope containing the strange card also had an address. It wasn't an address that made any sense, so half the papers scattered around the hotel room had Emrys's futile attempts to decode it.

Avenue Thierry

25th E div.

37

Stop – This is the Empire of Death

Emrys groaned loudly, tearing his fingers through his hair to force it off his face. He hadn't seen Lie since the masquerade, but he couldn't help wondering if maybe he would be able to help. Frustrated, he lay on his back, staring at the card in his hand.

"Once there was a traitor hidden at the table..." he murmured. Whatever the answer was, he had to figure it out *fast*. If there were forty-nine others competing against him to solve the treasure hunt, Emrys couldn't afford to fall behind.

He debated, if only for a split second, going to the Seer at le Cirque de la Rue to see if *he* could help, but the thought of cheating left a sour taste in the back of Emrys's throat.

There was no way he could solve this blasted riddle alone.

Tucking the card back into its red envelope, Emrys stood. He smoothed out his clothes and tucked the card into his pocket. Throwing on his coat and top hat, goggles hanging around his neck, Emrys left his hotel room for the first time since the masquerade, determined to find Lie and figure out the answer to the riddle before nightfall.

It was strange to see le Cirque empty during the day. No one lined up around it, hoping for a glimpse of the magic that was the Circus of the Street. It looked *abandoned,* forgotten as people shifted their focus to the Carnivale of Saints. Emrys kept his head down, hurrying past the circus to get to Notre-Dame.

When he arrived, the cathedral was strangely empty, devoid of any commoners, with just a few nuns here and there. Emrys, not being Catholic and unsure of how to properly approach them, deciding standing in the middle of the antechamber until one of *them* approached *him* was the best thing to do.

A crucifix stared down at him, painted eyes betraying a sense of agony that sent shivers down his spine.

"The House of God welcomes all, young man. Don't be afraid to come in. You'll catch a draft standing there," a woman's voice said, startling Emrys from his staring contest with the Lord.

He bowed his head to the nun. "I'm not Catholic, Sister, so forgive me for my ignorance."

"As I said, young man, the House of God welcomes all." She was around his mother's age, her brows thin and grey, eyes crinkled with crow's feet.

"I... There is a chasseur I need to speak with."

The nun's expression changed completely. It became...*solemn.* She nodded once and began walking, not towards the nave but to a side door hidden beneath columns and stained glass depicting Madonna and Christ. Their eyes seemed to follow him as he ducked through the door.

"Which chasseur?" the nun asked.

"L—Blaise. Blaise Beaumont. Please." Emrys inwardly cursed himself for nearly giving away Lie's true name, then cursed himself *again* for cursing in a *church.*

"Ah, yes. The quiet one." The nun chuckled to herself. "I believe he is in a meeting with the Archbishop and that D'Amiens fellow. Do you have a demon to exorcise?"

Right. Chasseurs were holy soldiers sent by God to eradicate demons. Because...because demons existed. The thought made his stomach queasy.

"With the Archbishop?" Emrys hesitantly prodded. "Is everything alright?"

"I believe the Archbishop simply wants to check on the D'Amiens fellow and see how he is progressing. He was sent to investigate the demons that make up that sinful circus." She scoffed as though just saying the words was an act of evil. "Wait right here. I'll fetch Monsieur Blaise and be right back."

"Thank you, Sister," said Emrys absently.

The hall she left him in was long and narrow, with only a few gas-powered lamps hanging from the ceiling. The dim orange glow lit up the stone walls and tiled floor. A few woven tapestries hung from the walls. The one closest to Emrys was a stitched copy of the Last Supper. It didn't have the intricate details da Vinci's painting had, but Emrys could still recognize Christ and the twelve apostles.

Wait, hold on –

"Emrys?" came Lie's hushed voice. Emrys nearly leaped out of his skin when he saw Lie sneak up behind him. "What are you doing here?"

Emrys pointed to the tapestry. "Which one is Judas?"

"You came all the way out here and specifically requested to speak with me to ask which one *Judas is?*" he hissed. *Right. He's supposed to be mute.*

"It's important, I swear," Emrys said. "Just...which one?"

Lie looked at the tapestry for a moment before pointing to one of the men on the left. "This one, I think. *Why?*"

"I need you to come back to my hotel room with me. I need your help."

Lie scrunched his face up but sighed. "Fine. But only because I don't want Olivier to scold me again."

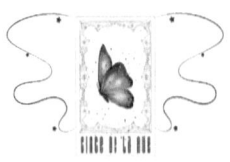

Lie frowned at the mess that was Emrys's hotel room. She carefully stepped over a few loose sheets of paper, unsure of where to even stand. Finding a single patch of carpet unobstructed by papers, she stood there, stiff and still as a statue.

Emrys reached into his pocket and pulled out the same red envelope he'd found at the masquerade. He took out a card and read from it. *"Once there was a traitor hidden at the table. Another cursed to sit under a snake in a gable. A king to return with a coven of knights. A blue moon to bathe the world in its lights. It is near yet far. Unto all it shall mar. It is the beginning that gnashes its teeth. It is the ending, a pale, wicked beast."*

Lie frowned. "What does that mean? And what does that have to do with Judas at the Last Supper?"

Emrys jabbed his finger against the card. *"Once there was a traitor hidden at the table.* Isn't that Judas? He betrayed Christ, and he was there at the Last Supper. So, how does that tie in with the rest of the clue? *What does it mean?"*

Lie had no idea what any of it meant. Frankly, she was struggling to catch up and figure out what, exactly, Emrys kept going on about.

"Slow down," she said. "Start over. What are you *talking about?"*

Emrys explained quickly. He'd found the card at the masquerade and figured out it was the clue for some sort of treasure hunt. He just had to figure out what the riddle meant and where the address was.

Lie sighed heavily, her whole body slumping with the motion. "Unfortunately, I think I know someone who can help," she said reluctantly. "But it would be better if *you* went to fetch him. He's not happy with me right now."

Emrys tucked the card back into the envelope. "I'll fetch him. Who is he?"

Lie, with a tight jaw, said, "Olivier Beaumont."

Loath as she was to admit it, Olivier was agonizingly brilliant. *And* he'd been at the masquerade the entire night, so if anyone knew any details that could solve Emrys's riddle, it would be him. Unfortunately.

Because involving him in the scheme would mean Lie's mute gig would be up. And then it would only be a matter of time before her true identity came out.

And then a matter of time until she was dragged back home to be stuffed in a wedding dress and married off like she was cattle.

She groaned inwardly. Well, all things considered, maybe Olivier would be so shocked that he'd forget to be mad at her for abandoning her post to sail the skies with Emrys.

"I'll try to figure it out in the meantime." She crouched down and picked up one of Emrys's rambling notes. She stared at the illegible handwriting and sighed softly. "Just...hurry. And don't tell him I'm here." *I don't need him ruining things for Emrys because he's upset with me.*

Emrys gave a lazy mock salute before hurrying out the door, leaving Lie alone with his dozens of notes.

She crouched down and got to work organizing his chaos.

Half an hour later, all the papers were organized into three neat piles. She set the last leaf of paper down just as the door swung open. Instantly, she reached for her pistol, only relaxing when Emrys and Olivier walked in.

The irritation on Olivier's face when he saw Lie aged him by a decade, if not more, and Lie, with a gut-sinking dawning, realized this probably wasn't the best idea. Neither was what she was about to do, but then again, Lie *had* run away to France, clear across the ocean, pretended to be a man, and joined the chasseurs d'Paris just to avoid marriage. Her track record for *best ideas* had to be the worst in the world.

She took a deep breath, and when she exhaled, she spoke. "My name is Lie. I *can* talk. I'm sorry for abandoning you at the masquerade, I'm sorry for not contacting the authorities about the body, and I'm sorry for being a liar. But all of that aside, we need your help."

Olivier stared at her, completely still, like Michelangelo descended from the heavens to carve Olivier Beaumont's likeness out of marble. For a split second that lasted between a heartbeat and an eternity, Lie panicked that she had somehow shocked Olivier to death.

Emrys took the envelope out of his pocket and spoke quickly, shattering the uncomfortable silence but only scraping away the topmost layer of mud-thick tension that stretched taut through the hotel room. "Lie says you're clever. I got an invitation to the Carnivale of Saints, but neither of us can figure it out. I think one of the lines is in reference to Judas at the Last Supper."

He awkwardly handed the envelope to Olivier, who hadn't blinked once. Lie wasn't sure he'd even taken a *breath*.

To her surprise, though, he stiffly took the envelope and pulled out the card. His gaze lingered on the address printed inside.

"'Stop – This is the Empire of Death,'" he read. "This is on the plaque at the public entrance to the catacombs. Avenue Thierry is one of the lanes in Cimetière du Montparnasse. The plot must be some sort of entrance to the catacombs."

Lie and Emrys exchanged a silent glance. Awkwardly tense as it was, having Olivier come clearly was a good idea.

Olivier looked at the card next. He silently read the riddle, his brow creasing as he concentrated. "A king to return with a coven of knights... That's referencing King Arthur, isn't it? In some stories, he has a hundred knights. In others, he has twenty or so, or even twelve..." he gnawed on his bottom lip, ignoring the lock of dark hair that fell over his face.

He began pacing, eyes glued to the card like Lie's lies and sudden, shocking truths hadn't just frozen him in shock moments before.

"There were thirteen at the Last Supper... It's part of why people consider the number thirteen to be unlucky..." he murmured as he paced, treading a path into the rug with enough vigor Lie worried it might get a hole. "And the blue moon... There're twelve full moons a year unless there's a blue moon..."

Lie inched closer to Emrys, both of them watching Olivier with rapt fascination.

"A pale, wicked beast..." he muttered something in hurried French, too fast for Lie to translate back into English, as she had been doing this whole time. *At least one good thing came from all those French lessons as a child...*

Olivier smacked the card with the back of his hand. "The answer to the first part is thirteen. The second part is death."

His gaze slid to Lie. "Now that I figured that out for you," he said. "I want an explanation. Blaise – Lie, whatever – when were you going to admit to the duke here that you're a *woman?*"

Chapter Sixteen

Armed with only a pistol and the bullets it contained, his coat over Enoch's shoulders, and his heart in his throat, Nicholas stepped out of the abandoned house and onto the abandoned street. A layer of snow coated the ground, but atop *that* was a blanket of ash, more of it floating from the dark sky to settle on his nose and hair.

"Clear," he said once he was certain they were alone.

Trembling like a newborn fawn, Enoch slowly crept out of the house. Nick flexed his artificial hand before shoving it into his pocket. The dull glow from the astrium tubes inside would give them away in a heartbeat if they had to hide.

"Stay close to me," Nick hissed. Snow crunched beneath his feet, the sound too similar to the snapping the bodies of his comrades made when the demonic beasts trampled them. He swallowed a bout of bile.

"Don't need to tell me twice," Enoch whispered. Still, he stepped closer to Nicholas until, if he stepped any closer, they would resemble a set of conjoined twins.

Pistol drawn, Nicholas led Enoch down the liminal street. He hadn't fought here, but he knew the place was ravaged and abandoned because someone *else* had. A different squad, maybe, a different platoon led by some other lieutenant colonel. Had they walked from the battle victorious? Or had they perished in a painful blaze, a slow death no man should ever have to endure, just like Nick's platoon had? He could see obvious signs of a fight – holes blown into buildings, dried blood crusted on doorframes, the heavy scent of gunpowder still lingering thickly in the air – but...where had they gone? The humans, the demons, either of them.

If the human army walked away with victory, there should at least be demonic bodies scattered about. And if the demons had won, why hadn't they stayed to occupy the space they so vigilantly defended?

There was something...off...about the whole situation, something that raised the hairs on the back of Nick's neck and kept his stomach in a hibernacle knot. Something acrid on his tongue but something he couldn't quite place.

"How will we prove to the soldiers that we're human?" Enoch whispered. "What if they think we're demons? *I* thought the cast at the circus were all human..."

Nick glanced down at him. He was rather short, the perfect height for Nick to rest his arm atop his wild curls. His fingers itched to touch those curls...

"If you're in the army, you've been trained to identify demons quickly," he said, gripping his pistol tighter to resist the urge to rake his fingers through Enoch's hair. "It's easiest to identify them in photographs since they...blur. But in real life, their eyes are usually wrong. And they have features no humans have. Like the acrobats at your circus – if you look closely, they both have silvery wings."

Enoch blinked. Clearly, *he'd* never looked closely. Nick suddenly felt weird for having done so.

"And I can vouch for us. I did serve for many years," he added.

Even though he had been (honorably) discharged and was no longer a soldier.

He didn't deserve that honor. He'd gotten his entire platoon killed with his poor decisions. And now here he was, back in this other not-here, not-there place, Enoch's life balanced in the mismatched palms of his flesh and metal hands.

Nick was a fool.

"Would it be in poor taste to write an article about all...this?" Enoch asked softly, providing Nick with the false guise of a distraction.

"This?" Nick arched a brow.

Enoch gestured vaguely, unhelpfully. *"This.* This *Otherland."*

Journalists had a reputation for devouring wartime stories. Stories of tragedy, of far-off bravery sold. A story about a war against demons in a realm that shouldn't exist would make the front page of every newspaper across Europe – across the *world*.

Maybe it would help raise support – funds and soldiers, better hospitals, better weapons – if more people knew. Maybe it would send the world into a mass hysteria.

Well, it wasn't like Nicholas was fighting in the army anymore, so what did it matter?

He lifted his shoulders in a lazy shrug. "I'm not a journalist," he said plainly. "I don't know what is considered *in poor taste*. I just don't want to be in any interviews."

"You're just like Lenore," Enoch grumbled.

"Who?"

"Lenore – Doctor Therese. She's an undertaker. She helped me with this article on a body that turned up. She wrote it off as *organ failure* because she didn't want to incite panic because it was clearly a murder. She always asks that I don't mention her name."

Well, at least that hadn't changed while Nick was away. Murders happened all the time.

Crunch.

Nick threw his arm out, halting Enoch before he could take another step. Pistol drawn, Nick listened for another crunch in the snow, another sign that they weren't alone.

Wait...

The air before him...shimmered.

Nick touched the barrel of his pistol to the shimmery veil. It went through, vanishing from sight.

Crunch crunch crunch –

He turned to see the outline of a not-human shadow dip behind a building. They were being followed, and Nick didn't have enough bullets to save them both.

For the second time, he grabbed Enoch's wrist and dragged him into the unknown, slipping through the veil and deeper into the Otherland.

Emrys stared at Lie blankly, unable to conjure up the will to even blink. A girl? No. There was no way. What respectable lady would not only dress as a man but *infiltrate the Church* to fight demons? Sure, Lie didn't have the deepest voice, but he – she? – was still young. He glanced, ashamedly, at Lie's chest. Flat. No corset lines peeking out beneath Lie's shirt.

"I –" Lie started, glancing between Emrys and Olivier nervously.

Then, without offering to explain, Lie bolted from the hotel room.

Olivier, despite being a God-fearing holy soldier, cursed. Loudly. Abashedly. To Emrys, he said, "Her voice. It's feminine."

Then, he, too, ran out, leaving Emrys standing there, unable to process what had just happened.

Well, he thought since he couldn't fathom doing anything else. *I know of one person who knows about tarot cards. I suppose I should ask them for help.*

It's not cheating, he reasoned as he grabbed his jacket and hat. *It's just...using my resources.*

As if le Cirque de la Rue's Seer counted as a resource.

Fifteen minutes later, Emrys stood outside the gates of le Cirque de la Rue. He knew he couldn't get in, but he wasn't sure how to politely call for the Seer.

"Ah..." he started. "M. Seer? I... I would like to ask you a question! It's about Tarot cards, not about the past or future or any of that."

Maybe the Seer wasn't even awake. Maybe this was a terrible idea, and he should have gone after Olivier and Lie – *damnit*, why hadn't he gone after Olivier and Lie?!

"Louis Toussaint," a voice said, startling Emrys.

He turned to see a woman in a red dress, golden curls clouding around her, her face shielded by a porcelain mask.

"The Seer," she said. "His name is Louis Toussaint. You could try calling that."

Emrys stared. She was a beautiful woman, from what he could tell without actually seeing her face. But there was a sinister aura to her, one that instantly triggered the adrenaline-fueled fight-or-flight (or freeze, in Emrys's unfortunate case) response engrained deep in his primitive psyche. There were three things instinctively wrong about the woman: she was alone without a chaperone of some sort, she had her face completely covered, and her eyes...

They were greener than absinthe. The same abnormal, toxic brightness that the Dreammonger's eyes were, green to his blue. Poison to his astrium.

Frozen in place, his heart galloped against his ribs, painful and numbing.

"Zarifa!" a singsong voice chirped.

There he stood, the Dreammonger himself.

Under the astrium lights and guise of magic and miracles le Cirque de la Rue offered, the Dreammonger was an extraordinary man – a man who transcended every meaning of the word, teetering on the edge of *god*.

In the daylight, though, cheeks flushed and rosy from the cold and snow landing around his slim figure, he was a simpering fool. A *child*.

"Oh, there he is," said the woman – Zarifa (oh, *why* was that name so achingly familiar?) – in a tone so flat Emrys could land an airship on it.

Before the Dreammonger could turn into a gushy puddle of one-sided affection and exclusive pining, Emrys said, "I need to speak with Monsieur Seer. Please. It's...it's important."

He reached for his card.

The Dreammonger's face became a cold mask, not unlike the one Zarifa wore.

"The Seer has not figured out the clue," said Zarifa. She brushed a snowflake off her shoulder. "He will not offer the help you seek."

Perhaps, Emrys thought, *Lie truly is a woman because if* this *woman can be as brazen as a man, surely Lie can be, too.*

He cursed inwardly, scolding himself for thinking of him – *her* – then.

Emrys knew what Lie was – a *distraction*. One that had wormed its way into his brain, his heart, the lowest pit of his belly, coiling around his stomach in an infestation of bloodthirsty papillon that clogged his arteries and nested in his throat.

"I know you," the Dreammonger said, scattering a few of those invasive butterflies. "You have come to more than a dozen of my shows. *How?* How do you know?"

Emrys's mouth went dry.

(Papillons sucked the moisture from his tongue with their needle-thin proboscises).

"I... I fly," he stammered. "My airship. I have someone tell me where it appeared, and I fly."

The Dreammonger stepped closer, the tip of his pointed nose nearly meeting Emrys's. He could see the astrium-blue veins through his irises, his pinprick pupils, each individual black lash.

The makeup he wore – the black slash through his eye – looked more like a scar.

"Do you know someone named J–" the Dreammonger started, but a ball of snow hit him on the side of the head and he stumbled, caught off guard.

"Come along," said Zarifa. She packed another snowball between her gloved hands and reeled back to throw it. "There's something I wanted to discuss with you. Alone."

She angled her porcelain mask toward Emrys. A chill rushed down his spine, a vicious ice-spider that devoured the papillons. He stood there, ice-spider frozen, as Zarifa, with her absinthe eyes, led the Dreammonger with his astrium ones into the snow.

"Death," said Svetlana, a woman well-versed in the topic. She picked at her claws as nonchalantly as someone burdened with the realization of Hell could.

Louis might have met her gaze, but with his eyes hidden by the aviator goggles he always wore, Svetlana couldn't tell. If he was going to try to pry into her past, she would pry those goggles off his face and see what delectable things they hid.

Unfortunately, one of the rules Séb had given her was *do not eat any parts of any humans, no matter how delicious they may seem.*

Her stomach grumbled at the thought, a mournful whale song desperate for the salty crunch of cartilage between too-sharp teeth.

Men once feared you, the voice she'd learned was her subconscious chided. *Now, you can't even have a taste. A little nibble. Do men fear you? Or do you fear them?*

Preposterous. The only thing Svetlana feared was one day stepping into her box, her bucket, her cup, her thimble, and having a lid shut tight overtop. She feared her taste of freedom was just that – a *taste.*

"What?" he asked, lowering the card he'd been staring at.

"The answer," she said smoothly. "It's death. *It is near yet far. Unto all it shall mar. It is the beginning that gnashes its teeth. It is the ending, a pale, wicked beast.*"

When she grinned at Louis, it was all teeth – too sharp, too many, too inhuman for the red slash of her human mouth.

"It is me," she said.

Louis gripped the card tightly, his gloves creasing around the knuckles. The lump in his throat bobbed as he swallowed hard, and *there* was that delicious fear everyone ought to have toward Svetlana.

"Death thirteen," he whispered. "Death is the thirteenth major arcana card in the tarot deck... But... What about the address?"

Svetlana smiled coyly. She was quite clever. She had to be, after all, because what made a predator all the more terrifying than if it was *intelligent?*

"Where do the people of Paris go to die, Louis darling?"

She knew he thought about the body in London, the woman's corpse devoid of vital organs, frostbitten and trapped in an abandoned state of rigor mortis.

"The catacombs," he whispered.

She grinned wider, teeth just right. "The catacombs, Louis darling. The catacombs."

He stared at her behind those goggles of his. She could see her reflection in the opaque glass. Human.

Around them, the circus groaned, shuddering like it was feverish, sick, ill with a plague that rotted its bones and slurped out its core like cooked marrow.

Oh, Sébastien, that *fool.*

The things Svetlana knew about his past and the circus were few and far between, yet she knew more about it than anyone else, save for the *Dreammonger* himself.

Yet it did not take her knowledge of the five years in the forest to understand that something ostensibly was wrong.

"Death, Louis darling," she said with a forced calm. "Do not forget it."

She turned to leave, to run, to dart through the air in a shape she had not taken in lifetimes, but Louis stopped her, calling out, "Where are you going?"

She smoothed out the front of her gown, the emerald green catching in the astrium light. "To save our circus. To keep our ringmaster from damning us all."

And, in a blink, she was gone.

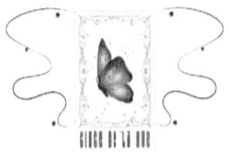

The plan had been to tell Zarifa to leave him and his circus alone, to find a different stomping ground untouched by the miracles of le Cirque de la Rue, but that plan had crumbled to hourglass sand the moment Sébastien saw her, in her red dress and Venetian mask and gilded crown of curls.

"I'm surprised," said Zarifa, "that your circus doesn't have a sideshow. Isn't that all the rage over in America?"

Séb flinched. Those words bore the weight of a broadsword swinging toward his exposed neck.

(Or a particularly slim and sharp knife).

Do not let her distract you. You cannot let the circus fall apart. Remember the contract. The bargain.

The deal.

The deal.

The deal.

The –

"No sideshows," said Sébastien. The twins flitted across his mind then, brief flashes of moonlight flesh and crimson hair and tears that burned like acid against red-painted cheeks.

A cage meant for animals but became the home for two non-animals. A hellhole for hellspawn not originating from Hell.

Nobody in the le Troupe de la Rue condoned sideshows, especially Noa and Sasha.

Especially Sébastien, who stole them away from one the way their kind would steal human babes and leave changelings behind.

Zarifa tutted. "Why a circus?"

Remember your place. Remember why you are here. Remember remember remember remember remember –

He did not wish to remember. He wished, not for the first time in his miserable existence, to forget.

"Why do you wear a mask?" he asked. Zarifa stopped walking. Snow did not fall on her the way it fell on Sébastien, clinging to his hair, to his shoulders, to his gloves.

"Why do *you* wear one?" she nodded to his gloves, masks for his hands. "My...*heritage* is not typically welcome here."

"That's not the full answer."

"No, it is not. But it is an answer. I come from Kenya. I know you're curious."

He was.

He said, "Can I see you?"

She stepped into an alley, and for a moment, Sébastien worried she would become the next desecrated corpse, but he followed her in, the reprieve from the snow not welcome.

"If I remove my mask," she said, "I require something from you. A secret of equal weight."

Were his soul his to give, he would have borne it to her then and there.

"I *can't* tell you how the circus works," he pleaded.

You fool!

"Tell me," she said, tapping one gloved finger against the side of her porcelain mask, "what exactly you are."

There were a number of loopholes Sébastien had memorized to get out of truthfully answering that question because he was bound *not* to truthfully answer it.

"*I* am human," he said. And he grinned a wide Dreammonger grin.

He had flat teeth and round pupils, curved ears, a human body through and through. It wasn't exactly a *secret* that he was human (rather, it was a secret that he was the *only* human in le Troupe de la Rue), but Sébastien had plenty of other things *he* kept secret.

His age.

What he hid under those gloves.

What he kept in his Tent Noir.

Zarifa reached up, taking her mask carefully. Séb's heart thudded against his ribs hard enough to bruise. When she delicately removed the straps and clasps, pulling it off her face, Sébastien forgot completely why he had followed her into the alley. He forgot the taste of magic on his tongue, vomit against his teeth, the weight of his soul, and how his body had been that much lighter for so long.

You fool!

You incompetent fool!

Do you know what this means?!

Séb ignored that voice, instead focusing on Zarifa's face. Her *face*. He had never seen such beauty before, and he lived with Svetlana, with Antara, with Odette and Alice.

Her eyes were almonds, slanted and catlike, with absinthe irises and thick lashes so long they resembled golden spider legs. Her full lips had a smear of red paint on them, not unlike that on her mask, and painted dots as white as snow lined her cheekbones.

Beneath her right eye, curving like a sickle just above those painted marks, was a scar, puckered and thick.

You are breaking the terms of the deal! He stepped closer. She did not shy away, not even as he took her chin between his thumb and forefinger, angling it up just enough that her lips met his when he leaned down.

She tasted of honey, of rouge and sugar and that undeniable tang of magic.

Fine, then, you simpering fool.

I will take things

Into my own hands

A shock jolted through Sébastien, hot and violent like he'd grabbed a live wire with his bare hands. His eyes flew open, and he stumbled back, body stiff as though he'd gone into rigor mortis.

Rigor vita. His knees hit the ground hard, the blanket of snow doing very little to cushion his fall.

Someone called his name, or perhaps they didn't, because everything sounded distorted and watery. His vision blurred, and his eyes rolled back into his skull.

As Sébastien lay there, supine in the alley with Zarifa standing over him, shaking his shoulders and trying to wake him up, le Cirque de la Rue shuddered.

For the first time in its two years of existence, the chokehold grip the contracts held over its troupe waned ever so slightly, and all nine un-humans within its confines felt it.

CHAPTER SEVENTEEN

OLIVIER DASHED DOWN THE stairs, his heart racing faster than an airship. Jumping down the last few steps, he ran into the foyer of L'Hotel. Glittering lights shone from the high ceiling, and people lounged in the lobby, sipping from flutes of champagne and dainty cups of tea.

Not among them was Blaise – *Lie*.

His shoulder collided with something solid – metal. Cursing, he stumbled back.

"No running," chided the automaton – a humanoid creation dressed in a copper suit.

He ignored it and continued running, squeezing through a throng of people to get outside. Standing on the snow-covered walkway, he scanned the streets, looking for the familiar Chasseur uniform Lie had been wearing.

"Lie!" he shouted. "Lie, where are you?!"

No answer. Only a few odd stares. *Great.* He'd been reduced to a noisy madman all because of Lie – if that was even her real name.

Her.

How had Emrys not realized it? She kept her hair tucked up, even though it wasn't unusual for men to have long hair – his own hair reached far past his shoulders. And her voice...

If that wasn't a giveaway, Olivier wasn't sure what *was.*

"Excuse me, monsieur," a man said suddenly. His French was so thickly accented it hardly even sounded like the language, but Olivier turned nonetheless and faced a tall blond man. He continued, "Are you looking for someone?"

Olivier narrowed his eyes. The man was...well, he seemed human enough, but there was a strange aura to him that simply was *not.* He tucked a hand behind his back, fingers poised to draw a sigil at a moment's notice.

"E nomine Patri et Fili et Spiritus Sancti," he whispered under his breath. *God, help me.*

In the legal hierarchy of France, chasseurs didn't make the list. Not because they didn't have power – they were, after all, God's holy soldiers, blessed by Him to eradicate evil and sin – but because they were a secret kept from the public by the Church. If someone had a demon they needed exorcised, they would ask the Archbishop, who would send one of the chasseurs to do the dirty work.

Because the public was not supposed to know about the existence of demons.

And unless Olivier planned on exorcising the strange man in the middle of the street outside one of the busiest hotels in all of Paris, he couldn't do a thing about the blood splattered on the man's otherwise pristine, starched collar, mostly hidden by his coat but *just* visible enough to raise alarm bells.

There could be a mundane reason for it. Maybe the man had just visited the butcher or the doctor, or perhaps he'd gone to the dentist and had his gums poked and prodded at until they bled. Maybe he *was* a butcher or a doctor or a dentist. Perhaps a woman had spontaneously gone into labor, and he delivered her babe.

But a nagging voice in the back of his head – one that tugged the hairs on his neck erect, one that spawned adrenaline in his veins, one that sounded a lot like how he imagined God would sound – said that was not the case.

That nagging voice said to run.

That nagging voice screamed *Lie!*

Olivier took a step back, putting a breath of distance between himself and the man.

He had his rosary and his Bible, and he had his sigils, but he did not have a syringe of holy serum to give him the ability to grab a demon once exorcised. And he was alone.

(Once again abandoned by Lie in his time of need).

He narrowed his eyes.

"Do I know you?" he asked the man, who...almost looked...familiar.

The man chuckled. "I imagine not. My name is Herr Johann Engelstein. But you may call me *Jack.*"

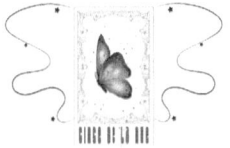

The day Enoch received the key to his flat, Mrs. Taffy took his hand in hers and said, "One day, you'll go to Hell, and you'll find me there, sitting on the throne with the Devil at my beck and call." She firmly believed, for whatever reason, that Enoch would end up among the fire and brimstone himself one day.

He didn't quite understand why.

And he didn't quite expect Hell to look like... *This.*

Gone was the snowy town, liminal in its abandonment. In its place was grandeur. A souk straight out of *Arabian Nights,* with tents and awnings in every shade of red lining a cobblestone street. String lights stretched overhead, illuminating the street in a bath of warm light. Gas light, not astrium, casting a soft orange-yellow over everything. Hiding the sky was a swath of fabric so dark it might have actually been the outside world, but amidst the twinkling stars and swirling constellations was the gentle ripple of satin or silk or some other luxurious fabric.

And at the stalls...

If Enoch hadn't believed in demons before, he did after seeing the people at each of the stalls. The diversity amongst humans was *nothing* compared to the diversity of the Otherland beings.

There was a woman with a hibernacle of writhing snakes atop her head selling little carved statues. Next to her was a tall creature with a single eye on their face trying to talk a couple with goat legs into buying a shimmering amulet. There were small beings with wings and talons, massive ones with serpent tails for their lower halves, and even one with six arms and eight eyes and fangs that gleamed in the warm light when they grinned at Enoch.

"*These* are what you fought?" hissed Enoch as he took a step closer to Nicholas. "These are what took your hand?"

"Technically, an explosion took my hand," murmured Nick. A man – Enoch *assumed* it was a man – with twisting ram horns eyed them as they passed. Nick continued, "But, yes. These...are the demons we are at war with."

The demons that made up le Cirque de la Rue's cast. Unease twisted his belly like a towel being wrung.

"You boys," came a voice suddenly. Enoch turned to see an old woman beckoning them with a knobby, too-long finger. Her silver hair hung down her back in a tight braid, and while her nose was hooked and her skin marred with wrinkles, she wasn't ugly. If anything, there was an otherworldly aura to her, a beauty not up to par with human standards, but she was not human.

Her tent, like the others, was made of dark red canvas. Outside it, framing either side of the parted entrance, were two sticks with glowing skulls atop them.

Enoch shot Nick a glance.

"Let me do the talking," he said through clenched teeth, then led Enoch to the strange tent.

The woman sat behind a table, grinding something in a mortar. A rag doll sat propped against a basket of glowing flowers.

"Did Alucard send for you?" She looked up from her grinding. When she grinned, her teeth were sharp, bearlike.

"Whom?" asked Nick. Enoch stared at the doll. He wondered if watching it would make its button eyes blink.

"Severin Alucard," said the woman. "No? Eh? Then why are you here?"

"Someone named Benedict sent us instead," blurted Enoch, who never really knew how to keep his mouth shut.

The woman's silver eyes widened a fraction. "Ah," she sighed. "What is that name he goes by instead? Saint... Bah, I don't care for Catholic saints. There was a time when *I* was considered a god." She resumed her grinding.

Inside the mortar, coated in white dust, were teeth.

Enoch took a step back, quickly swallowing his nausea. This was a mistake. Coming here was a mistake, talking to the woman was a mistake, everything was a blasted mistake. He should be at home, nestled up in his flat with a cup of tea and his notebook. He should be thinking about what to write at work; he should be figuring out how to get his assistant, Miss Gertrude, to hate him slightly less.

"I won't ask for your names, because I know you humans are attached to them," continued the woman as she grinded the teeth. "But I will offer you mine, free of charge. I am Baba Yaga. Welcome to the Crimson Market."

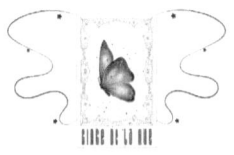

Cold seeped through Louis's body, his blood turning to ice for a momentary heartbeat. Without thinking, he ran for his tent. Once he was alone, he tore off his gloves, then his goggles, sight desperately searching for an answer to the shudder of *wrongness* that had gripped him like a vise.

A kiss, a smear of red paint, a body collapsing in the snow.

Blue – astrium blue – gleaming through the dark, like the eye and grin of his Devil tarot card.

Sweat beaded on his forehead. He pressed the back of his hand against the wall to keep from collapsing.

He looked harder, searching through the future to find more answers, to figure out when his inevitable death would catch up to him and if it was *now*, but... Nothing. Nothing, nothing, *nothing*.

God damnit!

He balled his hand into a fist and slammed it against the wall, feeling the reverberating shock all the way in his toes.

The world fishbowled around him, distorted and muddled and so wrong. His head swam, his eyes searched, tension built behind his sinuses and in his temples.

He unclenched his hand, alleviating some of the headache-inducing pressure. He dug out his deck of cards and, with shaky hands, shuffled them until three fell out, landing on the floor in a perfect fortune.

The Tower, crumbling against a lightning-stricken sky, the decrepit building looking eerily similar to the Big Top of le Cirque de la Rue.

Death, with his shining scythe and dark cloak and face hidden by a mask of shadow.

And the Devil. The *Devil*, of course, the single sliver of an eye and a grin glowing blue.

He closed his eyes and opened his other eyes, and delved into the future.

Fire. Flames licking an overcast night sky, singeing snowflakes as they threatened to fall on the smoldering remains of the black-and-white tent.

Blood on the snow, hot and coagulated.

A body nearby, dark hair strewn about, lips reddened with blood, and cheeks flushed from the cold.

A man in a top hat and an overcoat standing over the body, a grin on his face as he watched the life fade from spoonsful of honey eyes.

Louis gasped, yanking himself back to the present with a closing of his eyes and an opening of his other eyes. His heart stuttered against his ribs, his insides telling him to run, to flee, to break the contract because the contract had no control over him anymore, but logic... Logic told him to stay, to not move, to huddle in the darkness that soothed his headache and kept his eyes from seeing too much.

He took the invitation out of his pocket, smoothing out the red envelope. Death, Svetlana had said. It had to be another card that he was looking for – Death Thirteen. And somehow, it was hidden in the catacombs, the maze of bones tucked beneath the Parisian streets, a crypt of ancient death and –

"M. Louis Toussaint!" A rather familiar voice called, shattering his thoughts like a thin sheet of ice.

Quickly, he pulled on his gloves and his goggles, ignoring the dull throb accosting his head, and hurried outside to see what the commotion was.

Even without his sight, he recognized the man standing on the other side of the fence surrounding le Cirque de la Rue – though the top hat adorned with a pair of aviator goggles was a giveaway.

Duke Emrys Wilde stood there, holding a familiar red envelope. That same envelope was tucked in Louis's pocket, right next to his cards.

Competition, the street urchin in him screamed.

Help, the slightly wiser part of him rationed.

"You have one, too," he said, nodding at the envelope.

Duke Wilde frowned. "Too?" he repeated. "Never mind. I need your assistance. Nobody knows Tarot like you do, and that's the last part I can't seem to figure out."

Help, that wise part said smugly, quashing the street urchin's competitive antics.

He stepped closer to the fence. "If you tell me what the address means," he said, "I'll answer your Tarot questions?"

"You can't just peer into the future?" the duke joked.

Louis just sighed. Everything would be much easier if he *could.*

The duke shook his head. "Never mind. The address leads to one of the plots in the Cimetière du Montparnasse. We think it's an entrance to the catacombs."

So, Svetlana had been right about that. A chill ran down his spine at the thought of being surrounded by millions of bones. He had no real reason to be afraid of skeletons. After all, the dead couldn't harm the living the way the living could.

Well, that wasn't necessarily true. Louis knew that better than most.

"We came to the conclusion that the first part of the riddle is *thirteen,*" Duke Wilde continued. "And the second part is *death.* But...how do those tie together? How are we supposed to find another Tarot clue?"

"Death is the thirteenth card," Louis murmured around the sinking feeling of necrosis nestled in his core. "Do you know how to get to the Cimetière du Montparnasse from here?" He didn't, but he wanted – *needed* – to get there now, to find the Death Thirteen card, to win the Carnivale of Saints game to get his wish.

Since the day he was born, Louis had carried death with him, and that death would become his if he didn't rid himself of it soon. His cards turned leaden in his pocket, grim reminders of the fate he kept drawing for himself.

"I..." the duke faltered. Then, slowly, he nodded. "There are people I would like to pick up before we go. They will know how to get there. If you come with me to find them..."

If Louis had to kill the duke to ensure the wish was his, so be it. For now, he needed the assistance. "Deal," he said. Then, he climbed over the fence, ignoring the shuddering sense of dread he got from leaving the circus.

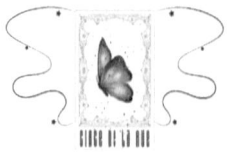

Svetlana tore through the air, darting through the streets and around automatons and carriages, tracking the scent she knew as *Sébastien.*

The moment she spotted him in the alley, she changed, becoming bestial, and stalked in. A woman crouched next to him, shaking his shoulder desperately as she begged him to wake up. A discarded porcelain mask sat in the snow.

Svetlana towered over them, her dark hair loose around her face, tumbling to her mid back and billowing in the winter wind. Where she once had soft curves, bones protruded, ribs and limbs sticking out in a malnourished, feral way – like a rabid wolf who hadn't eaten in a *very* long time. Her eyes, forest green, pierced into the absinthe green of the woman's. She took a jagged step closer.

"What have you done," she hissed, not in Russian, but in the language of the trees. The Circus struggled to translate, especially with Sébastien unconscious, chopping her words into a harsh tritone.

"I didn't do anything!" the woman pleaded. "He... He kissed me, and then –"

And then the woman was against the brick wall, gasping for air as Svetlana held her by her throat. Her nails had lengthened to talons – bear claws – and from the very tips of those claws to just shy of her elbows, her vanilla skin was black like she'd dipped her forearms into a vat of logwood dye.

The woman choked, writhing like a worm under Svetlana's grasp.

"Do you *know* who that is?" hissed Svetlana. The flesh around her mouth tore like parchment, revealing a set of razor-sharp teeth. "Sébastien de la Rue. The Dreammonger. Do you understand how *unstable he is?*"

The woman couldn't answer, not with Svetlana's iron grip around her windpipe.

She continued, not bothering to wait for an answer. It was not Svetlana's place to expose Sébastien's secrets, but the contract that kept her from talking was loosened, and with it loosened her tongue enough to explain the situation to the asphyxiating woman. "He is human, but atop his shoulders is a *very powerful* demon who feeds off attention. If he doesn't meet the *quota* of entertainment, it will take his soul. Do you *understand now?* Do you *know what you have done?*"

She let go of the woman, letting her fall to the ground. Before she could hit the snow, Svetlana swooped in, grabbing Sébastien and cradling him against her chest.

"I will kill you," Svetlana promised.

Then, clutching the Dreammonger, she darted out of the alley and back to le Cirque de la Rue.

Even with the contract loosened Svetlana had enough respect to avoid the Tent Noir. Instead, she took Sébastien into her own black-and-white-and-green tent, settling him down on her bed atop the pile of furs and blankets. She brushed his hair off his face with her vanilla finger, her nails back to their usual almond shape. She sat on the edge of the bed, watching with hawk eyes the steady rise and fall of her master's chest.

The contract couldn't stop Svetlana from eating him right now, but she knew that if she gave into that urge and tasted his sweet flesh, she would end up right back where she'd been two years ago.

In a box on a shelf in a caravan in Moscow, forgotten, abandoned, weak.

She curled her nails into her palm. Thinking about her past was...well, she'd spent too long – four hundred fifty-two years – with nothing but her thoughts.

In a certain tsardom, in a certain country – though it wasn't yet a tsardom and not quite recognized as a country – there was a forest. Northeast Rus' had plenty of forest, but this one...oh, this one was special. In the dense stretch of Siberian pines and spruces, larch trees and aspen, birch, and beech barren as they prepared for winter amidst the thick snow and glistening ice, there lived Svetlana.

(She was not called Svetlana then because *Svetlana* was a human name, and she had not yet forged a human tongue to shape the harsh consonants and sharp vowels. But she is called Svetlana now, so Svetlana she shall be).

She came into existence before mankind touched her forest, and she was appointed its guardian. She learned every tree, every root, every creature that made a home out of her wood – from the tiniest of mice to the lumbering bears she liked to mimic.

Time was a fickle concept to an ageless being immune to it. Instead of counting the passing years, Svetlana counted the seasons. In the spring, when the snow began to thaw, she would take the form of a bird – an owl, a raven, a curious lark. She would perch on the branches, singing a song that wasn't quite a birdsong but was recognized as being something more lyrical than the rumbling Language of Trees.

In the summer, when the snow was gone, and the air had a warm sweetness to it, she would lumber along the forest floor as a bear, pausing to scratch her back against the bark of a tree or to dip her paws in a stream. She liked being a bear the very most because bears were powerful. They were feared. They were beautiful, and she loved beauty.

In the autumn, the leaves above her turning a crisp array of gold and red, petrichor sifting through the air with the impending promise of winter's ice, she would be a wolf, howling longingly at the moon, or a white tiger, pouncing on unsuspecting rabbits and chasing after crunchy leaves. She would run with the wind, reveling in the way it raked its fingers through her thick fur coat.

And in winter, the snow thick and deep and unforgiving, she would take her second favorite form: that of a deer. A graceful, slender thing with a high neck and limber legs, light on her feet as she pranced through the snow.

And when she wasn't a raven or a bear, a wolf, a leopard, a deer, she was...

Well, *Svetlana.*

She was bigger than the trees themselves, strong enough to uproot them with both hands if she truly wanted to. She could pluck a spine from someone's back and pull it – and their skull – free from their flesh. She was an amalgamation of limbs, not quite bipedal, but she could be if she desired. She had antlers, razors for teeth, four eyes with eight pupils that could see all. Her own spine stuck out of her back like a mountain ridge of solid bone, holding a cage of ribs that bent outwards, not quite right since they didn't have any squishy organs to protect.

That was the form she should have taken when Ivan arrived, but she was a naïve fool then, one who spent too much time at the hut on chicken's legs.

She was not Svetlana back then.

In the dead of winter, she wandered through the woods as a girl, barefoot and naked with only her ankle-long hair to cover her milky flesh. That's when she found the glow. It was an unusual glow, so she followed it, only to find a ring of skulls on stakes, creating a makeshift fence around a house atop fowl's legs. The skulls, Svetlana had realized, were the source of the light.

An old hag stood on the porch, a loaf of bread in her hands, and she yelled at Svetlana. "If I wasn't so stressed about my house being a mess, girl, I would march right out there and eat you. You look like you'd taste good with carrots and potatoes."

Svetlana blinked. This was not the Language of Trees (or *any* language she had heard in her wood before). Yet, she understood it perfectly.

The hag bit into the bread, chewing crassly.

"I..." Svetlana's human voice sounded strange in her throat, deeper than the hag's but...lighter. Younger, with a youthful lilt to it. "I would eat you first."

The hag cackled, sending half-chewed bread spraying. "Who are you? We should hunt together. Humans taste *delicious.*"

Svetlana just blinked. "What are you doing in my forest?"

"Your forest, girl? Ha! Don't be a fool. These woods are mine."

Svetlana's form rippled. The hag dropped the bread.

"Baba Yaga," the woman said. She was not human, that much Svetlana could tell, but whatever she was, she was weaker than Svetlana.

She had seen a human once. A girl whose body she now wore. She had heard the girl talking to a snow-white rabbit, which is how she knew the girl's name.

She borrowed that name now. "Svetlana," she said, mimicking the way the girl had said it.

"What are you?" Baba Yaga picked up her bread. Her hands shook. "You're not human, but you're not a witch, either."

Svetlana's form rippled again. It would become her default human skin – green eyes, brown hair, skin the color of vanilla milk. But now, she was still getting used to it.

"I am the forest," she said. "You are not welcome here. Leave."

The next day, the hut on chicken's legs would be gone. The only proof that it had ever been there was the fowl's footprints in the snow, leading out of the wood. The next time Svetlana would meet a Baba Yaga would be many, many, *many* years later, just before she met Ivan. Just before she was locked away in a jar for centuries before Sébastien came along to save her with a contract.

When Sébastien finally woke, Svetlana was still perched on the bed, nursing a cup of Russian Caravan that was at least a third vodka. She peered through her lashes, schooling her face until it was an expressionless mask.

She could count on one hand the number of things she knew about Sébastien de la Rue.

He was obsessed with coffee (especially if it was French in origin).

He was a human in a dangerous contract with a hungry demon who fed off entertainment, one who, if the quota wasn't met, would devour his delicious soul.

He was being hunted by a man in a black coat who was not from France but lurked there like a stain.

And that was all.

Of course, she knew other things, too, like how he hated sugar and had the opposite of a sweet tooth, or how he actually had horrible stage fright, or how he collected astrium brooches despite how expensive they were.

Or how she knew, deep, deep, deep down, that *Sébastien de la Rue* was not his real name, just as *Svetlana Vasilievna* was not hers. She had borrowed the name and never bothered to return it.

But who

(or what)

had Sébastien borrowed his name from?

"You," she said over the lip of her teacup, "are not in love with that woman."

Because he wasn't.

Séb blinked, still half-asleep, a veil of delirium coating his eyes. Astrium blue, just like the bright cyan-turquoise brooch at his throat. His lips were smeared red.

"She is not human," she continued, finally lowering her cup. "She is not from Elphame. She is not from Earth. She is from the Otherland, and she is a succubus. Her only desire is to devour you, Sébastien darling, and there is no contract to prevent her from doing so."

CHAPTER EIGHTEEN

LIE PRESSED HER BACK against the brick wall in a secluded alley and slid to the ground, not caring that her trousers were almost instantly soaked by the snow. If there was an award for being the biggest fool in Europe, she would have won it three times over.

She was a fool for running away from her estate to avoid marriage.

She was a fool for thinking joining the chasseurs would work in her favor.

She was a fool for believing she could get away with it.

Of *course* her voice would give her away. She had been raised as a prim and proper lady, her soft-spoken soprano drilled into her at a very young age. Anyone who heard her butterfly-soft London accent would be able to tell she was a woman – a *lady*, one bred and groomed for the life of a duchess. She knew how to maintain a household and host tea parties, not how to exorcise demons and fly airships.

The tears burned as they slid down her cheeks. Lie buried her face in her hands, her shoulders trembling with each silenced sob she choked out. The worst part wouldn't be returning home and having to explain herself to her parents. The worst part wouldn't be the punishment, the expedited marriage, the expectation that she lay on her back and bear heirs for her betrothed.

The worst part already happened, in the form of the utter *betrayal* plastered on Emrys's face. She shouldn't have lied to him. But what was she supposed to say? *Hello, my name is Eulalie, but please call me Lie because I loathe my actual name. I'm the only child to a lord and lady, and I was born with the sole purpose of marrying a duke and squeezing out sons for him, and I didn't want that life, so I ran away to Paris and pretended to be a man named Blaise Beaumont so I could sneak into the Church and become an exorcist, please forgive me?*

High society had stripped away all of her rights – her freedom, her free will, her sense of self – the moment she came out of her mother's womb with a womb of her own. She was judged by the organ alone, not by what potential she might have had should she have been raised differently. No matter what other people made a claim to the ladder that was society – criminals, murderers, anyone who was *different* from what society deemed *human* – women would *always* be at the very bottom, barely making a foothold on the lowest rung.

Instead of climbing trees outside and running with her father's hunting dogs through the field, instead of poring over books about arithmetic and science, instead of coming home after dark with scraped knees and muddied trousers and windblown hair, she was expected to sit with her back straight and her figure dainty. She was expected to learn how to manage a household with dollhouses, to learn how to be a mother with the porcelain dolls she was gifted each birthday and Christmas, to be demure and pretty and obedient for her husband that was picked out for her the moment she came into the world with purple eyes and blonde curls and nothing worthwhile between her legs.

And as terrifying as it was walking through the catacombs, the tools for exorcising demons at her hip, she *loved* the freedom she'd tasted these past few months. She enjoyed Emrys's company and, hell, Olivier's company, too. She enjoyed fitting in with them, being treated like she was their equal.

But it was ruined now. That tiny sliver of freedom was gone forever, and it was her fault.

She hugged her knees to her chest. Snot and tears streaked her trousers. Frustrated, she yanked her cap off, letting her curls tumble over her shoulders.

"Lie!" a voice shouted, startling her enough that her heart fluttered to her throat. She looked up, pale hair a veil over her tear-streaked face, to see Olivier standing in the mouth of the alley, the shadow of a monster behind him.

And then Olivier, who she knew hated her, did the unexpected. He ran over and wrapped his arms around her in a hug so tight she was sure her ribs would snap.

He leaned close, lips brushing against her ear, and whispered, so soft she wasn't sure if she'd actually heard it or if she'd simply imagined it: "The man who followed me is not completely human, and I cannot exorcise him by myself here. On my mark, we are going to run."

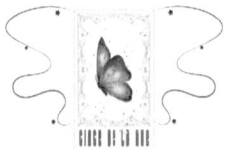

Most days, Sébastien could keep the voice under control. If he fed it enough entertainment, he received magic to eat, and the voice would remain quiet. But now...

Now he could feel it sitting on his shoulders, whispering in his ear, talons digging into his flesh.

You have made a grave mistake.

You are a fool.

A pathetic fool.

And I, too, am a fool for siding with you.

I told you, but you did not listen. You never listen.

You. Are. Not. To. Sleep.

He sat up and turned, vomiting all over the wooden floor of Svetlana's tent. Bile burned against his esophagus as he threw up again, his body seizing as it fought to gain some control.

"Are you finished, Sébastien darling?" Svetlana asked flatly. She dropped her teacup; the circus took it, putting it somewhere other than shattered on the floor. "Regardless. I do believe I am in need of an explanation."

"C-contract states –" Sébastien's voice was harsh, grating, like unoiled gears rubbing together in a janky automaton. He coughed. Magic fluttered on his tongue, sweet and blue.

"Darling, the contract is in place to keep me from eating you," Svetlana interjected. "And if I don't get an explanation soon, I will find where you keep it, devour it, then devour you."

He didn't doubt she would.

He locked eyes with her, his narrowed into predatory slits, and said, his voice colder than ice, "I will kill you, Svetlana Vasilievna. I will lock you in a box and ship you right back to Moscow to be forgotten again if you try to pry into my past."

When she spoke, her voice was so devoid of emotions that he knew she was furious beyond words. "Why do you do this. Why must you dig a grave for yourself and push the rest of us in while our backs are turned."

He dug his nails deep into his palms. The leather of his gloves creased, whining as his claws nearly punctured through. "Because," he said softly, "it's easier to make enemies of you all than it is to be vulnerable."

Something flitted across Svetlana's face. Or, maybe her appearance rippled, whatever hold she had on her current form waning ever so slightly.

"Who are you?" she whispered.

"Sébastien de la Rue," he answered. "Who I was before doesn't matter. Who I was before is dead, and I intend on keeping him that way."

He left Svetlana's tent, trudging through the snow to his Tent Noir. Halfway to it, he paused, then went to the Big Top instead, slipping through the back and onto the risers to watch his troupe.

The Flying Foxes, Alice and Odette, tumbled through the air, gossamer-thin silver wings barely visible behind them, fanning out to catch them before they could fall. He found them separately, even though they seemed to have a past he was unaware of. Odette had been trapped in a wealthy woman's house, exploited for luck. Alice had been wandering aimlessly, the only survivor of a circus fire.

Beowulf, Ilian, whispered to the drake Dakov, commanding him – *compelling* him – to walk laps around the ring – good exercise after he'd been cooped up for so long. Séb found him in Gévaudan, secluded in a manor with all his beasties and a thirst for blood that was only sated with a contract that protected Sébastien from being drunk dry.

Lady Kali, Antara, threw her knives at a spinning board, eyes covered by a blindfold. She was the oldest member of the circus, nearly two thousand years old, and the only one who was technically *not* inhuman in a negative sense. She had been trapped in an urn locked away in the British Museum. Nobody seemed to miss the urn after Sébastien stole it and freed her.

Strapped to the board was Noa, one half of the Gemini Twins, while the second half, Sasha, spun it. Uncanny and obnoxious as they were, they treated Sébastien as their hero – their god – because he had been the one to break into the circus sideshow where they were kept like animals to free them.

And El Cuélebre, Aurelio, who was likely still furious with Sébastien but was too busy inhaling oxygen and breathing out clouds of fire to notice his one-man audience. The dragon tattoo across his collarbones shimmered in the firelight. Sébastien found him in the woods of Spain, alone and afraid and desperate for companionship and a hoard to call his own.

Sébastien hardly knew anything about his troupe. He knew *what* they were, what their talents were, where they had been two years ago, and he knew whatever other information they cared to share. Why should *he* have to share more than that?

The Troupe de la Rue knew those very things about Sébastien: he was human, he could create miracles, he had been traveling Europe in search of inhuman talent, and he liked coffee and astrium brooches. Nothing else was important. Nothing else mattered.

Why should he tell Svetlana the truth?

"Newspaper," he whispered, holding his hand outstretched.

You don't get to use my powers like this anymore. You are treading on very thin ice.

"Newspaper."

If you don't consume magic, your soul will corrupt.

Fine.

Why should I care? Your soul is mine, regardless.

A copy of the *La Loi* appeared out of thin air, plopping right on his waiting palm. It was the same issue he'd already read earlier that day.

"I don't suppose you can give me tomorrow's issue?" He tossed the paper over his shoulder.

Ask your fortune teller.

"Louis..." he murmured. Then he sat up straight. Louis. Where was *Louis?* The Troupe de la Rue was in the Big Top, sans Svetlana, who was still in her own tent, but...

Louis was nowhere to be seen.

He is not here, the voice said. *Not here.* Which meant he wasn't on the circus grounds at all.

Sébastien stood up. "Help me find him."

As you command.

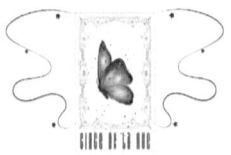

Louis had spent most of his life on the streets. He knew better than to blindly trust strangers and follow them away from his safe space. His parents had been killed in a one-way knife fight with a drunken stranger when he'd been too young to fend for himself. The very same *could* happen to him now.

Could. But wouldn't.

As he trailed after the duke, he tugged one of his gloves down, eye opening to peer into the future. After having it blocked so many times lately, it was strangely cathartic to see flashes of what was to come now.

Two people dressed in navy blue uniforms darting through the streets.

The shadow of a man in a dark coat.

A cemetery with mausoleums reached toward the dark sky.

A door opening.

A wall of clocks –

"These people," Louis piped up. "They don't happen to be dressed in uniforms, do they? One with black hair, one with blonde?"

The duke stumbled, tripping over his own feet. "My God, you really *can* see the future," he breathed. "Yes! Olivier and Lie. Do you know where they are?"

His eye strained, searching through the millions and millions of infinite potentials, futures that could happen if he inhaled too sharply, futures that would shatter if his heart decided to skip a beat.

"There...there is a white-and-red striped awning. They just ran under –"

Louis didn't finish his sentence. The duke grabbed his wrist and yanked him along, dragging him as he booked it through the snow.

Cold wind bit his nose and ears, snowflakes splattering against his goggles faster than he could wipe them away. The duke dodged carriages and automatons, ducking under hanging shop signs and squeezing past passersby.

"Ah! I see them!" Emrys exclaimed.

Just as Louis's toe found a chunk of ice and sent him sprawling to the ground.

"Go get them!" Louis shouted. He broke his fall with his palms, wincing as pain radiated throughout his body, his unprotected eyes taking the brunt of the crash. Emrys glanced back but nodded, solemn, and disappeared into the throng.

"Need a hand?" a voice suddenly said. It was not French the man spoke, though the circus translated the German into the language he knew.

Louis didn't answer. The stranger grabbed Louis's arm and hauled him to his feet, going so far as to brush the snow from his knees.

When Louis looked up, four eyes not covered by gloves (but hidden by goggles) met the gaze of a blond man.

And when he was thrown into the past, his stomach sank.

He knew.

He *knew* the past he was not supposed to know.

Louis Toussaint fell to his knees, the world bleeding black.

He knew he knew he knew he knew, oh *God,* he knew.

He knew *everything.*

His cards were right – he was going to die. Only, it wouldn't be the long-dead corpse of an angel dragging him down.

PART THREE

Welcome to

The Crimson Market

SEVEN CARDS HAVE BEEN HIDDEN.
CAN YOU FIND THEM ALL...
...BEFORE THE TIME RUNS OUT?

BE WARY, DON'T TARRY...
AND MAKE IT OUT ALIVE.

CHAPTER NINETEEN

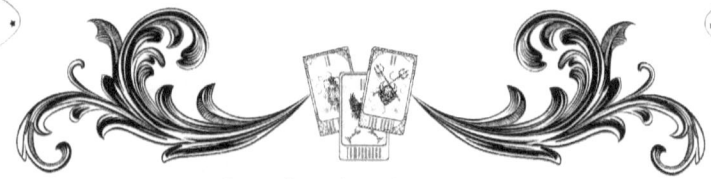

NICK STARED AT THE bit of cardstock in Enoch's hands. The hag – Baba Yaga – had plucked it from thin air, shooing them both off once Enoch held the card.

Red and black stripes covered the entire thing, save for a pale red square in the center. In deep gold letters were the words

WELCOME TO THE CRIMSON MARKET

SEVEN CARDS HAVE BEEN HIDDEN.

CAN YOU FIND THEM ALL...BEFORE THE TIME RUNS OUT?

BE WARY, DON'T TARRY...AND MAKE IT OUT ALIVE.

The Crimson Market. Nick hadn't heard of such a thing while he was in the trenches. He didn't even know where they were. This strange, canopied souk wasn't anywhere near the frontlines. That Baba Yaga – and the other demons in the Otherland – hadn't descended on Nicholas and Enoch like a pack of starving beasts was more unsettling than if they all eyed the two humans like they were walking cuts of meat.

Something was not right about this place beyond the fact that it was, at the very root, Hell, and it itched at the back of Nick's mind like a variola sore. The seam where his flesh and sawed bones met the warm, whirring metal of his prosthetic hand ached. He was nowhere near the trenches where he had lost his entire platoon and hand to a foolish, naïve mistake, but adrenaline began coursing through his body with each rapid beat of his heart, nudging him to the pinnacle of fight-or-flight. Copper and brass fingers – not fueled by adrenaline and blood, but by astrium and steam – twitched, nudging close to his pistol just in case.

"We need to get out of here," he whispered to Enoch.

A loud, robust laugh filled the market before Enoch had the chance to answer. Both Nick and Enoch whipped their heads up, following the belly-deep laugh to a red tent held up by bamboo stalks that looked too bleached to be anything but bone. Sitting in the shadows was, undeniably, a demon. Nick couldn't tell what it was or if it even fell on the gendered spectrum put in place by mankind. It had the grey head of an African elephant, nine tusks jutting out like spikes beneath a curled trunk. Its ears were full of gold hoops and jewelry. It had two elephant arms from its elephant-like torso, but beneath that was a thick, powerful serpent tail corded with muscle and coiled dangerously tight. It sat five times taller than Nick, and that was while its tail was curled up, acting like a chair for it to sit back on.

"You there," it said in an accent Nick had never heard, in a language he should not have been able to understand, but, like with Baba Yaga – like with the circus – he somehow could. It continued: "Come into my tent, boys. Let me have a look at you. Don't give me that look. I won't eat you. You're both too small and bony for my tastes."

Somehow, Nick felt a pang of offense at those words.

"Stick with me," he whispered, grabbing Enoch's hand. "We've caught its attention; if we run now, we'll only draw more eyes to us. We will not be able to escape then."

Enoch nodded once, using his knuckles to nudge his glasses up his nose. His hand was warm in Nick's, damp with nervous sweat but soft, uncalloused, unused to the horrors the Otherland had to offer.

Nick led him into the tent.

Up close, the demon was even bigger, its spiked back hunched to fit in the tent. Bones covered the walls. A massive ribcage hung from the ceiling, little lights draped from each rib in a macabre chandelier.

"You come under invitation of Severin Alucard, no?" *That name again...* "No? *Bwahahahahaha!* How did two scrawny humans like you make it here? Do you know where you are?"

"The Crimson Market?" Enoch asked at the same time Nick said: "The Otherland."

"*Bwahahahahaha!*" the creature tipped its head back, feet-hands pressed to its chest as it laughed, the whole tent shaking with its shoulders. "You are funny humans! Tell me, what are you?"

Nick squeezed Enoch's hand, hoping that subtle message would be enough to keep him quiet. "Humans," he said. "We are, as you observed, humans."

The creature laughed *again.* "No! You *are* human at your core, but what are *you?* I am a Grootslang at my core, but *I* am the Bone Merchant."

"I am a journalist," said Enoch, ignoring Nick's message completely. "And he's a –"

Nick squeezed his hand again. "I'm a guide."

Understanding glazed Enoch's eyes. He nodded solemnly. "He's my guide. A guide. An adventurous guide. He's been all over the world, exploring new places previously undiscovered by man."

The Bone Merchant leaned in close, its tusk curiously prodding the air around Nick's face. He stood statue-still, afraid to even think about reaching for his gun. "Y-yes," he stammered. "All over the world. I'm...yes, I'm a guide."

The Bone Merchant clapped their feet-hands together. "Have you ever been to Africa? No? For the best, truly. Too many white British men there now, hunting all the elephants before I can eat them. You white British men are not here to colonize the Otherland? Severin Alucard will get you if you are."

That name again!

"Who is Severin Alucard?" Enoch butted in. Nick could almost imagine the pen and notepad in his hands, ready to scribble down notes from this makeshift interview with the Bone Merchant. He could envision the headline now: *What is the Otherland? Exclusive Interview with the Bone Merchant Tells All!*

The Bone Merchant laughed. "Severin Alucard! He is the Archangel Gabriel. He is the Wishmaster of the Carnivale of Saints!"

"Is he human?" asked Enoch.

"Nobody knows! He looks human, but is he?" The Bone Merchant grabbed a rag from a hook on the wall with its trunk. "We make bets here – he created the Crimson Market. Granted a wish to give us this place! – on what he is. Between you and me, Journalist and Guide, I think he is the Devil."

Ice swept through Nick's body, freezing his core with permafrost dread. Demons he could fight. But the Devil?

He could not win a fight against the Devil.

Lie's hand was small in Olivier's, the leather of her glove fitting against his. She kept his pace as he darted out of the alley, dodging Herr Jack before he could grab them. She didn't question it, didn't argue, just nodded once, and when he took off running, his hand wrapped around hers, she followed.

As he ran, Olivier's heart thundered against his chest, beating impossibly fast. He'd exorcised dozens of demons since becoming a chasseur. He'd sent dozens of them back to whatever Hell they'd crawled from.

But ever since coming to Paris, everything had gone downhill.

The demons at the circus, the demon Firebird, now whatever Herr Jack was... Olivier should have known how to deal with it, yet...

Yet all he could do, clutching Lie's hand tightly to keep her close, to keep her from slipping on the snow and falling, was run.

He wasn't paying attention when he ran into a man with dark curls and goggles around his neck. It took him half a second to recognize the man as Emrys Wilde and half another second to realize Emrys wanted Olivier and Lie to follow him. Still clutching Lie, Olivier ran after Emrys.

He recognized the demonic presence of the Seer before seeing him kneeling in the snow, head in his hands. He had been at the masquerade ball, and while Olivier had ranked him as being one of the less dangerous demons within le Cirque de la Rue, he still bristled at the sight. There were too many civilians around, too many innocents that were at risk.

Lie tugged her hand free and ran over to the Seer, crouching down and offering him a hand. "Are you all right, Monsieur?"

Gingerly, the Seer took her hand, only to quickly recoil. He stood on his own, swaying like a drunk.

Olivier narrowed his eyes, but before he could say anything, Emrys piped up: "We're all here. Let's get to the Cimetière du Montparnasse before it's too late."

"Monsieur –" Lie tried, reaching for the Seer again.

"I'm fine, mons – oh, are you still going by mademoiselle now?" The Seer rubbed his temples. "My mind is a mess right now. Forgive me. I'm Louis Toussaint.

He almost called Lie monsieur, Olivier noted.

"Helloooo," Emrys interjected. "Cimetière du Montparnasse? Are we going to go?"

Lie, Olivier, and the Seer all turned to face him.

"The room," the Seer said, "we need to be in has a wall full of clocks. If we can find that, we are going the right way."

Naively, Olivier thought that would narrow it down and make it a lot easier.

"There's four of us, though," interjected Lie. "And only two invitations. How is that going to work?"

The Seer fidgeted with his glove. "We'll sneak in the way you've always snuck out of parties."

Lie's cheeks flushed deep pink. Olivier suddenly felt very naked and exposed. Could the Seer pry into *his* past, dredging up things best left forgotten?

Before anyone could ask what he meant, Lie sighed softly and said, "by pretending to be someone else. This is a terrible idea."

"But it's the only one we have," said Emrys. "So, let's get this over with."

A map appeared before Sébastien, the veining streets of Paris stark white against the black blocks that made up the city. There were no labels, but Séb knew the city better than he knew the back of his hand. A bright blue circle made up le Cirque de la Rue, and a blue line stretched out from it, showing Louis's path. The map itself wouldn't work outside the circus grounds, but all Sébastien needed was an idea of where to go.

He grabbed the winter coat the circus conjured for him, sliding it over his arms and buttoning it to his chin. A blue butterfly appeared then, fluttering a few feet away. Nobody seemed to have informed the butterfly that it was the dead of winter, and all the other butterflies had gone into an eternal sleep, only to reemerge come spring. The blue butterfly didn't care, not as a fine dust of glittering magic twinkled from its wings with each flap, misting into the air, visible only to Sébastien. Shoving his hands deep into his pockets – the gloves he wore did nothing to combat the cold – he followed the butterfly.

It fluttered through the air, dodging snowflakes and people, leading Sébastien through the labyrinthine city. He kept his head low, gaze focused on his feet save for a few fleeting glances every now and then to make sure he was still behind the butterfly.

Paris was a very dangerous city for Sébastien, and he did not want to be back.

It's a big city, he told himself, following the butterfly past a hulking automaton – its astrium eyes trailing Sébastien as he went – and down a side street. *The likelihood of you running into him is slim.*

You are safe. You are fine. You are –

He stepped over the threshold and into one of Paris's biggest cemeteries. His stomach sank all the way to his feet.

Ignoring the butterfly, he broke into a run, mazing through the city of graves, heart thundering against his ribs the whole time. It had to be a coincidence. It had to be a strange play of fate that brought both Louis and Sébastien to the Cimetière du Montparnasse.

Because if Louis had been prying into his past, Sébastien would have no choice but to kill him.

He picked up the pace once he spotted a flash of white hair disappearing into an open mausoleum. He slipped through just before the door could slam shut.

"It's *dark,*" hissed a feminine voice. "Why didn't we think to bring *lanterns?* I wish we had a light."

A cold tingle shot down Sébastien's spine. He couldn't help but grin. Holding out his hand, a lantern appeared, its flame glowing bright astrium blue.

"Well!" he said in his Dreammonger voice. "Your wish is *my* command."

Four people – three strangers, two dressed like *chasseurs,* one with aviator goggles like Louis's around his neck and one not-stranger, goggles and gloves right where they were supposed to be – turned around to face Sébastien, their faces aglow, bathed in bright blue light.

"Sébastien?" hissed Louis.

Sébastien grinned, though it didn't reach his eyes. His smiles rarely did. Perhaps the last time he truly smiled and meant it was ten years ago.

"Why did you come here?" he asked.

It was the curly-haired, goggles-wearing man that spoke. "The Carnivale of Saints," he explained. "The clues led here."

"The what now?" asked Sébastien.

Louis groaned. "Oh, for the love of God. The card? Remember? We were all trying to figure it out?"

Well, everyone *else* had been trying to figure it out. *Sébastien* had been too busy fantasizing about Zarifa. That was why he didn't recognize the red envelope Louis pulled from his pocket to wave in his face.

"You're the Dreammonger," the goggles man said suddenly.

"Yes," said Sébastien. Then, mustering up what little strength he had, he bowed dramatically. "Sébastien de la Rue at your service. Maître de la Rue, the Dreammonger, ringmaster of le Cirque de la Rue. None of that is important. You needed a lantern, correct? This is only good for as long as your wish holds, so we'd best get moving if we want to find this...*Carnivale*..."

He said the word like it was poison, acrid and sickly sweet on his tongue. That blasted *Carnivale of Saints* was ruining his life, ruining everything he'd spent the last decade building, the last two years perfecting. Le Cirque de la Rue was his *soul,* and now that was about to be trampled, worn to nothing but dust so useless not even the street rats would find comfort in it.

Pushing past the others, Sébastien ventured deeper into the mausoleum. He learned quickly that it wasn't a true mausoleum but a false one erected to house an entrance to the catacombs. He flashed the lantern across a plaque embedded in the wall.

ARRÊTE!

C'EST ICI L'EMPIRE DE LA MORT!

Stop! This is the empire of the dead!

"These catacombs are a lot less creepy than the ones under Notre-Dame," muttered the woman dressed as a chasseur. "Those ones have demon bones."

The hair on the back of Sébastien's neck stood on end. He said nothing, listening keenly instead as he followed the bone-lined path deeper into the ossuary. Eyeless skulls watched the five as they passed, evermore grins stretched wide and toothy, yellowed reminders of what fate waited for each of them.

Because they were all human – except for Louis, who wasn't *entirely* human – and they would all one day die, their flesh melted away and their bones picked clean and bleached and forgotten. Each skull – each femur, each abandoned bone stacked neatly into underground walls – once belonged to someone.

And once death claimed them, they lay here, forgotten.

"The catacombs under D'Amiens have demon bones, too," added the other chasseur.

"Your names," Sébastien said without turning around. Frankly, he could not care less what the names of the mysterious three were, but it would be easier if he had something to call them.

"Olivier," said the chasseur. "This is Lie, and that is Emrys."

He paused to stare at a skull that was far too small, covered in far too many sutures, to belong to an adult. His tongue turned to ash, crumbling in his mouth and forming an unswallowable lump in his throat.

"We need to find a room with a wall of clocks," Louis said, oblivious to Sébastien's stop. "I can't see anything else that might be helpful."

"If only someone needed a miracle," drawled Sébastien.

Emrys was the first to catch on. "It would be a *miracle* if we could find where to go. I *wish* we could have an easy path lined for us."

And just like that, another bright blue butterfly appeared. It flapped its wings, magic dust fluttering from the paper-thin membranes, and fluttered down the corridor.

"Magic," whispered Lie, so soft Sébastien would have missed it had he not been primed to listen to every – *every* – reaction his miracles drew.

As the five followed the butterfly, their footsteps against the packed dirt ground the only sound, unease knotted over and over again in Sébastien's belly.

He didn't fear bones. It was such a common fear, yet a silly one, he thought. Everyone had a skeleton in them. Everyone would inevitably die and be reduced to bones. The catacombs bodies were centuries old. Even if they could somehow be reanimated and cause destruction, they were so ancient that one swift kick would turn them to dust.

It wasn't the bones that had his hackles raised and his body one misstep away from fight-or-flight.

It wasn't even the fact that he was beneath a cemetery with *fresher* bodies buried under the dirt.

The butterfly rounded a corner and promptly dissipated into magic so fine Sébastien could taste it on his tongue.

There was nothing but a wall of bones to greet them. Sébastien groaned. That blasted butterfly leading him astray...

Olivier stepped forward, running his hand over the skulls.

"Maître de la Rue," he said as his fingers deftly searched the bones. "Before we go any further, I need to know. What are you?"

Sébastien de la Rue grinned. "You caught on quicker than most. Must be because you're a chasseur. What do you *think* I am?"

The only remedy for his unease would be having his ego stroked, and if Olivier decided he was something powerful – like Svetlana – or something legendary – like Aurelio – or something both – like Antara – his ego would grow triple its already massive size.

"I think... I think you're a puppet being controlled by something extraordinary."

Almost exactly what Zarifa had said...

He scoffed. "What makes you think that?" he asked, his ego having shrunk.

Olivier hooked his finger beneath a skull. "You act like you are God Himself, descended from the Heavens to grant miracles. But chasseurs are taught to identify demons. Demons can't be photographed well. They show up blurry, like...smudges. Everyone in the circus shows up like that except for you. You are just a man, and man cannot harness God's power. Or the Devil's, for that matter."

Beside him, Louis went stiff.

Sébastien lifted his shoulders in a lazy shrug, pretending that would mask how bruised his ego was. It would have hurt less had Olivier grabbed his ego and beat it with a stick. "You're right. I run a circus of demons. But *I* am nothing more than a human."

Click.

The wall of skulls, which was actually a *door* of skulls, slid open, revealing a gaping maw of darkness.

Sébastien stepped forward, holding out his lantern. The blue light did little to ward off the shadows. "Well," he said, stepping into the corridor. "Down the rabbit hole."

CHAPTER TWENTY

ZARIFA WATCHED THE AUTOMATON butterfly circle her room, unblinking. After fleeing back to Saint Gabriel's manor, she'd gone straight to her bedroom, flopped on her bed, and began having an internal crisis.

Groaning loudly, she rolled onto her side and pulled one of her red pillows to her chest, squeezing it tightly.

There was no reason for her heart to be racing like this. Succubi weren't even supposed to *have* hearts. True, she was only half succubus – her father had been an incubus who, far too many years ago for Zarifa to admit, decided to lay with a human woman. She'd grown up normal, being doted on by everyone in the tiny Kenyan village, until her teenage years. With the maturity of her body came the maturity of her abilities. Around her mid-twenties, she stopped aging completely, outliving everyone in her village before she fled to Europe, where she was found by Gabriel.

Succubi didn't have hearts. Half-succubi weren't supposed to have them, either. But Zarifa did, and her awful, horrible, terrible heart fluttered against her ribs. Butterflies – wasps, more like – filled her stomach, flitting and fluttering in a storm, angrier than the copper-and-steam model that flew around her room.

It was just a kiss. She'd kissed dozens of men before. She could dress and speak and act like a proper lady, but she'd done things that would make even the most seasoned ladies of the night blush.

So why – *why* – did one silly human man make her this *flustered*?!

He was just an excellent kisser, she told herself. He *had* been an excellent kisser, after all. The perfect amount of lips and tongue, no clashing teeth, all hungry softness and warm wetness. The kind of kiss that left her lips swollen and his lips smeared with her rouge.

Until he decided to faint in her arms, that is.

It had been *hours,* and Zarifa showed no signs of getting over it soon.

She dug her nails into her pillow, face buried in the silk-encased feathery down. Her mission had been clear: get close to Sébastien de la Rue and figure out how the circus worked. Gabriel didn't care how much seniority Zarifa had on him; if she didn't fulfill her end of the contract, she would be terminated.

But after the masquerade, it seemed clear that Sébastien *couldn't* disclose his secrets.

Couldn't, like *he* was held under a contract, too.

"He isn't allowed to share his soul with anyone else," Zarifa murmured to her pillow. "Especially not that Russian woman. He is *mine.*"

Knock, knock, knock.

Zarifa kicked her pillow away and scrambled to her feet, grabbing her discarded mask and slamming it over her face as she tripped over her feet to get to the door.

"*There* you are," said Gabriel, exasperated, when she finally swung the door open. He didn't wear his mask, his tired face on unfortunate display. He raked his fingers through his short, dark hair. "I'm sending you to the Crimson Market to supervise with Magdalene and Michaelis."

Saint Magdalene and Saint Michaelis were the youngest in the Carnivale of Saints – Mags being sixteen and Michaelis at seventeen. Zarifa didn't know their real names – nobody did. They were just Mags and Michaelis, changelings who ended up on the wrong side of the Veil with a talent Gabriel desired. They lived in the gardener's cabin behind the manor, relying more on each other than anyone else.

Zarifa didn't *mind* the changelings, but... To her, they were children. Infants. She didn't want to have to *babysit* them.

"Isn't Benedict usually the one to...supervise...them?" She toyed with a loose thread on her sleeve, wrapping it around her finger before yanking, snapping it right off.

Gabriel – whose unsaintly name was *Severin Alucard* – scrubbed his hand over his face. "Benedict has...run into some issues."

"Issues?" she cocked a brow.

"Apparently, two humans snuck into the library during the masquerade. He will not listen to any of my orders. Finding those humans is a higher priority to him – one that trumps the contract – because they *supposedly* ended up in the Otherland."

Zarifa wasn't from the Otherland. She was from southern Africa, just like her mother. But her *father* had come from the

Otherland. Succubi and incubi came from that other place that wasn't Earth or Elphame, that wicked place where law was scarce and chaos reigned above all else.

The Otherland was also where the Crimson Market was. An eternal night market with blood red stalls full of ephemera and occultic tchotchkes where demons could barter and sell and trade in corporeal goods and souls alike. When Severin decided to host the first Carnivale game there, Zarifa had argued. Sending helpless humans to a market for *monsters* would only end in bloodbath.

But he made sure every vendor and customer was aware of the game and allowed them to participate. So, he hid his cards and set the Crimson Market Scavenger Hunt loose.

"Have Mags and Michaelis meet me at Zozo's in half an hour," she said. Half an hour would be plenty of time to freshen up and use Severin's Bluebeard Door to get to the Otherland.

"Bossy," he tsked.

"I'm a lady, Monsieur Alucard." She smirked beneath her mask. "I must look my absolute *best.*"

Severin Alucard grumbled under his breath but left, leaving Zarifa alone with her traitorous heart and mutinous feelings.

Curse you, Sébastien de la Rue. Curse you!

Half an hour later, after walking through the oaken Bluebeard Door, Zarifa stood outside the red tent known as Zozo's, impatiently waiting for Magdalene and Michaelis to arrive.

Throughout his twenty-nine years of life, Enoch had learned there were two versions of himself. There was Enoch, the squirrely, awkward single man who rented a flat and drank too much coffee and found joy in typewriters and airships and circuses.

And there was E. E. Irving, the journalist who would do anything for a good scoop, who would go to Hell to chase an article that would make it on the second page under a photograph of the Thames if he was lucky.

Enoch would be afraid of the Grootslang – the Bone Merchant – but E. E. Irving? Somehow, erasing his name until only two letters and a surname remained gave him the confidence he needed to deal with a demon.

He pushed his spectacles up his nose. "The Devil?" he pried. "What makes you say that?"

If he pretended he held a pad of paper and a pencil, he could have all the confidence in the world.

The Bone Merchant laughed again, that awful, grating laugh that filled the tent and froze Enoch's insides to icicles.

(*Intesticles,* he thought, then promptly snorted at the lewd phrase).

The Bone Merchant leaned closer, trunk swishing through the air carelessly. "He thinks highly of himself. Has power. *Too much* power. Anything he wants, he gets. He has a herd that follows him

– his Saints, he calls them. Not a single one of them is human, but they follow him regardless. They can't say no to him, not at all. *Bwahahaha!* None of *us* can say no to him, either! If that doesn't make him the devil, then I don't eat elephants for breakfast!"

Enoch wasn't sure *anyone* ate elephants for breakfast...

Still feigning that E. E. Irving Confidence, Enoch asked, "What other vendors should we visit? Any that you recommend? I'm not sure either of us are in the market for...bones..."

"Silly journalist!" The Bone Merchant laughed. "I don't sell my bones to humans like you. My bones are farmed for devouring. For humans like you... Visit Baku to rid yourself of nightmares. Indrik has horns. Banshee, if you want to know when you will die. Basilisk has potions that could help you. If you visit the Basilisk, tell her she owes me another round of cards, and she is not allowed to cheat this time."

Enoch made a note to *not* bring that up to the Basilisk, should he and Nicholas come across her, but nodded regardless.

"Thank you, Bone Merchant," he said as politely as he could.

"Safe travels, Journalist and Guide!" the Bone Merchant laughed. "Try not to be eaten alive! You are good company. It would be shameful if you died."

Enoch wasted no time. He grabbed Nicholas's wrist and led him out of the tent, back onto the street of the Crimson Market and –

"*Oof!*" a childlike voice exclaimed. A...*familiar* voice.

The masked girl stepped back, brushing herself off. Though Enoch hadn't gotten a good look at the two teenagers while he and Nicholas hid from Benedict, he'd got enough of a glimpse at them to recognize the blonde ringlets and pale pink dress on the girl before him as one of the duo.

And she, apparently, recognized him, too, because she gasped and exclaimed, "It's you! Michaelis, I found them! Benedict is going to be so happy with me!"

"That's our cue," said Enoch at the same time Nicholas yanked on his arm and hissed, *"Run!"*

Perhaps blindly following four men she hardly knew down a dark tunnel deep in the Paris catacombs wasn't the smartest idea, but Lie was fresh out of those. She stopped having smart ideas the moment she decided to run away from her life and responsibilities in Wessex to pretend to be a man in Paris.

In her defense, she did not want to marry some duke she'd never met and be forced to be his broodmare.

And sneaking onto the airship destined for Paris *had* been clever...

Sandwiched between Olivier and Emrys, Lie stared at the backs of Sébastien and Louis.

After the lack of reactions from Emrys and Olivier, Lie realized only *she* could see the magic entwined in the two circus members. It sat heavily on Sébastien's shoulders, an overgrown cat wrapped around his throat like a serpent. It clung to Louis's shoulder blades, branching out in a pair of featherless, broken wings. His wasn't nearly as bright as Sébastien's, though. It was...duller. Washed out.

Dead.

She wanted, desperately, to grab Emrys's wrist and whisper in his ear *do you see it? Can you see what ails them, too? Am I crazy for seeing something that isn't there?*

Please tell me I'm not going insane. Nothing has been right since we saw the Rene Doe.

Emrys brushed his fingers against hers, loosening the knot of tense dread in her belly in a whispering instant. She grabbed his hand, squeezing it tightly.

"Aha!" Sébastien suddenly exclaimed. He held out his lantern. It wasn't enough light to see whatever it was that caught his attention.

"I dream of more light," she whispered, hoping that would do the trick.

It did. Even in the astrium glow, she could see Sébastien's feral grin. He snapped his gloved fingers and the antechamber – for that's what it was, she realized – exploded in light.

Three walls greeted her, for the fourth was the mouth of darkness they'd emerged from. On the wall opposite where she stood was a door.

And covering every available centimeter of space not occupied by the door were *clocks.* Hundreds of clocks – tiny stopwatches, cuckoo clocks, grandfather clocks, dainty alarm clocks, pocket watches, every type of clock imaginable, all tick-tocking out of sync, all displaying different times.

She let go of Emrys's hand, approaching a small clock with a mother-of-pearl face and hands that pointed to five-thirty. There was no hand indicating the seconds, no movement of the minute hand. But the hour hand ticked slowly, moving a hair, as though the minutes went by too fast to be perceived, and the hours came and went just as quick.

"This is it," whispered Louis. Whether he realized it or not, the magic-wings on his back twitched, blue feathers fluttering to the ground and disappearing into dust.

Lie sucked in a breath through her teeth. Now, she reckoned, she would have to teach these men the art of being someone they weren't.

Lie was sixteen years old and hiding in the powder room under the guise of fixing her hair and cosmetics when, in reality, she simply did not want to be at her debutante ball. Her mother had spent months picking out the blush pink dress and matching shoulder-length silk gloves. Attendants spent the entire morning piling her freshly-curled pale hair atop her head, painting her face white with splashes of rouge, fixing a veil of ostrich feathers to the back of her head, smoothing out her gown until there were no wrinkles, and she was too afraid to move in case she did wrinkle it...

And in the powder room Lie sat, nails dug deep into her palms as she tried to quell the oncoming panic. She was sixteen, *and she was being paraded around like livestock at an auction, ready to be given away to the highest bidder.*

The rats of the street longed for the life of luxury – to sink into the bliss of unending money and food, to succumb to the fate of power and influence and everything else that came with high society.

But the people at the top? The sixteen-year-old girls who were primed for marriage the moment they came out of the womb? For them, they longed for the life of the street rats. They desired freedom – free will, choices, a life of excitement, and romanticized poverty.

Lie would happily switch places with a gutter orphan if it meant getting out of this debutante ball. If it meant avoiding a loveless marriage to a man thrice her age for the sake of providing heirs to continue his bloodline.

But not hers. No. The Thomas bloodline was over the moment Lady Thomas could no longer bear children, leaving her husband with a single (foolish) daughter.

Lie wished she had been born a son instead.

Nausea roiled in her belly. She hadn't eaten since breakfast that morning, and even then, it had been a paltry serving of toast, fruit, and a cup of tea with no sugar. Because she had to maintain her figure. Because God forbid a sixteen-year-old girl, still in the throes of childhood, have anything more than a twenty-two-inch waist. There were refreshments, of course – tiny cakes and chocolates, petit fours, mousse served in dainty glass bowls – but Lie wasn't allowed to touch any of them.

She leaned against the wall, desperate for some balance. Her head spun, her vision becoming a motely kaleidoscope of overwhelm. The mint wallpaper of the powder room bled with the pink of her dress, the cream tile, the tacky Persian rug that was so out of place that it almost looked right.

Get it together, Lie, *she scolded herself, gnawing on her thumbnail to quash her inner turmoil.* It's just a party. Just one party...

And she had a scheme brewing, the storm clouds of teenage rebellion and deceit roiling around her like she was the almighty Zeus from lore.

All she had to do was make an appearance. Twirl around for one waltz. Make sure her mother saw her pretty dress and gaudy veil and clown-paint makeup.

And then she could slip away. There was one group of people that always went ignored at parties. The help. The servants. No matter how thick her makeup was, no matter how many pins were stuffed in her hair, all it would take was one glance at her uniform, and nobody would bat an eye. Lie just had to slip into the laundry room, snatch a uniform, and sneak out into the night before anyone realized the debutante herself was missing.

Steeling herself with a few deep breaths, Lie brushed her skirts out, straightened her spine, held her chin high, and strode out of the powder room and back into the ballroom to make sure every single person saw her.

So that they would know she had been there. So that nobody would think she skipped her party because everyone had seen her.

One waltz later, Lie wriggled out of her dress and slid the trousers and shirt of a male servant on. She grabbed a cap, stuffed her stiff hair into it, and slouched her shoulders, caving her chest inward.

When she walked through the ballroom again, holding an empty tray as a prop, nobody even glanced in her direction. She was outside before anyone could think to ask why Eulalie Thomas was nowhere to be seen.

Lie wrung her hands nervously. There was no telling what awaited on the other side of the door. There was no telling what would happen to those without an invitation – herself, Olivier, Sébastien de la Rue. The mangled, eviscerated corpse of the Rene Doe flashed in her mind. She swallowed her unease in two harsh gulps and turned to face the Dreammonger.

"If," she said, choosing her words carefully, like an assassin picking her best blades, "I was to dream a miracle that would disguise three of us with enough magic that we would be unrecognizable..."

The Dreammonger's blue eyes gleamed, wicked, dangerous, *inhuman*.

She finished: "Could you grant it?"

He grinned. In the darkness of the antechamber, his teeth glowed astrium blue.

"Ask," he said, "and your wish shall be my command."

She sucked in a breath, eyelids fluttering closed. There were so many things she *wanted* to wish for. So many miracles that would change her life for the better, miracles that would save her from the hole she'd dug around herself. But she was the only one who could see the magic sitting on Sébastien de la Rue's shoulders. She was the only one who could do this. It was her responsibility, so she shoved her own desires down – like she'd been doing since she was born – and made her wish.

"It would be a *miracle* if Olivier, Sébastien, and I could be cloaked with enough magic to make us unrecognizable and safe to pass through this door."

Sébastien snapped his fingers, his grin widening. *"Done."*

CHAPTER TWENTY-ONE

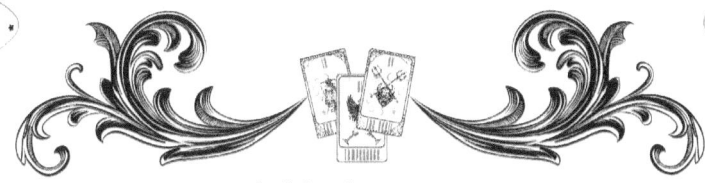

YOU ARE AN UTTER fool for this.

For entering this place.

I could smite you where you stand, and there would be nothing left of you.

For someone who wishes they were dead, you fight too hard to stay alive.

They will know. They will know about your contract. They will know about me.

You

Cannot

Hide

It

For

Much

Longer.

Sébastien, as he'd been doing for the past several years, ignored that voice. He watched as Olivier opened the door and stepped through first, ever the brave and valiant chasseur, followed by Emrys, then Lie. As Louis stepped toward the door, Sébastien grabbed his coattail and followed him through.

He had been to the Otherland once before, many years ago, but it was, somehow, just as he remembered it. Even if this part of the Otherland hadn't existed then.

The door spat them out in the middle of a night market. Indigo silk stretched across the sky, creating the illusion of twinkling stars. Lining the cobblestone street were tents in every imaginable shade of red – from pale pinks to maroons, vermilions, bright scarlets, brown reds the color of dried blood. In each of those tents were...

Well, demons.

All sorts of demonic beasts filled the tents – women with long, snakelike necks, a creature with a horse skull for a head, something that looked like a walking umbrella with eyes, a spider woman sitting in a red web, knitting happily like she was someone's grandmother.

Amongst the demon merchants and shoppers, scattered about with red envelopes clutched in their hands, were humans.

"Death thirteen," Louis said, fingertips nervously messing with the edge of his glove. "Do you think there's only one card? How are we supposed to find it?"

"Perhaps *I* could be of assistance," a new voice sounded.

Sébastien turned to see a man no older than himself, a porcelain Venetian mask covering his face. Fangs poked out from the red-painted lips. Despite his apparent age, he was dressed like a young boy.

"I am Saint Januarius," he said. "But you can call me Janu." He said his name with the Latin pronunciation – *Ee-an-oo.* "Welcome to the Crimson Market! Here, take these. It'll help you with the game. And while the Carnivale game should be your top priority, it *is* a carnival, after all. Shop around! Eat delicious food, buy souvenirs, enjoy yourselves! This isn't Elphame, after all. As long as you make it through the door at the end, you won't be stuck here forever."

Saint Janu gave a dramatic bow after handing two cards to Louis and Emrys. His gaze never met that of the other three. The *invisible* three. Then, he marched off, vanishing into the crowd.

"Saint Januarius," whispered Olivier. "The patron saint of Naples, known for his annual blood liquefication."

"What does the card say?" Lie leaned over Emrys's shoulder. She read aloud: "'Welcome to the Crimson Market. Seven cards have been hidden. Can you find them all...before the time runs out? Be wary, don't tarry...and make it out alive.' So, there're *seven* cards? In total? Or each *person* has to find seven?"

Sébastien glared at the card. The red-and-black stripes were *too* similar to the black-and-white stripes of *his* circus. If Noa and Sasha saw that someone had stolen their red color, they would throw a fit not even he could calm.

"Wait," Olivier said. "What did he mean by *Elphame*? Where are we?"

Sébastien bit his tongue, resisting the urge to say *the Crimson Market, obviously*. Instead, he answered: "There are three worlds. Earth, Elphame, and the Otherland – Hell, as you Catholics know it. Elphame is the fairyland. It exists on the other side of the Veil. Louis, you should know this. The Gemini Twins and the Flying Foxes are from Elphame. Where are *you* from?"

Louis toyed with his glove. "Lyons. I... I'm more complicated than the others."

A not-answer answer, then. He wanted – needed – to know more. It wasn't unusual for demonic beasts to be born on Earth. As far as he was aware, every other member of le Troupe de la Rue came from Earth, except the four fae folk.

"We are in *Hell?*" hissed Olivier.

"More or less." Sébastien shrugged. "Now! How about we find those cards so we can get out of here? I still have a circus to run, after all."

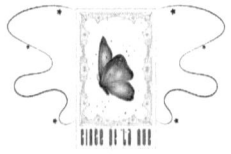

Nick pulled Enoch through the crowd, his grip iron-tight as he held Enoch's wrist. His years in the infantry taught him how to make decisions faster than a blink, and the second he saw the masked girl, his mind was made: don't draw attention, evade for as long as possible, and lose her trail. Whipping out his pistol and shooting the girl would only draw attention – unwanted attention.

And he couldn't be sure regular bullets would work on her. She wasn't human. He was willing to bet she came from Elphame, which meant iron was the only thing that would be fatal. His pistol didn't have iron bullets in it. There was only so much a mortal man could do against a hoard of demons.

Behind him, Enoch's ragged breathing could be heard. He stumbled over his feet, relying heavily on Nick to get them to safety. Nicholas's heart hammered against his ribs. The last time anyone trusted him, he got his entire platoon killed, and he lost one of his hands. He couldn't lose Enoch. Not him, too.

Nicholas turned down a side alley without any warning, vanishing into a thick throng of people. Through the crowd of demons, a few humans lurked about, waving red envelopes as they went from stall to stall.

Forgive me, God, he thought. Then, he scoffed. *If You even exist, which I'm starting to doubt.*

He shoved Enoch aside and ripped his pistol from his belt. He grabbed one of the humans – one who had an excessive amount of wealth based on the luxury clothes he wore. Clothes Nicholas could never dream of affording on his honorably discharged soldier wages.

Nick shoved the barrel of his gun under the man's chin, forcing his head back. "That envelope you have," he said through gritted teeth. "If you value your life, you will hand it over."

"E-excuse me!" The man scoffed. "How dare you! Don't you know who I am? Get your filthy mitts off me!"

Nick shoved the gun harder. "I know more than a thousand ways to kill a man," he said, his voice dangerously low. For the first time since waking up in that hospital bed, hands missing, platoon dead, he felt...

Powerful. Worthy.

The way he was supposed to be.

He continued: "Unless you want a demonstration, I suggest giving me that envelope. *Now.*"

The man paused, debating internally whether Nick was bluffing (even Nick wasn't sure. Perhaps he *was* bluffing, and he wouldn't kill an innocent man in cold blood. But, perhaps, dangerously, he *wasn't*, and unless he got that envelope, he would add a fresher shade of red to the Crimson Market when he painted the cobblestone street with the man's blood and brains). Then, with a shaky hand, he held out the envelope. Nick snatched it and kicked the man away.

"Take this," he said, shoving the envelope into Enoch's hands. "If anyone asks, you're meant to be here."

"Wait!" Enoch cried. "I... Where are you going? Are you *leaving me?*"

His stomach cramped. It was the only way he could describe the fluttery tightening in the organ, squeezing his thoracic cavity like laundry being wrung dry.

"I'm dangerous, Enoch," he said. "Being with me will only lead to your demise. I promised to keep you safe, and I plan on doing just that. I'll be back soon. Once I find a way out of this place."

Nicholas didn't like goodbyes. He refused to think of this as one.

So, he didn't look back, not as he ran back into the crowd, not as Enoch stayed behind.

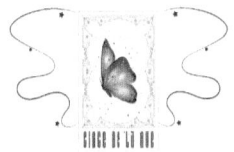

Svetlana did not come from the Otherland. She hadn't been since before she was trapped in a jar for centuries, and she hadn't had the time after joining le Cirque de la Rue to stop by. The Otherland was one of three places she could shed her stolen skin – besides her forest back in snowy Rus' and her tent at the circus. One of the very few places where she could be herself and not the mirage of *Svetlana Vasilievna* or *the Firebird*.

She wasn't even the actual firebird! That wasn't her story. That was foolish Ivan's story, yet again.

As she tore through the air, her body that of a crow, she shook the thoughts of Ivan away. Her dreadful ex-lover would do her no good, especially not when he'd been dead for centuries and reduced to little more than a fairytale.

Louis was missing. That was tragic in itself because Louis was a good kid. Svetlana wasn't sure what he was, but he treated everyone in le Troupe de la Rue equally, and that was worthy of being good in her book. Still, she'd been the one to tell him about the meaning of the strange tarot riddle, so she felt some semblance of responsibility for the boy.

(No matter how old he really was, he would always be a boy to her. Only a few centuries younger than Antara, Svetlana was amongst the oldest in the troupe).

Tragic as Louis's disappearance was, the main issue, as it usually was, was *Sébastien*.

The second he stepped into the Otherland, the circus decided to give up. Her contract loosened enough that if Sébastien was there, there would be nothing keeping her from ripping his spine from his back and devouring his flesh. It wasn't just hers, either.

Aurelio confined himself to his tent. Svetlana could smell the smoke and brimstone. She knew even the tent's strange properties couldn't hold his massive size for long.

Antara sat in the snow, the area around her melted completely as she burned, rambling in a tongue so ancient the circus couldn't translate – though Svetlana knew it was something about being called a demon despite being worshipped as a god once.

Alice and Odette, their bloodlust for human flesh only, set their wings free. Gauzy, gossamer-thin membranes of liquid light trailed behind them. Svetlana didn't know the details of their contracts, but she suspected there was a clause about keeping their wings glamoured.

The twins Noa and Sasha... Well, when Svetlana left, they were just as chaotic as usual, running about the Big Top, screaming as they tore strips of canvas from the walls.

Ilian locked himself in his menagerie. Svetlana knew better than to bother him. She liked her blood in her veins.

She flapped her midnight-dark wings, urging her little corvid body to fly faster. Finding a Gate shouldn't be *this* hard, but it had been centuries since she'd last used the thin veils between worlds to cross from earth to the Otherland. There were Gates leading to Elphame, too, though they were simply known as the Veil. She didn't come up with the names. She'd just been spawned into her forest one day.

There. Above the packed human cemetery was the shimmering, rippling Gate. She tucked her wings against her body and dove through.

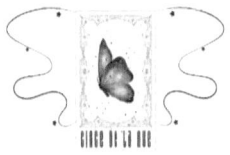

Enoch watched Nicholas disappear into the crowd. He counted to thirty, then sixty, then a hundred before he shoved his glasses up his nose and took off running, too. He wasn't built to run. He was built to sit at a desk and drink (coffee or booze, depending on how tight his deadlines were) and type away on his typewriter. He was built to eat sandwiches from his favorite shop and sleep early and travel by airship if he absolutely must go anywhere fast.

He'd hardly made it two blocks before his breathing ran ragged and he had to stop, doubled over as he gasped pathetically for air. The red envelope grew damp from his palm sweat, crinkling in his grip.

Nick will find you again, he thought.

And then, sobered, he scoffed and thought, *Why are you calling Mr. Lockhart that? You shouldn't be so familiar with another man! Mr. Lockhart. Nicholas, if you must. Not Nick.*

"Oh!" Came a strangely familiar voice. "You!"

Enoch turned to face Duke Emrys Wilde, the man who had seen the circus eighteen times and had figured out it would be returning to Paris.

Even though it was most likely some sort of demon trick, he nearly burst into tears at the sight of a familiar face.

With him were two chasseurs, a Seer and a Dreammonger. He recognized the chasseurs, too. M. Beaumont and... Blaise.

"Mr. Irving?" Duke Wilde prodded, stepping closer and putting a hand on Enoch's shoulder. "I'd say it looks as if you've seen a ghost, but I think a ghost would be tame compared to what's around us."

The Dreammonger frowned. Enoch did, too. Up close, the Maître de la Rue looked...young. Younger than Enoch. Too young to be running a circus, to be in *Hell*.

"Who is this?" The Dreammonger asked.

"E. E. Irving," Emrys introduced for Enoch. "Enoch Ezekiel Irving. He's a journalist. But where's Mr. Lockhart? Isn't he usually with you?"

Blaise Beaumont shuddered at the name. Right. He'd been in Nicholas's subconscious at the Symphony Hall a few nights ago. Had it truly only been a few nights? It felt like an eternity had come and gone since that fateful trip to le Cirque de la Rue.

He took his glasses off and busied himself with rubbing a smudge off the lens, the mechanical motion keeping him from breaking down and sobbing right then and there.

"He...ran off," he finally said, throat tight with tears that threatened to spill. "To protect me. R-regardless, I'm here, and I have one of these cards. Does anyone know what we are supposed to do with them?"

Emrys was quick to catch Enoch up, explaining the clues, the passage through the catacombs, Saint Januarius, and the cards he handed out. They were the same as the card Baba Yaga had plucked from thin air – the one that sat in his pocket heavier than lead.

"We have to find this death thirteen card," the Dreammonger interjected. "I'm on a tight schedule. If you want to socialize, fine. Just do it while we search. *Please.*"

Banshee, if you want to know how you die. The Bone Merchant's words slammed into Enoch at once.

"I know where we can start," he said. "I don't know what a Banshee is, but I think they might help. They should have a tent around here somewhere."

The Dreammonger threw his hands in the air dramatically. "Wonderful! Simply fantastic! Let us just *waltz* around this place aimlessly. Louis, can you find it? Or are you – *shut up!*" He clapped his hands over his ears.

"Excuse me." Emrys walked up to a stall with a fuzzy, mothlike creature. "Do you know where we could find a Banshee?"

The creature lifted a wing, gesturing to the left.

"Thank you kindly!" Emrys beamed and returned to the group. "Come on. In theory, we can find the Banshee over here."

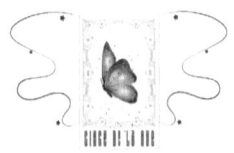

Louis could not see into the future. He couldn't use his six eyes to glean the location of the Banshee. Sébastien didn't even need to finish his sentence – Louis knew what he was going to say. *Or are you too useless?*

He was.

But regardless, there was a curtain around his vision. He couldn't glimpse the past. He couldn't peer into the future.

Useless.

He kept Olivier between himself and Sébastien as if *Sébastien* had the six eyes and would be able to see what Louis knew. If Sébastien knew that Louis knew, he would kill Louis. He didn't doubt that for a second.

He inched closer to Enoch just to be safe.

"Once I can," he said quietly, "I will look into the future to make sure your friend is safe."

He tugged his gloves down a fraction, but his eyes were met with solid darkness. He started to think it wasn't a block on his vision but the future itself.

He was, after all, destined to die.

"I'm curious," said Enoch, pulling Louis from his thoughts of inevitable demise, "you say you're from Earth, but...what are you, exactly? How do you see the future?"

"I have six eyes," he said flatly. *"Be not afraid."*

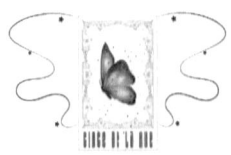

"Be not afraid," Louis, six years old, said, his eyes wider than saucers. Those were the first French words he ever spoke, for up until he was six, he spoke only in ancient tongues.

He had not been born to wealthy parents but parents that were a step above the bottom of the food chain. His mother worked at a factory, sewing clothes until she came home with bloody fingers. His father lit lamps on streets too poor to afford astrium lights. They were hardly more than children themselves, both young teenagers when Louis came to be. They lived with Louis's father's mother, an elderly woman with hair as white as snow and six eyes, though all but two had been carved out when she was younger and desperate for money, leaving fleshy scars on her cheeks and hands behind.

It was late at night. Late enough that Louis should have been asleep, but he wasn't because the other presence in his body decided to finally speak up. It would be the first and last time he ever heard the holy creature dwelling in his body, nestled against his ribs and organs, speak.

He blinked innocently, confused as to why his mother had dropped the bowl she was holding, letting it and the porridge inside splatter against the floor. Confused as to why his father fell over in his chair.

He held up his left hand, his first two fingers pressed together and his thumb out at an angle.

"Be not afraid," he said again, all six eyes – blue, blind, green, and gold – blinking slowly. "Oh. It's gone now."

Then, he helped clean up the porridge and bowl shards; the future told him that if he did, his mother would give him a spoonful of cream and sugar before bed.

That night, as he lay in bed pretending to sleep, mind plagued with thousands of visions – black and white stripes, a blue smile, red tents, blood, knives – of the past and future, he listened to the hushed whispers of his parents.

"He's like your mother," his mother said.

"But my mother coexisted with hers. She could talk with it. They were two souls living in one body. Louis seems to be fighting with his. He can't control it."

"He's six years old! He needs to be playing with other children his age. God knows if we had the money, we would send him to school. He shouldn't have to deal with this!"

"We could bring him to the Church."

"They would cut him apart! You know what happened to your mother when the wrong person saw her eyes. Don't tell me it was for the money because I don't buy it."

His father groaned. "The best we can do is hope they get along."

Louis decided to sleep. The future he saw if he stayed awake wasn't pretty.

Be not afraid, the angel in Louis's body had said before it went quiet – before it died, taking Louis's body with it.

Be not afraid, Louis said now, the irony of it grating because he was, in fact, *very* much afraid.

He thought of every moment leading up to this – the cards, the butterfly, the audition, the body in London torn to unrecognizable shreds not unlike the Rene Doe, the masquerade, Saint Gabriel, the card leading him to death thirteen.

Louis Toussaint was always going to die, but perhaps he'd misjudged the idea of dying spectacularly versus dying alone in an alley.

The Banshee's stall came into view quickly, after no more than a few minutes of walking, and with it, the Banshee herself. She was tall and lithe, wraithlike with snowy flesh and hair just as white as his. Like Louis, she had her eyes covered, though instead of goggles, she wore a strip of fabric. Her teeth, jagged and sharp, were on display, her lower jaw too broken to close.

The only thing on her red cloth-covered table was a deck of cards, their backs the same crimson as her long nails.

"Clever little poppets," she said. She spoke the same language as the Gemini Twins, as Alice and Odette, though Louis hadn't the faintest clue *why* he knew that. "You found your next clue."

Louis bit his tongue. Of course it wouldn't be that easy! Of course! It wasn't a scavenger hunt if the treasure was found after only a single clue.

Sébastien swiped the top card off the deck. He turned it over and frowned. "It's blank. Why is this blank? Is this some sort of *trick?*"

Death, Louis thought. The card meant a dozen things – change, demise, sickness, secrets, a new path –

Wait, that was it!"Secrets," he whispered. "One of the card's meanings is secrets. Miss Banshee, do you require us to give you a secret?"

"Saint Gabriel said you would be clever," the Banshee tutted. "Make a tarot reader find tarot cards." Her unhinged grin stretched wide. "One secret, and the card is yours."

"Oh, that's –" Enoch started.

"One secret," the Banshee interjected. "From *each* of you. A secret so deep, so dark, that only *you* know it. A secret that you have never written down, a secret you have never whispered to the wind, a secret that rots in your mind, forever known only to you. Until now. A secret for a card. And you will *each* need a card to proceed."

Sébastien scoffed. "Fine. The walls inside my tent are all bright pink." He grabbed a card from the deck and frowned. "It's blank."

The Banshee gnashed her teeth. "It *must* be true. A lie is not a secret. A lie will get you killed."

Sébastien dropped the card, recoiling as if it was burning.

Nobody moved. Nobody spoke, nobody offered up their deepest secrets. Not that Louis blamed them. He didn't offer his secrets, either. Dread twisted in his belly like a serpent.

It was Olivier who finally spoke. "I am a chasseur not because I wanted to be one but because I had a promise to fulfill. I don't know if I believe in God anymore."

He grabbed a card, a shadow crossing his face when he saw what was on it. Not blank, then. That had been a true secret. A chasseur devoted to fighting for the Church didn't even believe in God...

Louis's stomach soured. If God didn't exist, then why did angels? Why did demons? Why did Louis have a celestial holy being in his body but was classified as a monster? Because of his six eyes? Because he could see the past and the future? Because of his white hair? Because he was something *different,* and humans loathe abnormality and nonconformity more than anything?

He rubbed his eyes through his gloves. They were closed, of course. Even if he had them open, he'd see nothing but darkness. He wore gloves and goggles to keep the headaches from seeing too much at bay.

Emrys raked a hand through his unruly black curls and said, "It's my fault my grandmother died. I brought her cookies that had been left out because I thought she'd enjoy them. They weren't meant for her. They had nuts in them, and she... She didn't realize until her throat closed up and she died."

His hand trembled as he picked up a card. The color drained from his already pallid face. He hugged the card to his chest.

The Banshee grinned, her pale teeth whiter than snow. She leaned closer, absorbing the secrets like they were her life force.

"I prefer the company of men to women," blurted Enoch. He tensed, bracing for an attack that never came. Hesitantly, he took his card.

The Banshee chuckled. "You humans have such pathetic laws about those things," she crooned.

Only Sébastien, Blaise, and Louis hadn't shared their secrets.

"There's –" Louis started, deciding to just get it over with. At the same time, Blaise – who could *speak,* apparently – said, "When I –"

He turned to face the other chasseur. For a moment, neither of them spoke.

Blaise sighed. "When I was eighteen, I was bedridden and ill for two months. People assumed I had consumption. I didn't. I...sterilized myself. I was stuck in bed because I nearly died. Nobody noticed."

"You *what?*" Olivier exclaimed. "Lie, are you...are you an *idiot?!* Sterilizing yourself... It's a goddamn *miracle* you didn't die."

Blaise – Lie – snapped, "And I thought you didn't believe in God."

He – she – grabbed a card.

Only Louis and Sébastien.

Louis sucked in a breath and said, "There is an angel inside of me. It has been dead for many, many years now."

The last thing Nicholas wanted to do was leave Enoch alone in the Otherland. But his gut told him to separate, to run and get the kid to chase *him,* and the last time Nick ignored his gut twenty-five good men died, and he lost one of his hands.

Fall back, his instincts had screamed. *Retreat. Flee now to live to fight tomorrow.*

"*Stand your ground, men!*" he had ordered. "*If we die, we will die on our feet.*"

He tore around a corner, daring to glance behind his shoulder. The girl was still chasing him, her face hidden by a mask, her speed far too inhuman to belong to a child.

"You're a snoop!" she shouted, shoving a human aside to get closer. "You saw things you weren't meant to! I will kill you!"

Nick pulled his gun free. He didn't hesitate. Didn't think. He just aimed and fired, emptying the barrel into the space where the girl had just been. No body hit the ground. No blood painted the cobblestone crimson.

An arm wrapped around his throat, wrenching his head back.

"*Gotcha,*" the girl hissed in his ear.

Nick shoved the barrel of his gun into the soft, unprotected area of her stomach.

Bang!

Clatter!

The girl's mask fell to the ground in two broken pieces. Her grip tightened; he dared to glance back.

She had no face, only a grinning skull, an ash cross painted right on her bony forehead. Her jaws did not move, not as she spoke. "Silly human," she purred. "Your mortal bullets won't hurt me. Only iron and silver can harm the fae."

Her face shifted then, rippling, shimmering as it fell apart and became *otherworldly.* Her flesh became bark, her teeth stone, and when she opened her mouth, she sank those stone teeth right into the softness of Nick's exposed throat.

He struggled, writhing in her grip as blood surged from his neck.

Please be safe, Enoch, he thought.

And then the world went dark.

CHAPTER TWENTY-TWO

Svetlana kept her wings tucked close to her body as she flew over the sea of red tents, her inky feathers nearly brushing against the silken fabric designed to look like the sky.

Perhaps being trapped in a jar for centuries softened her. Perhaps being rescued by a strange man who fell to his knees and begged her to join him chipped away at the enamel that was her metaphorical armor. Ivan had taken her heart and crushed it into a million unfixable pieces. Sébastien built her a new one and offered it to her with only a contract for a caveat.

Even though she could feel the iron grip of the contract wavering – the bloodlust built primordially into her body, the bloodlust that transformed into her borrowed forms with her gripping her in the throes of desire, the starved urge to *devour* all but taking control – Svetlana searched for Sébastien.

She owed him that much. Two years ago, he had unsealed her jar and begged her to join him. Two years ago, his face was the first she had seen in centuries. Two years ago, she had asked, *"What year is it? Where is Ivan?"* and when she'd learned that several hundred years had gone by since she was stuffed into a box and carted around Rus', and Ivan's name had faded from history, she felt a weight lift from her hunched shoulders.

Cursed Sébastien and his habits of rescuing those who desperately needed it.

Suddenly, a glint of something white caught Svetlana's eye. She knew that glow. It belonged to her oldest enemy.

She dove, shifting back to her human appearance before her feet hit the ground.

"Baba Yaga," she said coldly, approaching the old hag. Glowing skulls on spikes surrounded her stall.

"You," the old witch hissed. "I'm not in your forest. I haven't stepped foot in there at all. You can't kill me."

Svetlana's face rippled. Baba Yaga took a step back.

"I can," Svetlana said, "if you refuse to help me. I'm looking for a man. My height, black and white hair, a scar through his eye, irises the color of astrium. Where is he."

The hag glared. "I've only seen two humans today. A man with glasses and a man with an artificial hand. I haven't –"

Svetlana's hand shot out, grabbing Baba Yaga's throat. She lifted the hag up. "You will tell me," she said, her voice split into a cacophonous tritone. "Or I will rip your spine from your body and devour your ancient flesh. You know what I am. You know better than to upset me."

Even with a crushed trachea, Baba Yaga laughed – a raspy, hissed laugh. "You forget, little Vasilisa, that while you were locked away, *I* became the most fearsome beast in Rus'. *You are nothing now.*"

Her other hand darted out. Claws longer and sharper than Antara's knives tore through fabric and flesh, hooking around the hard bone of Baba Yaga's vertebrae. With a flick of her wrist, Svetlana pulled the witch's spine free. Blood spurted, hot and red, drenching the tent and the cobblestone and Svetlana's rippling onyx form.

"You forget, Baba Yaga," a voice that was not Svetlana's but came from her mouth all the same growled. *"I am of the trees. My power does not depend on whether people believe in me."*

As she unhinged her jaw, slurping down the limp, bloody body of what was once Baba Yaga, a shudder wracked Svetlana.

She had just killed and devoured someone.

Her contract with the Dreammonger specifically stated she would not be allowed to do that.

Her form shifted. A cloak of crow feathers lay over her bare shoulders, trailing behind her as Svetlana Vasilievna started to run.

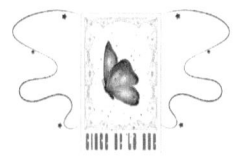

You know you cannot confess.
  There are sins
  Sins that remain buried
  Sins that you cannot share
  Sins
  That

Will

Destroy

You

Once

Again.

Choose your secret wisely, for I will remove your tongue if you reveal too much.

Sébastien's heart fluttered in his throat. He swallowed around it. His stomach tightened, his legs went weak, and no matter how hard he tried, he could not quench the papery dryness of his tongue.

Do not.

Do not.

There was no need for him to reveal a secret. He wasn't playing this game. But Louis was here. But all the people of Paris who cared about le Cirque de la Rue were here. But *he* was here, and it was too late and if he didn't meet his quota, he wouldn't get magic, and if he didn't get magic, he would lose whatever semblance of a grip he had on his soul and Sébastien de la Rue did not, despite all the terrible decisions he continued to make, want to die.

He had to win this stupid Carnivale game. He had to remove Saint Gabriel from his shiny red pedestal and put le Cirque de la Rue back in the spotlight.

A secret came to mind then. Technically, other people knew about it, but they didn't know the exact wording, so it fit into the Banshee's rules. Two years of running a circus and five with *it*.

He clenched his hands into fists, the fine leather of his gloves creasing. He *could* take them off. Now *that* would be a secret, but it didn't count.

Two others already knew about it.

Then again, *it* knew all of his secrets because *it* lived in his mind now.

"My name," he said, mustering all the grandeur of the Dreammonger, of the Maître de la Rue, "is Sébastien de la Rue. That is not my secret, even though that is not my real name."

Seven sets of eyes all turned to him, the eighth belonging to the Banshee never once having left.

He held out a hand, an astrium blue flame erupting, dancing around his fingers.

"And I killed the Rene family ten years ago."

He swiped a card from the deck.

THE EVENING STANDARD

1875   JUNE 18   LONDON

TRAGEDY IN PARIS
by F. S. Pierre

Of all the notorious families in Paris, France, there is one that always stood out: the Rene Family. With wealth that rivaled the coffers of her Majesty Queen Victoria, the Rene Family sat comfortably at the top of the social ladder. The family of four, Lord and Lady Rene and their twin sons, were loved by all, staking investments in several places -- a toy shop, a candy shop, a few factories, and more.

In the evening of 15th June 1875 a fire broke out at the Rene Manor in Paris. Firemen were called, but by the time they arrived on scene the flames were all but gone. All the staff had been set home for the weekend, leaving on the four Renes behind. Two bodies were found in the manor.

Autopsy reports identified the bodies as Lady Anne Rene and Lord Jean-Léon Rene. Despite the fire and their charred remains, there was no evidence of smoke in their lungs. Perhaps they perished before the fire took control of the manor? If so, how did they die?

Neither of the twins have been found. Search efforts have proven futile. The Bank of France has taken to observing the Rene vault. They are to contact the constabulary if any money is added or withdrawn.
If you have any information on the whereabouts of the Rene twins, please contact the local authorities.

HAVE YOU BEEN HAVING STRANGE DREAMS? DO YOU SEE THE DEVIL WHEN YOU CLOSE YOUR EYES? PLEASE CONTACT SILVIA GEORGE, MEDIUM, TO BANISH THE UNHOLY.

Editor wanted - please visit the Evening Standard building to learn more.

Cheapest and best groceries are at R. S. Jones and Co's Main St. near foot of church London, England

Sébastien did not know the first thing about Tarot, but he knew that the card in his hand was...*wrong.* Bile stung the back of his tongue, acrid and hot, only adding to the unease that he suddenly felt.

Painted on the card in oil brushstrokes that looked too real to be anything less than uncanny was a man wearing a hat and a black coat. His face was hidden, save for a sharp-toothed grin that shone through the shadow. In one hand, he held a knife that dripped still-fresh blood onto the snow. In the other was the bloody severed head of a woman.

This is what happens when you play with fire.

You get burned.

You know all about getting burned, don't you, Sébastien?

He shoved the card into his pocket, then looked over Louis's shoulder to see what was on his card. It was blank. Frowning, he checked everyone else's cards. Blank, blank, blank, blank.

"You lied. They're blank. You –" He turned to the Banshee, but the Banshee was gone, her tent vanished with her, as though she had never existed at all.

"Mine isn't blank," said the chasseur Lie, her voice soft, delicate, and fragile like snowflakes. "It... It has a bride, but the bride is pregnant. I..." Her hands trembled as she clutched the card. "What does this mean?"

Emrys's dark brows knit together. He stepped closer to Lie, a strange air of protectiveness about him that left a sour taste in the back of Sébastien's throat. He said, "Mine just shows fire."

Olivier was more hesitant to speak up, clearing his throat twice before saying, "Mine has a Bible and an angel." Then, he added, quietly, the man of God he was, "A Throne angel. The protectors of Heaven."

Enoch swallowed thickly. By the paleness of his face and the sheen on his forehead, Sébastien could only guess he was choking down vomit. Now he *really* wanted to see what was on that card.

"A dead body," he choked out. "With no head. I... It looks like Nicholas. And there are spiders all over the body. Oh, *God*, I don't like this."

"God can't help you," said Sébastien, unhelpfully.

He used sarcasm as a shield, the fear of the man on his card too much to bear without it.

"Mine has me," whispered Louis. "Alone. What does this mean?"

"You're the Tarot reader, Seer," Sébastien shot. "Figure it out."

He started to grow restless, pacing circles around the group as he dug his nails deep into his palms, claws biting into the leather of his gloves. Black and white strands of hair fell over his forehead, but he could not care less to blow them away.

He was the *Dreammonger*. The only things he was supposed to worry about were what astrium brooches to wear and if Svetlana would let him sneak a fourth (fifthsixthseventhtenth) cup of coffee before a show. Not... Fiery deaths and Otherlands and not-Tarot Tarot cards that didn't make a lick of sense and beautiful women with masks and secrets and...

And men with dark coats and dark hats and darker souls hidden by the mask of an inviting smile.

Ten years ago, the Rene family died in a housefire, even if that wasn't the technical cause of death. Days ago, a woman was found mutilated at the manor, not unlike the mutilated corpse Louis had stumbled upon in London. Not unlike the bodies that had been popping up across Western Europe, excerpts of poems not written in French left behind where organs were missing.

Not for the first time, Sébastien wondered why he even bothered working so hard to stay alive after all these years.

Because if you die, I lose my vessel, and I am quite fond of this one.

Because you have to find him.

Because you don't want him to win.

Because we have a deal. A contract. An oath that will not let you die. Why do you think the clauses in all your contracts state your little troupe cannot kill you?

For someone, Sébastien thought angrily, projecting his thoughts as loud as he possibly could just because he could, *who seems to enjoy my suffering and failure so much, why do* you *care?*

I do not.

I do not, you fool.

He stopped pacing. Not because he wanted to – he would keep going if he could until a circular path was worn into the cobblestone – but because something solid grabbed him.

Clawed hands stained black to the elbows. A green day dress beneath a cloak of black crow feathers. Forest green eyes and blood red lips – *Svetlana.*

Svetlana grabbed his upper arms, forcing him to stand still.

"Sébastien, darling!" she exclaimed.

He saw the flecks of blood on her face a moment too late. Blood meant she'd eaten. And that meant the contract was null.

Before he could move, she struck, her teeth sinking into the soft flesh where his neck and shoulder met.

CHAPTER TWENTY-THREE

PAIN FLOODED SÉBASTIEN'S EVERY nerve, reaching all the way to his toes and sending splotches of black across his vision. He stumbled, nearly collapsing under her weight. From the corner of his eyes, he saw the others move – Louis tugged down his gloves; Olivier reached for something in his pocket, his other hand quickly tracing something in the air; Lie traced the same symbol, murmuring something in Latin; Enoch stepped behind Emrys, who put himself in front of Lie.

"Svetlana," Sébastien groaned, voice stiff as he tried not to move too much, lest he find his carotid artery severed and his life surrendered to Svetlana's mouth. "Let go. You've made your point, you fiend."

She pulled back, lips and chin crimson, slick with blood that was completely human in appearance. She rubbed her clawed, stained-black thumb across her bottom lip and stuck it in her mouth, sucking it clean.

"Just making sure, darling. Come along, then. I'll buy you a cup of coffee. We need to get back to the circus," she said plainly as if she hadn't just bitten a chunk out of Séb's throat.

He pressed his hand against the wound, trying to slow the steady flow of blood. He could already *feel* the dozens of inhuman eyes homed in, the scent of fresh blood too tantalizing to pass.

"What are you?" Olivier demanded. "Are you going to kill him?"

Smooth as liquid, she slid over to the chasseur, wrapping herself around him. She traced a bloody claw along his jaw.

"There is a name for me in the Language of Trees," she purred. "But your pathetic human tongues cannot fathom it. I am the forest. I am every pine needle, every raindrop, every deer and bear and bird. I am the roots that feast on the bones of the forgotten."

Without the contract keeping her on a lead – she proved it had broken by biting Sébastien – there was nothing keeping her from devouring Olivier. Sébastien couldn't move. He didn't *dare* move because while the man in the coat scared him more than anything, Svetlana was a *very* close second.

Svetlana grinned a crimson grin. "There is a word that man has coined for me. A word akin to terror, a word spread across Rus' by Ivan himself. You can call me Leshiy."

Gross, thought Sébastien. He pulled his hand away from his neck, grimacing at the sticky sheen of blood left on his glove.

"We need a plan," Enoch said, his warbly, mousy voice barely more than a squeak and hardly enough to draw everyone's attention.

Séb pressed the heel of his palm against the wound again. He mustered that Dreammonger strength and said, "Here's what we know: each of us has a card with something else on it. We cannot see each other's cards. We had to give up a secret to get them. All my contracts have been nullified. That means two high fae, two low fae, a dragon, a vampire, and a god are on the loose in Paris, with nothing to keep them from eating everyone. Oh, and a dead angel and a Leshiy, but they're the least of my concerns right now."

Two high fae. Alice and Odette, faerie creatures from Elphame whose real names were close-guarded secrets and whose ability to soar through the air came from their silvery wings.

Two low fae. Noa and Sasha, the púca twins who could shapeshift at will but liked their clown faces.

A dragon. Aurelio, who only ever shifted in the brimstone cave of his tent.

A vampire. Ilian, the beast tamer who used his compulsive tongue to whisper to his creatures, whose taste for blood was so strong that Séb had to write three separate clauses in his contract.

A god. Antara was considered a demon now, a Hindu monster based on her nickname, but she had been a god once, centuries ago, one made of fire and one who all but faded from history with the birth of Christ.

A dead angel – Louis – and a Leshiy – Svetlana.

And one measly human commanding them all as the ringmaster in a magical circus.

With the hand not pressed against his open, bloody wound, Séb pinched the bridge of his nose. The past twenty-four hours alone were almost as stressful as the past ten years of his life.

"Svetlana," he said, shedding his Dreammonger voice for his Sébastien voice. "My card. It has *him* on it."

Svetlana said something that was almost definitely a curse in her Language of Trees. Then, in a language the circus could translate – except it wasn't really the *circus* anymore – she said, "We need to leave, then. Now."

The heels of the woman's boots struggled to find traction on the thick layer of ice beneath the snow. All she wanted was to get back to the flat she called home – the flat she shared with three other women of the same promiscuous profession as her. She hated her job. She hated laying on her back for filthy men. She hated the mistress of the brothel she was indebted to. She hated the snow, she hated the cold, she hated the *stupid* boots she wore – the leather pinched her toes, and a hole in the sole let freezing snow seep in, soaking her wool socks.

She took a miscalculated step, her foot sliding across the ice. She threw her arms out, trying to break the fall before she could break her knees – and a hand grabbed her.

"Are you alright, mademoiselle?" an accented voice asked.

The woman looked up through her tangle of dark curls to see her savior – a tall man with a heavy coat, a top hat, and a smile brighter than the sun itself.

In all her years of work, she had learned how to tell a man's wealth by the way he dressed and to always trust her instincts.

Her savior was a wealthy man, and her gut instincts told her to run.

"Here, let me walk you home," he said, letting go of her arm and offering a hand instead. "It's awfully dangerous for a young lady to be out alone. Haven't you heard of the body they just found?"

The woman's literacy was subpar at best. She'd seen the article, but she could only pick out the smaller words. People were murdered all the time. Her flatmates had talked nonstop about the mysterious Leather Apron killings in London earlier in the year. Another string of murders was unlikely.

"I'm fine," she said, refusing his hand. When she took a step, though, pain blossomed from her ankle. She stumbled again; the man, once again, caught her.

"It looks like you must have twisted your ankle," he observed. "You're in luck mademoiselle, because I just so happen to be a doctor. My office isn't too far from here. Please, let me treat you. It could get worse if left untreated; you may even lose your whole leg."

A shiver ran down her spine. She couldn't lose a leg. Wenches with missing limbs went for less.

"I can't afford it," she whispered.

"No charge," he said, flashing that sunshine smile. "After all, it was my fault for not catching you sooner."

Run! Her instincts screamed.

She took the man's hand. "Oh, all right. As long as I don't have to pay."

"Excellent," he said. "My name is Johann Engelstein, but you may call me Doctor Jack."

Forcing a smile to hide her unease, the woman followed Doctor Jack through the snow.

In a room above the Crimson Market, Severin Alucard observed. He set his Saints out to assist the players, to remind them of the rules. Saint Geneviève – Zarifa – was in charge of his youngest Saints while Saint Benedict was off on his revenge-fueled campaign.

"Saint Gabriel," came a mousy voice.

He turned his head to see the small Saint Gertrude groveling at the base of his seat. She was a fae creature, an Oakshee from Elphame, with large eyes, larger ears, and a penchant for sneaking around unheard and unseen. She was the perfect spy.

"What do you have for me, Gertrude?" Severin asked. His voice was muffled behind the porcelain of his Venetian mask, but he refused to take it off. He had not shown his face to anyone except Zarifa in ten years.

"The Dreammonger is here," Gertrude squeaked. "And the Seer. And the Firebird. They have found the second card, they have. All of them. Each of them."

Severin gripped the edge of his seat tightly, knuckles turning white beneath his gloves. He wanted to know the Seer's secret, but the Dreammonger... If he could learn *his* secret...

"Did you speak with the Banshee?" he pressed.

"Yes, yes, yes. She and I don't get along." Gertrude shivered dramatically. "Told me her secrets, yes, she did."

Severin had learned early on that he had to be specific with his wording when speaking with the demons of Elphame. His patience, worn thin, could not keep up with Gertrude's faerie antics.

He sighed heavily, irritation weighing down on him. "What was the Seer's secret? And what was the Dreammonger's?"

Gertrude sat down, legs crossed. Even though she was the size of a small child, she was old enough to be his great-great-great grandmother, and even *that* was being generous.

"The Seer has an angel in his body," she said after thinking long and hard about it. "But the angel is dead. It is a rotten corpse within him."

For the longest time, Severin refused to believe in God and his angels. They had not descended from the Heavens to pull him from his darkest moments; why should he believe they existed at all?

"And the Dreammonger?" he prompted.

"Oh! He did not want to give it up, no, he did not." She twirled a strand of brown hair around a lithe finger. "But he did because he got his card. He said ten years ago he killed the Rene family."

Severin stood so fast a wave of dizziness washed over him. He *knew* it. He knew there was something about Sébastien de la Rue that rubbed him wrong, and now he had it. Ten years ago, a fire had broken out at the Rene Manor in Paris. The lord and lady were found dead, but they'd been dead long before the flames started. Their twin sons were never found.

Ten years Severin spent living on the streets, scraping together deals with devils to finally figure out what had happened. It was a mystery that itched the back of his brain, one that he wanted, more than anything, to solve.

And now he had half an answer. A culprit. All he needed was a motive.

"Torment the others all you want," he said, "but leave the Dreammonger to me. He is *mine.*"

Gertrude grinned, her mousy smile widening and widening when Severin said, "Let the others know. They are not to leave this place unharmed. They are not to leave alive."

"They will not," promised Gertrude. She scurried off to rally up the rest of the Carnivale of Saints.

CHAPTER TWENTY-FOUR

"I'M NOT LEAVING." SÉBASTIEN pulled himself free from Svetlana's grip. "I'm going to see this through, and then I'm going to dismantle the Carnivale of Saints."

Svetlana narrowed her eyes, the edges of her corporeal form blurring as she struggled to hold onto her current image.

"You aren't supposed to care about me," he continued, touching his fingers to his neck and grimacing when his glove came back red. Was he going to bleed out here? He couldn't – he absolutely couldn't. Not now, not after he'd fought so hard to stay alive.

He hadn't given up his humanity to die in some Otherland hellscape teeming with inhuman monsters that would tear him apart the second his corpse hit the cobblestone ground.

He stumbled, dizzy. Hands grabbed his shoulders, steadying him – Olivier's or Emrys's. He couldn't tell – but Sébastien shrugged them away, the thought of being touched less desirable than having bugs crawl across his skin, burrowing in his flesh.

"Why?" Svetlana demanded. "Why are you so stubborn? Why can't you just go back home – back to the circus – and just…just forget about all of this?! Why can't you pack it up and move it like before? Why *now*, why are you stuck *here*?"

Because he was, beneath the bravado, still a child.

Because the circus wasn't his home, and he couldn't return to it until he made things right.

Because *it* was too fatigued to use its magic.

Because he had fallen asleep when he was told not to, and now everything was ruined.

He shoved his hands through his hair, forcing it off his forehead, away from his astrium blue eyes that were wide and wild.

"You want to know why?" he said, voice teetering on hysteria. "You weren't the first demon I made a deal with, Svetlana. I'm not even the first Dreammonger. I am human. Human! And all the magic and grandeur and miracles are just *borrowed power!* I'm a nobody, you see. A gutter rat who tasted fame and will do anything to cling to the power that comes with being at the very top!"

He threw his head back and laughed – laughed and laughed, a cackling witch's laugh, a hysteric laugh, the laugh of a child wearing shoes far too big for his urchin feet.

A flash of red bled into the corner of his vision, followed by warm arms and lips at his throat, licking and suckling the blood spurting from the bite wound.

Zarifa.

"We have to go," she whispered, her tongue hot and wet against his sensitive flesh. His entire face flushed, his stomach doing acrobatics that would make Alice and Odette look like amateurs. His heart sputtered, stuttering in a helpless arrhythmic tempo.

She pulled away and licked his blood from her red lips. "They're coming after you all – the Carnivale of Saints. Gabriel wants all of you – except for you, Sébastien – dead."

"How are we supposed to trust *you?*" Olivier growled. He lifted his hand – forefinger and middle finger pressed together, thumb bent at an angle, the remaining fingers tucked against his palm – and began tracing in the air.

Svetlana was on him in a heartbeat, hand wrapped around his throat. She stood taller than him – almost twice his height, and he was a tall man.

"Do *not* attempt to exorcise us in our own domain, Livi darling," she said calmly. "That will not end well for you."

Zarifa tugged on Sébastien's sleeve. Between her, Olivier and Svetlana, and Emrys, Enoch, Lie, and Louis, there was a...a rift in Sébastien's mind.

He'd wasted too much time. In a heartbeat, they were surrounded by a host of masked Saints.

"Orders to kill," said a small, mousy saint with whiskers on her mask. "Kill all but the Dreammonger. No survivors allowed, no survivors, none."

And then she attacked.

She went for Lie, taking the smallest opponent down in a tackle.

Zarifa grabbed Sébastien's wrist and ran, dragging him along. "There are no Bluebeard Doors that would lead to someplace safe," she said as she pulled him down another street, then another. "But I can hide you for now. You just need to keep a – *duck!*"

He ducked, narrowly missing the soaring blade that whistled through the air right where his bleeding neck had just been.

"A low profile?" he gasped out, regaining his footing quickly. "Do you know who I am? I'm incapable of subtlety!"

Zarifa yanked him into an alley and shoved him against the wall hard enough to set his teeth rattling.

"You will listen to me, Sébastien de la Rue, if you want to live," she hissed, absinthe eyes narrowed behind gilded lashes. He wanted to kiss those lashes, but he wanted to live first.

But, instead of agreeing, he just said, "You know, that isn't actually my real name."

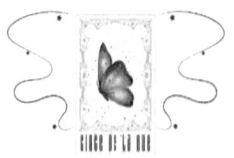

Enoch pressed himself closer to the others, wishing desperately that Nicholas was with him – or, at least, that Nicholas had left his pistol with Enoch.

There were two chasseurs – one real, one a fraud – with rosaries and Bibles, an unarmed duke, a fortune teller trembling like a reed, and one single non-human beast with blood smeared across her jaw.

And Enoch, the journalist who had bitten off more than he could chew. Oh, how he wanted to go home. How he wanted to curl up in his bed with a newspaper and a cup of spiked coffee.

How he wanted to sit in the kitchen and listen to his landlady, Mrs. Taffy, reminisce about her youthful years.

He dug his nails into his palms. Nicholas would save him. He had to.

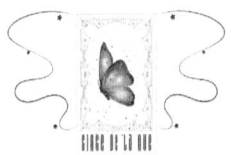

The corpse inside Louis's body had once belonged to an ophanim, or so it had told him before dying and dragging his mortal body with it, slowly, slowly, slowly. He had many eyes because he was a seer, and he had many eyes because a wheel angel had decided to make him its vessel. Louis kept his eyes covered to keep the extra light out, to keep the two extra sets from overstimulation.

He peeled his gloves off first, tucking them safely in the pockets of his coat. Then, he pushed his goggles onto his forehead, pinning his white hair back and blinking slowly.

The two eyes on the center of his face, where all eyes should be, were a mismatched heterochromia of green and yellow. Truthfully, his right eye was brown, but it was such a pale shade of brown that it looked more yellow than anything else. His green eye was pale, too, like a jade disc framed beneath thick white lashes.

Beneath those eyes, tilted on his cheekbones, were the eyes that looked into the past. Blind eyes, milky and opaque but able to look all the same. They saw the world in blurs of black and white, halftone smudges of what once was.

On his palms were the eyes that looked into the future. Each iris was bright blue – not quite astrium blue, but a deadly cyan with X-shaped pupils.

All six eyes blinked out of sync, adjusting to the sudden accosting brightness. Then, slowly, he raised his hands and placed them over his face, palms – eyes – facing outward.

"Be not afraid," Louis said, the ophanim charade wobbly.

The angel inside him might have been dead, but he still had its six eyes, so nobody else – except Lie and Emrys, Enoch and Olivier and Svetlana, and the Banshee – would ever suspect that he was a fraud.

The Saints faltered. Beneath his hands, the eyes on his cheekbones strained, seeking the past that was buried by gauzy layers of organza blackness piled so thick it was nearly impossible to see through. But...he found it. Rather, the *lack* of it. The lack of humanity. The Saints were all demons and demons...

Well, they feared angels.

He took a shaky step closer. If he could ward the Saints away from the others –

He was on the ground in a heartbeat, blood rushing to his head. A willowy man straddled his waist, his mask painted with pale purple lilies.

"There is no angel in you," he hissed. "You dare come here and flash your eyes at us? For that, you will die."

The Saint's hands descended, thumbs pressing into the flesh beneath Louis's Present eyes. Dull pain erupted, pulsating along his optic nerves as the Saint dug deep into the membranous skin of Louis's eyelids, trying desperately to gouge his eyeballs out.

Blood sprayed across Louis's face, metallic and hot, and his heart stuttered, fear gripping his loins with the dreadful realization that he'd just gone from six eyes to four.

Except...

Except he could still see the Saint straddling his waist. He could still see the shadowy silhouettes of Olivier and Emrys as they corralled Enoch and Lie against the looming threat of more Saints.

The masked head of the Saint, whose body was still, dreadfully, attached to Louis, rolled across the ground wetly.

A foot came down, stomping the head.

Squelch!

Brainy pulp and bone-thick blood sprayed, mixed with shreds of ceramic and stringy mats of bloodied hair.

The monster removed her foot, shaking brain matter and skull shards from the sole. Fear surged, squeezing Louis's heart and yanking the breath from his lungs.

She stood taller than le Cirque de la Rue's Big Top, back hunched and spine protruding in a picket line of thorny vertebrae. Two sets of branch-line antlers sprouted from her head – which wasn't a proper human head anymore, but a blackened animal skull with rows of sharp teeth.

She reached a clawed hand out and plucked the headless Saint from Louis's petrified body. Her jaw crackled and unhinged, opening like a snake's, and in one gulp, she swallowed the corpse whole.

In a ripple of smoke, the beast was gone. And in its place was Svetlana, her hands still blackened and antlers still curving from her skull.

"Rotten," she murmured, her face scrunched up in distaste. Like she'd just eaten a moldy piece of bread and not a body. Still, she licked her fingers clean and turned toward the others – toward Olivier. "There is nothing holding me back anymore. No contract keeping me from devouring all of you. Take them and go, Livi darling. I will make sure you are not followed. Find Sébastien and bring him back to me."

Someone – Enoch – grabbed Louis's arm and dragged him to his feet.

The Devil, he realized weakly, stumbling after Enoch as he started to run, *is real. And her name is Svetlana Vasilievna.*

CHAPTER TWENTY-FIVE

IN LESS THAN A heartbeat, Sébastien and Zarifa had gone from being in the alley to sitting on the wooden floor of a small cottage. Zarifa peeled herself away from him and dashed to the tiny kitchen on the other side of the room, busying herself with rummaging through the cabinets.

"What –" Sébastien started, barely able to hear his own voice over the thunderous tattoo of his heart. His mouth went dry. Fear. Of course, it was fear. He hadn't been in a cottage like this in two years.

You're safe, he told himself. *It's just you and Zarifa.*

"Bluebeard Doors are doorways that lead in and out of the Otherland," she cut him off. Opening another cabinet, she made a soft *aha!* Clutching whatever she found, she hurried back to his side.

A medical kit rested in her hands, pried open as she sat down. She pulled out cotton gauze and pressed it against his neck.

"There's a Bluebeard Door in the catacombs," she explained. "It's what brought you to the Crimson Market. They're all over the world and nearly impossible to find unless you know where to look. But Bluebeard Doors can only lead to and from the

Otherland. All the doors in the Crimson Market would take you someplace Saint Gabriel – Severin – would be able to find you. Time and space don't really exist in the Otherland. Demons can move about it freely. We're still in the Crimson Market. This is Severin's next game. Since it hasn't started yet, we'll be safe here. There are no Saints here yet."

She peeled the gauze back, frowned, then grabbed a new wad to press against his neck. He winced at the initial sting of pressure against the bleeding bite but soon melted.

He was tired. So damn tired. All he wanted to do was close his eyes and simply give up. What was the point in trying so hard anymore?

Suddenly, Zarifa's hands were on his face, palms cupping his wet cheeks. *Wet.*

Oh. He was crying.

Absinthe eyes searched his.

"I want to know," she said softly. "I want to know who hurt you. I want to know why Severin hates you so – why he had me follow you and plant notes he knew would scare you, why he was desperate for you to show up at the masquerade, why he wants to know the secrets of le Cirque de la Rue. I –"

Sébastien leaned into her touch. His movements were slow, hesitant, like a street dog finally accepting the outstretched hand coaxing him home. He squeezed his eyes shut, forcing beads of tears to fall from his dark lashes.

"But," Zarifa continued, "I won't force you to tell me."

There were certain things Sébastien was forbidden from saying. How the circus worked. What he had done in those years spent tucked away in the cottage in the Foret de Compiegne. Who the Dreammonger was, because it certainly wasn't Sébastien – it was a borrowed moniker, an epithet lent to him by the demon on his shoulders. What was hidden in the inky confines of his Tent Noir.

Logic told him not to trust Zarifa. She was a demon, one of Severin Alucard's Saints. Sébastien did not think with his brain when faced with Zarifa, though, so he ignored logic and tried his tongue at what few things he *could* explain.

"I can't say who hurt me," he said through fat tears. "I don't know why Severin hates me. I've never even heard of him until now. All I can think of is that Severin works for *him*. I... I am a human. I am a human who made a pact with a demon. My soul is not my own; I'm living on borrowed – stolen – time. I've made too many mistakes, Zarifa, and I keep making more. I'm so *tired.*"

"Then sleep," she said, flicking away more of his tears with her thumbs.

Sleep and you will regret it, said the true Dreammonger, its claws digging deeper into his shoulders.

"I *can't,*" Séb choked out. "I want to. I want nothing more than to sleep and not dream, but I can't. I..."

He squeezed his eyes shut tighter and swallowed hard, forcing the lump in his throat down.

Zarifa tugged the ribbon from his hair, letting the black and white locks tumble over his shoulders and chest. She combed it back with her fingers, pushing it off his forehead.

"Take off my gloves," he whispered.

Slowly, he pried his eyes open, watching as Zarifa took one of his hands. She loosened the fingers, then slid the leather glove off his arm, letting it fall to the floor with a whispered flutter.

"This," he croaked, "is why I can't sleep."

It was a human hand, but... without flesh and muscle. Held together, not by ligaments and tendons, but by a dusting glow of magic, Sébastien's hand was skeletal. Phalanges and metacarpals, carpals, a radius, and an ulna, all pristine and white and utterly impossible, but it was the least of the impossibilities that made up Sébastien de la Rue. Just before his elbow, before his humerus could be exposed, too, his flesh bled back in.

It was disgusting. Horrific. The worst thing Sébastien had ever seen, and yet...

And *yet*.

Zarifa peeled off his other glove, exposing another skeletal hand. His right hand was bone up to his wrist instead of to his elbow like the left.

"The deal was that I can have the Dreammonger's power, but I cannot sleep."

You cannot say those things! You cannot tell anyone!

"When I sleep," he said, ignoring the Dreammonger, "this happens. If I keep it up, I'll die. And when I die, my soul... It isn't mine..."

She took his skeletal hands and kissed the bony knuckles of each – all then, letting her lips linger, her breath warm enough to wake the butterflies in his stomach.

She trailed kisses up his arm, across his clavicle, along the fluttering pulse in his throat. She kissed his jaw, both corners of his lips, the wet tears on his cheeks.

When she kissed him, she sucked the breath from his lungs, the tension from his shoulders. He melted against her, kissing back like it was the only thing in the world that mattered. And, just then, it was.

She took his hands, holding them tightly, her skin soft and warm against the cold bone of his, and when she pulled away, her absinthe eyes searched his astrium ones.

"You are not the Dreammonger," she breathed.

He shook his head. He wasn't.

"You're Sébastien de la Rue."

He wasn't that, either, but that didn't matter. The boy he was before had died ten years ago. Sébastien de la Rue was all that was left.

Sébastien de la Rue was all that would remain.

Epilogue

Lieutenant Colonel Nicholas Lockhart pried his eyes open slowly, blinking against the harsh blue lights that suddenly accosted his vision, making the pounding in his head that much worse. He tried to rub his eyes, but his hands were chained, locked against the wall with heavy shackles.

Blinking again, he looked around, trying to make out his surroundings. Iron bars. Cold stone floor. Chains. An astrium spotlight on the other side of the bars shining directly in his face. His gun gone, his clothes removed and replaced with rough-hewn fatigues.

He was in a cell.

Taking a deep breath, he yanked on the shackles. If he could dislocate his thumbs, he could free his hands. Then it would only be a matter of finding a way out of the cell.

Where even *was* the cell?

The stench of mildew and rot was thick, weighing down the stale air. Each breath made him want to vomit, but he didn't know when – if – he would be fed or watered, so he kept it down.

He pushed his thumb down with his middle and forefingers, trying to force the joint to pop out. Each time his metal hand scraped against the metal shackles, a shiver ran down his spine. That one would be harder to free...

He pressed harder, adrenaline outweighing anything else.

Then...footsteps.

He froze, then let his hand go limp. The last thing he needed was for his captor to figure out his schemes.

His captor. How had Nick even ended up here?! The last thing he remembered was pushing Enoch away and running. Then pain and... He'd been knocked out, hadn't he? Someone struck him against the side of the head. As if on cue, another painful throb radiated from the injury.

Deep breaths, Nick, he told himself. *You've been through worse. At least Enoch had the chance to get away. Nothing else matters. Please, God, let him be safe.*

The footsteps stopped. Tipping his head back, Nick met the gaze of his captor. Astrium light gave him an angelic aura, reflecting off the porcelain of his mask. He'd seen that mask before – at the masquerade. That cursed masquerade. If he and Enoch hadn't gone...

No. It was too late now. Now, Nick had to figure out how to escape and find Enoch again.

"You're the little rat who slipped through the Bluebeard Door, hm? The one who evaded my Saint Benedict?" The man spoke French, yet Nicholas understood every word.

"Go to Hell," Nicholas spat.

The man chuckled. "I'm already there. And you are one step away from joining me. Tell me, Englishman, what's your name?"

It was the creatures from Elphame that would take Nick's name and twist it into theirs, but he didn't trust the Otherland creatures one bit. He'd rather bite his tongue clean off than tell the masked man who he was.

Click.

The cell door swung open, slamming shut once the masked man was inside. He crouched down and grabbed Nick's face, gloved hand gripping his jaw *hard.*

"Stubborn," he crooned. "I'll make it fair. My name is Saint Gabriel, Wishmaster of the Carnivale of Saints. But, of course, that's nothing but a pseudonym. You may call me Severin Alucard."

Nick spat on Severin Alucard's masked face.

He bristled. With his face covered, Nick couldn't see the way his expression twisted and contorted. Severin let go of Nick's face only to swing his fist, knuckles colliding with Nick's jaw in a white-hot burst of pain.

"Oh, you are going to need quite a bit of training," Severin said tightly. "It will be a lot of work, but I'll make an obedient dog out of you yet. Perhaps I'll make you Saint Francis. I don't have a Saint of obedience yet. Then again... You are human, and there is little I can do with humans."

Severin straightened and clasped his hands behind his back.

"I know what happened to your platoon," he said, and Nick stiffened, his blood running ice cold.

No. His platoon. The mistake he made that cost their lives and his hand. Telling them to hold their ground instead of retreating...

"I know it's something that haunts you," Severin continued. He reached into his pocket then, slowly extracting something. A syringe filled with a golden liquid that seemed to glimmer in the blue light. He said, "Do you know what this is? Of course, you don't. This is a drug used by the chasseurs of France. It's what allows them to grab the incorporeal forms of demons during exorcisms and banish them."

"I'm no demon," growled Nick.

"No," Severin mused, tapping the end of the syringe against his jaw. *Click, click, click.* "But you have a mortal body, and *I* have a demon in the next cell. What, pray tell me, do you think would happen if, perhaps, I injected this serum into myself? What would happen if I exorcised the demon and, instead of destroying its soul, put it inside *you?*"

Nicholas's legs went numb.

No. No, no, no, no, no.

He yanked on his shackles, desperate to get free, as if brute strength alone would rip the anchors from the wall. As if he could will the chains to break.

"You monster!" he screamed. "You bastard, don't you dare! I will not be your puppet! I won't join your Saints! Just kill me now!"

If his heart beat any faster, it might just burst.

Severin dragged the needle against his throat.

Then, he plunged it in, filling his veins with the serum that would be Nicholas's demise.

"Oops," chortled Severin. He dropped the syringe.

Then, he peeled the mask from his face – a face that Nicholas *knew*. He'd seen that very face before – those brown eyes, those dark lashes, that pale skin marred only by a few beauty marks.

Bile rushed up his throat again.

When Severin left the cell, he kept the door wide open. Nick yanked his wrist against the cuff. Skin tore, blood wept from the raw wound, slicking metal in a hot lubricant. He yanked again – again, again, again – and –

Pop!

His hand slid free, the flesh of his wrist torn in thick, meaty shreds, his thumb broken at an angle so unnatural it caused him to stare. Pain hadn't registered yet, and he hoped his adrenaline would keep it at bay for a moment longer, long enough for him to escape.

As he reached for his artificial hand to pry it off, footsteps entered the cell.

"Naughty boy," tsked Severin.

I'm sorry, Enoch, Nick thought. Severin let go of the black shadowy mass he'd been holding.

I'm so sorry.

Cold flooded Nick's body, followed by a heat so blinding that all he could do was claw at his face. His back arched, and a scream tore from his throat.

I'll find you again.

Dark spots flicked against his vision – blurring the world until he simply couldn't *see* anymore. Couldn't speak, couldn't hear, couldn't feel, couldn't do anything but think.

I'm sorry.

When Severin Alucard spoke, his voice was distorted, like he was underwater. "What is your name?"

The voice that came from Nicholas's mouth was not his. *"Raum."*

"Will you make a deal with me, Raum?" Severin grinned. "A contract. You join my Carnivale of Saints, and I will give you as many souls as you wish to eat."

Nicholas-Raum licked his lips. *"As many as I wish?"*

"As I said."

"And I just need to join your Carnivale?"

Severin pulled a scroll from his inner pocket. "Just sign on the dotted line."

Nicholas-Raum swiped his finger against his bloody wrist and scribbled on the paper without even reading it.

"Mm," sighed Severin. "Welcome to the Carnivale of Saints. I am your Wishmaster, Saint Gabriel. And you... You will be Saint Judas. There is a man I want you to find."

"Who?" asked Saint Judas.

"His name is Sébastien de la Rue. The Dreammonger. Find him and bring him to me."

Saint Judas stood, ripping the chains from the wall. "As you wish."

Inside, trapped within his own body, the still-there soul of Nicholas Lockhart screamed. But Raum ignored him, and the Wishmaster did not hear him.

You are Lieutenant Colonel Nicholas Lockhart, he repeated in his mind, desperate to control his thoughts as Saint Judas controlled his body. *You will not die here.*

On the morning of December 28, 1888, another body was found. Her ribcage had been pried open, revealing an empty chest cavity to the world of Paris, France. Her stomach was missing, too, as was her uterus. Her intestines spilled into the snow, picked apart by carrion crows and stray dogs. Rigor mortis locked her legs in a bent, awkward angle, and her face had been removed, leaving only a pulpy mess of meat and muscle and bone. Unlike the other bodies, tucked away in alleys or hidden where no one could see, this one had been placed right outside the fence surrounding le Cirque de la Rue.

Ilian Agreste had found the body, smelling the blood before anyone else could. He stood on the other side of the fence, shoulders gripped by Aurelio. Antara held Noa and Sasha close, refusing to let them climb over the fence to taste the stale blood. Alice and Odette covered their noses, their faces pale.

"What does this mean?" Antara asked weakly. When her contract broke, her powers surged. The snow around her feet was melted and steam curled around her bare toes.

"We need to find Svetlana and Sébastien," Aurelio said grimly. "We need to bring them back."

"Hungry!" cried Noa, writhing against Antara's grip.

"Hungry, hungry!" echoed Sasha.

"Shut up!" hissed Ilian, his fangs flashing in the light. Aurelio tightened his grip. The last thing the circus needed was for a vampire and four fae-things to be unleashed. If the murder somehow landed on their shoulders...

"That much is obvious," grumbled Odette. "But I think she meant the writing."

"It's easier to see if you're airborne," said Alice. Only four of the circus members could fly – Aurelio, in his dragon form, the Flying Foxes, and Antara, now that her godly powers were at their full potential.

The murderer, whoever it was, had used the woman's blood to write a message in the snow – one that made no sense to Aurelio, Antara, Ilian, Alice, Odette, Noa, and Sasha.

I FOUND YOU.

TO BE CONTINUED...

I cannot keep the tears back;
The tears, that should not flow
For the one who wantonly could grieve
A heart that loved him so.

I cannot keep the tears back;
The bitter, bitter tears,
For the sweet memories of the past,
The fond, fond love of years.

For many days I doubted—
Would God it still were so!
Would God there were a gleam of doubt
O'er all that now I know!

For many days I doubted;
But when he soothed my grief
With fond assurances of truth,
Could I deny belief?

It is not that another lures
His loyal love from me;
Though well I know she's lovelier far
Than ever I could be.

And well I know the little grace
That won his passion brief,
Is worn from *my* frail form and face,
By sickness and by grief.

No thought like this could make them flow,
Those bitter, bitter tears,
O'er the dear memories of the past,
The fond, fond love of years.

Not this—though it has blighted
The one sweet hope I knew,
That if a world beside were false,
His generous heart was true.

It is the unexplain'd distrust,
The studied, strange neglect;
Ah! only for a lover lost,
My pride these tears had check'd!

But with his love, his friendship fled,
And that I scarce can bear;

For I would be a friend to *him,*
Through every joy and care.

And oh! I pine to see his face,
And hear his gentle tone;
And he is near—yet comes not here,—
And I must weep alone.

I would not blame him by a look;
For if I e'er had met
A more heroic heart than his,
I also might forget!

But I cannot keep the tears back,
The bitter, bitter tears,
O'er all the memories of the past,
The fond, fond love of years.

I cannot keep the tears back,
And yet they should not flow
For one who wantonly could wound
A heart that loved him so.

Zarifa, Frances Osgood, 1850

Acknowledgements

Once upon a time (14ish years ago), hidden away in my Definitely Haunted Bedroom with YouTube playing Taylor Swift, I sat down with my Green Notebook (the one with the wire spiral that always cut my hands) and a pencil my grandma got at the Grand Canyon and I created the very first ever version of Sébastien. Fourteen years later, he has been reconstructed and pulled apart and shoved into so many different stories that now he is nothing but a faint echo of that original version. He was in a dystopian about mutant outcasts. He ran three (3!) different circuses (all titled le Cirque de la Rue, of course). He was a woman. He was in two different musicals. He was two people. But he has always been the same at the core. And we grew up together. We went through middle school together. High school. College. I am proud to say that he finally has a home in *The Dreammonger*. We did it, Ten-Year-Old-Me. This is for you. For the hopes you scribbled into that Green Notebook all those years ago.

As always, I want to thank my mum. For reading this, for encouraging me to be a writer, for raising me, for being the best mum in the entire universe. I love you, Mama. And thank you, Dad. Thank you for not questioning me when I randomly text you "hey, how would you perform an exorcism?" and actually giving me the steps. While writing, I kept thinking about when we read all the *I Spy* books EXCEPT the funhouse one because, back then, neither of us liked clowns. How the tables have turned...

Thank you to my sister, Penny, for coming up with the nicknames Wonkus and Goober, and for saying "smash" every time I sent you character art.

Okay, Raven, your turn! THANK YOU. THANK YOU. THANK YOU. For the cover, for loving this story fiercely, for being TDM's biggest fan from the start.

A very special thank you to my assistant editor, Mephisolou, who simply decided to sleep on my arm whenever I tried to work. You're lucky you're so darn cute. And thank you Lysandra and Andarna, who are also very cute and very bad at helping me work.

Anyone who picked up this book: thank you. Thank you for visiting le Cirque de la Rue. There have been so many different readers over the years. The ones who read the music I wrote for the musical version. The ones on Wattpad who read that (horrible) version. And you. Yes, you! You very special you. I love you. It may take me a while, but my DMs are always open if you want to tell me your theories, who your favorite character is, all of it.

I know I'm forgetting tons of people, so... Everyone else! Hi! Yes! THANK YOU!

And Dani. I love you. I miss you. You went out like a firework: brightly, loudly, over all too soon. Not a day goes by where I don't miss you. Rest in peace, my love. This story is for you.

About the Author

Emma T. Shannon has been writing since before knowing how to actually write. On the rare occasions where they are not writing, Emma can be found hunched over a drawing, circling the same shelf at the local bookstore, obsessing over 2D men, and singing loud enough to annoy the neighbors.

Emma lives in the dreary PNW with their tiny house tigers Lysandra and Mephisolou, their tiny house dragon Andarna, two cursed dolls, and more tarot cards than they know what to do with.

Instagram @goth.witch.writes

Threads @artem.mxrtis

ko-fi.com/artemmxrtis